In loving memory of Ann Ford.
Dearest aunt, who heard this story first.

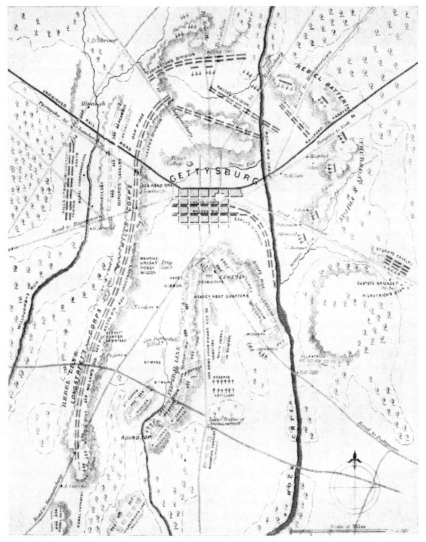

Map of the town and troop positions during the Battle of Gettysburg, 1863

Chapter One

Breanne Walker

A HOLIDAY WASH-OUT.

I looked out my apartment's large picture window and onto my slabbed-concrete, rusted-railing balcony, now flooded from the gushing rainspout pouring directly onto it from the third floor above.

What a shame. I thought of all the ruined Labor Day Weekend barbeques — ones that I hadn't been invited to.

Back home in the bone-dry state of Nevada, a passing cloudburst was a real storm. Rain was always welcome. We'd line buckets on our front lawns to collect every droplet, so we could wash our cars and water our plants: two things outlawed during droughts. But since I moved cross-country nine weeks ago for a job at the National Military Park in Gettysburg, Pennsylvania, it had been a nearly nonstop downpour.

The rain was getting old. Even for me.

From the looks of it — the black, ominous clouds building in the sky overhead, the gale force winds ripping through the trees, the booming thunder—and the hour—four o'clock—this storm wasn't about to let up.

I pressed my forehead against the window; the heavy pitter-patter of rain vibrated the glass against my skin. The vindictive part of my personality was thinking fondly of all the soggy hamburgers and saturated potato chips abandoned on backyard picnic tables. A small smile cracked my pursed lips.

I turned from the blanketing mass of storm clouds, leaving my spiteful thoughts out on the flooded balcony. I picked up my worn copy of Emily Brontë's *Wuthering Heights* and plopped down on my plush couch. I cracked my favorite novel's spine to the opening page for the sixth time, and my dull apartment was transformed into the foreboding moors of Yorkshire. *Alone with a book; my kind of night.*

Hours later—which felt like the bat of an eye—I was violently woken by a foghorn, blaring inches from my ear. My body jerked in fright, sending Brontë's masterpiece crashing to the carpeted floor. My hand shot out to my coffee table—I had fallen asleep on the couch…again—and groped for my ringing cell phone.

"Hello," I said groggily.

"Breanne, it's Greg."

Who? Everything in my head was fuzzy. I sat up and glanced at the clock hanging on my living room wall. It was 3:45.

"Hello? Are you there?" the voice asked.

Oh right, Greg Ransome. My boss. "Yes...I'm here. Sorry." I stifled a yawn and tried not to sound overly annoyed. *This better not be another ploy to get me to socialize with my coworkers.* He'd been loading my email's inbox with Happy Hour invites. All of which I declined and deleted.

"Well, throw on your tennis shoes. This can't wait till morning," he said.

"It *is* morning, Greg. Very, very early morning. Listen, I'm not in the mood—"

"You need to see this." His voice was breathless and squeaky—almost crazed.

"See what?" I whined.

"Can't explain over the phone. You'll have to meet me."

"At the museum?" I asked, knowing there was no going back to sleep now. Still dressed from the day before, I grabbed for the shoes I had kicked off and bent over to pull them on with my free hand.

"No." He paused, and I heard his sharp intake of breath. "Little Round Top."

My spine straightened as he named the infamous battleground.

"You there?" Greg asked.

"Yes. Yes. I'm here," I said. "I'm on my way." Heart pounding, I grabbed my messenger bag and darted for the door.

Chapter Two

Breanne Walker

L UCKILY, THE RAIN HAD STOPPED BY THE TIME I STEPPED ONTO MY balcony and locked my apartment's door. A thick fog hung in the air — typical after a heavy downpour on warm days in Gettysburg. The intense winds had left a mess: leaves, branches, and empty trash cans littered the black asphalt of my apartment complex's parking lot. And as I drove away, I found that the surrounding streets looked no better. *Am I in an active war zone?* I thought, maneuvering my car past the strewn debris and wishing I was still in bed. *Or the couch.*

But when Greg called, I jumped. I owed a lot to him.

At the age of twenty-five and after two decades of education, my institutional learning had abruptly ended. I had a bachelor's degree in American history and a master's in anthropology — with a focus on the preservation of 19th-century American artifacts. My bright future — dwelling on the past — was within arm's reach.

Then I graduated, and life smacked me upside the head.

My plan had been to move right into a doctorate program at the University of Arizona. But I had maxed out the amount allotted for educational purposes—which I hadn't known was possible. Every single loan officer in the state denied my application for additional funds. One laughed when I explained my plan to become an accredited historian who traveled the world in search of long-lost artifacts. A *real-life Indiana Jones*. As one rejection letter explained, my future was "monetarily unrealistic" in terms of eventual repayment.

Instead of moving on to a higher level of education, I moved home to Nevada.

Nothing quite knocks the wind out of you like moving back in with your mother at the age of twenty-five. All I had was my ambition—I had no friends, support structure or hobbies; school and my career were everything to me, my way of escaping the world. Without it I was a fledgling, wading into the water too soon. I swan-dived into a bottomless depression—a pit of hopeless longing for what could've been. I stayed locked in my old bedroom; I only moved from my bed to use the bathroom and eat. I avoided mirrors—specifically my horrific reflection—and kept my bedroom dark and dank. I accepted my new life: living at my mother's, with nothing to fill my days but day-time soap operas and frozen dinners.

After two months of my sloth-like existence, my mother burst into my room. "Alright that's enough!" she screamed. She threw open the curtains, letting in the bright Nevada sun. I shrieked as the light burned my unaccustomed eyes.

She pulled the covers off my bed and gripped the mattress, threatening to flip it with me still on it.

"Are you crazy?" I hissed as I scrambled off the bed and to a shaded corner.

"No, Breanne. I am perfectly sane. But this," she said, pointing to me and my room, "this is crazy. And it ends today. You are getting up. You are going to brush your teeth and that tangled mane you call hair. You are going to burn the clothes you've been living in and you are going to start working. This pity party is done."

She stomped out of my room, leaving me utterly shell-shocked.

Truthfully, I hadn't considered looking for a job. My reality was school and continuing to research anything and everything in hopes of making a truly significant historical discovery. A job meant being around people. I didn't want a boss or co-workers, weekly office meetings, or water-cooler gossip. People in the present were pointless. I just wanted to be left alone.

But there was no arguing with my mother—if she said more than two consecutive sentences to me, she meant business. She wanted me out of her house. For good.

So, I stalked job boards for assistant curator or preservationist positions at every American history museum. Then started submitting my resume. I didn't think much would come of it. If all else failed, I'd crawl back to the University of Arizona—I would've been perfectly content living in the stacks of their library.

Then I got the call from the Gettysburg National Military Park.

A recruiter had reached out to one of my professors, looking for a recent college grad to fill a vacated staff position. That professor dropped my name and submitted my senior thesis—without my permission. After, he called me to explain what he'd done, and said that the museum wanted an in-person interview. Initially, I was irritated; it was a dream job, one that I wasn't qualified for. I assumed I was the laughing stock of Gettysburg. My professor thought differently. He convinced me to purchase a plane ticket, with money I didn't have, and fly across the country, to a place I'd never been, to meet with the assistant director of Exhibits and Collections, Dr. Greg Ransome.

My mother was thrilled and even drove me to the airport.

With only a backpack, I climbed out of her beat-up station wagon at the departure gate, feeling rather bewildered. I'd never been on a cross-country flight, so I turned, hoping for a bit of encouragement, only to see the back of her head in the rear windshield of her station wagon. She beeped twice, stuck her hand out the window and maneuvered away into airport traffic. Like she was just dropping me at the library, as she'd done every summer weekday of my childhood. Crestfallen, I walked towards the ticketing counter, knowing no one really cared what happened to me next.

After a turbulent plane ride and a sleepless night at a cheap motel, I arrived by taxi and stepped into the museum's administration office fifteen minutes early; my

outfit—approved and partially paid for by my mother—
had survived the cross-country plane ride with no wrinkles.
I looked over my thesis—*The Excavation and Preservation
of Pioneer Artifacts on the Oregon* Trail—one last time before closing my portfolio and leaned back against the wall.
I'm going to kill this, I'm going to walk out of here with a job, I
repeated to myself over and over with my eyes closed. I
started to sway with my repeated mantra. Everything was
perfect, and it felt good.

"Ms. Walker?"

My eyes shot open and I jumped to my feet, forgetting
that my perfect portfolio—meticulously organized to emphasize my research and restoration skills—still sat on my
lap. The white pages scattered all over the marble floor;
I just managed to stifle the expletive escaping my lips.
Horror-stricken, I dropped to my knees and started grabbing at my papers.

"I'm so sorry." He bent down to help me. "I guess I
should put bells on my shoes or something." As I gathered
my pages, I stole a few looks at him. He was young and
very handsome. His hair was ashy blonde, his eyes were
like sapphires, and he was very tall and fit. *Did he just walk
off the cover of GQ?* Despite my limited knowledge of fashion,
I noted a Rolex on his wrist and equally expensive brown
leather shoes on his feet.

"First time on the East Coast?" he asked as he scooped up
a few sheets.

"What? I mean—yes. How did you know?"

"An educated guess." He pointed to the University of Arizona alumni button on my backpack. "I assume you grew up in Arizona and not California? No one from California would kill *this* many trees." He laughed, pointing to his building pile of papers.

I forced a laugh but was suppressing my building aggravation. Why was he helping me? No one who looked like him ever took a second glance at me. My mousey-brown and barely brushed hair, unexceptional hazel eyes, skin that freckled but never tanned, and below-average height have never stopped traffic. He had nothing to gain by being nice to me. Plus, I didn't want anyone touching my portfolio. The only people permitted to touch it were myself and Dr. Ransome.

"It's really okay, I have this. I don't want to hold you up," I said, gathering my portfolio in a haphazard pile and standing.

"Can't hold an interview without the interviewee." He stood and handed over my last few pages.

"Excuse me?" I was speedily reorganizing my portfolio and only half listening.

"Oh, sorry. I'm Dr. Greg Ransome. The assistant director of Exhibits and Collections. You can call me Greg, everyone does."

My papers—along with another expletive—nearly dropped again.

An hour and a half later, I had talked through my expertise in journal transcription and conservation. Dr. Ransome stared and made the occasional observation, but he took no notes — which irked me. In fact, there wasn't a pen or a pad of paper to be seen in his Lysol-smelling, pristine office.

"I spent two months traveling the trail and really put myself in the mindset of a pioneer," I blabbered on. "Afterwards, I stayed in Oregon, searching every box in the state's archive. I hoped to discover a journal kept by a woman that gave accurate details of life. Obviously, the travelers had much more on their minds than detailing their experiences — like disease, famine, and the unfamiliar environment. But it's so rare to hear a woman's perspective of that time."

"Did you ever find one?" he asked.

"Unfortunately, no. Outside of a few buck-shot shells and arrowheads, I found very little on the actual trail. But an estate sale in Oregon became my personal gold mine; I found six handwritten death records at the bottom of a steamer trunk. I authenticated and preserved the documents, and then I was able to find the living descendants. A few death records weren't what I was envisioning but it was fulfilling in its own way."

"I envy your experience," he said, adjusting the cuffs of his tailored, button-down shirt. "Field work is the one thing I never got to experience in college. I geared more towards the business side of anthropology: administration, gallery planning, the procurement of research funding," he said, flicking his hands through the air. "Following in the old man's footsteps, you could say."

"How so?"

He cocked his head in confusion, as if I should've known. "My family's collection makes up most of the museum's holdings. And my father sits on the Board of Trustees."

Greg Ransome, of the Robert Ransome Collection. Trust-fund baby. It took everything in me not to roll my eyes.

Dr. Ransome continued to smile and stare. *He's not taking me seriously at all,* I thought.

"I just have one last question, Breanne. Why?"

"Why?"

He leaned forward in his chair, looking me straight in the eye. "Why any of this? Why are you pursuing a life of history?"

Is this a trick question? So, I blurted out the first thing the neurons in my brain flashed. "I want to leave my thumb-print in this world. I want to bring a part of the past into the present." It was the most cliché, Miss-America-contestant response a person could give. Unoriginal and uncreative. I had just blown my one chance.

The smile plastered on his face grew, and he started to nod.

A few minutes later, I walked out of the museum feeling disoriented. Because I got the job. *My dream job.*

"The board requires the interview and a screening pro-cess," he'd explained, "but the truth is we need some young eyes on this antiquated topic. And after I read your thesis, I knew you'd be a perfect fit. Hopefully flying back with a solid job offer makes the trip worthwhile."

"I...I'm...I don't..."

"Just say yes!"

11

"Yes! Yes! Thank you, Dr. Ransome." My self-worth was soaring high above me, higher than it had been my entire life.

"Please call me Greg, Breanne." He reached for my hand, shaking it vigorously, then showed me to his office door. "Now go home and pack up your life. We need you on the East Coast."

"Thanks?" I managed to utter as I stumbled out of his office, praying I'd make it outside without fainting.

"Oh, and Breanne," Greg called from behind me, "the question I asked? My answer would've been the same; making history is why we pursue history." He shot me another million-dollar grin and closed his office door.

He gave me back my life.

So, like I said, when Greg calls—even at 3:45 in the morning—and says to meet him in an unknown location near Little Round Top, for a reason he can't explain, you jump over that gaping gorge. No matter how far the fall or how crazy it sounds, you jump.

After driving on a branch-littered road for fifteen minutes—at senior-citizen speed, with my body pressed up against the steering wheel in paranoia—I was finally at the junction of Warren and Sykes. I turned left onto Sykes, squinting into the deep darkness ahead. This was the reason the National Park was closed at dusk; there were no lights lining the battleground paths, and if you got lost, you were out of luck. The directions Greg had given were vague at best. "The monuments will be on your left—pass them and drive for five minutes, "he said. No "go right on a gravel road," or "look for an odd-shaped boulder." Just "drive on a dark, extremely haunted road and hope you run into me." I inched past Little Round Top and tried to steady my pounding heart.

Little Round Top was one of the bloodiest battlegrounds of the American Civil War. A stone face surrounded by jagged rock that looked out onto an open field, it had been the high ground of the battle. Union sharpshooters picked off their enemies from a thousand feet away, firing into Devil's Den—a boulder formation in the open field at the base of the rockface—where many Confederate soldiers were taking shelter. The forested land atop the hill was where Col. Strong Vincent stalwartly led his brigade of Pennsylvanians and found infamy only in death. Where the 20th Maine Volunteer Infantry Regiment bayonet-charged oncoming Confederate troops. Where the Confederates formed ranks again and again and could not get the upper hand. The site of so much bloodshed, Little Round Top was beyond ominous.

Driving in the dark on Sykes Avenue—the road that split the wooded battleground in half—was spooky, to say the least.

"How the heck am I supposed to find him?" My voice echoed in my car. Momentarily, my fear dissipated and was replaced with overt annoyance.

The forest on either side of my car only got thicker, and the darkness bore down on me. The shine of my headlights seemed to stretch only a few inches beyond my front bumper. I knew from the curve of the road that I would soon pass Wheatfield Road and that Sykes would become Sedgwick. But was that too far?

I seriously contemplated turning around, but then I saw something up ahead. Huge spot lights beamed into the woods and sky — reminiscent of the last scene in *E.T.* — eating the darkness and bringing light to the suffocating trees. The lights appeared to be shining on a single spot, in a circular pattern — like in *E.T.* They appeared to be about a quarter mile into the woods.

Jesus, Greg, I thought as I pulled off the road. My anxiety was replaced by excitement; my gut told me I was about to step into something big.

Chapter Three

Breanne Walker

I PARKED ON THE OPPOSING-TRAFFIC SIDE OF SYKES AVENUE, GRABBED my messenger bag and climbed out of my car. The car door slammed much harder than I intended, and the harsh sound reverberated off the trees, making my bones jump and probably waking a few woodland creatures.

Cautiously, I crossed the road and stepped into the woods. My steps were short, my arms outstretched — like the mummy in those black-and-white horror films — and fear was pulsing in my veins. The only sounds were the soft crunch of the debris beneath my feet and the pounding of my heart. I chided myself furiously for not having grabbed the flashlight stored in my trunk. Leaves rustled on either side of me, but I didn't dare look to find out why. Instead, I stared straight ahead and repeated "I don't believe in ghosts," until I almost believed it. Finally, a bit of light found its way past the massive tree trunks and lit the area in front of me in a hazy, orange tone.

Then the path in front of me was blocked by yellow police tape. **DO NOT CROSS,** it yelled out to the world in big, bold letters. I looked to the right and left; the entire area had been barricaded off. Undeterred, I ducked under the plastic tape.

"Wow! Wow!" someone screamed from my right. I turned to the right to see a park ranger emerging from the darkness and stomping towards me, flashlight raised and walkie-talkie at the ready.

"The park is closed! On the other side, girl!" he screamed, shining his flashlight directly into my face.

"I'm an employee at the museum. Dr. Ransome called me." I pulled my ID badge from my bag and batted the blind spots from my eyes.

He popped his walkie-talkie back into his belt loop and accepted my ID. He looked it over and shone his flashlight into my face three more times before he believed I was the person pictured. *Do I look that disheveled?* He motioned for me to open the flap of my messenger bag, which I did. He pointed the light inside, looking through my bag without actually looking through it. He turned from me and walked a few paces away, radioing over to someone else and speaking quick codes in hushed tones.

Am I breaking into the Pentagon, I thought as minute after minute went by and still, I stood on the outskirts of...well, whatever was in front of me.

"Okay, Ms. Walker. You're free to go on ahead. Dr. Ransome is waiting for you." He handed me my ID and ushered me forward like someone from air-traffic control.

"Thanks for your time," I said, tipping my imaginary hat. I walked away with a chip on my shoulder, feeling like an anthropological badass.

Once passed the armed guard, I stepped onto a grassy hill, promptly lost my balance, and slid onto my hands and knees. *Definitely misjudged that one,* I thought, hoping the ranger hadn't seen. After slipping two subsequent times, I crawled up the slippery incline on all fours, digging my fingers into the drenched earth.

Once the ground had leveled beneath me, I stood and found myself in a small clearing, lush with green grass, surrounded by massive oak trees, and emblazoned with artificial light. I wiped my slick hands on my sodden jeans — trying not to think of the creepy crawlers I had probably squished when I fell — and looked around. Hurried, loud conversations and the drowning buzz of four electric generators — powering multiple, massive construction lights — filled the air. People rushed here and there, reading notes from clipboards and making frantic phone calls. The cleared space wasn't large — 3,000 square feet at the most — but every inch was jam-packed with rangers, a backhoe, and complete chaos.

How the heck did they get a backhoe up here?

Before I could speculate, I heard Greg yelling my name. I looked around and saw him waving his arms frantically. He was dressed in basketball shorts and a white tee-shirt and running towards me like a little boy on the recess yard.

"So…. glad…. you…. found it," he huffed when he finally reached my side. He took a few gulps of air and then hunched over. From his pocket he pulled an inhaler and took a few puffs. *Another surprising characteristic.*

"Kind of hard to miss," I said. I patted him on the back. "Are you okay?"

He rose slowly but clutched at his chest. His face was crimson, and he was still gasping for air, but he managed to say, "I'm fine. Great. Just great. This is some night!"

"I can see that!" I pointed to the commotion around us.

"It's beyond exciting. You'll be thanking me for pulling you out of bed for the rest of your life." He beamed from ear to ear.

"Well, I don't know about that, I do like my sleep." I stifled a yawn.

"You can sleep when you're dead," he said, taking my elbow and guiding me forward.

He walked — rather, pranced — on his tiptoes, like he was afraid to bend the blades of grass. And he was talking a mile a minute. So fast, in fact, that I couldn't understand more than half of it. *If he keeps this up, he'll need his inhaler again before we reach our destination.* He maneuvered his way among the throngs of people. Then, without warning, he stopped dead in his tracks and almost tripped me. Without an apology — or a single word — he dropped my elbow and stepped ahead to what he had pulled me out of bed for.

It was a gigantic, overturned tree, pulled up to the roots.

"Is that...supposed to be tipped over?" My voice was high-pitched and whiney. I felt stupid for asking, but I was completely dumbfounded. Steam was rising from the tips of the branches, and there was a strong smell of burning wood.

"No, not at all. That tree has stood tall and strong for over one hundred and fifty years, until Mother Nature decided to pound Gettysburg tonight. A bolt of lightning went straight through her." He pointed to the charred split in the upper branches.

"So that's a—"

"A Witness Tree. Survived the battle and thrived in this very spot."

I felt cemented to the spot. He motioned me forward. My eyes bugged, and I obeyed like a mind-controlled zombie. From my minor knowledge of Gettysburg and its arboreal inhabitants, I could tell the tree was a white oak. They were known for large branches that shot out at abnormal angles, thick trunks—gray, scaly, and covered in moss—and warty acorns. Their bowers were bountiful and adorned with glossy, green leaves, lobed and symmetrical from the center vein. Most of those leaves now littered the ground beneath my feet. Undoubtedly this tree had been breathtaking when it was standing upright. The park rangers circled the tree like buzzards scouting prey, clipboards in hand. Some were taking exact measurements of the circumference of the trunk, its height, the length of its roots, and the branch span. I stepped closer and inched between two rangers. I ran my fingers over the trunk, realizing I was touching a piece of history. These trees were the only living witnesses to a time gone by. They were living monuments. "The trunk hasn't been cut for carbon-dating?" I asked, reverence striking me hard.

19

"No, not yet." He stepped beside me and waved the surrounding rangers away. "They are waiting on me. All Witness Trees are registered with the Arbor Society. But that's not what's important right now," he said guiding me back to the base of the trunk, where the roots were more exposed. The roots extended deep into the ground, some still grasping for dirt, as gravity took the rest sideways. He pointed down into the hole the tree had left behind. A hole, eight feet across and maybe six feet deep. I crouched down to get a better look. There wasn't much to see, so I looked back to Greg with a *so what* expression.

"Pass me that," Greg instructed a ranger at his side, who obediently passed him a small dust brush. He jumped into the hole. Placing his feet in a wide stance, he bent forward and began to brush away the remaining thin layer dirt from a point directly in the middle of his stance. To reveal what appeared to be a cloth, covering a sphere. An elongated sphere that thinned out towards the bottom, then broadened out.

Like shoulder blades and a skull...

I gasped so loud that I woke the birds nesting nearby.

"There's more." He looked up and shot me another toothy grin. *More than a freaking body?* He pulled himself out of the hole and motioned for me to follow him to the opposite side of the felled tree, where the roots were splayed upon the ground like two-feet long fingers. He looked to his sides—making sure no one was watching—then dropped to his knees and reached among the roots.

"When I arrived, I did a walk around the tree's entire circumference," he said, his voice muffled. "I saw something dangling among the roots. So, I halted the proceedings and rushed everyone out. I wanted you to be here when I pulled out whatever it is." He crawled among the roots, obstructing my view; all I could see were the roots shaking as he grabbed at something deep within. Then he shimmied out from the tree and got to his feet. In his hand was a square-shaped object, wrapped in burlap. "Time to be part of history," he said as he handed over the bundle.

"It could be trash."

"Okay!" He threw his arms up like he'd been caught cheating on a test. "I peeked. But only enough to know it was worth calling you, and then I put it right back."

The package was light, hard, but also pliable. Carefully, I slipped the rough burlap down, and my breath caught in my throat again. Beneath the burlap was a white cotton cloth. The fabric — like the burlap — was weather worn, stained and old. My fingers acted on their own accord; I removed the burlap and pulled back the cotton fabric, to reveal brown leather.

A brown, leather-bound book.

Chapter Four

Breanne Walker

A BODY. A LEATHER-BOUND BOOK. SWEAT WAS POOLING ON MY forehead and my palms. The very same palms that were holding the small bundle. Frantically, I looked for somewhere to place the long-buried book, knowing that every second my bare hands touched the leather, they were damaging a potential historic artifact.

"Take these," Greg said, handing me a pair of white gloves.

"Oh," I said, thankful that he'd had the same thought as I. Gently, he took the book from me, and I slipped my hands into the gloves. "Has anyone else been here to inspect the findings?"

"No, just us. The Park Service called me first, and I wanted to see the site before waking all of Gettysburg." He looked over his shoulder, making sure no one was close enough to overhear.

"What about the body?" I asked, tearing my eyes away from the item in his hands and back to the tree. "No one has disturbed it? Are there markings on the tree to give any clue as to who it could be? How long has it been lying there?"

"I need approval before I touch any witness trees. The bark will need to be completely removed to be sure we don't miss carvings, if there are any. The body is in its original state—or so I would guess, based on the gravesite and its surroundings."

Hands properly gloved, I handed the burlap to Greg. Then he handed back the bundle. My fingertips barely touched the cotton cloth, when an icy jolt passed through me. I felt my eyes roll and then close. For half a second, a scene flashed in my head.

A shrouded face. Eyes. Pleading eyes, reaching out and drawing me in.

In complete and utter terror, I forced my eyes open. I turned this way and that, searching the field for what I'd just seen. But there was no sign of that haunted face. Greg was staring intently at his iPhone and hadn't noticed my reaction. My entire body was tingling from shock, but I shook the vision from my head. *Sleep deprivation. Must be.* "What happens now?" I asked.

He slipped his phone into his pocket and stepped closer to me. "A whirlwind, naturally. The last time this happened—fifty years ago, when General Meade's bible and some personal letters were found beneath a pile of rocks on Cemetery Hill—the entire country converged on Gettysburg. But for now, the body will stay where it is entombed—nothing can be touched by unsupervised hands. Once it's uncovered, samples will be collected: clothing fibers, teeth, hair, bone fragments, all for carbon dating and

DNA analysis. The best of our staff will be pulled in to assist with the research." He sounded excited and exhausted at the same time.

"And this?" I lifted the bundle into sight.

"Well that lies, literally, in your hands."

I stared back at him in confusion.

"Transcription and conservation of manuscripts is your expertise, correct?"

"Yes, but—"

"You're the only preservationist not currently assigned to a project. Peggy Cupples won't be available for weeks."

Peggy Cupples, the lead archivist and the foremost expert on antiquities at the Gettysburg National Military Park. Her name had been associated with every major discovery made in the last twenty years, particularly with the Battle of Gettysburg. She was responsible for the majority of the research grants and annuities that came into the museum. Her ego and reputation were as big and colorful as her resume—she was controlling, domineering, demanding, and hard to work with. Once, I heard her assistant say, "She's a viper in a three-piece Armani pant-suit." She walked the museum's hallways with an air of superiority and a gaggle of research interns trailing behind. If ever I saw her coming, I'd melt into the wall, pretending I was wallpaper.

If she ever found out I'd swiped this research opportunity from her, her wrath would be unimaginable; I'd be blacklisted in the research world. I'd lose my job—my dream job, my lifeline and reason for existing. "Peggy is way more qualified, Greg. I really insist you call and at least offer —"

"Yes, she is more qualified. Unbelievably more qualified. But her time is precious and is better suited to her present grant. This," he said, placing a light hand on the bundle, "needs someone's complete attention."

"I've never done something of this magnitude, Greg! I'm too junior! I don't have the right to even breathe near it. I don't...I can't." I wanted, more than anything, to keep what I held in my hands — I felt an unnatural pull to it, a responsibility to keep it safe. But the professional risks were too great, and I knew the possibilities that could lie beneath the leather cover. How history itself could change when buried and forgotten passages were brought to light. One slip-up could harm the manuscript and damage history itself. I'd be responsible. That scared me more than anything. Suddenly, my knees felt very weak.

"You'll never know if you don't try. So why don't you start, right now." He pulled back the cloth, revealing another inch of the leather beneath.

My hand snapped up in shock. "Here? Now? Absolutely not!"

"Why? Aren't you curious at all?" he asked, a mischievous grin planted on his lips.

"Of course, I am! Who wouldn't be? You just pulled this from a tree that stood during one of the most important battles on American soil. And then there's that." I pointed to the unearthed grave.

"All the more reason to unwrap this now." He reached again for the bundle, but I snatched my hands back.

"No! We need to get this back to the museum, into a temperature-controlled environment, and call Peggy!"

"We don't need to set up a full laboratory, just to open a book cover. We need to know what we're getting ourselves into. This is history, Breanne. Isn't this what you always wanted: to find a manuscript and leave your thumbprint? Here's your chance."

He was looking at me with a stupid grin, challenging me, urging me on. *Bad, bad, bad idea*, I repeated to myself over and over. I should hand him the bundle, walk away, and go straight back to my apartment. I should let this amazing, life-changing, career-affirming—*or damning*—discovery wait until I reached a climate-controlled environment. It'd be easy.

But I couldn't get away from that stupid, movie-star grin of his.

I caved. I closed my eyes—*if I can't see myself, possibly, defiling a historic artifact, then I'm not, possibly, defiling a historic artifact, right?* With my free hand, I peeled off the cotton cloth, then carefully stuck my gloved fingers between the cover and what I assumed was the first page. I could feel my heart pounding harder, as if the skin across my chest was stretched too thin, and my heart was going to rip right through.

I ripped off the Band-Aid and lifted the cover.

From the nearness of his sharp intake of breath, I sensed Greg had moved closer to my side. My eyes opened and beheld a page of weatherworn, yellowing parchment. These words were all that was contained there — in precise, elegant handwriting:

Written Accounts of

A.M.P.

1863

My hands went weak and almost dropped the precious book, which I now knew was a diary.

Chapter Five

Breanne Walker

Y OU KNOW THOSE "FIGHT OR FLIGHT" MOMENTS THAT SOLDIERS talk about when they know their life is at risk? Physically, they are about to drop from exhaustion, but the adrenaline sets in, and they are unstoppable. They keep fighting because they know the enemy is at their back, and the need to protect their comrades becomes more important. So, the physical exhaustion disappears, and they fight until they drop.

Well after reading that first page, my first panicked impulse wasn't to fight; I slapped the cover shut, clutched the diary close to my chest, and ran from Greg.

I just fled, like a rocket was slapped on my back and then ignited. I needed to take my precious cargo to the safest place possible. Where that was, I wasn't too sure, but it wasn't on that patch of clear land past Little Round Top. I felt no control and completely reckless; Peggy and my future at the museum were pushed to the furthest part of my brain. I could hear Greg screaming, calling me every synonym for "lunatic" as he desperately attempted to catch up.

I was ducking beneath the yellow tape at the bottom of the hill when he finally did. He yanked my arm back—not too gently—to force me to turn and face him. I yelped in pain, almost dropping the diary.

"What the hell, Greg!" The pain in my arm grew like a brush fire. "You could've pulled my arm out of its socket!"

"You need to calm down!" he yelled back, catching his asthmatic breath. His eyes were pulsing—it was frightening.

"I can't stay here. This," I waved the diary in his face, "can't stay here."

"I know! I get it! But you can't just take off like you're in the middle of a bank heist!"

I nodded like a little girl, scolded after touching a hot stove. "What now?" I asked.

He took a long breath and looked back towards the brightly lit excavation site. "In a few hours, this area is going to be a zoo: museum employees looking for additional artifacts, reporters snooping for exclusives, the museum trying to micromanage it all. And that," he said, turning back and pointing to the diary, "will only add to the mayhem." Defensively, I stepped back from him; the need to run was building within me as he continued. "But as my father always says, 'It's better to ask for forgiveness than permission.'"

"I'm not sure I understand."

He took the diary from me, rewrapped it in the cotton cloth and gently placed it inside my messenger bag. "Go home, get some sleep. I'll hold off the museum for as long as I can. I'll let them believe the body was the sole discovery — that will tie them up for at least a few days. And by then, hopefully you'll have something earth-shattering to report."

"I can't work from my apartment, Greg! Everything I'll need is at the museum. Peggy will — "

"I'll handle it! I'll reserve one of the back labs and make sure no one disturbs you for a few days." He lifted the yellow tape and ushered me beneath it.

"I'll need to send specimens for testing," I said as I ducked under. "Carbon dating. Ink samples. I'll need access to — "

"Everything will be arranged," he said, sounding more stressed with every second. "You need to trust me with this; I won't leave you in the lurch. Now go home before I change my mind. Go!" He dropped the tape, turned me away from him and pushed me into the woods, in the direction of the road.

I stumbled out into the dark, knowing that Peggy's wrath was now unavoidable. *Kiss your job goodbye, Breanne!*

Chapter Six

Breanne Walker

T HE SUNRISE WAS A FIERY ORANGE AND DEEP PURPLE WHEN I FINAL-
ly got back to my apartment's parking lot. It was
breathtaking. I hadn't seen a sunrise since my time on the
Oregon Trail—*sunrises on open, virgin land are an emotional
experience,* as I claimed in my thesis—and if I hadn't been
so tired, I would've stopped and marveled at its brilliance
from the safety of my balcony. But I was like the Tinman
awaiting Dorothy's application of oil; my joints were stiff,
unbendable and in desperate need of lubrication. Mounting
two flights of stairs was a feat.

After my door was closed—and locked—I bee-lined
straight to the kitchen and rummaged inside my cabinets,
looking for a large Ziploc bag. I found one and slipped the
rewrapped diary inside it, then returned my stowaway to
my bag. In my bedroom, I placed my belongings on my
desk—half asleep but fully aware that in my bag was something priceless—and belly-flopped into bed. My shoes and
jacket were still on, but I didn't care as I cocooned myself

beneath my blankets. In my current state—complete mental and physical exhaustion—touching anything of historic importance was not wise. I lifted my head to look at the clock on my nightstand—5:45 a.m.—and set my alarm for ten a.m.

Instead, I got a solid forty-five minutes of tossing and turning.

I urged myself to sleep. I did muscle exercises beneath my covers, I closed my eyes and tried to think of things to dream of, I counted sheep—I got to about fifty and gave up. I even prayed—something I hadn't done since grammar school. I think I combined the Our Father and the Hail Mary, and I couldn't remember how either ended. Nothing worked.

My brain was overly wired from all that had transpired, whirling with endless questions concerning what lay in my messenger bag across my bedroom. I lay there in the dark, analyzing the smallest details of all I had seen: the tree on its side, the size of the hole, and particularly what was beneath the tree's roots. Then my mind started dissecting the word 'accounts': could the book be a record of the season's harvest, the amounts of fabric woven, or a financial ledger? But given the year—1863—I hoped it'd be the personal writings of someone who lived through the Battle of Gettysburg. Then, lingering in the far corners of my subconscious was the reality and repercussions of what I'd just done—*though virtually forced, you just committed a crime by stealing an artifact off a dig site; an act that will assuredly get you fired from your dream job, possibly arrested, and end your career in the preservation field.* There was no escaping my torturous anxiety.

I looked at my alarm clock. *Only 6:32?* The seconds became longer — *30 seconds have gone by, why aren't you at 33 already!* The clock became my enemy, and I was very tempted to smash it against the wall.

I watched the time change from 6:32 to 6:33 and realized sleep was pointless. My only option was to get to work; dazzle Peggy with my authentication skills and force her to forget my alleged crime. *Save your job, Breanne.* I sat up and swept my blankets to the side. My feet hit the floor, and fatigue was replaced by resolution. I stepped over to my desk and carefully slung my messenger bag over my shoulder. I didn't bother to change, to brush my hair or my teeth; at this hour, I didn't care who I ran into at the museum. As for later, I intended to stay well away from my co-workers.

I grabbed my keys and headed for the door.

Chapter Seven

Breanne Walker

A T 7 A.M., THE GETTYSBURG NATIONAL MILITARY PARK WAS AS
silent as an off-season amusement park. *Where is everyone?*
The custodians should've been clustered around the
main entrance, emptying trashcans, running vacuums, and
squeegee cleaning the windows. After using my ID to get
inside, I saw no one. I called out and listened to my voice
reverberate against the walls and the twelve-foot ceilings.
The hum of the industrial sized air-conditioner was the only
thing that answered. Then I remembered it was the Sunday
of Labor Day weekend. All museum employees were likely
in bed or on mini-vacations with their families.

Divine intervention had dropped this privacy into my
lap; I had no family on the East Coast, no holiday plans to
call me away from Gettysburg. I smiled and confidently
walked through the vestibule, with my shoes squeaking on
the pristine marble floor.

A persistent squeaking that was painfully pointed out
my first week on the job.

When I moved to Gettysburg, I figured I'd forego buying a car until the winter, which I heard were cruel and unrelenting. Pennsylvania had arid, Indian Summers that lasted until mid-October, so I bought a bike to get back and forth from work.

I quickly regretted that decision.

Day after rain-soaked day, I'd arrive at work, soaked to the bone. There wasn't a poncho or umbrella big enough to keep the rain out — trust me, I bought four different sizes. I also didn't have a dryer, so my radiator became a makeshift Laundromat and my no-brand sneakers never quite dried out. Now, they make a permanent squishing sound — like a rubber ducky.

That first week, I found a note on my desk;

> *Buy a car*
> *555-685-6482*
> *Ask for Jimmy*
> *—Your Co-Workers, who wish they were deaf*

I was mortified. It took me back to high school and the traumatizing notes taped to my locker; *Do you ever* WASH *those jeans* — their pink, gel-penned notes asked in a mockingly-girlish, Valley-girl accent. Rather than face further ridicule in the cafeteria, I'd spend my lunch in a bathroom stall—which I repeated after finding the adult version of that note. You never get over that kind of humiliation and bullies never really become adults—they only find new, age-appropriate targets.

I bought a car that same day; a 1999 Pontiac Grand Am with over one-hundred thousand miles on it. It was a total junker and probably wouldn't see me through the year, but it solved my immediate rainy-day problems. I also stopped wearing those sneakers to work.

Except today.

I squeaky-stepped past the galleries, gift shop, and wall-to-wall advertisements for the 155th anniversary of the Gettysburg Address—our next big event. I continued down a long hallway lined with employee offices, conference rooms, and paintings of President Lincoln and Jefferson Davis. I opened and stepped through the **Employees Only** engraved set of doors that led back to the administration offices and labs. I was already halfway down the hall when the doors closed behind me—I walked with a fire at my back.

My hands were shaking as I slid my badge through the next ID sensor and stepped into a TSA-like body scanner that was used as a decontamination chamber. The chamber was glass-plated, 8-feet in height, and used pressurized steam to remove outside contagions. With my bag slung over my shoulder, I stood in the center of the chamber, hands above my head and waited. The footpads beneath me sensed my weight and the door closed, then the machine buzzed to life. My first few weeks at the museum, I'd jumped out of my skin every time the door closed behind me — I've never been comfortable with small spaces. But this time I barely flinched as steam streamed from a small nozzle by my feet and moved up the length of my body three times. The air and moisture were then sucked out and pumped through the vents above my head. A green light blinked, and a second door slid open to my left.

Ready to go, I thought as I stepped into a white-washed, décor-free hallway. Four doors off the hallway led into basic labs. They were identical in size and orientation: 13-feet by 16-feet deep, with floor-to-ceiling glass walls facing the corridor and lit by fluorescent dome lighting. The first two were research labs. An aluminum-topped worktable ran down the center of the room, with small stools beneath for seating. Three walls were lined with filing cabinets, and the fourth held a computer station. On the tables were microscopes, magnifying glasses, beakers, brushes, extraction needles: everything a conservator would need. These rooms were designed for the extracting of evidence and the dating of materials. The facts uncovered were used to prove the authenticity of anything from clothing and pottery to art work and ammunitions — including bullets and sabers, which most natives of the county claimed to own. Also, specimens were extracted from human remains and ink — from handwritten accounts like diaries or maps — so they could be sent to our labs in Harrisburg for more in-depth analysis.

Next were two preservation labs, where artifacts were moved once their authenticity was proven. In these labs, the microscopes were replaced by sewing machines, cutting supplies, pins, seam rippers, clear rulers, bottles of leather oil, and air-controlled clothing racks. Here is where uniforms were repaired—their hems, buttons, holes, and any other aspect that were damaged. Wood and other furniture was reinforced and returned to its original state. Art was cleaned, jewelry polished, leather treated, and handwritten documents rebound and preserved. Artifacts already on display were brought back frequently for maintenance.

At the end of the hallway was an elevator shaft that only went down and up one story—down to the archives beneath the museum. Stretching the entire length of the building, this was where the most precious items were kept under lock and key. The museum's collection of Civil War artifacts—the largest in the country—included rare books that were too delicate for display. Duplicates were painstakingly created, and these were displayed in the public areas, with most people never knowing the difference. The archives was temperature controlled and access was sparingly granted by Greg, Peggy and one other curator.

I stepped into the first research lab, shut the door and turned on the lights. I took a long look around. Greg was right; once news of the discovery hit the museum circuit there would be rubberneckers and a lot of questions. So, I had to get the initial examination done and be out of the lab as quickly as possible—*part one of keeping my job.*

I exhaled a long, held breath and placed my messenger bag down on the smooth worktable. I had two, maybe three days before Greg had to tell the board and Peggy about our second discovery. Three days to prove I could lead the project and silence anyone who thought I was unqualified.

My hands and mind worked methodically, collecting everything I needed. Manila folders were dropped on the lab table, along with a pencil—ink was a dangerous tool on delicate materials and was strictly forbidden in conservation labs. I lined up hypodermic needles, vials and stoppers, filter paper, and pipettes. From my bag I pulled my personal cloth gloves—my lucky pair that had seen me through undergrad and graduate school—and my preservation kit—inside a *My Little Pony* pencil case that my mother gave me for my fifth birthday. Childish, yes, but it was tin and lightweight.

With my tools in order, I pulled a stool from beneath the table and took a seat, then retrieved the diary from my bag. I opened the Ziploc bag; my pulse quickened the moment my fingers touched the hard surface of its cover. I pulled on my cloth gloves, and slowly removed the outer cotton fabric. *Okay, cloth first.* When it came to the age, the cloth was as important as the actual text. The smallest of specimens could pin-point an accurate date.

With tweezers in hand, I ran my fingers along the edges of the cloth. In the right corner, I found a tiny bug, smaller than my finger tip, and likely a deer tick. If it was a tick, evidence from the inside could be valuable—especially if it had a meal right before dying. *Like the amber mosquitos in Jurassic Park.* I secured the specimen between two microscope slides and labeled it. I also found a few blades of grass stuck in the fabric. I managed to scrape a dirt sample from the middle of the back of the cloth, as well as a few fragments of what appeared to be rock sediment—carbon dating could be drawn from both.

I sat back and looked at the small pile of collected samples. *Not bad,* I thought. Ready to move on, my hand happened to graze the lower left corner. There was a slight raise and edge in the fabric beneath my fingers. I grabbed my magnifying glass and studied the spot. Barely visible was the etching of a design—I brushed my finger over it and felt a different pattern than the rest of the cloth.

"Embroidery?"

I looked closer and could see a faint design of swirling curls and what appeared to be flowers. The center of the pattern seemed different and script-like. *The thread's dye has faded,* I assumed as I continue to look at the corner. I ran my gloved finger over it again and closed my eyes—letting my mind guide me.

"R.M.A." I opened my eyes.

A monogram? With my cell phone, I snapped a picture of the corner, zooming in as far as the lens would allow. These were different initials than those inside the diary. If I was finding anomalies before even opening it, no doubt the diary held many mysteries.

After examining every inch of the cloth, without ripping it apart and sewing it back together, I clipped a small piece of fabric from the corner. Then I sat back and cracked my knuckles. My specimens were all lined up, labeled, and ready to be shipped to the lab in Harrisburg for further analysis.

Now it was time to dive into the diary.

The leather was of a reddish-brown hue. Almost the color of redwood bark — California trees I've only seen in pictures. The material was soft to the touch and flexible. As I ran my gloved fingers down the cover, imprints formed beneath my touch. Thankfully my fingers left no marks. The leather was well-treated with oil — pliable and glossy. I held it to my face and breathed in, smelling leather, dirt, and a tinge of mold.

The spine was still intact — slight wear and tear on the side edges, but it had a firm hold on the pages inside. There were hundreds of volumes in the archives that had seen many man-hours and still weren't in as good condition as this. Most had needed to be re-sewed page by page. Some didn't survive the conservation process and were left in pieces. The fact that this diary had been protected from human contact for over a hundred years — or so I assumed — worked to its advantage. Humans cause the most damage. *To everything.* I removed the scalpel from my kit and cut a tiny square of the leather from the spine. I picked the piece up with tweezers and placed it inside a vial.

I turned the diary front to back and looked closely with my magnifying glass. Maker-marks or dates were usually found on the backside cover, but this didn't appear to have one. *Locally made,* I thought turning it back to the front cover.

I inspected the spine closely. The stitching appeared to be sinew, which was sturdier than regular thread. Most likely it was deer sinew, which was commonly used as threading material in the 19th century. It was sewed in a very close, cross pattern with uneven gaps between the stitches, a mistake that a machine wouldn't make. I applied a small amount of pressure to the thread with my tweezers. From my kit, I grabbed my scissors, pressed into the spine to make the thread bulge. Carefully, I snipped a piece of the sinew thread — another piece of the puzzle collected.

One more scan of the cover and I knew there was nothing left to do but open it up. I adjusted my gloves, slipped my middle and index finger beneath the front cover, and lifted. Revealing, once again, the title page.

Written Accounts of

A.M.P.

1863

I picked up my magnifying glass and lowered my face to the page.

The paper was off-white — pure white paper was rare before the turn of the 20th century because removing striations, bleaching, and preparing the paper was a more arduous task. The weathered edges were tinged a darker color — like a tea bag had been placed on the edge and the contents stained the paper. The paper towards the center of the book was probably still its original hue.

I made a few notes, then opened the diary to the exact center and placed a light weight on each side — making sure not to rip the binding or cause damage to the spine. I pressed down slightly, testing the weights. Then something caught my eye.

The light above illuminated something within the spine. But I couldn't see exactly what it was. I picked up my tweezers and carefully poked at the center of the spine until I saw the shine shift. I clamped down. I retracted the tweezers while my other hand fumbled for a vial. My hands were shaking but I managed to get the edges of the tweezer inside the vial without dropping its cargo. I loosened my fingers, and the item fell into the vial. I placed a stopper in the vial and grabbed my magnifying glass.

It was a very fine piece of auburn hair. An archeologist's dream discovery.

Though little, the hair was a clue to the time and could connect the manuscript to a person. Lab techs made daily stops at the museum, so the analysis could be started as early as tomorrow — with results as quickly as two days. *If only today wasn't the second day of a three-day holiday weekend.* I wanted to jump up on the worktable and do a jig. I was in a groove — one I hadn't felt since graduate school and missed terribly.

But it would all have to wait two more days.

I leaned back on my stool and stretched my aching back. *Now comes the fun part.* I pulled in closer to the table with pencil and notepad at the ready. My fingers reached for the manuscript and flipped to the title page.

"Written Accounts of A.M.P. 1863," I read aloud and turned the page.

Chapter Eight

A.M.P.

April 15th, 1863

I would like to preface this by clearly stating that I am not the usual type to use a journal to capture my life—I refuse, with every part of my being to call this a diary as I believe it sounds sophomoric. I assure you, I am not a fanatical little girl, who will fill your pages with daydreams and the first buddings of love for the preacher's son. Nor am I an old man, looking to recall his days of glory and to reaffirm his own importance in the world. It is the people who haven't lived and dream of their lives to come, or those who are nearing their ends that have the need to list the daily workings of their lives. Most don't have the time or energy to devote to writing; as life is full and busy for those with children or professions.

And when my dear baby sister presented me with you this past Christmas, I was uncertain of her motive.

"They're all the fashion," she said as I opened your leather cover and flipped through your light pages. "I worry about you, sister, out in those woods, all alone. I thought this would help fill the lulls in your busy day."

Indeed, her words—and gift—had an unspoken and hidden meaning but I thanked her for the gift. Inwardly, I assumed you'd collect dust on the bookshelves above my bed, or your paper used as fire-kindling on an especially cold night.

And you did just that—sat on the shelf with my medical texts and novels, collecting dust and completely forgotten. Truly, I felt my sister had wasted her—or her husband's, depending on how you perceive it—money on such a useless gift. For me, writing in this manner is a waste of ink, paper, and precious time that could be dedicated to nobler pursuits.

But nature has forced me to take desperate measures to keep boredom at bay.

It has been raining for almost a week, with no end in sight. Clouds piled in from the west, blowing a strong wind that hasn't stopped. The ground is soaked through—drowning much of my herb and vegetable garden—and the creek has nearly overflowed. Our sheep are penned and huddled together under a large oak tree at the corner of the property. Like everything else, their fleecy coats are dripping with rainwater. My mare and milk cow have been cooped up inside the barn, which seems pure torture. I've tried to maintain my normal schedule as much as possible; I've braced myself against the elements and ventured twice to town, only to return hours later, soaked through and chilled to the bone. A chill that even the warmest of fires cannot disperse—one that fills the body with shakes that rattle one's teeth. I am beyond surprised I haven't come down with a dreadful cold or influenza. If either comes to pass, I have stockpiled enough herbal remedies to combat both ailments.

Today has been the worst of it; the winds are howling, and I can barely keep a fire lit in the hearth. Besides rushing to the barn for the cow's milking, I dare not step from my front door. But there is only so much one can do when trapped inside. I scrubbed the floors and furniture, dusted the shelves until they glistened, ironed my tablecloths, washed the curtains and dishes, swept or polished every earthly possession inside the cottage. And the rain has continued to pour. I once read about what sailors describe as "cabin fever." I cannot rightly compare my single day, locked inside to the months upon months that poor sailors endure at sea, but now I understand the mental ague they face.

Which leads me to you and your blank pages. Yes, it is out of desperation that I begin to fill you with my thoughts. I guess I need some way to break the silence—the silence beneath the patter of rain splashing against the wooden roof. Loneliness made me pull you down from the shelf.

But how does one start something like this? Do I introduce myself? Describe my appearance? Tell you how I grew up and what brought me to this moment? Do I describe my day-to-day life—even if it is mundane and uninteresting? Do I tell you my deepest desires and passions? What about my beliefs? Give you every miniscule detail that makes up my being, leaving no secrets behind?

The notion of pouring ones soul into an inanimate object is very odd. Especially when I will receive nothing in return. Most friendships have a give and take—a mutual exchange of opinions and beliefs that you give in the hopes you will learn from each other and grow. That exchange is impossible between us. In addition, the trust needed to reveal ones' secrets is not easily earned.

I know I sound half bonkers, as you are without bones and blood. You are just a book, not even a "you." But I am giving you life.

For now, I will give details as they come and try to be as transparent about my life as I can.

I hope the rain ends soon.

—A

April 17ᵗʰ, 1863

The rain has finally passed! When I opened my eyes this morning and saw sun shining through my curtains, I jumped out of bed, dressed and grabbed my boots, and then flung open the back door. I stood in the doorway, bathing in the spring air—crisp with a chilly wind that rustled through the tree branches. I stepped from the house and my feet instantly sank into thick mud from the flooded creek. My once grassy lawn was now filled with shallow pools of rainwater. I carefully navigated my way around the divvied pools of water to the barn, hoping that the day's sun would dry-up much of the remaining ground water and revive my bountiful grass.

I opened the barn doors and the various sounds that greeted me confirmed all I suspected: anxious animals and an overwhelming smell of refuse—of which knocked me back a few paces. Mucking the stalls was a daily chore, but the weather kept me from doing a proper job that last two days. So, I left the doors open wide—to help with the smell—and immediately approached Barley's—our mare—stall. I opened the gate and she ran out of the barn with an eagerness that I couldn't blame her for. I milked Gertie—our cow—and filled her trough with fresh hay and water. But she cared little for sustenance and followed Barley out to the sun. I spent an hour thoroughly mucking the barn—an arduous and disgusting task—before joining them outside. Across the yard was the fenced paddock, where twenty-five pairs of eyes were impatiently waiting for me. Our sheep, who enjoyed the freedom of the entire property, were just as desperate to be out of their fenced confinement as Barley and Gertie. I pulled open the gate and they speedily bounded into the yard. I'd need to check them for foot rot this week, I mentally noted. All the muck in the paddock wasn't good for the flock's hooves, but I'd need Henry—my neighbor's young son, who I hired to help with the livestock—to assist me.

Now it is almost noon and I must be on my way. I hope the roads aren't too soggy and that my journey will not be burdensome. I live four miles from the center of town, past

Little Hill, and it will take me over an hour to get there. The storms have kept me away far longer than usual — three days have passed, when I'm usually in town every other day.

I am ending this entry in haste. I'll return tonight to finish. I hate to admit but recording my days' work is somewhat satisfying.

April 17th cont'd

Writing this now, I am half asleep; it took much effort to simply light my lamp. But I want to finish this entry before I retire.

As I headed towards Taneytown Road atop Barley and along a small path, lined with trees and only wide enough for a small wagon, I feared I'd need to turn back to retrieve my axe. The rain had brought down a great many trees. Luckily none fell directly on the path. All the same, I was sad to see so many old fellas — as Mam used to call them — on their sides, roots in the air and limbs splayed. The only positive — which I chose to focus on — was that firewood would be abundant. I will harvest bark from the oak, hickory, and poplar trunks for medicinal purposes, too. The path itself was soaked — the sun had yet to hit the shaded road — and I really had to hold tight to Barley's reins. She's angsty at the best of times and knew the paths better than I, but I couldn't afford her to throw a shoe on an unearthed root or to get stuck in the muck. She huffed, grunted, and tossed her head in annoyance which only caused the leather straps to dig more deeply into my palms. But once the towering trees were behind, the cloudless sky was above, and the dry-dirt of Taneytown Road was beneath, Barley relaxed and trotted without further complaint.

For there is nothing more splendid than nature in spring.

The air on the open road was soft and delicious. Birds soared overhead, rejoicing in song. Flowers reached for the heavens, glorying in the heat of the day. On either side of the road, seeded blades of winter wheat waved and rolled with the wind. I closed my eyes, leaned back in my saddle, and let my senses fill with the sound of bending wheat—I imagined it to be like the roar and crash of the tidal sea, though I've never seen the ocean—and my skin tingled beneath the heat of the sun. I felt reborn in the glorious rays of sunshine. Temptation to delay my trip to town stirred within me—would it be so awful to lie among the grass and give in to my daydream of sandy beaches?

But the sounds of mankind stalled my fantasy. Stress emanated from those twenty acres on either side of Taneytown, owned by the Rose family. Strained voices and conversations carried on the wind and the tension was palpable; field managers urged their men without whips, but their words were just as biting. I opened my eyes to see field-hands dashing back to work after a short, midday meal. The spring reaping was only a few weeks away, but work had been at a standstill during the storms. If the crop wasn't brought in on time, pay would be withheld. One bad harvest could destroy a small farm.

Suddenly, my eavesdropping felt like an intrusion. I turned my sights to the brick buildings on the horizon.

Compared to Harrisburg and York, the population of Gettysburg is small. But Gettysburg could become quite chaotic when all her townsfolk—a little over two thousand souls—converged in a single area. Today was one of those days. All the houses had their shutters open wide and the streets were bursting at the seams with people socializing in large groups or queuing at the tannery, blacksmith, and General Store. Everyone was enjoying the fine weather. Everyone but my poor Barley, who had a hard time navigating the crowds. She doubted her footing on the cobblestone streets and I could feel her shaking beneath me. My own feelings in large groups were similar and my ears ached from the onslaught of noise. I tried to calm her as much as I could—leaning close to her ear, speaking sweetly and appreciatively—and steered her away from the crowds. Luckily, I had planned my day and knew exactly where I was going.

Mrs. Rebecca Roberts was my first stop and I was most anxious to see her. Her due date was fast approaching. Before the storms, she had been spotting, and her husband— who had lost an arm at the Battle of Shiloh—panicked and rushed to fetch me. She was not hemorrhaging and not in labor; I'd seen this before with first pregnancies especially if the woman still chose to lay with her husband. I couldn't ask her if was doing this, naturally, but I gave her some black haw root and partridge berry for a tea.

Today, she was in good spirits, no longer bleeding but sleep deprived. Her birth pangs would soon begin, I informed her, as her stomach had dropped and was stiff to the touch, and her birth canal was stretching. I told her to send her husband to fetch me, if anything seemed amiss. I knew it wouldn't be more than a few days.

Jane Bradley was next. She was twelve weeks along. Her skirts only showed the hint of a bump at her abdomen, but she felt rather conspicuous and refused to leave her house on Steinwehr Avenue. Her smile was bright when she opened her door and invited me in. I followed her into the sitting room, where a small tea tray was waiting. Normally, I'd shy away from tea with patients — as I firmly believed these relationships should stay medically based — but she seemed desperate for company. Jane was often alone; her husband worked on one of the larger apple orchards in Gettysburg. Many of the women I see are in similar situations — confined to their homes by the embarrassing nature of their condition, but still needing normal human interaction. So, I try to be sympathetic with all my patients, especially when they seem to need more than medical care.

She undressed down to her shift and made herself comfortable in an armchair, with a stool to prop her feet. I examined her. Her pulse was strong at both the wrist and throat, and I could feel the steady heartbeat of her child as I palpated her belly. Her tiny bump had grown since last I saw her; two inches by the last measurement noted in my medical log. I asked for any changes in her diet, health, stamina, and pain. Her pain was minimal — except for the occasional cramping and sickness throughout the day. I gave her some chamomile and peach leaves, to brew a tea for her stomach. I notated all changes in my log and stayed for one cup of tea. Mr. Bradley arrived home just as I was taking my leave. He followed me out to the hitching post, where Barley was patiently waiting. The father-to-be looked tense and vexed; he was ten-years Jane's senior and his first wife had died in childbirth. I assured him that his wife was progressing beautifully, and I'd return in two weeks. He took my hand and shook it vigorously in thanks before dashing back inside, returning with a sack of potatoes that he slung over Barley's saddle. Despite my protests — I usually won't accept payment until after the birth — Mr. Bradley was adamant that I go home with something for putting his mind at ease. I acquiesced and accepted his gift

I crossed over Baltimore and saw three more patients — two in the first few months of pregnancy, and the third a new mother with feeding troubles. I gave her a salve for soreness on her nipples and taught her a technique for helping the baby latch.

I stopped in on Andrew McGuire to remove a finger splint from his right hand. He had jammed his finger while replacing a wagon wheel three weeks prior. I removed the splint and am glad to report his finger has full dexterity and motion. He presented me with seven candles, of which I was happy to accept.

My last stop was the post office.

A small bell rang above my head as I entered. Miraculously, there was no one waiting at the barred, front counter that separated the general concourse from the rows of wooden mailboxes at the back. A chair creaked, and I spied David Buehler, the postmaster, with his feet up on a desk, reading the newspaper.

He stood and walked up the aisle of mailboxes towards me. "Haven't seen you in a few weeks. How's life out in those woods?" Mr. Buehler knew everyone in town, but he had only recently taken the position as postmaster. He was a lawyer, a staunch Republican, and well known through-out the county. But the war had forced many of us to take on new professions — even Mr. Buehler, at the age of forty-two.

I stepped up to the counter. "Quiet as always. How are Fannie and the children?" I delivered three of the four Buehler children and I knew his wife, Fannie, quite well.

"Fine, just fine." He stepped from my sight and down a row of mailboxes. He returned shortly and handed me a square parcel wrapped in parchment. I didn't need to open it to know it was my copy of Rafinesque's, *Medical Flora of the United States*. I had sent away for it ages ago, and I was relieved to finally have it. I clutched the parcel to my chest and turned to leave.

"Pleasure seeing you," Mr. Buehler called after me as I opened the door, the bell chiming again. I hastily waved back, but my mind was already racing home.

Only when I stepped from the stoop did I realize no letters had accompanied my package.

My eyes drifted, and instinct made me step to the town's List—the seven feet tall, double-posted, wooden board where announcements, advertisements, and other important information were nailed for all to read. Over the last few years, the most pertinent information was the sheet listing the local casualties from recent battles. That list held a place of prominence, right at the center of the wide board. From where I stood the paper looked weatherworn and tattered. I'd heard of no new engagements but still…I needed to know.

My fingers flicked over the thick packet of names, listed alphabetically. I flipped to the P section, fearing that his name had appeared overnight. My finger drifted down and down until I reached the letter Q. I exhaled in relief.

The ride home was smoother and uneventful.

Now I must sleep. The oil in my lamp is considerably lower than when I started, and my fingers are stained black with ink. Effort aside, writing feels good. Your pages have drawn me in and I'd like this to become a nightly routine.

Chapter Nine

Breanne Walker

"…to become a nightly routine." She wrote the final line with long, fluid hand strokes. Her final stroke complete, she placed her pen down on the desk. Picking up her rocking blotter, she pressed the curved base onto the page and rocked it back and forth, line by line until the ink was dry. Satisfied, she carefully closed the small leather-bound book and tucked it inside the desk's drawer. She sat back and stretched her arms over her head.

She was young – her skin was a flawless ivory color, her cheeks a rosy red – but she had an air of maturity beyond her short years. Her eyes were large and blue. Behind them was a vast knowledge of life. She was dressed in a plain nightgown, with a shawl draped over her shoulders for warmth. Her hair was a deep auburn and was braided down the length of her back. Her face was dainty, and she was pretty – beautiful even.

She pushed the chair out from the desk and stood, pain showing on her face. Her hands were on her lower back, as she attempted to ease the aching muscles. She picked up the oil lamp that she had been writing by and carried it across the room to her bedside *table. Placing it down, she turned a small knob and the light extinguished. The one room cabin – furnished sparingly – was now only lit by a small brick fireplace in the corner.*

She was facing a full-sized bed with a colorful, cozy quilt. She turned down the quilt and top sheet and removed the shawl. With a weary sigh, she turned to sit. But the bend in her knees froze as another thought hit her. She stood back up and turned.

And looked directly at me.

Her eyes were blazing.

"Mrs. Walker? Mrs. Walker?" A voice pierced my ears, and I felt like I was falling. Only I really was falling; one second my body was feather light, and the next, my head forcefully smacked a hard surface with a loud THWACK!

"Jesus," I groaned. My eyes were spinning – *or is it the room?* – and my head was throbbing. As my vision steadied, I looked up and was blinded by a glossy, fluorescent light. *Where am I?* I looked to my side to shield my eyes and saw four, thick table legs. A few seconds passed before I realized the hard surface beneath me was the linoleum floor of the Gettysburg National Military Park's research lab and I was splayed out beneath a worktable.

And I wasn't alone.

"Mrs. Walker? Are you okay?"

"It's Ms." I managed to say as I detangled my legs from the lab stool and hoisted myself up.

"Sorry. Sorry. Take your time." I now recognized the voice of one of the museum's undergraduate interns, Vince McGill. He righted the stool and picked up a few loose papers that had fallen with me.

With dignity inching back into my psyche, I brushed off my jeans and felt the ostrich-egg forming at the back of my skull. *Great, now I have a concussion!*

"I didn't mean to scare you. I didn't know how else to wake you." He handed me the papers that had fallen.

"I was asleep?" My voice squeaked with shock as I snatched the papers from him.

"Yeah. You were out. Like D.O.A. out."

"No, I couldn't have been. I...I must've dosed off for a second. What...what time—" I swiped my bag from the table and frantically searched for my phone inside. I found it at the very bottom. *3:21* blinked from my home-screen.

"Oh my god," I whispered. *How long was I asleep?* I slunk back onto the stool in utter defeat. I dug my fingernails into my jeans and tried to calm down. The last time I'd checked the time was...around nine? *I wasted at least five hours.* I had precious little time to get this project off the ground, and I passed out on top of...

I jumped up and almost dove onto the lab table. The diary was still open to the page where I'd left off. And, with all probability, the same page had acted as my pillow for the last few hours. I hastily scanned the pages for facial grease, drool, or any other kind of human-produced moisture that could destroy a one-hundred-and-fifty-year-old document. Bodily fluid meeting the ink could smear the text. Mercifully, it was unaffected by my unexpected nap.

I sighed and dropped back onto the stool, feeling like I'd been granted a death row pardon.

A throat cleared behind me.

Oh, right. Vince. I swiveled on the stool to face him.

"You okay, Ms. Walker?" He looked like a person who'd entered a psych ward during lock-down—his hands were raised, and he took a step back. I looked half crazed, I knew this, and my reaction to him trying to wake me—freaking out, falling off a stool, and smacking my head—had sealed my insanity diagnosis. He was taller than me by at least a foot, with long, lanky arms and legs and flaming red hair—and could have easily overpowered me if I truly was insane.

"Yes—I'm fine! So sorry, Vince." I scrambled to clean up the mess I had made. "You caught me in the middle of a project, and—wait, why are you here?"

"Oh, right! Dr. Ransome called. He knows I'm from Texas and would most likely still be in the area over the long weekend. I've told him that I'm available for anything. Day or night, I'm your guy." He patted himself on the chest like some used-car salesman. "He figured you'd be needing some help and to head on over. And I'm always eager to be of service. Love to help!"

His voice exhausted me. He smelled of desperation and was green—as green as could be. He wanted a job post-graduation, with scholarship money to continue his education, and the only chance he had of getting that was to kiss every archivist's ass. Couldn't blame him—jobs were rare, and competition was stiff in this industry. But interns buzzing around, begging for work, were cumbersome and irritating.

Especially now.

"So, ah.... what you working on?" He looked to my work on the table. My body instinctually shifted in front of him, blocking a clear view of the diary.

Not a step closer, little man.

"Oh, just finishing up transcribing a...medics journal from the Wheat Field." With my left hand, I slid my notebook towards the edge of the table, and it tumbled to the ground. "Oh, so clumsy."

"I got it!" he said, diving to the linoleum floor.

I closed the diary and quickly shifted it beneath a manila folder.

"Well, I'm at your disposal," he said, standing and handing me my notebook. "Anything you need, anything at all, I'm your man." There was no getting rid of him; he'd only come back on Tuesday, more eager than before. And if Greg had called him, he must've had a reason.

But I needed him out of my hair.

"Um..." I drummed my fingers on the table. "Oh! Okay! Do you have a car, Vince?"

"Yes, of course! A 2011 Honda Civic. A graduation present from my MeeMaw. I drove it cross country to—"

"Great! That's great. I need some samples tested at the lab in Harrisburg. Our next scheduled pickup isn't until Tuesday, and that's too late. Can you drive them over?"

"Will they be open today?"

"I'll have Greg—I mean Dr. Ransome—call in a favor."

He shot me another toothy grin and replied, "Okay! I can get this stuff to Harrisburg! No problem."

"Okay, great!" I turned back to the worktable and gathered everything I had collected. From beneath the table, I grabbed a box, then loaded everything inside. I ripped a piece of paper from my notepad and scribbled down instructions for the lab tech.

"Oh, wow! DNA testing!" He peered over my shoulder watching every word I wrote. "What did you find?" I could feel his hot breath on my shoulder.

"We shall see," I said through clenched teeth. My personal space felt violated, and I was ready to throw him through the double-plated glass windows — *but if you do, you will definitely get fired, and the diary taken from you.* I finished the note and handed it to him. "Please tell the tech to follow these instructions to the letter. And I need the results in twenty-four hours, if not sooner. Here is the address." I handed him a business card for the lab in Harrisburg.

"Great!" He took the card, studied it, then slipped it into his shirt pocket. "Anything else?"

"Yes. Drive carefully and don't get pulled over."

"Got it!" He picked up the box of samples. "I'll get these over there lickity-split!"

"And wait for results, if you could?" Requesting that he sit in his car for up to twenty-four hours wasn't too much to ask. *He probably considers this his entrance exam.* "I'll need the samples back, too."

"Will do. I'll keep in touch." He turned towards the door.

I swiveled on the stool back toward the worktable and exhaled. Nothing like waking up from a deep snooze and being slapped in the face at the same time. But Vince was serving a purpose—*and I trust Greg.* I was a little nervous about handing off parts of my project but driving to Harrisburg would've drained a lot of my time—*and the errand got Vince off my back.*

"Oh, Mrs. Walker. I almost forgot." I turned and found Vince had double-backed and was lingering in the doorway. "I figure you didn't hear about the Witness Tree up by Little Round Top?"

Shit.

"No, I haven't heard."

"Apparently the storm blew the tree over. Could be the biggest discovery since that mass grave was unearthed beneath the high school's football field."

"Well, witness trees are old. Doesn't seem too big of a deal," I lied through gritted teeth.

"Yeah, but it's not every day you find the body of a Confederate soldier beneath one."

Chapter Ten

Breanne Walker

"I CAN NEITHER CONFIRM NOR DENY THE EXISTENCE OF A BODY FOUND beneath a witness tree. I also cannot confirm or deny that said body was dressed in a Confederate soldier's uniform."

The rubber soles of my sneakers were smacking loudly on the linoleum floor as I paced with seething anger. I had remained calm and passive until Vince officially and permanently left the lab. Once he'd stepped from the decontamination chamber and shot me a thumbs up, I counted to one-hundred and fifty-two—just to be sure he didn't double-back, again—and then grabbed my phone to punch in Greg's phone number. He took entirely too long to answer—five rings to be exact—and then finally picked up so nonchalantly that I wanted to choke him through the phone. One more blasé utterance from him and the blood vessels in my skull would burst.

"Greg, I don't have time for your bullshit press statement," I screamed, gripping my phone so hard that I could hear the plastic of my phone's case bending.

"Breanne, is that any way to talk to the man who signs your paycheck?"

"No, but it is the way a woman who was dragged from bed at 4 a.m., told to drive out to a historic battlefield, showed a tree on its side with a body beneath it, and given a diary to secretly authenticate while her boss is playing diplomat to the press."

"Touché. Feel better?"

"No! I mean yes, but no." I breathed for the first time in minutes. "Tell me the real details? Off the record, unofficial, whatever you need to say to tell me the truth."

He exhaled. "The final layer of dirt was removed from the grave. It revealed a cotton shroud, typically used with burial preparation in the 1800s. The fabric has intricate, colored embroidery around the edges and despite the elements, it is in great condition. The shroud was carefully removed from the site and, before you ask, yes, it was handled with care and placed into an airtight container. The human remains appear to be male, dressed in a uniform that is gray and tan in color—"

"The colors of a Confederate soldier," I cut in.

"Yes. I say that unofficially, of course."

I stopped pacing and pulled up a stool. With so much information swirling, I didn't want to miss any of it. I grabbed my pad and pencil and wrote furiously. "So, am I the last person in Gettysburg to unofficially know this?"

"Well, no. We've leaked a few details to the press to pique interest. The museum's press conference will be tomorrow at 9 a.m. Hopefully the world will know after. The board is seeing it as a major endowment opportunity."

"And you didn't think it'd be beneficial for me to hear these details? Especially that the sex of the body was identifiable?" Specifics of the body were crucial to my research; the battlefield positions of Union and Confederate brigades were well documented, and if I had known which side to connect the diary to—*and* that the female diarist couldn't possibly be the body beneath the tree—I could've had a hypothesis by now. But obviously there was no explaining that to Greg.

"I've been a little busy, Breanne. I figured I'd eventually hear from you about the secondary discovery, or you'd hear through the grapevine. How's Vince, by the way?"

"He's great! Perfect even," I answered sarcastically. "I just sent him with samples to Harrisburg—you'll need to call to have the results rushed, by the way. Did you think I couldn't handle this on my own? I don't exactly work well with others."

"Breanne, let's be honest. You don't work well with others because you've never tried. And I think it's about time you did."

I opened my mouth intending to give a stinging rebuttal—one so strong that Greg would immediately take Vince off my case. Instead, my jaw dropped and stayed that way, without a single word crossing my lips. I reached into the depths of my memory, looking for a simple group project from elementary school, or a team-building activity that adequately exemplified my ability to work with others.

But there was nothing. Every memory came back with the same result: teams assigned, me lingering in the back and then doing the entire project on my own, letting others reap the benefits. That same lack of trust followed me right through middle school, high school, and college. In fact, "lack of teamwork" was the consistent flaw on every one of my report cards.

I hate when he's right.

"Oh," he continued after my prolonged silence, "be out of that lab by 8 a.m. The staff will be informed via email of the discovery of the body before the press conference, and I imagine most will be rushing back. I've granted you access to the archives, which will be the only place — I assume — not crawling with people. I'd suggest hunkering down there. Totally up to you, of course. Pass on my regards to Vince."

The line cut out, so all I could hear was the dial tone and the sound of my own breath.

My brain melted into mush. With the phone still attached to my ear, gravity took my body, and my forehead connected with the cool aluminum of the worktable. I lifted my head and let it drop over and over, hoping to give myself a bigger concussion.

Chapter Eleven

Breanne Walker

I SLID MY ID CARD THROUGH THE SECURITY READER AND WATCHED as the tiny bulb in the center blinked green. A bell chimed, and the elevator door opened in front of me. I jumped inside—as if at any second the elevator would change its mind and slam shut—and pushed the lower of the two buttons on the inside door panel. The doors creaked shut, and I felt the floor beneath my feet drop.

I've been on many elevators in my life—too many, to be honest. I am a child of the instant-gratification generation, where impatience reigns supreme and the dial-up modem took entirely too long. But elevators are one thing I've always tried to avoid. Every time the doors close—trapping me inside—a vision of that ride at Disneyland pops into my head. Though I've never been, I've seen plenty of videos and pictures of the exact moment when the elevator plummets thirteen stories; the look on the riders face still scares the life out of me. Putting my life in the hands of a machine and being completely out of control isn't ideal.

But there was only one way down to the archives, and it was by elevator. Using the stairs would set off an emergency alarm, triggering museum security, who would call Greg and, worst of all, Peggy — which would be catastrophic. The elevator was very old and got stuck every few months — a fact I found out from a co-worker during my first week.

"Oh, make sure you always have your cell on you," she told me as the doors closed on us and she pushed the button to go down. "Sometimes the doors get stuck between floors. The only way out is to call the information desk and for them to call the repair guy."

"Has it ever happened to you?"

"No, but it did a few weeks ago to Bill in Records." The doors opened, and she gingerly hopped out. "Took three hours to get the repair guy here." I bolted from the elevator, and luckily haven't gotten trapped inside.

Yet.

I gripped my phone close to my chest and prayed that today wasn't the day. The car stopped with a short jolt, and the lights flickered. Another small bell chimed above my head, and the doors cracked open. Off the metal deathtrap I propelled like a swimmer from a diving block and I landed with solid footing on the other side.

I was standing in The Gettysburg National Military Park Archives. Home of the largest collection of military and historic artifacts from the bloodiest battle of the Civil War. Most of which — I now knew — belonged to Greg Ransome's family. "They're on loan," Greg told me once, with a snide grin.

The collection was massive and diverse; anything not on display was meticulously organized and maintained down here. Once a month, an archivist was given the task of taking inventory for every piece of history we held. An accounting sheet was provided, and at the end of the project—which could take up to a week—a report was due, with pictures and detailed descriptions of the artifacts. It wasn't a coveted task, and most of my fellow employees tried to pass it off on interns or assigned it as a form of punishment for minor infractions.

I'd volunteered every time the job was posted. The archives was the ideal place for me: no human interaction, just surrounded by history and books. Just the smell—that combination of sterility, old leathers, nature, and a hint of mildew—sent me over the edge.

Row upon row of artifacts were grouped according to description, then subcategorized by significance for the Union or Confederate side. Furniture, books, uniforms, ammunition, arms, and personal effects were grouped together using a highly scientific system—a barcode assigned to each individual artifact that, once scanned, could tell you the exact location, down to the row, shelf, placement, and the last time it was on display. The smaller items—like buttons, thread, or coins—were kept in air-controlled cabinets. Books were kept in similar cases; these were consistently swapped out and checked for changes in binding structure or removed for research. Clothing and uniforms circled the circumference of the room on racks in air-tight clothing bags, far away from air vents. Paintings were kept in wooden crates towards the back, as was furniture — covered in dust-repellent fabric and plastic — and larger items like window panes or building structures with bullet holes in their stone.

When displays were changed in the main gallery, it was a big to-do. Transporting the artifacts down to the archives was a delicate process, practiced and perfected by each member of the staff. One false move could destroy something irreplaceable. Usually we were given a few days' notice before a change would occur, and everyone was expected to clear their schedules.

The next change wasn't for three weeks. And an inventory had just been completed — by me, and my report was still under review. So, this was the best place for complete privacy.

I readjusted my messenger bag and walked down the center aisle, towards the table at the center of the room. Usually, I had a hard time walking by rows of history without stopping for a closer look. But today I put on imaginary blinders and only looked forward.

After ten minutes of walking — and not looking — I reached the work station. The area was simple: a rounded, wooden table with four chairs surrounding it, a free-standing lamp giving off just enough light to allow people to see the surface area of the table, a water cooler — the air was so dry in the archives that the water jug needed to be changed regularly — and a filing cabinet with cleaning products. I put my bag on the table and switched on the lamp. Next, I turned to the filing cabinet, opened a drawer, and took out a dust rag. There was no way I was putting the diary on a potentially dirty table, so I thoroughly dusted the flat service. Relieved, I sat down.

With my hands securely gloved, I took out the diary and placed it on the table.

I took a long, deep breath and started to think — really think — my current situation through. Peggy aside, I couldn't imagine the museum — *hell, the U.S. government* — would appreciate anyone taking a piece of its history from what was now deemed an archeological site. And even worse, without them knowing the artifact existed.

And now Vince was involved — *I wonder how that's going,* I thought, looking at my phone.

A sharp pain in my head and made my eyes water. *Oh right, you probably have a concussion,* I felt the fully formed egg on the back of my head.

The dream!

I remembered the eerie vision I had. Actually, both — the one when Greg first handed me the diary and again when I fell asleep in the lab.

The hooded figure. The young woman sitting at her desk and writing. The way she turned and stared right at me.

A chill wracked my body.

My brain told me the visions were just sleep deprivation or something I ate. A figment of my imagination. I do not, by any stretch of the imagination, believe in the supernatural — ghosts, specters, anything that goes bump in the night. I honestly felt bad for the fools on TV shows who brought "paranormal experts" into their homes, to solidify their belief that their squeaky pipes were in fact the previous owner who murdered his entire family and wouldn't pass on. My eye-roll was epic when the experts made the big reveal.

But this was different — I wasn't one of those idiots.

The logical side was not adding up; I couldn't be rational when deep down I knew what I had seen was real. Those eyes, the way they pierced and took hold of my heart, were real.

But why me?

If I continued down this path, nothing would get accomplished and I'd become a paranoid mess — like those couples listening to their rattling pipes.

"Okay," I told myself. I pulled my messenger bag towards me and took out my pad of paper to review my notes. One question plagued me above all: "Who is A.M.P?"

The question was a mosquito, buzzing around my head. Her name was a crucial piece of the puzzle, and the only piece that there was a slight chance I'd never find. Why would the writer of a diary mention their own name? In all my experience, I don't think I've ever seen a full name recorded. I had to hope this diary held an unintentional slip-up somewhere in its lengthy account.

I let out an exasperated breath. I needed to read.

With my hands fully gloved, I slipped my fingers beneath the leather cover and opened to where I had left my acid-free bookmark. I hunched closer to the page and found the next entry.

Chapter Twelve

A.M.P.

April 26ᵗʰ, 1863

FIVE NIGHTS AGO, A FURIOUS POUNDING ON MY FRONT DOOR WOKE ME. It is not uncommon for me to be woken at all hours. But of late, I've been more on edge to nightly disturbances as the woods around my home have been active with strangers fleeing Adams County. Fleeing because of mounting rumors of Lee's army crossing the Potomac, into Pennsylvania, and bringing the war to our doorsteps. Many believed — particularly, the freed negroes who feared retaliation — and were leaving under cover of darkness, heading further north. Fear forced them to pack up their homes and flee on foot. With my windows open, I'd hear their hushed voices — or sometimes, unfamiliar songs carried on the wind — and see the bobbing lantern flames, like fireflies dancing in the summer heat. The next morning, I'd see their deeply entrenched footprints on the path leading to my house and then away into the woods.

So, the pounding on my door at an obscene hour made me jump from bed and take a defensive position on the floor, on all fours, like a cat ready to pounce on a threatening dog — hair standing tall, claws stretched. The pounding repeated, but now louder struck. I gathered my wits and pulled my loaded shotgun from beneath my roped bedframe.

A woman living alone can never be too prepared, as Mam always told me.

With the butt of the shotgun cocked in the pit of my arm and the barrel stretched before me, I stood and walked the few paces to my front door. Fists pounded on the wooden door again, so hard that I heard a distinct cracking sound. I took one deep breath, gripped the brass door handle, and stuck the double barrel of the gun out into utter darkness. "Who's there? What do you want?" I yelled with a husky voice, faking brute strength.

"I'm sorry about the time, Missus. But my wife needs your help," said a faceless voice on the other side. I recognized the voice and opened the door further to find a startled Mr. George Roberts standing with his hand — he only had one — reaching for the sky.

"Good gracious, Mr. Roberts," I said, lowering my rifle, "you scared the daylights from me. Come in, please."

"There's no time to be wasting inside, missus. Rebecca's started. The baby's coming, and she is needing you." He urged me to follow him outside. A first-time father he surely was; I asked for one moment to dress and gather my kit and my collapsible birthing chair. When I emerged after ten minutes, Barley was fully saddled and waiting for her rider.

I secured my kit and the chair to Barley's saddle and pulled myself atop her. "Lead the way, Mr. Roberts."

"Yah!" he yelled to his horse, who shot onto the path towards Taneytown Road, the light of the silver moon guiding the way. I followed, awed that he was able to saddle and bridle Barley with only one hand. Watching him direct his horse left me with no questions; the war had taken his hand but not his will to live.

Mr. Roberts pace was manic, and we made it to town and to his home in half the time it should've. Mr. Roberts swung down from his horse with ease and offered his hand to me. I handed down my kit and birthing chair and jumped down on my own. He took both horses and tied their reins off to the rail post at the back of their house.

"She's right inside," he said, striding up the gravel path to his back door. He held the door open and waved me inside.

I stepped into the Roberts' kitchen to find Rebecca Roberts. Rebecca Roberts on her feet and pulling biscuits from the cast iron stove.

Once Mr. Roberts was standing beside me, confusion made his hand go limp and he promptly dropped my medical kit to the floor. I stifled a giggle—I couldn't help it.

"Rebecca? I...what...you..." Mr. Roberts started, pointing to the other room and then back to the kitchen.

"Well, I figured you'd both be hungry after a long ride. Would you like cream or sugar?" She handed me a cup of steaming coffee and pointed to a chair at her kitchen table.

I sat down, leaving Mr. Roberts gaping in the back doorway. Seeing her up and moving was a shock to him; in his mind, she should've been laid out on the parlor's sofa, languishing in pain. But as Mam would always say, "Keep those legs moving 'til the babe's in your arms."

"I'm sorry if it's not strong enough," she continued, as she poured some milk into my mug and offered me a spoon. "This is the fourth pot I've made from those grinds. So hard to come by, with the war on and all."

I swallowed the warm liquid. "It's lovely. Thank you," I said.

"How was the ride? George, sit," she barked at her husband as she turned back to the oven. Mr. Roberts obediently sat down, his mouth firmly closed.

"It was brisk. How are you? That *is* why I'm here?"

She turned back around and placed a plate of delicious-smelling biscuits in front of me. She heaped golden butter atop them and placed a plate in front of her husband, still holding one for me.

"Oh, that. I woke with a little pain," she said rubbing the bottom of her stomach, "and it lasted for just a few — " she keeled over in pain, and the plate she was holding fell to the floor, shattering on impact. Mr. Roberts was on his feet before I could form a proper thought. He was holding her from behind and steadying her arms as she grasped her stomach and convulsed. I jumped up and supported her from the front, knowing this was an intense contraction.

"Count aloud, Rebecca," I coached her, using a trick of Mam's; counting helped distract from the pain. She did, and after a minute her body relaxed. It was then that a rush of water poured upon my feet. Her water had broken.

She looked down between her legs in disgust. "I'm so sorry. Oh, I'm so....so embarrassed. I've ruined your shoes," she cried, grabbing for the dish cloth on the stove, wanting to mop up the mess.

"My shoes have walked through worse."

She immediately burst into tears, so I pulled her in to cry on my shoulder. "Let's get you upstairs."

She nodded and allowed me to begin leading her from the kitchen.

Mr. Roberts stood stock still, unsure of which way to go. His arms were held out, as if he was still supporting his wife, and his eyes were bewildered with fear. "Missus, what do I do?" he asked as his wife and I slowly walked from the room.

"I can take care of her now, Mr. Roberts," I called over my shoulder. "But could you boil some water and make sure you have clean linens for the babe?"

"I can do that," he said, and I heard the kitchen door slam. I pictured him running with all speed to the well and filling all the pails they owned.

Fresh, clean water was important in birthing, not only for the expectant mother to drink and to mop her brow, but to keep my hands and instruments sanitary. Dr. Ignaz Semmelweis's treatise on childbed fever opened my eyes to the need for obsessive cleanliness in the birthing room and I aimed to avoid delivery complications at all costs.

We took our time climbing the staircase—one step and a short pause after each—to the second floor and to Rebecca's bedroom. Once inside her modest bedroom, I proceeded to help her undress down to her shift and stripped the four-poster bed down to the sheet and spread a wax canvas over the mattress. With a pained sigh Rebecca laid down, supported by many pillows, and allowed me to examine her.

In a full circular motion, I pressed down on her stomach to find the position of the unborn child. The babe had dropped; his head was in the right position. From my case, I took my Pinard horn—like Dr. Semmelweis's treatise, an acquisition from a friend at Jefferson Medical College—and pressed my ear to one end, with the other pressed to her stomach. I listened and counted, hearing the tiny but hearty beats from inside her belly.

"Your babe has a healthy heartbeat, Rebecca," I told her with a smile.

"How many children have you brought into the world?" she asked.

"I assisted at hundreds with my Mam—my grandmother. Yours will be my forty-sixth on my own. The year after the outbreak of the war was my busiest." Enlistment babies, I called them.

"This will be my first for both," she said, shifting her bottom into a more comfortable position.

"You never sat at a labor? Not even one of your mother's?" I readjusted the sheet over her legs.

"No, I am my mother's only child. She died when I was young." She crossed herself as emotion filled her eyes.

"I'm sorry to hear. I will talk you through as much as I can."

"Thank you, Miss A—" her face contorted, and she collapsed forward. The convulsions wracked her body for twenty seconds and then subsided, leaving her breathless and sweating.

There was so little I could do for pain. All medicines—especially morphine and laudanum—were being sent down to the front. If given the choice, most women wouldn't take the few available medical supplies from the soldiers. They'd endure the pain as their mothers had; women were meant to suffer due to the 'curse of Eve' as our pastors preached every Sunday. I've been able to make do with many botanical substitutes—poultices and herbal teas made from local flora and roots. Alcohol helped and was easily accessible, but most women did not like the taste or rarely chose to partake even in normal circumstances. Unfortunately, Rebecca would need to bear the pain to eventually hold her child.

"Lie back for a few minutes, Rebecca. Catch your breath before the next contraction," I instructed. I retrieved bandages and a crock of grease from my medical kit, and then unfolded the legs from the birthing chair—a backless, three-legged stool with a hole in the seat and arm rests, designed by my grandfather for Mam—and set it atop another wax canvas.

From downstairs, I heard an alarming crash and a scurry of movement; I excused myself and walked to the top of the staircase. I peered over the banister to find Mr. Roberts staring back up at me like a little boy.

"Missus, Rebecca tells me not to bother with the stove as I don't know how to use it. The fire was still lit, so I just tried to add more kindling, but I don't know if it's enough. And then I dropped the pails of water." He was close to tears and I could see the front of his pants were soaked from the backsplash of water.

"I'll be right down, Mr. Roberts. Don't fret," I called to him. I returned to the bedroom to assure Rebecca that everything was fine, then gathered my skirts and descended the staircase to assess the situation in the kitchen — and clean up the mess Mr. Roberts had made. As I sent him back outside to fetch more water, I knew that this day would be very long.

Almost thirteen hours later, Rebecca pushed her first baby — a seven-pound boy — into my waiting arms. He let out a healthy scream, announcing to the world that he had arrived. His anxious father — who until that moment had waited impatiently outside the bedroom — burst into the room, tripped on the small area rug beside the bed, and landed face down on the hardwood floor.

He hoisted himself up and leaned over the bed, face a crimson red, he stammered, "Is it….is it…"

"Mr. Roberts, you have a son," I said as I cut the umbilical cord with sharpened shears. I cleaned the babe and wrapped him snuggly in a linen sheet and handed him to his waiting father, while I prepared for the afterbirth. Mr.

Roberts' eyes lit like a starlit summer sky. Never taking his eyes off his baby, he sat beside Rebecca on the bed.

"Our son, Becca," Mr. Roberts whispered to his wife as he handed her the babe.

She gently kissed the baby's forehead, her husband mirroring the action on hers. Their love was intoxicating, and I looked on with a longing curiosity. I always cherished that moment: the birth of a family. Two separate entities becoming one in the form of a child, both realizing that their whole lives have been a preparation for this one blessed moment.

The love I was witnessing between Rebecca, her husband, and the newborn child was limitless and pure.

After every birth, I always think of my mother. I ask myself, did she ever feel this way about me?

"Thank you, thank you so much." Mr. Roberts pulled me away from my inner thoughts and back to the bedroom. I smiled and nodded, gathering the soiled linens and water basin. There would be a few minutes before the afterbirth, and I needed some air.

A light breeze welcomed me as I stepped into the back alley. Fatigue was building in my legs—I had been kneeling in front of the birthing chair for almost the entirety of Rebecca's labor—and my body ached for rest. But as Mam said, "Better to rest when all is through." As I emptied the water basin's contents onto the lawn in the corner of the alley, I heard my name being called from inside the house. Holding the basin, I ran back inside. In the kitchen stood Mr. Roberts and a man I didn't recognize.

"Missus, another babe is coming," Mr. Roberts said. "In Cashtown. The midwife has been called to another birthing room and won't be back in time." I looked to the unknown man and saw another worried father, desperate for my help.

"Of course. Just let me finish here." I placed a reassuring hand on his shoulder, then returned upstairs to Rebecca to deliver the afterbirth.

Hours later, I delivered a baby girl in Cashtown to a family I have never met. They were more than appreciative of my assistance. The labor was long but easier on the mother as this was her second child, and I had assistance in the birthing room: her mother and aunt. Once the babe arrived, the mother knew what to do and I was needed for very little else, so I hurried back to Gettysburg and Rebecca—who was doing quite well. Her son—little Georgie—was thriving. He took easily to the breast and her milk was bountiful.

I received three dollars from each family for my efforts. The ride home was a blur, I am surprised I was able to sit in the saddle. As the sun rose in the east, Barley delivered us safely to my little cabin in the woods.

That was five days previous and finally, I've felt refreshed enough to record the details and am happier for it. Cashtown and Gettysburg are now two inhabitants richer.

May 1st, 1863

I am still trying to come to terms with something that occurred this morning. It brought forth many things I had long since buried. Now, I've realized I am still that little girl who is so unsure of herself.

I need to write it out. Write it out of my body.

My baby sister is pregnant with her first child. And because Gettysburg's doctor enlisted with the local Pennsylvania Regiment and is stationed in Georgia, I will be responsible for her care. "Only due to this unavoidable circumstance, I assure you," said Jonathan, her husband — the assistant pastor at Christ Church — with a huff of superiority. He didn't take me seriously; I was merely a girl playing at medicine and had no real business practicing it. To him, doctors were academically taught and male. Graduating from the Theological Seminary four years previous made him an expert in everything — even midwifery. He likes to hover within earshot while I'm examining Rosie and questions my methods. The last two visits were completely consumed by his thoughts on the use of forceps. "If this tool helps avoid cutting the mother, then why hasn't it become a standard? Tools are the way of the future, sister." Trying to explain the horrible risks to both the mother and child was pointless. My eyes permanently rolled into the back of my head and Rosie couldn't look at me for fear she would laugh.

I love my sister dearly and will not stay away from her for any reason, especially when it comes to her health and that of her unborn child. But I truthfully don't know how much more I can take of Jonathan Anderson.

Fortunately, her husband was absent when I called today.

"Oh, Jonathan has just run up to the church," she said as she ushered me through her foyer and into the parlor.

"Oh, what a shame," I said, with a sarcastic air. Knowing Rosie, she made sure he'd be absent, as I had not seen her for a few weeks and she'd want to talk freely. How she can suffer such a pompous, self-righteous man I will never know.

As she lay flat on her back on the loveseat in the parlor, I listened to her heart and that of her child with my Pinard horn and checked on the expansion of her stomach.

"The lower abdominal pain has subsided, I suspect?" She complained of cramping during our last visit, which was normal in the seventh month—she was due the beginning of July. Cramping usually worsens in the last few months of pregnancy and I had brought my sister some black haw and partridge berry to help with the pain.

"Yes. Your tea did wonders, sister. The taste was wretched, but I added a bit of honey."

I smiled. Rosie always had a sweet tooth. Every time I walked into Mother's house, she'd run towards me and root through my pockets, knowing I always carried candied pecans just for her. She'd look up at me with big doe eyes and hug my legs as she popped a piece in her mouth.

She hadn't lost those doe-eyes.

Rosie was as beautiful as her namesake. Everything about her—from the shine of her cocoa-colored hair, to the emerald sparkle in her eyes and her hourglass figure — was alluring to the male eye. From the moment she debuted in Philadelphia society at sixteen, she was courted by throngs of me. She had a gift for making men fall in love with her — as evidenced by the number of letters and male callers. Rosie would read the letters aloud to me with a giggle, impersonating the boy's voice. It became a little game to her — seeing how many men would vie for her attention. Until Jonathan, that is, who seemed to sweep in overnight and won her heart. Before I knew it, my baby sister was engaged and married.

And now pregnant and never happier. Fast approaching the end of her pregnancy, she was uncomfortable, and confinement didn't agree with her. She agreed to stay in her home — as most women did when they could no longer conceal their condition — but refused to remain in bed. I didn't agree with society's belief that lying-in helped calm the mother and prevent the risk of premature labor; in my experience, sticking to the tasks of daily life promotes an easier labor.

"How long before I'm back to my normal self?" she whined as I finished the pelvic examination. "My feet are twice the size they were! I can barely walk. And none of my dresses fit me!"

"Both are quite normal. The swelling in your feet will go down once the baby comes. Your weight is entirely dependent on you."

"Mother told me just last week that she was twice my size while pregnant with me. That I cannot imagine," she said as she sat up and straightened her wrapper.

"You received a letter from Mother?" I asked.

"Oh, no. Mother was here to visit. Would you like some tea?" Rosie stood and walked through the parlor, towards the kitchen at the back of the house. Her words left me instantly alert and confused at the same time. I shook my head. Why would Mother...I followed her into the kitchen.

"Mother was here?" I asked, leaning against the doorway's frame.

Her back was towards me; she reached up into her cabinets and tried to take two teacups from inside. She could not quite grasp them. "This stomach, always in my way," she grumbled to herself. I walked over, reached for the cups, and handed them to her. "Oh, thank you," she said, accepting the cups. "Yes, Mother was here. For about a week." She turned towards the stove and placed the kettle on the flat top.

My face flushed, and even though the room was quite cool for early spring, I became unbearably hot. I unbuttoned the top of my blouse and fanned myself. I stepped away from Rosie to the nearest window and opened it, hoping for a breeze.

"I did find it rather odd that you hadn't called while she was here. You knew, of course, that she was coming?"

"No. No, I didn't know she was in Gettysburg." My words were barely audible.

"Oh. I—I mean—I only assumed Mother had written explaining that she'd be in town. I—I didn't know—I'm sorry I didn't..."

Silence followed. Neither of us knew what to say. I heard Rosie nervously shuffling behind me—another personality trait that had followed her from infancy to adulthood. The clink of porcelain told me she had brought our tea to her kitchen table. I stared out the window at nothing, as my mind whirled with the images of the last time I saw Mother.

"I'm sure she didn't intend to—"

"Don't fret, Rosie." I swung back towards her and plastered a false smile on my face. "I really must be going. I need to visit Rebecca Roberts and a few others in town." I swiftly crossed the kitchen, kissed her cheek, and headed towards the parlor. Then I snatched up my kit and headed to the front door.

"Sissy," Rosie called as I opened the door and stepped onto her stoop. I turned back to see her waddling up the hallway towards me. Her smile was sweet and cooled my anger. She took my hand in hers and put it to her lips, kissing my fingers lightly. I smiled and reassuringly squeezed her fingers—letting her know I didn't hold her responsible for Mother's slight.

"I love you," she said. I nodded before stepping onto the street. As I climbed atop Barley, I could feel my hands shaking and knew my emotions were at the cusp of my control. I grasped the reins and urged Barley to turn and head north on the cobblestone street. I didn't have the strength to wave to Rosie, I urged Barley towards home without looking back.

I lied to my sister. I had visited Rebecca Roberts and my other patients in town before going to her. But I needed to get away with no objections or further conversation about our mother.

And now that I'm home and feel safe within this cabin's walls, I feel that I can fully come to terms with what Rosie revealed. That my mother—who currently lives in Philadelphia—was in town for a week and didn't think to tell me. My mother—whom I haven't seen in almost two years—was in the same town as her eldest child and didn't visit.

This hurt. Hurt more than I wanted to admit or would allow Rosie to see.

The hurt of being forgotten, passed over, found unworthy. The hurt of feeling unloved and neglected by the one person who is supposed to love you unconditionally. My mother didn't think of me; I was not important enough. I wasn't worthy of a letter or a quick visit. As I write these words, the tears well up in my eyes, but I will not let them fall—I haven't cried since Mam's funeral.

This has always been the essence of my relationship with my mother, so I'm unsure as to why this slight affects me so. I cannot recall ever having received a hug, a kiss, or an expression of love from her. There was a time—a time I can barely remember—when I was part of a very loving family. If I could, I'd go back to that time to see my mother and father together, when they were young and blissfully in love. To see her humanity, before grief turned her heart to stone. My mother blames me for a lot of hardship and heartache, which I have yet to accept or fully understand—heartache revolving around my father's death.

They were from different worlds. She was from an elite Harrisburg family: she wanted for nothing, had the best education a woman of her station could obtain, and partook in all the luxuries a city life could offer. He was an only child of a Cashtown apple farmer who had emigrated from Germany. While her parents were summering in Europe, Mother stayed with an elderly aunt in Gettysburg. After a chance meeting between the two at Papa's produce stand in the town square — Mother bought an entire bushel of apples, just so Papa would have to carry them home for her — they became inseparable. The summer months waned and soon Mother would return home to Harrisburg. But neither wanted their romance to end; so, they eloped.

It was terribly romantic but also quite the scandal. One that Mother's family didn't take lightly; they had all but disowned her. She remained in Gettysburg with her new husband, he bought a small farm with money his father loaned him, and she dreamed of the happy days ahead. And they had many happy days together.

Mother married, had a child, and was widowed all before the age of twenty. My father died suddenly from a disease of the heart — or angina pectoris, as I later learned. When he didn't return for supper, Mother sent one of the hands to look for him. He was in the orchard, beneath a ladder that was propped up against a tree. The doctor assumed he'd been picking fruit when the attack hit, and he had fallen. He was young, only twenty-five.

I have few memories of my father: how he kissed me goodnight, how I squealed in delight when he rubbed his rough beard against my cheeks, how he laughed with his whole belly, how he couldn't just say my name—he had to sing it. In truth, these could all be the imaginings of a little girl desperate to know her father; I was only two years-old when he passed.

What I do have are clear memories of the days following his death.

Of how my mother screamed when the news was broken to her. How she dropped to her knees and cried until the floorboards were soaked with tears. How she took to her bed and did not emerge, even for his funeral. How I was shooed out of the way by relatives—my mother's family had resurfaced to pick up the pieces—and how she looked at me with dagger-like eyes. "Take her away. Please, take her away," she'd cry, covering her eyes and shaking her head.

I remember crying myself to sleep almost every night, questioning why my mother didn't love me anymore. It was all beyond my understanding—in some ways, it still is. I was too young to understand the hurt my mother felt when she looked at me. She saw him every time she looked at me. My presence cemented her heartbreak, which only worsened when everything was taken from her.

The bank waited a full five weeks—until the first sprouts of grass had grown on Papa's grave—to tell my mother that there was no money. The farm was mortgaged to the hilt, and the taxes hadn't been paid for two years. Papa had struck a deal with the bank and promised everything would be paid in full after the harvest. This harvest would be our most plentiful yet, he was certain, and he believed he'd be able to catch up. But a late frost killed the budding apple blossoms and only a quarter of what my father anticipated had grown.

Mother had been in the dark. Money rarely crossed her fingers, and she didn't know where Papa kept his important papers. It took two weeks of pulling the entire house apart to find his account ledger. He must have been so confident in the crop that his demeanor and attitude never changed. Mother hadn't noticed a thing—he hadn't even asked her to curtail spending. To her knowledge, everything was as it had always been.

Mother cursed his name, cursed the day she met him. Her anger engrossed and drowned her love.

Mother's family, again, swooped in to clear the mess. They convinced her to cut her losses and give up the farm. The sale would pay the mortgage, taxes, and the farm-hands. She'd walk away with her dignity, all the way back to Harrisburg and her father's house. Which was the other part of their plan; she was young enough to find a suitable match in society—of their choosing, naturally—and to re-marry. She'd have a fresh start, and they hoped she would simply forget this first marriage. Money could throw a shadow on almost anything.

But not on me—the breathing reminder of her disastrous past. I couldn't be unborn, no matter how hard my mother tried to forget my existence. My presence could hinder her future; what man would want a woman with a young child hanging at her hip?

Mam became the solution.

Mam—my father's mother—lived alone on a farm in Cashtown. When my grandfather passed, he willed his land to her. Papa never questioned his father's intentions, so he allowed the farm to stay in her name and worked it with continued success. Many considered her odd, my mother included. She refrained from church services, liked to walk the woods in her bare feet in all weather, wore her long, gray hair loose around her shoulders with no pins or nets, and—as if that wasn't enough—served as the town midwife. She gawked at tradition and lived as she saw fit. Mother never pursued a relationship with Mam—to my knowledge, she stopped seeing her all together soon after their wedding. My father visited alone. Mother considered her a stain, impossible to remove and distanced herself from the embarrassment she brought on the family. Mam was not welcome in my parent's home—for an infraction I have no knowledge of. The first time I met her was when Mother brought me to her farm, two months after Papa's death.

We were waiting at the screen door of an unfamiliar plantation house, the biggest house I'd ever seen: with a wrap-around pillared porch, massive white-paned windows with red shutters, and wildflowers circling the house's perimeter. Mother was holding two suitcases and I was wearing my best travel clothes. I thought she was taking me on a trip. I was elated to be at her side for the first time in weeks; I remember leaning in and rubbing my cheeks against her warm skirts, feeling safe and happy. She had finally forgiven me, and our lives would go back to the way they used to be. It was only then—as we continued to wait for someone to answer the door—that I looked at the cases and realized the ones I'd seen her pack for herself were missing. They must have stayed in the carriage we'd traveled in. Suddenly, my happiness was replaced by dread; she was leaving me.

Tears welled in my eyes, and a sob escaped my throat.

"There will be no crying." She knelt before me. She didn't touch me, didn't pull me in to a heartfelt embrace—she was stone cold. "You will be a good girl and listen to your grandmother. Now wipe your face and hold your head high. No more tears."

I gulped down my fear.

A whirl of gray hair and skirts rushed through the screen door and swept me up into a warm hug. I was too stunned to react properly, but the arms around me were strong and full of love.

Crystal blue eyes took in every inch of me. "You look just like your papa, little one." She spun me around until my legs kicked out and flew. The air was filled with our combined laughter; that moment took away the dread. She stopped twirling me and extended me outward in her arms, taking another long look at me.

Mother cleared her throat.

"Rachel." Mam addressed Mother, gently lowering me to her side. She took my teeny hand in hers, gripping my fingers like she feared letting go.

"Thank you, Mother, for—"

"Never call me that again for I will never answer to it. Not to you."

Mother remained poised, but her anger was like dying embers that only had to be pushed to reignite. She was a lady, and ladies were not to raise their voices—that was the only thing keeping her silent. The hatred between these two women was undeniable. I am unsure—even now—of how my father was able to love such different women so fiercely. Now he was gone, and all pretense with it; they no longer had to bite their tongues out of respect for him.

"I thank you all the same," Mother replied through pursed lips.

"I do this for my son—my only son. This child—who you have kept from me all these years—is the last part of him on this earth. I will do right by her for him. Not for you."

Their eyes locked in a powerful glare. I looked back and forth between the two, unsure of where to turn, afraid of becoming the victim of their wrath.

Mother relented and dropped to her knees. "Come here, child." She extended her hand and beckoned me. Mam loosened her grip and urged me forward.

Mother took my hands in hers and looked me in the eyes. "Be a good girl. Say your prayers every night, and God will protect you. Soon you will come home to me, and we will be a family once again." She kissed me lightly on the forehead and stood to her full height.

Mother and Mam had no further words. Mam took hold of my hand, and Mother walked away and didn't look back. Panic suddenly filled my heart, and I almost ran to her as her carriage turned and drove away. No matter how badly she had treated me since Papa's death, she was still my mother. But Mam gripped my hand until she was out of sight.

After, she scooped me up into her arms. "Fresh apple pie is waiting for us inside, dahlin'. You like apples?"

I nodded eagerly.

"I thought you might. Let's go on in." She kissed me on the cheek then placed me back down, grabbing my bags and ushering me inside.

The pain of being left in an unknown place by my mother was replaced with the sweetness of apples and Mam. Soon, the pain was forgotten altogether and filled with something quite different.

Love.

When my mother walked away and, in essence, relinquished her role, she forever damaged our relationship. My mother became this spectral force in my life; she was never there, but I always felt her presence.

Did she resent the love I had for Mam, the love that formed over years by her own neglect? Maybe she could not accept that Mam became my mother figure? Maybe she believed I should have harbored some allegiance to her, simply because she birthed me? But no...that cannot be.

Everything that happened between us was her choice. She chose to leave me at Mam's. She chose to stay away. She never gave me the love a daughter needs. But why did she continue to punish me, even after she had started a new life in which I had no part?

These thoughts and doubts have plagued my entire life. They have only intensified with the years—especially these past four when she has stripped me of control entirely.

Tonight, I haven't the energy to delve any deeper into my past. I will come back to this another time. There is still much to purge. Til then.

Chapter Thirteen

Breanne Walker

G LUNK GLUNK GLUNK WENT THE WATER COOLER, FILLING the oppressive silence of the archives. I lifted the paper cup to my lips, and icy liquid hit the back of my throat, instantly zapping my senses. An immediate headrush followed, and I gasped for air. I massaged my temples and pinched my face until the pain subsided.

My throat hadn't been that dry since Nevada. I refilled my cup four times before my throat felt lubricated.

I'd been reading and closely analyzing for almost four hours. The clock hanging above the water cooler said 8:47. I took one last swig of water, reminding my aching eyes and back that sitting in an uncomfortable wooden chair was not the best for a slightly curved spine. Functioning on very little sleep didn't help either. *Four hours in and I haven't put a dent in what lies ahead*, I thought looking back at the thick set of pages to the right of the opened diary.

Instinctually, I reached into my pocket for my cell phone. The screen lit, showing no missed calls or texts. I had the ringer on vibrate, but a part of me was hoping I had missed something. *Really, Vince,* I thought. Him spending hours on his own, unsupervised, and with no check-in worried me. Yes, Vince was a fully capable intern, and even an idiot could drive samples to Harrisburg without issue, but he should've at least checked in by now. Based on his overzealous nature, I'd thought I'd be hearing from him every fifteen minutes.

I returned to my research station. I put on my white gloves again; they were almost a second skin. My hands inside were in desperate need of moisturizer, but any extra oil would seep through the cloth. Hands fully clothed, I reopened the diary to where I'd left off.

"There is still much to purge," I read aloud as I sat back in my chair.

At that moment—on May 1st, 1863—only her past seemed relevant. The battle was a month away, and there were only rumors of the war shifting north. Her day-to-day life—though fulfilling—was trivial; but such small details were what I needed to "crack the case" of whose body was beneath the Witness Tree, authenticating the diary, and who A.M.P. was.

I took up my pencil and jotted a few notes to myself concerning historical accuracies I found in the manuscript: war-time food rationing, the rarity of paper money or coinage, bartering as means of currency, medical care provided predominantly by midwives. And finally, the most important fact thus far: A.M.P's sister's name, Rosie Anderson.

As in R.M.A., the initials embroidered into the cloth wrapped around the diary.

My mind did back flips when I read her full name—reminiscent of the exhilaration I felt when I found those handwritten, Oregon Trail death records. This was the first full, traceable name of consequence to my subject. Birth certificates, a marriage license, census reports, even sermons by Rosie's husband—who was the assistant pastor at Christ Church, and obviously known in Gettysburg society—could all likely be found by searching the museum's databases or those at the library connected to the seminary. I didn't have my author's name, but this was something.

"I'm coming for you, A.M.P."

And I was introduced to Mam—her surrogate mother, who seemed to pass on her spunk, independent nature, and calling.

I wish I'd had a Mam, growing up.

I put down my pencil and let my head fall into my hands. I rubbed my palms over my eyes and attempted to ease the strain building in my head—which was both a physical and emotional strain. *This manuscript is different.* Reading about A.M.P's life—particularly her painful childhood—struck me deeply. Her loneliness and isolation had roots in her strained relationship with her mother.

Our mothers should trade notes.

I had to sympathize slightly with her mother—she married young and was cut off from her family, her husband died suddenly, and he left her with a young child and tremendous debt. The death of a husband in the nineteenth century was disastrous. From my undergrad knowledge of feminism, women's suffrage had beginnings in the 1850's but everything curtailed with the advent of the Civil War. Society was based off marital status, and that included property rights; in Pennsylvania, married women weren't permitted to own property independently of their husband before 1846. A woman's wages weren't her own before the Act of 1855 — passed after so many men never returned from war. A.M.P's mother was left without much of an option; she had no means to keep the farm, especially if it was mortgaged and her family was unwilling to support her. Her only hope was to remarry and try to start over. And doing so with a child would be more difficult.

All of which A.M.P. seemed to understand.

But the part that hurt her — the part that time couldn't mend — was her mother's lack of affection. The loss should have drawn them together, but her mother pushed her away. She took her anger out on an innocent child, who wasn't old enough to understand what was going on.

In my gut, I knew the breakdown of their relationship wasn't solely based on that separation. Something else happened to further destroy their relationship.

I wanted to reach through the pages and hug her close, to tell her everything would be okay — *even though I have no clue if it will*. Our childhoods were similar in so many ways that I —

No, I'm not ripping that bandage off yet.

I had to keep reading and not dwell on the similarities between us. I pulled the diary closer and flipped the page to the next entry. But there was an additional piece of parchment folded into the spine. I carefully picked the page out of the diary. The paper was different from the diary's. It was of a cheaper quality and more transparent. It was so delicate that I was almost afraid to touch it. I placed the paper down on the table and opened the page at the fold. After a few minutes of trying to decipher the tiny penmanship, I recalled stashing a magnifying glass from the labs in my bag. I rummaged through my bag and found it at the bottom—naturally.

The paper appeared to be a letter.

But from whom?

I grabbed my notepad and pencil. While holding the magnifying glass with my left hand, I wrote down what I read. I wrote blindly; I read the words but chose to not comprehend the sentences. Much of it was guesswork—the handwriting was barely legible, just enough so that I could make out the bigger words and guess at the rest to string sentences together.

After a few minutes, I put my pencil down and picked up the notepad.

I read.

Chapter Fourteen

A.M.P.

February 19th, 1863

Dear Wife,

I know not when you will receive this letter, as many things seem to be delayed. For the time being, I am safe and in good health. My regiment will soon move out.

Please see to the shearing come May. The fleece must be cleaned and spun in time for markets. Hire three hands in town—Negroes are best. I hope the weather is fine and the rains will not delay your endeavor.

Joseph

May 10th, 1863

Shearing has consumed every moment of my waking life for the past week. My hands are blistered and raw. My legs are covered in bruises from the kicks of difficult ewes. And my knees and back are sore from kneeling for hours on end.

I had a hard time finding hands to hire this season. Migrant workers who frequent town this time of year were snatched up almost immediately by larger farms. And fewer arrived with the warm weather. Negroes were even harder to hire; Lincoln's proclamation freed the slaves in January, but the fear of Southern retribution towards freed slaves, or any Negroes they came across, kept away even those who were northerners by birth. They feared being dragged south and forced onto plantations. Daily, news circulated of the impending invasion of Johnny Reb and the death of us all. And it isn't just idle gossip on street corners; newspapers printed stories similar in nature — which only worsen people's trepidation. Yet life continues — with no Southern army marching down our streets or burning our barns.

Unfortunately, these same whispers have kept workers from our town at the height of growing season, and I could only find one man to do the work of three. Henry — my neighbor's son and my livestock hand — and I made up the deficit as best we could. My body feels as though I've aged ten years. How I'll muster the energy for tomorrow's tasks, I know not: combing and washing the wool will consume the next three days. I am already anticipating the odious smell of greasy, wet wool that will bloom and engross the barn, the painful blisters that will form on my hands from repeatedly dipping a pitchfork into boiling vats of water, and the ache in my hands and wrists from wringing dirty water and combing debris from the wool.

Fortunately, my patients had no emergencies. I've had a few people come to the house, needing remedies for common ailments — aches mostly — but my pregnant patients have had to do without our visits, as have I.

These sheep are the bane of my existence. The chain, dangling from my neck.

It is almost a cruel joke from the heavens that Henry delivered my mail today, including a letter from my husband with instructions for my current endeavor — an endeavor that I have completed on my own for the last two years. I know not why I expected kinder words from my husband after receiving nothing for over three months.

I've received four letters from him since he joined the 90th Pennsylvania Infantry and left for the front over two years ago. Every time Mr. Buehler has handed me a tiny, sealed envelope marked with a military insignia, my heart has skipped a beat. In hope or despair, I cannot distinguish between the two emotions. Each letter has been much of the same: concern over the farm, instructions on the proper feed for the livestock and caring for the sheep. Always the sheep. No concern over my welfare.

I know he cannot say much about the war — letters are easily intercepted at the front — but more than a few stoic words would be appreciated. I knew only from the papers that his regiment was engaged at Second Bull Run and later at Antietam. My stomach was in knots for weeks, not knowing if he was dead, captured, or suffering in a field hospital in Maryland. The news of the battles was so oppressive and frightening, my mind wandered, and I was sure something terrible had befallen him. Unsanitary conditions within the camps bred sickness — dysentery, typhoid, consumption — and these took more men than the Rebels. Then his letters arrived — speaking only of our hay supply and preparing the barn for winter — and I was reminded of the basis of our relationship.

Our marriage was a business arrangement, nothing more. No love, no emotional bond bound us to one another. Really, it wasn't his fault, and I cannot hold him responsible for how things fell into place. The war made many do things they normally wouldn't, like marrying a girl you met at the altar.

I've accepted it: the marriage, the cabin far from sight, the sheep. The moment I was back under Mother's roof, she stripped me of everything: my independence, my further education, and a life of my own.

Maybe God granted me all the love I was meant to receive early in life — that my childhood memories were to keep me warm when all else was ice cold. Almost like our sheep. Their winter warmth and protection has been stripped from them, and tomorrow the wool will hang from the beams in the barn to dry, then be sold to keep another warm. I wonder if the sheep look on sorrowfully as their wool is shorn from their backs, as I am now thinking of my past and the love I have lost. What I received from Mam was love that always kept me warm.

My hands and head ache, but I must write of this tonight.

From the moment Mother left me on her porch, Mam was devoted to my upbringing. She gave me structure and purpose, showered me with love, and provided a happy home for the entirety of my childhood and adolescence. She lived on sprawling fifteen acres, with four groves of apple trees and a dairy barn housing seventeen milk cows. The farm was the vegetable provider for two taverns within Cashtown and employed a slew of farmhands. But Mam wasn't above doing the work herself; she counted herself as their equal, we ate our meals with the hands and helped bring in the harvest. Hard work and dedication were paramount in her house, and laziness was unacceptable. Everything she did, I soaked in and learned from. She taught me to read before I started schooling, as well as keep accounts and a bank ledger.

Most importantly, she passed down the art of midwifery.

I was eight years old when she came to me in the early morning and told me to dress warmly. We were heading to town for a birthing. "Labor is the one thing men can never truly understand," she told me, "and their place is outside the birthing room."

That day, I watched with awed patience. And Mam allowed me to assist—I held basins, fetched water, supported the expectant mother's back in the birthing chair. When Mam brought that little soul into the world, she handed her to me. I looked down at the child just as she opened her eyes and a sudden lightness entered my head.

"Hand the child to his mother, dahlin'. She's waitin'," Mam gently reminded me as the mother looked on greedily. Reluctantly, I placed the baby into its mother's arms, and I watched as her eyes lit. I knew, even as a young girl of eight, that this was my life's calling. That my hands were meant to do this work.

Once Mam knew I was suited to the work, my instruction began. She trusted me to study her journals—which detailed local plants that could cure most ailments—and showed me how to create poultices and pumice my own herbs. She sent me to forage in the woods and pick the plants myself—after she'd taught me how to distinguish like plants and know their properties, and how to cut the roots without damaging the plant. And when I turned sixteen, she arranged an apprenticeship with Doctor Watkins—Cashtown's physician. He was reluctant to train a girl, believing the female sex was "squeamish." He refused until Mam insisted he witness a birth at which I took the lead. He was impressed and agreed to train me.

But the arrangement wasn't one I wanted. I loved midwifery in itself, but I loved learning from Mam even more. I was scared that leaving her instruction would damage our bond. I also feared the theoretical and advanced knowledge of medical care; I'd seen the damage left by doctors, desperate to use the latest instruments without proper instruction. Forceps, in particular, could lacerate a patient's cervix if applied in the wrong manner, and also mortally mutilate the unborn child. Mam was called many a time to try and salvage these dire situations; we'd walk into a blood-soaked bedroom, only to pull the cotton sheet over the deceased mother. These were the stuff of my nightmares. Dr. Watkins was rarely called to a birthing room—he left that to Mam—but I feared his teaching would require use of those same instruments. I was terrified that my blood-soaked nightmares would leach into my waking life.

"There's so much more to learn, so much more available to you than I. And I can't teach you," she said to my vehement protests.

I shook my head in anger—shaking the gore-filled memories and her words from my mind. She stepped forward and took my head in her hands. "When hatchlings are ready to leave the nest, what does the mother bird do?"

"She doesn't return with food. They starve—"

"But she's never far away. She forces them to fly out into the world. You need to take this and fly. And I'll still be here. Always." She kissed away my tears, replacing my fear with confidence.

Dr. Watkins applied theory to my medical base. Where Mam's lessons were spent foraging in the woods, Dr. Watkins taught with books and method: he introduced

Hippocrates, the humours, and the evolution and study of anatomy, surgery, and infectious diseases. He had modern instruments and books on almost every imaginable subject. He didn't outright oppose Mam's natural remedies — "They are tried and true." — but he saw the full potential in taking those components and adding an element of modern science. Modern instruments weren't so scary: like the stethoscope, used to hear the beating heart.

My life became so full. Mam truly let me flourish.

It hadn't taken long for Mother to remarry — to a wealthy banker in Harrisburg, twelve years her senior. He had houses in Harrisburg, Philadelphia, New York, and Gettysburg, and Mother took on the running of each. She was always moving from one to the next — whether with the seasons or when the mood struck. She was happy, incredibly happy with the life my stepfather provided her.

I stayed with Mam. And it seemed I'd be there indefinitely, which was what we all wanted.

Whenever Mother was in town, a coach was sent, and I was taken to her house. I'd cross her threshold, and oppression bore down on me like the sun on a hot day. There were no warm hugs or questions about my life. She'd stand me in the middle of her parlor and inspect me from head to toe; she'd look at my clothes, shoes, fingernails, and hair with such a critical eye and tone that it took everything in me not to cry.

"How often does she make you bathe?" she'd ask.

"Every other day, Mother," I answered.

She snatched up my hands and looked closely for dirt beneath my fingernails. "Even a pauper can keep himself clean, as my mother always said. You must be clean and poised, even if you are rolling around in the mud."

"Yes, Mother."

In her presence, I had to remind myself to breathe. She was on the prowl, waiting for any mistake to ream Mam about—though it was never Mam who was forced to listen to her condemnations. I'd stand for what seemed like hours as she complained about this and that. I learned to block out her voice, to make my mind go blank. After endless reprimands, I'd be presented with a new dress or gift and sent on my way. Gifts made her feel more like a mother, I suppose.

My stepfather was rarely present for our visits, and if he was he'd be sure to leave after a cordial hello and kiss atop the head. He asked that I call him Benjamin, which was his given name and I never questioned his reasoning. He was not my father, as his absence and overall ambivalence to my existence demonstrated. Perhaps he would've been warmer if I had grown up under his roof or if Mother showed any true interest in me?

Much changed with Rosie.

Our darling Rosie, born in Harrisburg when I was five years old. I only learned that Mother was pregnant after; she sent her butler to bring me to Harrisburg to meet my new sister. I had never been to my mother's house in Harrisburg and I wasn't comfortable being alone with someone unfamiliar, headed to a place where I was not welcome. But the thought of a baby sister raised my spirits.

Roseanna Marie was the name Mother gave her. *The name fits perfectly*, I remember thinking when I peeked into her cradle and saw her sleeping peacefully. I leaned close and breathed in her fresh, baby scent. The crown of her head had wisps of brown hair, the tip of her nose was the perfect button shape, and her eyelashes were long.

She was mine.

In the farthest corner of my heart, I had prayed for a sibling. Someone to love and be loved by unconditionally, a companion to go through life's every trial with. Once I started school, a deep-seeded jealousy grew within me towards my classmates who had younger siblings. They mistreated them in front of their friends—acted like they were insignificant or a bother. But once we were dismissed for the day, they'd walk home holding hands, like the slight had never happened. "I'd never be like that," I told myself. If God granted me a sibling, I'd love and cherish her or him at every hour of the day.

And at last I had Rosie.

"Rosie, Rosie, Rosie," I whispered to her, standing on my tiptoes and reaching into the cradle to pick her up.

"Don't you go touching her now."

Mother's voice sent a frigid chill went down my spine and I dropped down to the flats of my feet. "The wet nurse just finished her feeding and I'll tan your bottom if you wake her. Go downstairs for your dinner."

"Yes, Mother." I retreated from the nursery with my head so low I almost grazed the floor.

Later that night, I snuck back into the nursery and again peeked into the cradle. "Rosie," I whispered. She turned her head, and our eyes met. She smiled. I poked my fingers inside and between her tiny fingers. She curled her hand around my pointer finger, and we stayed like that until the sun was streaking in through the windows; I told her all my secrets and my hopes for the things we'd one day do together.

I worried that Rosie would be the victim of the same treatment and neglect from Mother. But my anxiety was unfounded—Rosie was raised primarily by her wet nurse, then by a governess as Mother continued to travel with Benjamin. But they both doted on Rosie and spoiled her with presents and trips. I doubt she realized that they were rarely together for more than a few days at a time—at least when she was younger. I was relieved that Rosie lived in a household where her parents cherished her.

When Rosie turned seven, Gettysburg became her permanent home. I'm sure my proximity had nothing to do with the decision, but I was overjoyed all the same. Mam took me to visit twice a week, and we even convinced her governess to bring her to Mam's on Sundays after service—all unbeknownst to Mother. I introduced her to my world—to Mam's house, the woods, midwifery. Rosie found freedom on Mam's farm. She could run, yelp, and do things Mother would never allow. She grew attached to Mam, and Mam smothered her with as many kisses and hugs as she did me. And if Rosie was visiting while we had to make a call to a patient, she came along and assisted where needed.

Mother would be furious if she knew Rosie was assisting Mam in any fashion. She believed—and told me on quite a few occasions—that I was going down the same embarrassing route as my grandmother; that I was fit to make my life "as much of a public spectacle as she has." She wasn't present enough to change my course.

Years passed, and I grew. And on my eighteenth birthday—May 26th—Mam outdid herself.

At the stroke of midnight, she woke me with a mischievous look in her eye and beckoned me to follow her downstairs. I lumbered out of bed and followed her through the dark house. I didn't know what she was up to, but her excitement was ricocheting off the walls. Yawning, I stepped into the kitchen and gasped. The entire room was lit by flickering candles—like a summer field filled with fireflies—and there was vase upon vase of every color tulip imaginable— my favorite flower. Strung across the entranceway was a banner wishing me a happy birthday. I looked around the room in disbelief.

Mam took my hand and guided me to the kitchen table, where a three-tiered, vanilla cake—decorated with tiny blue, sugar flowers—awaited me. She sat me down and covered my face with eighteen kisses.

"Mam," I whined as I batted her away, pretending to be annoyed.

"I have another surprise for you." Her face beamed as she crossed behind me, and then placed a large box, adorned with blue ribbon, in front of me. I untied the ribbon and lifted the lid to find my very own medical kit. It looked like a small steamer trunk—a sturdy, leather-lined wooden box with three brass locks on the front, metal trimming, and a shoulder strap.

Mam hugged me from behind. "I figured you'd be wanting one of your own. Open it."

Inside were storage compartments of different sizes for vials, instruments, and jars. Mam reached over my shoulder and pulled up the center tray to reveal more storage beneath—perfect for bandages and cloth. Next, she handed me a piece of paper, wrapped in a second strand of blue ribbon. "What's this?" I asked. Turning to face Mam, I unfolded it and saw train tickets inside

"You are booked on the morning rail to Philadelphia." Mam's smile was so wide that I could see all her pearly teeth.

"Today? But what about Mrs. Whiting? She could deliver." I was now Gettysburg and Cashtown's primary midwife—Mam's eyesight wasn't what it once was.

"I will be here to take care of that, don't you fuss."

"But I couldn't possibly go alone, Mam! How will I—"

"Of course, you can't, dahlin'. People would talk even more than they do! Dr. Watkins has agreed to accompany you. This was partly his idea."

"His idea?"

"Yes. To to visit his alma mater, Jefferson Medical College. He's arranged for you to see a surgical procedure. And then to go on to the Female Medical College of Pennsylvania."

"Female Medical College?"

She took my face between her hands and stroked my cheeks, kissing me once atop my head before kneeling before me. "You aren't that little beansprout of a girl anymore. Time for you to fly."

I had only ever been as far as Harrisburg — a world away from the farmlands of Gettysburg and Cashtown — but after four hours, two separate trains and countless stops in between, we arrived at our destination: Philadelphia, a true metropolis. With its cobblestone streets packed with carriages and people, storefronts with huge windows that displayed the latest fashions and things to buy, peddlers walking the streets offering ripe apples, cooked meats on a stick, or newspapers, Philadelphia was a city of wonderment. I had never seen so many people in my entire life. My head turned to and fro, not wanting to miss a single sight or smell in this wondrous place. I would've walked the streets all day if it weren't for Dr. Watkins reminding me of our appointments.

Jefferson Medical College breathed advancement and enlightenment. The school focused on the demonstrative approach to medical education; clinical classes were taught in the attached hospital, and students tended to the sick in its one hundred and twenty-five beds. The hospital had served over four thousand patients in its first year of operation, and many of the best physicians in the country came to teach and work there. Or so Dr. Watkins told me on our walk to the main building on Walnut Street. He was walking with such urgency that I had to hold my skirts almost above my knees to keep up with him. These were the streets of his youth and being in Philadelphia seemed to bring vigor back to his aging legs.

With its dark brown brick facade, Jefferson took up nearly a city block. Dr. Watkins and I fell in line with other students and followed as they strategically maneuvered through the halls. On my own I would've gotten horribly lost. Thankfully I was with someone who knew where he was going—to the "pit" for a leg amputation. The pit had amphitheater, tiered seating that circled an operating table at the very center, all lit by a massive, low hanging chandelier. As I took my seat, I garnered many stares and whispers from the male audience—I was noticeably not a student, and women were rarely admitted to the surgery. But their stares didn't deter me; I was there to learn. The patient was wheeled in and placed on the operating table. Dr. Watkins explained that the patient was a railway worker who had injured his left leg. Infection had spread, and an amputation of the lower extremity would be performed. The chief surgeon gave a brief explanation of the surgery to the audience. The students were hastily writing notes, and I instantly regretted having nothing with which to do the same.

The operation began. I leaned over the row in front of me, hoping to observe as much as I could. I watched a nurse place a small mask over the patient's face and sprinkle a liquid onto it. I assumed the liquid to be morphine, but I had never seen it administered this way.

"What is that they're using?" I whispered to Dr. Watkins, pointing to the glass bottle.

"Ether. Similar effects to morphine, but the patient inhales the fumes of the gaseous state. After just a few breaths, the patient falls to sleep, and the operation can proceed without interference."

I watched in awe. Awe that was still affecting me two hours later, when the procedure concluded. Students were filing out of the pit, and the patient was wheeled from the room, but I wasn't ready to leave. It took everything in me not to dash down the amphitheater stairs to the center; to beg the surgeon to answer a few questions. I was fascinated with how he staunched the bleeding after removing the leg—he hadn't cauterized the incision but used some sort of tourniquet—and how the ether was measured in its gaseous state. As I stood and stepped into the aisle, the surgeon left the room. I was disappointed—I felt I had lost the chance of a lifetime.

Dr. Watkins touched my elbow. "Ready?"

I smiled and turned towards the door. Before leaving, I looked over my shoulder, back to the center of the Pit and the peak of my imagination.

If Jefferson was my imagination's peak, then the Female Medical College of Pennsylvania was the fruition of my dreams.

We walked the halls of the small building on Arch Street, lingered in doorways, and overheard lessons. Instructors stood at the front of classrooms, showing anatomical diagrams, describing the chemical properties of medicines, and giving demonstrations of surgical instruments to rows of women—women like me who were eager to learn what had always been denied them. The instructors—all male—believed education shouldn't be denied due to sex. Though, the space was small—the entire school was housed inside a few rented rooms—the classrooms were filled to the hilt. There was promise within the program; female-inclusive medical programs were expanding quickly across the country.

So much was shown that I could feel my brain turning to mush. I had questions to ask, but I couldn't verbalize a single one. I just kept smiling and nodding, looking like a prim and proper fool with a hollow head. I truly wonder, even to this day, what a few of the instructors—who were colleagues and classmates of Dr. Watkins—thought of me. Once we'd left, I apologized to Dr. Watkins, knowing he'd gone out on a limb for me and I had embarrassed him horribly.

"I don't know what happened, Dr. Watkins. I just couldn't...I couldn't—"

"I'll hear none of that. Everything went fine. Better than fine, because I got to experience it through you. Your wonderment reminded me why I went into medicine."

All I could do was nod.

It was well after dark when Dr. Watkins's carriage returned to Mam's house. An entire lifetime seemed to have passed since that morning. I saw the promise of the world and knew I'd never be the same. I took a deep breath as Dr. Watkins jumped down from the carriage and helped me down.

"I hope you had a happy birthday," he said.

"The best. I can't thank you enough."

"Ah...I almost forgot," he said, reaching back into the carriage for a package beneath the seat. "One last gift for today." He handed me the package.

I untied the twine and removed the brown paper to find a book—*On Bandaging, and other operations of minor surgery*, by F.W. Sargent. We'd been discussing his methods for weeks, using Dr. Watkins's battered copy. I lunged into Dr. Watkins and hugged him. Initially, his body was rigid; his hands were tight at his sides in shock. But he gave in, relaxed, and returned the embrace.

We pulled apart, and I wiped the tears from my eyes. "Thank you. Thank you, Dr. Watkins."

"No, thank you," he said. From behind us, Mam's screen door creaked. I turned to find Mam standing on the porch in her nightgown. I gave Dr. Watkins one last look of appreciation and ran to Mam's open arms.

"How was it, dahlin'?" she whispered into my ear.

"Everything. Everything I could ever want," I cried into her shoulder. I was shivering -from the cool May air and the exhilaration bubbling inside of me—so she wrapped me in her shawl, and we sat down on the porch steps. I told her everything—speaking at a rapid pace, with no pauses until I was through.

"Your mama will not agree with this, now. But is this what you want? Is Philadelphia and the medical college what you—"

"Yes! Yes! A million times yes!"

She pulled me into her lap, like she had when I was a little girl. She laid her cheek upon mine and whispered, "Then dahlin' it's yours."

"But how will we—"

"Let me worry about that." She rocked me back and forth.

I had never given a thought to the future. But after being to Philadelphia, seeing the Female Medical College, and Mam telling me she would make it possible, I felt free. Life was no longer so suffocating. Once the place of my abandonment, Mam's porch became the place where my dreams had taken flight. We sat there for hours that night, eating my remaining birthday cake and giggling. We talked about submitting an application to the college, reference letters I'd need, where I would live in town, where life would take me after completing my courses. In that moment, I couldn't imagine being any happier.

But I've learned emotions are fleeting.

Not long after my nineteenth birthday, Mam passed.

She wasn't sick, nor in pain. In the days that followed her death, I racked my brain trying to remember any abnormal occurrences in our daily routine. There was nothing, nothing out of the ordinary. In fact, just two days before, she had assisted me in setting a farmer's broken leg in town. Mam simply went to sleep on a Thursday in October and never woke the next morning.

I found her.

In all the years I'd lived in her home, never once had she slept past 6 o'clock. So, I was surprised to walk into the kitchen that morning and not to find her mixing porridge or flipping hotcakes. I climbed the stairs, approached her bedroom, and knocked softly. There was no answer. I waited, staring at the door for minutes, hoping the doorknob would turn or hear a shuffle of feet on the other side. My hands were shaking as I turned the knob and opened the door.

I didn't need to walk beyond the threshold to see the truth.

She looked peaceful: lying in bed, her eyes open, hands folded across her chest.

My knees buckled, and I fell to the floor. That's where Ulysses—one of our farmhands—found me, hours later. He carried me to the barn, while another worker rushed to fetch Dr. Watkins. But there was nothing to be done.

I have no recollection of the events leading to Mam's funeral. As if I was drowning in the deepest of lakes, only to be pulled from its waters and revived while standing in the graveyard beside her casket. Almost all Cashtown and Gettysburg—even those who despised her—had come to the small graveyard on the hill where Granddaddy and Papa had been laid to rest many years before. She may not have been well liked, but no one could deny that she was a prominent figure. The number of mourners was truly a sight; one Mam would've enjoyed every second of. I saw former patients, the farmhands who were more like family, business owners who bought their produce from our farm. They stood shoulder to shoulder, with no breathing space between them.

I couldn't help but smile at the pastor who presided over the service; the very same pastor had made almost weekly visits to the farm to try and bring Mam back to his flock. I had to swallow a laugh as he called for the mourners to pray for Mam's mortal soul—which he had damned to hell a month before. Mam would have howled with laughter if she heard his impassioned speech. Her loss was momentarily filled with the joy of her memory. I felt she was there, standing beside me and holding my hand.

I looked over the crowd and locked eyes with Mother, who stood with Rosie on the outskirts of the graveyard. The look of contempt in her eyes made me shiver and swept the smile from my face. I became that little girl dumped on a stranger's porch all over again.

As the service ended and people started to drift back to their homes, I dropped to my knees beside Mam's casket and rested my forehead on its lid. The tears streamed down my face as I wrapped my arms on either side of the wooden casket. Our last hug. I relished the moment and soaked the wood beneath me with tears.

"Stop making a spectacle. Stand up," Mother muttered harshly from behind me.

My body went stiff, and I let go of Mam. I was no match for Mother; I no longer had Mam—my strength—to urge me forward. Before I stood, I kissed the wood separating us.

"I love you, dahlin'," I whispered with the last of my tears. Mother had already walked from the graveyard, but Rosie was waiting. Her cheeks were streaked with tears, which I dabbed away with my handkerchief. We walked from the cemetery hand in hand, silently comforting each other.

At first, I stayed at the farm. October was waning, and winter was upon us. I had no intention of allowing our farm to go under—I could hear Mam's voice telling me to "buck up and get on." So, I did. I put my feelings aside and worked in the fields alongside the farmhands, laying seed for the winter crop and wrapping the orchard's trees trunks in burlap. I managed the accounts, paid the creditors, and kept house. My patients were always a top priority and I continued my studies with Dr. Watkins. He became a true friend and confidant. We didn't speak about the medical college. I had sent my application—with Dr. Watkin's letter of recommendation and testimonials from former patients—a month before Mam passed but there was still no word. Not that it mattered; even if I was accepted, I had no means of paying the tuition.

But then a lawyer arrived.

I welcomed Mr. Brooks and showed him to the sitting room. From a case, he removed a stack of papers. "I apologize for taking so long to come to you, Miss. Customarily, we wait a month before calling on a beneficiary, but there were special circumstances involved," he explained.

"Beneficiary?"

"Why, yes. Beneficiary in your grandmother's will." He handed me a copy of the documents. I touched the paper and my hands started to shake uncontrollably. I knew people of wealth created wills, but I never counted Mam as one of them. But, the thought of Mam dying hadn't crossed my mind either.

"Your grandmother came to me six months ago. She informed me of new circumstances that needed to be addressed. Now, if you'll turn to the third page your inheritance is clearly outlined."

Obediently, I turned the pages and scanned the document. At the beginning of the fifth paragraph was my name. "And to my granddaughter—" I began reading aloud but was quickly absorbed by the words to continue. I read the half-page paragraph again and again, unsure of some of the legal ramifications. Mr. Brooks impatiently cleared his throat.

"I'm sorry," I said, looking up for the first time in a few minutes, "but if I'm reading this correctly, it means—"

"She left everything to you. The house, barn, livestock, and land."

The room started spinning. I placed the papers down on the table in front of us and fanned my face with my hand.

"Shall I open a window, Miss?" he asked.

"No, no. I'll be fine. It's a lot to take in," I said. I'd feared much in the days following Mam's death. I feared being thrown on the streets and having to resort to Mother for charity. But now, my future was assured. Mam was an independent woman, and she just bestowed the same gift to me. I smiled for the first time in weeks

"There are a few stipulations to the inheritance. Just a few formalities, due to you being unwed," Mr. Brooks went on, taking the document from the table.

"Unwed? What does marriage—"

"Your inheritance has been placed in trust until your twenty-first birthday. Your grandmother agreed twenty-one would be the appropriate age for bequeathment and agreed to an executor."

"Who would that be?"

"Legally, the executor needs to be next of kin: your mother and stepfather."

My heart dropped. I had hoped another would've been named—maybe even Dr. Watkins—but my mother and Benjamin were family. And if she hadn't been named, I'm sure Mother would've kicked up a fuss.

"She also left you this," he said, handing me a sealed envelope. I recognized Mam's wax seal, the one that sat on the rollout desk behind Mr. Brooks. "I trust everything is now in order. I will leave you with a copy of the will. Please call on me in town if any questions cross your mind." He stood, and I showed him to the door.

As the door closed behind him, I looked down to the envelope in my hands. I turned it over and opened the seal. Inside was a letter from Mam—a letter I no longer possess. But I read it so many times that I will never forget the words she left behind:

Sell the farm.

Go to school.

Fly.

Mam gave me more than I could ever hope for. And now with her death, she assured my dreams. She gave me permission to create my own life—not stay on the farm and continue hers. And what's more, she did so without my knowledge; no one but God knows the day he will call them home, but she prepared, knowing death was inevitable.

The next day, Mother arrived at the farm. She wouldn't enter the house—or even get out of her carriage. I hadn't seen or heard from her since the funeral, but I didn't expect a warm word. And I wasn't disappointed; her face was stern and devoid of feeling when I approached the carriage.

"She left you the farm," she said, never meeting my eyes.

"Yes. Mr. Brooks called yesterday."

"Well." She straightened her skirts and her silk gloves. "The woman had some sense after all. Now, you have a dowry and a man will want you."

"No...that's not what...that's not what Mam wanted. Not what I want," I stammered, and my mind started to race. Had Mam not written a letter to Mother, informing her of her intent for the money? Mother's face snapped towards me with anger.

"Oh no? What's your plan, then? To live in disgrace as your grandmother did?"

"She didn't...I want to go to school. I want to be a doctor. That's what Mam intended—"

"I care nothing for your grandmother's intention! I am your mother, and I know what is best for you."

"Then why wouldn't you want me to have a life of my own? A life where I can support myself." This was what I always wanted to say when we argued about midwifery but had never had the gall to utter.

Her anger was palpable. She would've struck me if she had a firm footing on ground. She took two long breaths and said, "Do you not think I had gifts at your age? I had no other option but to marry, and then remarry when your father left me bereft and straddled with an ungrateful child. What makes you think you are better than I?"

We had no further words. Mother ordered her driver on; he flicked his reins and the horses jolted forward, down the drive and away from the house.

A year passed with no change. One last year of freedom.

Whispers of impending war had many on edge. Gettysburg was staunchly divided on the issues at hand. Some believed, as our president did, that slavery was immoral, others saw the economic advantages and did not wish for anything to change. Discussions were often heated, and a great many physical altercations had to be broken-up by the sheriff. I was called to dress the wounds after such arguments — the worst being a minor stabbing. The country was a pot on boil; more flame would make everything spill over. Many left town — including Dr. Watkins, who returned to Philadelphia, where he accepted a teaching position at Jefferson.

"I'm needed there, especially when the world seems so uncertain. We will need doctors if this war comes to pass," he explained when I accompanied him to Hanover Junction. He gave his practice to his son and sold his home — he didn't know when or if he'd ever return. He asked me to join him — practically begged me — but much was still up in the air with my inheritance and I couldn't risk leaving the farm. I promised to join him in Philadelphia as soon as I could — my twenty-first birthday was less than a year away.

Our goodbye was devastating. I watched with bated breath as his train pulled from the station. In a way, I felt like part of my soul was wrenched from my chest and was being dragged along the tracks behind the train.

I should've gone with him; I regret not having done so to this day.

Yet I had little time to dwell as I was still managing the farm and seeing patients in both Cashtown and Gettysburg. If I wasn't working in the fields, I was almost on constant call in town. So, I guess it was little wonder that I hadn't noticed strangers on the farm. Ulysses informed me after the third group came in one week.

"Yous' was in town, Missus. I thought you known who it was, so I let them through. Yaw Mama and Mr. Benjamin was with em," he explained.

"My mother?"

"Yessum. Brought em right on through the house. Looked at the barn, too. Mr. Richards from next door was with em, too."

"Thank you, Ulysses."

My heart told me she couldn't possibly do something so underhanded. But I was reminded of her last words and the look in her eyes as she had said them. I prayed that interest in the farm would be moderate — once I turned twenty-one, I'd be in control of the fate of the farm.

I lost all hope on the day — four months before my birthday — Mr. Richards arrived at the farm, accompanied by Mr.

Brooks, Benjamin, and my mother. The bill of sale had been written up, and all was in order. Mr. Richards bought the farm in its entirety, including all the livestock, current crop, the house, and most of its furnishings. I would be allowed to take furniture and trinkets of personal value, but nothing more. I had one month to settle my affairs and then would need to vacate the premises. Benjamin and Mother signed the agreement in front of me, and then she handed me the pen — driving the knife further into my heart. I took the pen and hesitated, with the ballpoint hovering above the page. I could've refused, I realize that now. But Mother impatiently cleared her throat and I shuddered beneath her unspoken demand. I signed my name with ink that might as well have been made of my blood.

They were gone before I could collect myself. I sat down in the doorway and stared out the front door. Anger, sadness, betrayal: none of it mattered. Emotions wouldn't bring Mam back, wouldn't stop the wheels that had already turned.

I packed my bags, said my goodbyes to the hands and the animals, took one last walk through the house — through the rooms that made me a woman — and walked away from Mam's porch forever. Mother sent her carriage. I would move into her Gettysburg house with Rosie until "other arrangements" could be made. I didn't look behind as the carriage turned onto the road. The farm was nothing but a piece of property where I had once lived.

As my world fell apart, so did the country. On the 12th of April, Fort Sumter in South Carolina was attacked by

Carolinian artillery. Union forces surrendered the fort and evacuated in haste. President Lincoln called for volunteer troops to defend the capital and the country. He asked for seventy-five thousand troops for three months to wage a war within our own boundaries, against our own country, a war that our forefathers would have been ashamed of. The streets of Gettysburg erupted — with exultation from those who sided with the South, and with despair for those who sided with the North. Carts were lit on fire and rolled down the streets like fiery demons from hell. It was only midday, but drunken men took to the streets and screamed obscenities. Flags were ripped down, defecated on — or in stark contrast, worn like capes.

Rosie and I watched in silence from the front windows of Mother's house. It was frightening to see such heathen antics from grown men. Rosie wrapped her arms around me; she was shaking like a leaf.

"Will we be safe here, sister?" she asked.

A loud boom sounded in the distance — the fire of a cannon. I felt the sound deep in my chest, and it made my stomach queasy. "Of course, we are," I lied. I didn't know if we would ever be safe. Anywhere, ever again.

Almost all our young men enlisted — some with the local Pennsylvania regiments, some crossed the border and headed for Virginia. A town watch and militia were established, allowing older men to take part in the cause. The streets were quiet again. Compared to the chaos, the quiet was almost more disturbing.

Mother arrived two weeks after, in an oddly cheerful mood. She swooped into the house with a flurry of flowers, hat boxes, bags, and a high-pitched voice calling for Rosie and I. Rosie ran to her waiting arms. I hung in the doorway, unsure if my presence was truly wanted. But from her warm embrace with Rosie, her eyes found me.

"Come and kiss your mother," she requested. Meekly, I walked forward, and my dry lips brushed her cheek. Then she grabbed my hand and ushered me into the parlor. "I have something for you," she said as she sat me beside her. She called to Rosie to bring her the parcels she had left in the foyer. She snatched one of the garment bags from Rosie and opened it, revealing a golden-yellow satin gown.

"Here, let's see it against you," she said, urging me to stand. She asked Rosie to hold the dress against my frame and stepped back for a better view. "Oh perfect. I had to guess at your measurements. Maybe a slight hem in the skirt, but the waist and neckline will do. The color...well, it does nothing for your complexion, but you need only wear it once."

"Once? What is this for, Mother?" Rosie asked innocently.

"Her wedding, of course."

"My...my what?" The fabric made my skin itch uncontrollably, and I backed away as if the gown were crawling with ants.

"You will be married within the fortnight."

My legs lost their strength, and I had to grip the armchair to keep from falling. Rosie dropped the gown and grabbed my other arm, ushering me into the chair and asking if I needed her to open a window. I stared up at her dumbly. I thought—and prayed—I had misheard Mother. Rosie saw my struggle and spoke.

"How could this be, Mother? Who is she to marry?"

"It's all been arranged. I placed an advert in the Adams County Sentinel, and a man answered. Benjamin and I met him, and he has accepted. He has a small piece of land outside of town, and he's very pleased with our offer."

"Offer?" Like I was cattle.

"Your dowry. The money from the sale of the farm. Part of the funds have already purchased livestock and feed that will be delivered after the ceremony."

I didn't know it was possible for my heart to drop even further. I had nothing now; I was nothing. I was something to be pawned off on another person.

"That was for medical school, Mother! That was Mam's wish!" Rosie exclaimed.

"This does not concern you, Roseanna," snapped Mother.

Rosie took my hand and gripped it tight between hers. How could she do this to me? How could she force me to marry out of spite, to a man who knew nothing but the money our marriage would bring him? Mother turned back to me and glared with malice and contempt, daring me to argue.

"And if I refuse?"

"Then you will have nothing. No money. No home. No family." Her voice was cold, and she never broke her stare. My mind raced, trying to think of ways I could avoid this undesirable fate. Then it dawned on me why there was urgency behind this arranged marriage; my twenty-first birthday was four weeks away.

"Why?" I cried.

"You know why." The conversation was over; she stood and walked from the room. I crumbled into Rosie's lap.

"We will think of something, sister. I promise," she whispered into my ear as she stroked my hair.

But there was nothing to be done. My last shred of hope had dissipated. My future was no longer my own. In my pocket was the acceptance letter to the Female Medical College; it had arrived only the day before—long delayed due an influx of applications and the outbreak of war. I pulled out the letter and ripped it to shreds, letting the pieces scatter to the floor.

Two weeks to the day, I wore the gown Mother bought me to Christ Lutheran Church, where I met my husband, Joseph. I couldn't look him in the eye, nor he me. He wore a plain suit, and his face had a slew of cuts—he must've shorn his beard just for the occasion. It has been so long that now I can hardly recall any distinguishable attributes. He was not repellant, but my stomach turned, and I recoiled when he took my arm from Benjamin and guided me towards the altar.

I remember nothing of the service; my body was there but my mind was hovering in the choir loft above. I was the convicted, standing on the gallows, staring down the rope meant to extinguish my life. I nodded, responded when asked, and moved when instructed. I only remember when Joseph leaned in to kiss me. His lips were chapped and only briefly touched mine—thankfully.

We proceeded back down the aisle, and Benjamin took Joseph's hand, shaking it gingerly. The smirk on Mother's face broke my heart. She pulled me into an awkward hug, but I was limp in her arms. She stepped back, holding tight to my arms and looked long into my eyes—something she has never done. She said, "You look like him." A memory seemed to pass before her, and a smile curled at the corner of her lips. But just as quickly as it came, the moment was gone.

She released me and said, "This is for the best." She turned, took Benjamin's arm and left the church, leaving me with my new husband.

And then Joseph, my husband, took his own leave. He had enlisted with the 90th Pennsylvania and was anxious to join his regiment; they were moving out in the morning, and he had only enough time to escort me to our home.

Our conversation was light on the ride back to his homestead in his horse drawn wagon. He asked me many questions about the running of Mam's farm. He asked nothing about myself or was forthcoming about his own life; his only concern was my willingness to work. Once we arrived at my new home, he showed me the barn and the animals and gave strict instructions on their care. He had procured another horse—Barley—and seemed disappointed when I wasn't overly thankful. I followed him behind the barn to the spring house, which he seemed rather proud of as he built it himself. The ramshackle shack was dug a few feet into the earth and on top of a spring, and he used it store vegetables and the milk from our cow — Gertie. We returned to the house and went in. The house was heated by a brick fireplace and furnished only with a bed, a table with two chairs, a potbelly stove, and a rocking chair. Piles of dirty clothes and uneaten food littered the hardwood floor, and a musty smell lingered in the air. I'd seen pigsties in better condition. He showed me his account ledgers and his important documents — which he kept in a crate beneath the bed. He didn't want a wife; he needed a farmhand to keep things in order. And with my experience on Mam's farm, I was just that, with a large monetary reward, to boot.

"I will be home by Christmas. Be sure to stock up on hay before the freeze," he said as he put his saddlebags over his horse and mounted. Then, he nodded his head and reined his horse away. I stood there, in my wedding gown and watched the horse gallop from sight.

And that is how I arrived here. On the small parcel of land beyond the Little Hill. Inside a cottage that a strong wind would likely blow over. Living among a stranger's possessions. With a barn that is in desperate need of a new roof. Taking care of sheep that my freedom bought.

After his three-month volunteer enlistment, he reenlisted. With the war raging on, President Lincoln required another three years. Joseph wrote and told me after it was done. If given the chance, I don't know, even now, if I would've asked him to come home. And that is worrisome — no matter the circumstance, he is my husband and I should want him home.

Dr. Watkins sent me many fervent letters in the months following my wedding, offering to hire a lawyer to seek an annulment, to pay my tuition himself, to retrieve me in all haste. After a while, I stopped responding and he stopped writing—my sadness and a sense of worthlessness consumed me, and I felt there was no use. I was trapped. Happiness was not meant to be mine and I have no control over anything in my life. It all changed with the seasons—like the wind blew my hope away with the leaves.

Three Christmases have passed, and I have tried to keep the darkness of my past hidden deep within. I am isolated here and prefer this—my patients and my sister are the extent of my social interaction. Solitude has become my companion, and in that way, I am glad of my situation. This is my life now and I've tried to make it full; I've made Joseph's house a home, bringing items from Mam's house—like her rollout desk, area rugs, books, and curtains—to remind me of happier times.

But I no longer dream.

I try not to think of Mother or the path that brought me here. I go to real pains to live in the moment. Hearing news of Mother being in town or receiving a long-awaited, lackluster letter from Joseph provokes my emotions. Sometimes I feel my past will swallow me alive. I hope documenting my heartbreak will release some of my darkness. Maybe one day, my past will remain so.

I have written longer than I intended, and my hands are stained with ink. I must rise early for another back-breaking day of work. I look forward to the end of shearing and will not look at the sheep for some days after.

Till I write again.

— A

Chapter Fifteen

Breanne Walker

A VOICE COMING FROM MY LIVING ROOM WOKE ME FROM A DEEP, dreamless sleep. *Who is in my apartment?* I lay there in silent terror for a few seconds, allowing sleep to clear from my eyes and trying to convince myself that I had only imagined it. Just as my pulse started to steady, the voice got louder and multiplied.

Great, I'm going to be robbed and murdered in my own bed.

If an intruder was about to rush into my bedroom, cowering in bed wouldn't help. I peeled the blankets off my body — still fully clothed and wearing my shoes from the day before — got out of bed, dropped to all fours and crawled to my bathroom quicker than a baby on steroids. The exit was blocked by whoever was in my living room, so my only option was to try and ward off whoever it was. Blindly, I opened my sink's vanity cabinet and rummaged inside, grabbing the first sizeable object my hand bumped against.

Which was a can of Lysol.

Really? Not even a plunger to bludgeon someone with? One day, this would make a rather comical or gruesome story, but now my only option was to step out into my living room, armed with an aerosol can of bathroom cleaner. Still on my hands and knees, I crawled from my bathroom to my closed bedroom door. I stood, positioned the can in the best defensive position I could think of — in my right hand, out in front of me, pointer finger firmly planted on the nozzle — and turned the doorknob. I took one large gulp of air, pulled the door open, and thrust my body out into the living room.

To no one. I was completely alone.

Silly, stupid idiot, I dropped my arm and allowed my weapon to fall with a soft thud to the carpeted floor. To assume I was being burglarized was a complete overreaction from an overtired mind — *thank god no one is here to see it.* Then the voices started again, coming from the large, curtained picture window by the front door. I crossed the room and opened the curtains just enough to peek onto my balcony.

"You said you paid the electric, Billy! Where's the money?"

"I paid it, Marge. I don't know what — " I pulled my curtains closed, hoping to block out my neighbor's domestic spat — a common occurrence when the utilities were due at the beginning of the month. I retreated to my plush couch in my living room and slumped down onto its cushions, wishing that I was still comatose.

Then I spied the analog clock, hanging above my television, and realized the time. It was 9 a.m.

"The press conference!" I'd been so entrenched in the diary that I'd nearly forgotten about my pressing timeline and the illegalness of my contraband.

I lunged for my remote and turned the television—that I hardly used—on and turned to the local news station. On screen appeared a small stage, in front of the picturesque, white pillared façade of Gettysburg College, in front of a sea of reporters and camera crews. On the stage were several people from the museum—I recognized a few board members, curators, and most importantly, Peggy Cupples. Her snow-white, cropped hair made her stand out among her counterparts—that and the fact that she was close to six feet tall and towered over the short men beside her. She was wearing a smart pantsuit—a stark contrast to the khakis and white button-down combo she usually wore. Her face was stern and all business—*the Ice Queen returneth.* Standing near her, behind a microphone, was Greg Ransome—dressed in an impeccably tailored suit, no tie, top button undone. He could've easily passed for a politician on a disaster-relief tour. He also looked well rested and devastatingly handsome—*per usual.*

Bastard.

In the research world, it is very uncommon to alert the press to anything until concrete evidence can prove the discovery beyond a doubt. No one wants to back-track a lofty statement because the contrary was later discovered. Careers had been ruined by such mistakes. Obviously, the Gettysburg National Military Park had enough to prove the historical significance of the body; otherwise all of this would still be a huge secret — *a huge secret, on top of the one held between Greg and me.*

Greg was speaking, but I could only pick up every few words; the microphone he was speaking into kept cutting in and out. The way he was waving his hands and gesturing made me guess he was explaining how the body was discovered. He was in his element and had no problem with public speaking — he had the face and charisma that easily translated to television. Which I'm sure was the reason he was chosen to give the presentation. Then he started pointing to people in the audience, fielding questions. Reading lips was definitely not my forte but luckily many of the reporters spoke clearly.

"The Park Service are doing all in their power to preserve the tree and the surrounding area," the sound came back as Greg responded. "Witness trees are considered historic artifacts, and we take their care very seriously. Each tree is logged and monitored on a monthly basis, ensuring its health and stamina." He pointed to another reporter and another question was asked offscreen. "No, the body will not be transported to another site for study. Further disturbances will speed decay, and we are fully capable of completing the needed research at our onsite labs. Yes, the museum will have exclusive rights to any future exhibits, as outlined by Congress regarding any and all artifacts found on government land."

The camera panned out to a woman sitting in the audience. She asked, "There are reports of a second discovery at the Witness Tree and that the two are linked. Can you validate this?"

My eyes popped out of my head. *How could they know?* I leaned back on my haunches, peering into my bedroom. I could just make out the desk and my messenger bag lying on top—the secondary discovery was safely inside. I breathed with relief. Thankfully, I was not presiding over the press conference because my non-existent poker face would've given everything away. Greg, on the other hand, didn't miss a beat.

"At this time, there is but one discovery. Further excavation of the area will be scheduled, and as such the area of Little Round Top will be closed to the general public. That's all for today. Thank you." He turned to those standing behind him and motioned for them to leave the stage.

"A huge announcement made here today, on the steps of Gettysburg College," the reporter stated as she stepped back into frame. "If you are just joining our broadcast, Dr. Greg Ransome, the Assistant Director of Exhibits and Collections at the Gettysburg National Military Park has just informed us of the discovery of a body beneath a felled witness tree on Little Round Top. It is believed that the remains are those of a soldier, present during the battle that took place here in 1863. This is a developing story, so be sure to stick to WXPR Gettysburg for round the clock updates. Back to you, Brad."

"Thanks, Mackenzie. History being made here, in Gettysburg, on Labor Day. Now—" I pushed the power button on the remote and the screen went black. From my bedroom, I heard my phone ping. I stood up and went to find my phone. On my nightstand, the ping sounded again. Two text messages were in my inbox from Greg:

Where are you?

Staff meeting in 20

"Great. Just what I need!"

After a four-minute shower and a quick throwing-on of clothes, I emerged from my apartment with sopping wet hair. Sunlight hit my face, and I thought I was going to burst into immediate flames. Vampires had the right idea and this former Nevada girl wanted nothing more than to crawl back into her black hole of an apartment and stay there forever.

Even more so when I saw my car—which I'd parked sideways, taking up three spaces.

"Jesus," I whispered as I quickstepped through the parking lot, looking around sheepishly. Luckily, the lot was empty of people. *Well of course they saw it! How could they not,* I thought as I shoved my key into the lock and opened the driver's side door. I climbed inside, put the car into gear, and began my drive to the museum. I knew what my parking job seemed to indicate — *the aftermath of a night of partying*. It's the conclusion I would've jumped to if I'd walked out to that sight first thing in the morning. And I wished with all my might that that was the reason for it.

But my obscenely poor parking job was the result of extreme exhaustion and emotional turmoil.

I can't remember leaving the archives, getting into my car, or even driving home. For all I knew, I could've flown back to my apartment on a winged horse. I remembered closing the diary and feeling extreme despondency. Reading material in that long, unbelievably detailed, and heartbreaking diary entry felt like a head-on collision with a concrete wall. My entire body was overwhelmed. All I wanted was to get far away from the archives.

Fleeing the scene of duress must be a new habit of mine.

I didn't know her name, but I knew her deepest pain. I could see her life clearly: the beginnings of her medical career, her dedication and work ethic, the touching relationship with her grandmother and Dr. Watkins, the excitement books brought her, how and why she mothered her dear sister. But that deep seeded pain — the death of Mam, being stripped of everything she gave her, her forced marriage and her husband's absence — had crushed her soul. She was a shadow of what she could've been. Now things made sense; her solitary life, lack of relationships and trust were all hard-learned defense mechanisms to keep her heart safe. And all of it, every god awful, heart-wrenching thing was because of her mother.

I've never wanted to reach into a manuscript so desperately. Reach in, tightly hug, and then immediately smack some sense into A.M.P. Tell her mother to kick rocks or go play on the freeway—*yes, both middle-school insults easily translated into 19th-century language.* I'd march A.M.P. to Philadelphia and force her to take Dr. Watkins's offer. How could a mother be so cruel? To destroy any hope of happiness she had, then force her into a life—and a marriage—she never wanted. Resentment and jealousy bubbled beneath the surface of everything her mother did.

Recalling her past was difficult. Carrying the baggage of an unloving mother was something I was way too familiar with. Reading had awoken my own pain. Which was why I fled the archives.

Now I was back at the museum, pulling in to a parking lot that strongly resembled the scene of a blockbuster movie premiere. Every local news affiliate and quite a few from the tri-state area had brought a camera crew and enough supplies to camp out for a few days. Lawn chairs, pop-up tents, and massive satellite antennas took up more than half the rear parking lot. *Slow news day?* I parked my car—in one space—far from the vans and crowds. On foot, I glided past with my head down. I clutched my bag close to my chest, praying the strap wouldn't rip and dump the diary onto the hot asphalt. I hustled up the back patio's slate steps and headed straight for the rear entrance.

The atmosphere inside the museum was just as jarring.

All staff was on deck, congregating in the vestibule and saloon. *Didn't know this many people worked here,* I thought as the automatic doors closed behind me. Small groups were huddled together and frantically whispering—but the number of groups and whispers turned into a combined roar. Everyone seemed excited, wide-eyed, and acutely aware of the enormity of the given situation.

My anxiety was on overdrive.

After the soggy-shoes period, I'd never really made friends—*other than Greg.* So, I stood on the outskirts of a group of research assistants, like the loner I always had been. Truthfully, I was so high-strung that I was liable to blurt out the existence of the diary to anyone in earshot, and then where would I be? *Fired and possibly arrested.* Better to stay put and keep my mouth shut.

Then, above all the chatter, I heard someone calling for everyone's attention; we were to file towards the Cyclorama. I followed the masses past the ticketing booth, the vestibule, and the main gallery. The line slowed and thinned in the small hallway—decorated with paintings and original diagrams from the construction of the amphitheater. We stood in two, single file lines to take the escalator up to the second floor. As the escalator steps started to incline beneath my feet, the ceiling's recess lighting lit the amphitheater, illuminating the entirety of Paul Philippoteaux's painting of Pickett's Charge. The painting was a 360-degree oil-on-canvas experience; everywhere you turned, there was the battle from a different angle, revealing the entire landscape and the brutality that was the Battle of Gettysburg. I had seen the painting multiple times—I'd sat through the multimedia presentation on my first day—but seeing it in my current mindset made the painting more compelling. I stepped off the escalator and looked around in a newfound awe. But I stayed well away from my fellow employees.

Be invisible.

Then the crowd parted down the middle, as if a movie star or the Queen of England had arrived. Both were the case; Peggy stepped off the escalator and sauntered down the break in the crowd, to take her place at the center of the cyclorama. She was not surrounded by her usual gaggle of interns and looked as calm and collected as she had at the press conference. In her hands was a thick pile of manila folders, which she smacked against her palms as she looked out on her fearful audience. Greg was close behind, silently scanning the room. We locked eyes for a split second—long enough for my heart to skip a beat—and then he looked away, urgently whispering to a colleague standing beside him. His look said nothing. There was no hidden message or warning in his eyes. I was almost hurt.

"Alright, kids," Peggy said, loudly smacking the folders one last time. Few were actually talking, and no one's attention needed to be drawn; she'd had it the second she walked in. But Peggy tended to treat us as if we were schoolchildren and she our teacher. She dangled her power, daring anyone to question her authority.

"I hope you all had a restful holiday weekend." Her eyes darted from left to right, waiting for a rebuttal. "I trust that the news has circulated. I don't have the time or energy to repeat what was said, so please speak to your neighbor after I leave if you don't know what was discovered on Little Round Top. In the meantime, I'm going to make this really easy. I am overseeing this discovery." She started walking back and forth, marching like an army general, hands behind her back. I half expected her to pull a wooden walking stick from her pocket and start waving it around and smashing it against the safety metal railings bordering the standing area.

No one spoke. No one moved. No one blinked. We were in a stalemate of nerves. The room suddenly became very hot, and I could see perspiration building on many foreheads; that was the effect Peggy had on people.

"All current projects are hereby suspended. Focus will be redirected to this project, which is of the highest importance," she continued. "Assisting me will be everyone's main objective. If my name is to be associated with this discovery, I expect nothing less than perfection."

Again, no one spoke.

"With the increased media coverage, additional confidentiality agreements will be required. We feel this is necessary given the magnitude of the discovery. No information of any kind is to be released or discussed outside of these walls. This includes phone calls, text messages, e-mails or any digital communication. As such, we will be monitoring your work-related use of these interfaces. Those who do not comply will be immediately terminated. Suspicion of noncompliance will also result in termination. This is not negotiable. Gregory," she said, motioning to Greg, "will distribute the agreement forms."

Big Brother much?

"Alright." She clapped the folders against her palm, filling the room with a sound like a bolt of lightning; quite a few jumped in response. "The world is watching. Don't embarrass me." With that, she swept back down the escalator.

The room erupted in chatter. Sequestered in my corner, I continued to clutch my bag. *Be invisible.* Slowly I started to back step towards the exit, which would've been successful if my phone hadn't blared to life. The text-message alert was louder than I remembered it ever being. I fumbled with the strap of my bag as the attention of the entire amphitheater was drawn to me. My fingers touched everything inside my bag but what I was looking for. Then, to my horror, the strap slipped from my shoulder and my bag fell to the ground.

The flap opened, splattering everything on the floor, and revealing the diary—rewrapped in the cloth and inside a large Ziploc bag.

Shock froze me to the spot, and my mind went blank. One of my coworkers walked over and he reached for my bag. I smacked his hand away, and barked, "I got it, thanks!" He stepped back, with his arms raised.

I steadied my heart and shoved everything back inside, retrieving my phone in the process. Two text messages were waiting for me. *Hopefully Vince, with the lab results.* But they weren't from Vince — the texts were from Greg.

> **Slept lately? You look like shit.**

> **Get out of here. I'll stall Peggy.**

I didn't know whether to laugh or cry.

Chapter Sixteen

Breanne Walker

I RAN FROM THE AMPHITHEATER LIKE A CRIMINAL CARRYING A CASH-filled potato sack.

My colleagues resumed their heated discussions about Peggy's speech and hardly noticed as I stealthily hopped aboard the escalator and took it straight down. I bolted from the Cyclorama, through the Gilder Lehrman Special Exhibit, past the Camp Life Relic gallery, and straight to the rear entrance. I hadn't run that fast since I was nine and my neighbor's nasty dog got loose and chased me for blocks, nipping at my heels and barking furiously. My mom only caught up to me after the dog had latched onto my leg — I still have the scar from the six stitches I got as a consolation prize. But now I was running from something more ferocious than a dog — *Peggy Cupples.*

Outside on the patio, I composed my frenzied run and walked down the slate steps into the parking lot. I made it past the news vans and to my car without a single person looking up from their morning coffee. *Okay,* I thought as I fumbled with my keys, *you have very little time and a lot more to do.* I unlocked my door and climbed inside. I put my head down on the steering wheel to think.

With Peggy's totalitarian lockdown, I could no longer use the labs or facilities at the museum. Even the archives were out. If I tried to go down there, Peggy would know immediately and question what I was doing. *And that can't happen.* I needed to get the authentication completed before letting anyone else know about the diary. My job—my dream job—still hung in the balance, but I was more concerned about the diary being taken from me. *They can't if I already completed most of the work, right?*

I needed to make myself scarce.

Where can I go?

Oh, I'm an idiot!

I pulled my head off the steering wheel, started the engine, and put the car in reverse. I maneuvered around the news crews and out of the parking lot of the museum, heading towards Gettysburg College.

Specifically, the Musselman Library.

Gettysburg College was nestled in the heart of the historic downtown. The twenty-acre campus was surrounded by battlefields, and students were quite literally educated on history's doorstep. It is enough to make a history enthusiast weak at the knees. I always felt at ease on campus and being among academia gave me a thrill. On Sunday mornings, I'd pick a bench by Breidenbaugh Hall and camp out all day with a book. I liked to pretend I was still a student.

After parking, I bee-lined straight to the Musselman Library. Libraries are my safe place; my refuge and babysitter during the summer. Handing me five bucks for the vending machine, my mother—who raised me alone, on a secretary's salary—would drop me at the local branch every week day, and then head to work. She never worried—or truly seemed to care—that I'd be unsupervised for hours. Books became my babysitter, its characters—Jo March, Dorothy Gale, Frodo and Sam—became my friends, and the dusty racks were my magic carpet, transporting me to my heart's desire. The library and books bred the stability I so craved as a child; no matter the circumstance, chaos and torment always ended with a happy ending. And there was an endless supply—row upon row, shelf after shelf—of new stories and adventures, just waiting for me to pick up and crack their spine. It's one of the few things my mother unwittingly gave me. The coldness of my life was warmed inside its walls. And I loved it.

A feeling that still rings true, even at twenty-five years old.

As a museum staff member, I had unlimited access to the Musselman. The building was designed by Hugh Newell Jacobson and its distinctive design meant to emulate the grain silos scattered around Adams County. Four floors in total, the topmost housed the Special Collections—including

John Stuckenberg's extensive map collection—where the art of bookbinding and preservation is taught. The Musselman's databases, catalogs, computer labs, and precious texts were available to us and served as a secondary source for the museum.

I swiped my ID through the card reader outside the library and the door unlocked. My head rushed with fears of Peggy monitoring their systems. I imagined siren lights and buzzers going off, and Peggy arriving with a cavalcade of police and curators. Thankfully, nothing happened when I walked inside; Peggy's reach was far but trolling the college security cameras and door access didn't seem a huge priority.

For the time being.

I headed straight to the reference computers on the first floor. The library enforced a strict half-hour research time limit on these computers, as there were only so many allotted log-ins. There was a sign-in sheet at the circulation desk that the librarians checked regularly to make sure no one went over their time limit. Staff was no different—we had to abide by all college rules while on campus. I pulled up a stool and laid my bag down on the high-top table. I pulled out my notepad and flipped through the first few pages until I found the passage I wanted.

"Okay, Roseanna Anderson." I traced the line I made under her name. "Let's see where I can find you."

I hoped that whatever official records I found would branch out and lead to what I really needed: specifics on A.M.P. I was staunchly against ancestry websites that helped ordinary people access their past for a small monthly fee—solely due to the fee. Heritage shouldn't be given for monetary gain. Ever. But in this instance, I was pretty tempted to do a trial. I imagined one particular site and its use of the family tree; I'd enter Rosie's name, and her tree would bloom with A.M.P's vital information. The use of those sites was a cop-out. And discredited everything I stood for. Laziness was the only reason to pay someone to do it for me.

So, I pulled up the National Archives and Records Administration's website in hopes of finding census records from the time; the records would confirm whether Rosie Anderson had lived in Gettysburg at the time of the battle. All records and documents were public property, unless those records were an issue of national security and needed to be concealed for other reasons. Original documents were held at specific locations and libraries. But with the digital age, almost everything could be accessed through the internet.

I clicked through the browser until I found the search engine, then entered my terms: Adams County, Gettysburg, 1870. Since the census was completed every ten years, I rounded up to the next decade—if the Anderson family lived in the area during the battle, most likely they would've stayed put. *Well, hopefully.* After a few minutes, a huge number of documents were available for download. Thankfully, I had a further option of filtering by name. *Saving me hours and paper.*

I typed in Jonathan Anderson and pressed enter. The database buffered. A few seconds felt like an eternity. As I took breath after breath, dread sunk in. Perhaps Pastor Anderson — and subsequently his wife, Rosie — didn't exist. Rosie could've died in the ten-year interim, and this could all be a dead end. But then a PDF file materialized.

Please let this be something.

The first page was a picture of an original document — weather-worn, with faded ink and illegible writing. The second page was a transcribed copy of the original. *Thank God for transcribers.*

And there they were on the Adams County Registry.

Number in Household	Name	Sex	Color	Age	Profession, Occupation, Trade	Place of Birth
6	Jonathan Anderson	M	W	30	Pastor	Gettysburg
	Roseanna Marie Anderson	F	W	26	Wife	Gettysburg
	Mary	F	W	7		Gettysburg
	Emily	F	W	6		Gettysburg
	Elizabeth	F	W	6		Gettysburg
	Jonathan Jr.	M	W	4		Gettysburg

I wanted to hug the screen. It was a vast document with a lot of questions broken down — like, "Was the person's father of foreign birth" and "Did the person attend school within the last year," or shockingly, "Is the person deaf and dumb, blind, insane, or idiotic" — but the main gist was exactly what I needed.

Jonathan Anderson and Rosie lived, breathed, and walked the streets of Gettysburg. And with four children, the Andersons seemed to have been thriving. According to their ages and the timeline given thus far in the diary, Rosie was currently pregnant with Mary. Emily and Elizabeth soon followed.

"Twins?" I wondered as I looked at their ages. *Intriguing.* I'm sure A.M.P. was thrilled with the prospect of delivering twins, as it was so rare and high risk. Hopefully Jonathan allowed her to deliver his other children, even after a so-called real doctor had returned to Gettysburg.

I was ecstatic and clicked the mouse to print the documents. This was a start. A very, very good start. The census didn't mention anyone with the initials A.M.P. The diarist had not lived under Jonathan Anderson's roof at the time of the battle, and probably hadn't seven years later. But the census documents proved the existence of A.M.P's relatives.

Next, I needed Jonathan and Rosie's marriage certificate. The date would prove they were married in Gettysburg before the battle. This official document would help authenticate the diary, and the more I could find the better.

Records were kept by the local municipality and the church where the wedding took place. Local clerks documented marriages on a civil level and the church filed their own paperwork. In addition to the certificate, newspapers usually printed public announcements of intended marriages—which I'm sure happened in this case, given Rosie's father's money. *Her mother would want nothing more than to boast of her daughter's marriage, especially if it was advantageous.*

The only issue would be finding the document; marriage and death certificates weren't documented officially by the state until 1906. Funding and man power was more prevalent on the state level, so if the document was only stored by the county, then there was a chance that technology hadn't caught up yet. But, being married in Adams County—an area of historical significance—and during the Civil War may be the winning combination.

The Pennsylvania State Archives had a section dedicated to birth, marriage, and death records. Their site even broke down inquiries by county—expectedly, Gettysburg had a massive section for all three during the 1860s; largely due to the number of deaths in 1863. I typed in their names and waited—fingers, toes, and shoelaces crossed.

"Bingo," I said as the PDF appeared on my screen.

Rosie had been a June bride. On June 22nd of 1862, accompanied by her mother and father—Rachel and Benjamin Forrest were listed as witnesses on the certificate—Roseanna Marie Forrest married Jonathan Michael Anderson—of the incredibly affluent Gettysburg Anderson's, who helped establish the theological seminary—at Christ Lutheran Church. It looked to be a sizeable affair, as all Gettysburg and Harrisburg society were in attendance—at least that's what the *Adams County Sentinel* wrote in their article about the event.

"But no mention of a sister."

Jonathan's brothers—both being New York politicians—were mentioned in the Sentinel write-up, as well as the rest of the Anderson family. But nothing was said about Rosie's family, aside from who her father was.

Damn. Rachel Forrest had a sick sense of vengeance. She hadn't allowed her eldest daughter to attend the wedding of her only sister.

I pressed *print* and papers started spewing from the printer to my left, adding to my pile. My eyes wandered back to the computer screen.

To the death records icon.

As a rule of thumb, I would see a story through, in chronological order, without skipping to the last few pages. But now, with the pressure I was under, the lack of sleep, the slow pace of the diary, and Peggy's tyrannical gaze, I was tempted to search for Rosie's death record. Her story would at least have a period on the end, even if A.M.P's was still up in the air.

What's the harm?

I didn't think; I typed Roseanna Marie Anderson in the browser search bar. The page buffered for a few minutes. Then a PDF popup appeared on the screen. I stared at the download, my hand moving the mouse pointer to the document.

"Not yet." I clicked the X on the top right corner immediately, taking away the temptation.

From the printer bin, I picked up my printouts and put them inside my bag. My hand brushed the plastic of the Ziploc bag containing the diary. For an instant and I felt a zap in my fingertips. *She's calling me.* That, or static electricity. A few hours of undisturbed reading was all I needed to finish the diary, and I knew exactly where I'd find a quiet place to read.

I packed up my things and hurried to the fourth floor, then to a far corner of the Special Collections that was usually empty. When I'd needed some solitude a few weeks back, I found a small cubicle among the stacks and never saw another student. I hoped today would be no different. I plopped my bag down on the desk and retrieved some antiseptic wipes from inside, to wipe down the top for good measure. As I let the desktop dry, I looked around and stood stock still—waiting for the sound of footsteps or voices. When no sounds came, I put on my cloth gloves and retrieved the diary from my bag. Carefully, I pulled the diary out from the Ziploc bag and removed the cloth. Then, I flipped through the pages to where I had left off.

In my entire life, I've never felt so connected to another human being. It had only been a few hours since I'd closed the diary, but I missed her. Initially, I read to keep my job but now…now it was different. A.M.P. filled something inside of me; she was becoming the friend, sister, confidant that I'd never had.

"May 28th," I said, reading the date on the next entry. I settled in my chair and started to read. Secretly, I hoped this entry would be lighter material.

Chapter Seventeen

A.M.P.

May 28th, 1863

Our wool has been sold, every last bale and fleece.

And not soon enough.

Everything has been forfeited to shearing, cleaning, and then selling the wool. The calluses and burns that covered my hands have now blistered — the pain is unbearable, and I find it difficult to merely hold my pen. Most of my wool went to market in town, but I only received half of what we usually earn, with the Union army's weaver buying most of it. I tried my best to haggle with the man, but all industries have been hit hard with the war stretching on and on; as the weaver kindly reminded me after rejecting my attempt at haggling. No one should be selfish with a war going on. My heart was heavy as I accepted the money. The man was kindly and thanked me; many farmers weren't as willing to budge with their prices. Scoundrels are made in times like these.

I know not if Joseph will care much about this now.

We had news of the latest engagement, and Joseph's regiment—now part of Major General Joseph Hooker's Army of Potomac—was involved. From April 30th to May 6th of this year, our Union soldiers met the Rebels in the small village of Chancellorsville, Virginia. The fighting was fierce, the losses heavy, and General Lee took the battle as his own. The papers wrote of the creek beds flowing red with blood. There weren't enough stretchers or men to carry the wounded from the field; many died of their injuries where they fell, left to fester and bloat in the blazing sun for days before they could be properly buried. The Philadelphia Inquirer printed photographs of the horror. I was able to obtain a copy from Mr. Buehler and now wish I hadn't. Some were too gruesome to describe, and I was able to look only briefly. The blankness in the eyes of the dead struck me hard. Their eyes have haunted my dreams ever since.

How can we do such things to our own kind? Inflict such pain to our own countrymen? Brothers even. No cause, no matter the justification, is worth so many lives. I feel in my heart that there is a way to end this fighting—negotiation tactics that can be used, just like my haggling with the weaver. Nothing is worth so much loss.

Yesterday, I joined other women at the Lists. The casualty sheet was short for our county, the wounded list much longer. I allowed others to go before me, as I knew their plight was truer than my own. The other wives who were sick with worry; I watched as their fingers traced down the names, looking for a familiar one. With each cry of grief, other women rushed to their sister's side and whispered calmly. Tintypes were retrieved from breasts and clung to, as if they were the real person. I hung back and bowed my head, waiting for the crowd to lessen.

Joseph's name wasn't there.

I sighed and walked away, leaving many making plans to travel down to the Washington peninsula. Union soldiers were being shipped to the capitol, to be cared for in the hospitals established there, but no one could care for their loved ones better than their own kin.

Rumors are as persistent as ever about the Rebels turning our way. Robert Bell and Colonel Jennings have enlisted many students and older men—who were turned away from proper enlistment—to create emergency infantry and cavalry divisions to protect the town. Sentinels and watches were established on the outskirts of our borders, which I'm sure gives ease of mind to some. I am unsure of the usefulness of these divisions; I may be one of few, but the war will be fought and won in the south.

I pray every night for the war to come to a swift end. The thought of Joseph returning makes my head spin, but my own discomfort means little when so many of our boys are dying daily.

— A

June 9th, 1863

Seven days ago, I moved house and am now writing from the guest bedroom at Rosie and Jonathan's. Rosie, in her final weeks of pregnancy, has taken to her bed. She has the will of a warrior, and I believed she'd be on her feet until the end. But I had cause to be alarmed after our last visit; she complained of a lingering headache and a decrease in the need to urinate, both coupled with her sharp weight gain and pain in her abdomen led me to believe she is toxemic. Rest and a change in diet can help alleviate the risks, but the fear of an eclamptic fit forced her to the dullness of her bedroom.

Her house still needs tending, and I am only too happy to assist my sister. Running back and forth to the farm is not ideal, so Henry's father, Daniel Larsen, has kindly agreed to mind my sheep in his own paddocks and to barn Gertie with his cows while I am staying in town. And Barley is in a stall next to Jonathan's gelding in his private stable outback. But Barley frightens easily and is still not accustomed to this environment. Even from inside, I can hear her whinnies.

I also am not accustomed to the symphony of sounds in town—especially at night when I'm looking to store away my worries. Calm is hard to maintain with carriages rumbling down the cobblestones, delivering goods to local businesses and homes; doors opening and closing at all hours; and high-pitched voices from the tavern down the road. I cannot voice my frustrations as Barley can. I am happy to be here for Rosie and will stay as long as she requires, but I yearn for the quiet solitude of my cabin in the woods.

And Jonathan has given me no peace since I arrived.

He sees me as an unpaid servant, rather than a sister helping his wife. He has taken to ordering me around and slipping lists of chores under my door at night, detailing everything from how he likes his tea—two lumps of sugar, a drop of milk, and when he expects it—to the proper way to launder his clothing. "See the crease there," he said this morning, demonstrating how the pleats should lay on the kitchen table. "Be careful with the iron, sister. I wouldn't want you to burn through the fabric and ruin one of my good shirts." I have grinned and nodded my way through his demands. I have had to remind myself, almost hourly, that I love my sister.

I love my sister.

But his expectations have made me wonder: does my sister regularly cater to him in this way? Does she fulfill his every whim without a second thought?

And will Joseph expect me to be at his beck and call without question? I am sure Rosie does all for Jonathan out of love, but will I be able to do the same for Joseph?

Thoughts of his return often worry me. I do not think I can be a wife without true love or mere affection.

Another sleepless night awaits me, filled with nagging questions and accompanied by an orchestra of sounds wafting in through my bedroom window.

—A

June 16ᵗʰ, 1863

The hysteria that can rise in idle minds never ceases to amaze me.

Early yesterday morning while out visiting patients, I happened across a small group of townsfolk gossiping in hushed tones outside the Post. I have seen such a group gathered there often, especially when the weather is fine. With the current state of affairs, any bit of news is of great concern. But hours later—with suppertime fast approaching—I happened across a much larger group in the square, and the conversation seemed livelier and more heated. I approached and tapped a man on the shoulder, asking for the news.

"The Rebel army has invaded," he replied hastily, and he turned back toward the center of the group.

"This again," I said, a bit louder than I'd meant and I was instantly shushed by those standing around me.

I stood on my tiptoes to see the source of the booming voice at the center of the group. Rounder than he was tall, Mr. Ricgard, the butcher, was holding court. For probably the hundredth time, he recalled the latest rumor with fervor. "They're past the Potomac and headed our way. My brother arrived this morning, and he saw them with his own eyes. Saw Ole' Lee on his great white stallion leading the way like Moses." He lifted his arms, parting the crowd like the Red Sea. He continued, describing the army in such detail that it was hard to believe he hadn't seen them himself.

"I'm getting out of town," said a bewildered man to my side. Many around me seemed of similar thought and began discussing plans to leave in haste. Perhaps Mr. Ricgard looked to benefit from such hysteria, as the same man to my side asked how much jerky he had in his shop. I walked away, shaking my head at the lunacy of it all.

But cries from the street close to midnight woke me from a deep sleep and drew Jonathan and I from the house. The skies were lit as if the sun was rising hours before its time. I was dumbstruck, stepping down from the stoop into the street, staring up at the orange sky with my mouth open wide—it was lovely yet terrifying. The streets were full of crazed citizens, pointing to the sky and claiming that the Rebels had set Emmitsburg—ten miles away—on fire and were headed to Gettysburg to do the same. And Mr. Ricgard was back, his plump cheeks glowing as bright as the sky. He had an even larger audience around him, only now with a magnificent backdrop and seeming proof of his earlier statements. "See! See, I told you they was coming," he said pointing to the sky with a massive grin.

What else but fire could cause the sky to turn such an eerie, warm color? And who else but the Rebel army could be responsible? I'll admit I was scared.

"The first train is a quarter past six. If we hurry we should make it," I heard a frantic couple say as they hurried past me and on to their home. Many left that night—they packed up their families and possessions and headed to Hanover. Jonathan suggested taking such action.

"Rosie can't be moved in her condition," I said once we were back inside the house. "She too close to the end of her pregnancy to risk a journey." He didn't argue but retreated to his study, where I'm sure he kept a steady gaze on the sky. I checked on Rosie; she was fast asleep and heard none of the commotion outside.

This morning, we woke to a hazy gray sky and news.

A large fire in the direction of Emmitsburg. The Rebels had nothing to do with the flame. Mr. Ricgard's news of the Rebels passing over the Potomac were all false; the Rebels were nowhere near the Mason Dixon, as members of the local militia informed me later in the day as they rode the streets to assure all of our safety.

From my bedroom window, I watch now as many of our ashamed neighbors return from Hanover. I haven't yet spied Mr. Ricgard — who will undoubtedly hide his face for a few days. We have all become accustomed to the yell of a Rebel invasion, but I hope after this last stir, we know the difference between truth and rumor.

—A

June 20ᵗʰ, 1863

Yesterday morning, I was across town, caring for a young boy who had taken a nasty fall straight into a patch of poisonous ivy. I used a salve of sweet gum and Gilead buds to clean the scrapes on the boy's legs and a poultice of red-oak bark and alum to bring down the irritation of the spreading rash. Suddenly, Jonathan came bursting through the door with a look of pure panic.

"Why Pastor Anderson!" My patient's mother rose from her chair, ushering him inside. "How nice of you to call. Have you heard about my Benny's accident? May I offer you some refreshment?" She seemed thrilled to have one of the town's dignitaries in her home.

Jonathan stared at her blankly. He was trembling, and his face was drained of color.

I knew he'd come about Rosie.

I finished with my patient—giving his mother specific but hurried instructions on changing the bandage—and collected my things. Jonathan was hitching Barley to the back of his carriage when I emerged outside. I placed my kit into the carriage and stepped into it. He followed suit. The moment his feet hit the floor, every word he'd been holding inside came pouring out like an undammed river.

"I was preparing my Sunday sermon, when I heard a crash from the second floor. I rushed upstairs, and from behind the closed door she told me to fetch you home immediately. I begged her to let me inside, but she insisted I not enter. She said, "It's time." I ran from the house and searched every street for Barley. Should I have stayed? Her voice sounded so...different. You said the middle of July, and it is just June. Will she...can...will they both be safe?"

We hadn't moved an inch from my patient's house. His hands were stone-white from gripping the reins so tight. I placed my hand atop his — hoping a gentle touch would soothe his panic — and took the reins. He turned and looked at me, fear swimming in his eyes.

I flicked the reins of his horse and we pushed forward on the cobblestones, with Barley trotting behind. We were silent the rest of the ride, but my mind was sprinting a mile ahead of us.

If I couldn't stop the labor, I'd deliver Rosie's child in the next few hours. A pre-term delivery wasn't abnormal — I'd delivered many early babies with no complications — but this wasn't just another pregnancy. This was Rosie. My Rosie. Would I be able to keep a clear head if something terrible happened?

Once we arrived home, Jonathan saw to the carriage and horses while I ran upstairs to their bedroom. I was expecting to find her in bed, breathing heavily, possibly even sleeping. But she was not in bed or asleep, but on her feet, stripping the bed of its sheets.

"Rosie! What on earth?" I cried from the doorway.

She jumped at the sound of my voice and turned to face me. Almost instantly, she bent forward with pain. I rushed to her, steering her to the plush armchair in the corner of the room.

"I didn't want the bed to be ruined. Jonathan only just let me purchase the feather mattress and I'd never hear the end of it," she said as she sat down in the chair and put her feet up on the stool I placed in front of her. "I just...I didn't know there'd be so much water! I thought I had...well, you know." I crossed the room and picked up the discarded sheets—they were soaked all the way through. The aroma filled my nostrils, a smell as familiar as baking bread.

"How is your pain, Rosie? Have you been timing the contractions," I asked, dropping the sheets to the side and picking up my medical kit.

"Should I have been doing that?"

"Well, yes. But no matter; I will know for myself shortly." I opened the brass clasps of my kit and took out my Pinard horn. "But the pain, Rosie?"

"Tolerable."

I pressed gently on her stomach, feeling for the child. The babe had dropped further into Rosie's abdomen. I placed the horn on her stomach and listened closely. I heard a hurried but strong heartbeat—usually the sign of an impending birth. I stepped in front of Rosie and knelt, instructing her to raise her knees so I could do a pelvic examination. For physical exams, I always carried a small crock of cooking grease as a lubricant for my hands. I greased up and inserted my hand inside her vaginal cavity. With my fingers, I could measure the opening of her cervix—which had already stretched, in preparation for the birth. My heart almost stopped when my fingers grazed against what I knew was the spine of the child. The child was breech.

"Is everything well, sister?" Rosie winced with pain as I removed my fingers from her womb.

I steadied my breathing and painted a smile on my face. "You will be a mother soon, Rosie. Stay and rest here. I'll prepare everything we'll need." I pulled down her shift and allowed her to lower her knees. She eased into the chair, her face full of innocence and anticipation. My legs were shaking as I stood and walked back to the bed. Quickly, I pulled a wax canvas from my kit and spread it over the mattress—the mattress wasn't completely sodden, and the wax canvas would protect Rosie's precious bed. My mind was racing with the implications of a breech birth. It could still be hours until she was ready to push, and I could try and turn the babe. There was a technique of palpating the abdomen to turn the baby into the proper, head-first position. I had seen Mam do it dozens of times with great success and knew the steps by heart. Only two options remained if I was unsuccessful: deliver the baby breech; or perform a cesarean section, cutting the babe from her womb and risking the child and mother. The latter being the absolute last resort, as I hadn't the proper tools to perform the surgery—and the nearest doctor, who had the tools, was in Emmitsburg.

I shivered, thinking of the one instance I had witnessed Dr. Watkins performing a caesarean. Neither the hemorrhaging mother nor the child could be saved. She had lost too much blood even before he'd cut her. The bedding and floor boards were soaked in blood, and her eyes were lifeless. After, I mopped up the bedroom and cleaned her body, hoping to save her family from experiencing the horror of her death.

I heard Jonathan clear his throat. I picked up the soiled linens and briskly exited the bedroom without waking Rosie—who was dozing before her next contraction. Jonathan was cowering in the hallway. His usually proud and tall figure was hunched with the worries of every first-time father. And his jet-black hair—which he meticulously combed and styled every morning—was tousled and sticking up at every angle.

"How is she?" he asked.

I closed the bedroom door and said, "Her labor has begun."

I needed to be honest with him, but delicately honest. "But there is a complication. The child is breech." He tilted his head to one side, confused. "The child is facing the wrong direction in the womb. Ideally the babe needs to be born headfirst; your child is positioned buttocks first." His eyes widened, and his clean-shaven chin twitched. "I know what needs to be done, Jonathan." I took his hand as his strength left him. "I will need your help. Can you help me?" His eyebrows furrowed, and he nodded, looking very similar to the injured little boy I had just tended to in town. "Please take these down to the laundry." I handed him the soiled sheets. "Boil some water. And I'll need lots of clean linen, cut into strips."

He hurried downstairs to start his tasks. Given the last few days, ordering him around was admittedly gratifying. I ran to my bedroom and changed into a clean apron and retrieved my birthing chair. Before returning to her side, I took one long breath outside the bedroom, then stepped back inside to explain all to Rosie.

As hard as I tried and with all the pain Rosie could endure, I was unable to turn the baby. I palpated her stomach, massaged her abdomen and groin with cooking grease until my palms were numb, had Rosie pace the room and lie in different positions, and was finally able to inch the baby's buttock away from her birthing canal. But then the baby would shift back into his original position.

There was nothing further I could do. She needed her strength to deliver the child. Breech births were dangerous, but not uncommon. I had done it only once before and the technique was all about timing. And I would need help.

I walked out into the hallway and softly closed the bedroom door. I called down the staircase for Jonathan, who instantly ran up to the second floor. Hours had passed since we'd last spoken; he stayed out of the bedroom, but I sensed he was always within earshot.

"Has the baby arrived?" he asked, breathlessly.

"No, not yet. Bring me clean water and cloth. And I will need your help for this next task." His eyes bulged, and his limbs trembled; I grasped his shoulders to steady him. "You need to be strong now. For Rosie and the babe." He nodded and turned back down the stairs to fetch the supplies.

I returned to the bedroom and Rosie was sound asleep upon the bed—I helped move her from the birthing chair and into bed, hoping to give her a few minutes respite. With my Pinard horn, I listened for the baby's heartbeat. The beat was steady, which was a relief after the mounting stress of the last few hours. I wiped down her sweating brow, thinking of the beautiful little girl she once was. Soon she'd be a mother.

Rosie's eyes shot open, and she lunged forward with a guttural scream. I gripped her shoulders and eased her back into the pillows. "Breathe through the pain, Rosie." Her cries continued as I rubbed her shoulders. Jonathan entered the room with his arms overladen; he dropped everything when he saw the state of his wife.

"Jonathan," I called his attention back to me. "Come take a seat beside her."

He turned, did exactly as told, and then took a seat upon the bed.

I made the last few preparations for the birth: cleaned my hands and instruments, checked that the cloth was cut into thick bandages, and removed the pillows and other obstructions from the bed. I set up my instruments on a serving tray next to the bed and placed a pillow on the floor.

I wish Mam was here, I thought as I knelt upon the pillow.

"Jonathan, I'll need you to brace her," I said in my most nurturing voice. "She needs to swing her legs over the side of the bed and sit up; you need to support her back."

"I...I don't know if I—"

"Jonathan, your wife is going to be in tremendous pain and will scream quite a bit. You cannot flinch, you cannot cry, you cannot move. You need to be her rock and help her through this last bit. Are you ready?"

He gulped down the knot in his throat and whispered into Rosie's ear. What he said, I could not hear but her eyes fluttered open and she stroked his cheek. With help she sat up, inched her bottom to the edge of the bed, and swung her feet over the side. She looked at me, her lips curling in a mischievous but tired smile. "Are we ready, sister?"

I returned her smile. "I am if you are." She nodded, and I examined her one last time. I inserted my hand—causing Rosie to cry out in pain—and I could feel the child was curled up in the fetal position. Her birthing canal was now fully open and once I delivered the baby's bottom, the head would easily move beyond the pelvic bone and release from the womb.

"Lean back into Jonathan, Rosie. And grip his arms. Bear down like you are trying to move your bowels. Relax your jaw and drop your head. Lean in to the pain and push. Ready? Okay."

Rosie let go and screamed so loud that I heard the vibration of the crystals in the hallway chandelier. She screamed until her face was red, glistening with sweat.

"Well done, Rosie. Keep going."

Jonathan cooed loving words of encouragement into her ear; she caught her breath and prepared for the next push. She took two long breaths and pushed again, her screams never losing their vigor.

This continued for over an hour—her screams, pushing until her face was nearly purple, and Jonathan and I uttering words of encouragement. She never complained of the pain. Not once. Finally, the buttocks emerged. I grabbed Rosie's hands, so she could touch her baby. "You're nearly there, see. Feel his skin. Keep going."

Her purpose renewed, Rosie pushed harder and the babe's torso emerged. The labor would proceed quickly if Rosie kept her strength. I looked up and saw the anguish in her face; she had very little left to give.

I held the baby's legs steady and gazed up at Jonathan. "I need you to help her stand. She's exhausted and can only suffer a few more pushes. If she stands, gravity will make the baby fall."

He nodded and roused her into a standing position. Her legs were shaking, and she was whimpering, but she looked as resolute as ever. Once she was steadied in Jonathan's arms, I prepared to catch the babe.

With Rosie's feet firmly planted on the hardwood floor, the babe slowly inched into the world. Part of the umbilical cord descended from Rosie's womb and my heart started to race. The umbilical cord was the baby's oxygen source; once the cord completely dropped, the baby needed to take its first free breath of air almost immediately. Four minutes was all that was allotted.

"I know you're tired, Rosie, but one last push. Bring your child into the world."

She pulled herself forward and gripped my shoulders, letting out one last ear-piercing scream. Jonathan screamed with her, filling the room with such a ruckus that I thought the walls would burst. And the babe slid free and into my waiting arms, taking its first full breath and releasing a hearty cry.

For just an instant, I felt the world stop. I was holding Rosie's daughter: my niece. Looking down at the child, I laughed and cut the umbilical cord. I placed my lips over my niece's and sucked the fluid from her lungs. After spitting the refuse into the water basin by my feet, I wrapped the wriggling child in a clean cloth.

"Rosie, you have a daughter."

Rosie — who had slumped back onto the bed — embraced her daughter and immediately burst into tears. Jonathan pulled Rosie into his lap and kissed both his wife and his child with affection that I never knew he possessed. Mother and father looked at each other with awe-twinkling eyes, declaring their admiration for each other and their daughter. The afterbirth came quickly and, thankfully, it was intact. The new parents hardly noticed as I quietly gathered the dirty sheets and the water basin and exited the room without a word. Once outside the door, I sighed and a smile swept my face — a smile that still remains.

And that is how I brought my niece Mary into the world.

She is perfect in every way and is already the apple of her parents' eyes; she has her father's strong jaw and his button nose, her mother's lips and wisps of her beautiful, brown hair. She and Rosie are both doing well.

Having completed this entry, I can now fully rest.

Goodnight.

June 23rd, 1863

The Anderson household has been a whirlwind of activity since the birth of darling Mary.

Three days have passed since her birth and my feet are in constant motion; they hit the floor in the morning and don't stop until well past dusk. I am once again Jonathan's personal servant — the birth of his child has not curtailed his schedule or requests — I've visited all my patients in town and, of course Rosie and the baby need my attention. Rosie is anxious to be up and moving, but the labor took a lot out of her and I prescribed — actually, demanded — that she stay in bed for at least another week. She is bleeding slightly, which is normal, but my black haw root tea seems to be helping. I know the fear of hemorrhaging hovers in her mind — accompanying Mam and I to births taught her much about the post-labor risks — so she objected very little to the extra days in bed.

Also, staying still has granted her bonding time with Mary.

I entered the bedroom this afternoon with fresh sheets, only to find the living embodiment of motherhood; Mary was nestled against Rosie's bare chest as she rocked her to sleep. Rosie's face…oh, it's hard for me to describe…but she radiated warmth. She rocked her, humming a soft lullaby — one I didn't recognize — and littered her daughter's eyelids with kisses. I don't know how long I stood there watching, I was so mesmerized, but eventually Rosie felt my presence.

"Is all well, sister?" she asked without taking her eyes from Mary.

"I just love to watch you two."

Motherhood seemed so easy for her, and yet the notion seemed foreign and fearsome to me. I've always feared that Mother destroyed that part of me—the ability to deeply and completely love another person. We were born of the same woman; shouldn't she hold the same fears as I? Shouldn't she fear that history was bound to repeat itself; that we'd treat our children as Mother treated us? It occurred to me then that even though we shared a mother, there was a deep chasm between us.

"How do you do it? Know how to be a mother and love her so completely?"

She smiled and lifted Mary from her chest and gently placed her back in her cradle. Once safely settled, Rosie leaned back into her pillows and looked straight at me. "Don't you know, sister? I love her as you love me."

My knees almost buckled, but I kept my composure. I curtly nodded and left the room. As my sister, she knew not to call after me—for that I am thankful. I didn't want to become emotional in front of Rosie; fore my heart was both breaking and overflowing with her love. Since the moment I laid eyes on Rosie—asleep in her crib, delicate as a tiny rose—all I wanted was to protect and love her. To be worthy of the gift of sisterhood that God bestowed upon me. But...there has always been a vacancy and lingering doubt in my heart. Left by Mother.

Rosie's words temporarily lifted the living despair that always lingered in my heart. Though not completely gone, the memory of her words has helped remind me that I am worthy of love. I love my sister. My niece, Mary, even more. And that love is enough to fill my heart for two lifetimes.

But now hours later, despair has returned to my heart.

I know I must announce Mary's birth to Mother. Rosie cannot be expected to write in her present condition. She'd never ask it of me, but I know I must. Fresh paper sits beside this diary but the mere thought of writing her name fills me with dread.

I will put it off one more day.

− A

Chapter Eighteen

Breanne Walker

I LEANED BACK FROM THE LIBRARY DESK AND STRETCHED MY ACHING back. There was a building stiffness in my spine and I felt like the Tinman all over again. But that was nothing compared to the number I was doing on my eyes. A.M.P's handwriting was tight and tiny; every inch of every page was filled. The space between words and sentences was virtually nonexistent; since A.M.P. was a pragmatic individual, she wouldn't want to waste anything.

Pragmatic and tortured.

I was glad to read the diarist's account of Mary's birth. There could not have been more at stake for her. And a breech birth was not a joke. Cesarean sections were practiced more and more by undertrained doctors who knew nothing about obstetrics and consequently killed their patients. Their cuts were too deep, and they could not staunch the bleeding or remove the child without damaging the mother.

She brought Mary, her niece, into the world with sure hands.

"'Don't you know, sister? I love her as you love me,'" I read aloud. Rosie's words melted my heart.

But as always, a dark cloud swept over the narrative. That dark cloud being Mother. I could feel her sadness seeping from the page and into my soul. But that despair turned to anger. Anger that such an ominous and overpowering entity had a way of tarnishing every beautiful thing in her life. Just the thought of having to write to her—not even seeing her in person—made her take a nosedive into the abyss of depression. *Why?* Why couldn't she just never interact with her again, write her out of her life?

If it's that easy, why haven't you done it?

I stood up from my work station and walked to the window. I looked out on the college campus—to the rolling grass lawn and the vertical sidewalks that stretched to Washington Street. There still wasn't a soul in sight; it was after 3 p.m. on Labor Day, surely some students would be crawling back to campus by now? People watching would've quieted the little voice in my head, reminding me that I couldn't be angry with A.M.P. for something I couldn't do myself.

My mother is my one weakness.

I could be strong and assertive in every professional aspect of my life, but around her I felt invisible. Her presence knocked the wind from my sails, and I learned quickly to stay quiet and out of her direct eyesight. And that's where my love of books began; reading was my escape. It's no coincidence that my favorite book from childhood was Roald

Dahl's *Matilda*—the story of a neglected and unwanted child who discovers she has magical powers and uses them to punish the bad adults in her life. But there was no magic in my veins, no Miss Honey to save me from the loneliness of my home.

I had no buffer. I had no Rosie or Mam to give the love my mother could not. I was completely alone in her icy world. Trapped, just as she felt she was with me.

My mother has been estranged from her family since the day I was born. And I was the cause of this.

She told me once—I was five and she was drunk—that I was a teenage mistake that she'd pay for the rest of her life. She was seventeen, naïve, and so in love that she didn't think to take precautions. When she told her parents of the pregnancy, they demanded she have an abortion. She refused, and they promptly kicked her out of the house and all but erased their names from her birth certificate. My father took off soon after, so that left her alone at seventeen and with a child.

She punished me every day for existing—not with violence, but with a cold demeanor. She fed and clothed me and put a roof over my head but that was the extent of her parenting. To her, I was a parasite: clinging to and living off her essence. Later, she saw in me everything she could've had—a college degree, financial security, and a passion for my career—and she hated me for it. I've always wondered why she didn't terminate the pregnancy.

And when I tried to find my father, she stopped me.

She prevented me from finding him.

I shook the memories away.

But I couldn't go back to the diary just yet. I needed some space from A.M.P's emotions—*and my own.* Researching would keep my mind from drifting. I sat beneath the window and pulled out my phone. The library had the best Wi-Fi connection in town, so I could save myself a trip downstairs and do some light research on my phone.

I typed *"Emmitsburg Fire, 1863"* in the internet search browser. A.M.P's mention of the fire was a minor detail in the scope of her story, but it was major in the history leading up to the battle. A fire large enough that the citizens of Gettysburg could see it from ten miles away would have been recorded in some form. And if I could confirm the details that A.M.P. described, I'd be an inch closer to proving the diary wasn't a forgery.

"And we have a match," I exclaimed. My browser compiled six links for various articles involving, *"The Great Fire of June 1863."*

The Gettysburg Sentinel covered the event. The fire began around 11 p.m. on Monday, June 15th at the Gunther and Bean's stable. The cause is still unknown, but a strong headwind spread the flames eastward over two blocks and destroyed everything in its path. The flames were not quenched until 7 a.m. on the 16th and thirty families were left homeless.

I read through a few more articles and then forwarded the links to my email. If it was up to me, I'd declare the diary authentic now. I had no doubts that A.M.P. was a real person, present during the Battle of Gettysburg. But I needed indisputable evidence of the diary's age.

Vince! I could kill that kid.

I opened my text messages, hoping I had missed an alert from him, but there was still nothing. I checked my emails, too; nothing from Peggy, which was a good sign. *Greg is still holding her off.* Once I could authenticate the diary through the lab samples, I'd need the proven link between the body and the diary. All this before Peggy got involved. I looked up from my phone, back to my workstation and the diary.

No more stalling, get back to work.

I stood and trudged back to the library desk. I sat down and put my gloves on and flipped to the next page in the diary.

Chapter Nineteen

A.M.P.

June 26th, 1863

The Confederates have come. They have crossed the Mason Dixon, the borders between the North and South, and into our very town. We are overrun by a large company of Lee's army of Virginia.

This afternoon, while I was laundering in the kitchen, I heard a loud commotion from the street—a stampede of footsteps, followed by a rush of hooves. It had just started to rain, so I found it odd. I paused in my work for the briefest of moments. Rosie—who had ventured from her bed for the first time—was seated in the parlor, singing softly to Mary when the cries began. "The Rebs are coming! The Rebs are coming," flooded in through the open windows. The cries had never been so loud, never so pronounced. *If they wake the baby there will be hell to pay*, I thought as I stomped through the house and past Rosie. I flung open the front door and stepped out onto the street, fully prepared to reprimand whoever I saw first. Instead, I was almost run down by Mr. Buehler.

"Good heavens, Mr. Buehler. What on earth is the matter?"

He looked out of breath and haggard: his suit jacket was only half on and his hair was wild and unkempt. When we collided, he had kicked mud onto my skirts and dropped everything he was holding at my feet—including an umbrella and a large bundle of papers. I bent down to retrieve the paper—mail from the looks of it, which would be ruined from the steady raindrops falling from the sky—but he batted my hands away.

"I must get away. The Rebs are coming! They will hang me if I stay." He stuffed whatever he could grab into his pockets; the majority he left on the ground, in the puddle they fell in.

"Mr. Buehler we both know the false repor—"

"No! Listen to me!" He grabbed my shoulders and shook the condescending smile from my face. "This time, it's true. With my own eyes, I've seen a Rebel infantry division marching down Chambersburg Street. More are streaming in from Cashtown. We've been invaded. I must away before I am seen—they hang postmasters. And they'll burn all this mail."

"It can't be true." I felt faint and looked over his shoulder, expecting to see soldiers massing like ants at the end of the street. I didn't want to believe, but for as long as I've known him, Mr. Buehler has never told tales. It was then that I heard the drums and fifes of the Rebel army.

"Take to your house and don't leave. Have Jonathan hide your horses, for they will steal everything not nailed to the ground. I'm heading for Harrisburg on foot—they've torn up the rail tracks." He took my hands in his, eyes pleading. "Please, look in on Fannie and the children? I need to know they will be safe."

"I promise. Go! Run!"

He kissed my hands and ran down the street with the speed of a much younger man.

My heart dropped to my stomach and I darted back inside, dead-bolting the door behind me. Rosie was still in the parlor, darning socks, with Mary in the cradle by her feet.

"Is it raining, sister?" she called.

As I was deciding how to break the news to Rosie, the kitchen door swung open and Jonathan dashed into the kitchen and then the parlor. He stood before us, crouched over and desperately trying to catch his breath; by the look of him, he had sprinted all the way from church. Between his staggered gasps for air, he managed to utter, "I've seen them. They've come."

"Seen who, dear?" Rosie looked back to her mending and continued to sew, as if nothing was amiss.

"The Confederate army."

The sound of drums and heavy footsteps filled the room. Rosie stood slowly and walked to a window. Jonathan and I stepped to her side, and she pulled back the curtains.

As steady as the falling rain that accompanied them, an onslaught of Rebel soldiers pounded down the cobblestone street in front of the house. We watched in silent horror as they filed past. Rosie reached for my hand and held it so tight. The three of us were shaking.

The soldiers were far from the glory of the South that my imagination had painted; they were tired, dragging their feet and weapons; dirty, with torn uniforms sodden with dirt and dried blood; hatless with sunburn and scabs covering their faces; shoeless and seemingly bereft of emotion save the determination to keep moving. These were proud men ravaged by war. I pitied them. They were our enemy, but their condition looked deplorable. I wondered if what I was seeing was a mirror of my husband's plight.

"What should we do?" Rosie whispered, looking back to the sleeping form of Mary. Releasing the sound we were all holding back, Mary woke from her innocent dreams and let out a screeching wail. Rosie dropped my hand and rushed to her, picking the baby up from the cradle, clutching her close.

"We…we should pray," squeaked Jonathan. I rolled my eyes and grabbed Jonathan's arm, stopping him from retreating to his study.

"Prayer will not stop the soldiers from coming, Jonathan. They are here." I pointed back to the window. "We must safeguard the house."

Over the next few hours, Jonathan and I stripped the house of valuables and hid them in the cellar. Rosie and Jonathan had many family heirlooms and jewelry, the smallest of which we buried in the dirt floor of the cellar. Upstairs, Jonathan shuttered all the windows, and then he went outside to see to the horses — he bridled Barley and his gelding and hitched them to the carriage at the back of the house. We did not know what the next few hours would hold, but we needed to be prepared for anything — so we loaded blankets and food into the carriage, as well. With the Confederate Army camped just down the street, it was too late to try and run — we'd be sent back before we got very far — but if things got out of hand, we may have no choice.

I write this now from the cold, hard kitchen floor — I fear sitting at the kitchen table because of the windows. Rosie, Mary and I moved here once the gunshots and joyous celebrations began — the Rebels have set up their camp in front of the courthouse and are celebrating their conquest. And our neighbors who sympathize with the South have joined them. The sounds were too much for Rosie; she broke down in a fit of tears when she heard the first gunshot. Jonathan has barricaded himself in his study and will not join us. I believe he doesn't want us to see the fear in his eyes.

I cannot blame him. It is taking all of my strength not to fall apart in front of Rosie.

Stories of southern brutality have reached our ears; the newspapers have been full of their like since the war began. Reports of entire towns being set on fire as their army marched through, with inhabitants locked in their homes, burned alive. Mass lynchings and rape. We are both quiet; our overwhelming fear has struck us dumb.

I don't know what to do. I fear that most of all.

June 26ᵗʰ cont'd

Raiding parties began soon after I laid down my pen.

A loud pounding on the front door brought Jonathan from his study. Rosie and I hung back in the kitchen doorway as he opened the front door to a group of Confederate soldiers. Neither of us breathed as Jonathan stepped aside and allowed the soldiers to enter the house. I backed Rosie and the babe into a far corner of the kitchen, shielding them with my body.

They said nothing as they ransacked every room, looking for firearms and food. They didn't believe Jonathan when he told them he was a man of God and didn't own a gun. They were desperate—I could see it plain when they pulled open our cellar, then stuffed apples and other produce into their pockets like half-starved children. The pity in my stomach grew as I watched them scavenge and eat.

After the cellar, they looked through each drawer and cabinet in the kitchen—taking the silverware I hadn't hidden in the cellar. Then they looked to us, cowering in the corner. One approached with a toothless grin.

"Give us your rings, missus." With grubby, dirt-encrusted fingers he pawed at Rosie and the babe. I saw red; I slapped his hand away with a force so powerful that he stumbled back a few feet and almost fell to the ground.

"You touch her, I'll choke the life from you," I said through gritted teeth. I became a mother fox, snarling and spitting at the mouth of her cave, protecting her cubs inside. Surely, he had a gun and could shoot me dead in an instant and still claim Rosie's wedding ring. But I meant every word; if he touched her or Mary, I'd kill him without blinking an eye.

Rosie saw reason.

"Here," she said, removing her ring, "take it and get out." She threw the delicate, gold circle to the ground.

The ring bounced on the wooden floor, and he clambered after it—jumping with every bounce it made. Scooping it up, he clenched it between his thumb and pointer finger, then tested its durability between his four remaining teeth. Satisfied, he slipped the band into his pocket; he shot us another toothless grin before dipping his hat in thanks and exiting through the back door. We followed him, gripping each other's hands for dear life.

From the doorway, we watched as they unloaded the carriage we had meticulously packed a few hours before, and then they took our horses: Barley and then Jonathan's gelding. The toothless man led Barley from the yard at a slow trot. She was more than a horse to me, she was my dearest friend. I wanted to run out and beg them to leave her. But I knew my words would fall on deaf ears. I'd never see her again.

After, we stood in the front doorway and watched as they continued raiding our block. Every door was pounded on and every house barged into. Clothes, hats, livestock, and sacks of grain were hauled from homes and shoved into rucksacks and onto waiting carts, with the bewildered inhabitants giving no objection. Horses were the most needed, and while many of our neighbors had previously had the forethought to hide their steeds far from town at the slightest whisperings of invasion, some were still to be had. I locked eyes with our neighbor across the way as her mare was led down the street. Her look was very much like my own: helpless and defeated.

We retreated back into the house. The silence inside was heavy. The three of us — and Mary, still in Rosie's arms — returned to the kitchen and the cellar to take stock of what food the soldiers left us.

They missed most of what I hid in a dark corner of the cellar — I had draped empty burlap sacks over a second bushel of apples, potatoes, and corn. Our eggs and meat were taken from the kitchen. Mercifully, they hadn't checked the cupboard next to the stove, where I'd hidden our flour, oats, and sugar.

"We will need to be careful," I said finally, "but I think we can stretch this for a few weeks."

"What if they come back?" Rosie's voice was flat.

Almost immediately, there was a soft knock at the back door. The three of us looked at each other, silently asking one question: what else could they possibly want? Hesitantly, Jonathan approached the window that overlooked the backyard and peeked through the curtains. Tension melted from his shoulders as he opened the door to Mrs. Greinhold.

"I had to come," she said, pushing into the kitchen towards me. "My Henry is all actin' up. He aches all over. I told him it was 'cuz of the soldiers and in his head but he won't listen to me and says his hands and feet are all seizing up. He is crying in pain. You made that poke tea for him last month. I had to come, I'm so scared, and Henry, he—"

"Yes, yes of course, Mrs. Greinhold. I believe I have some phytolacca. Please, sit." I left the room to retrieve my medical kit. Henry Greinhold had rheumatism and he'd been under my care for the better part of two years. The symptoms in his joints flared up when it rained or with stress. I returned to the kitchen and set my medical kit on the kitchen table. I opened the metal clasps and rooted through my supplies, finding one vial of phytolacca leaves.

"Brew this in tepid water," I said. "You can use the leaves more than once. I will come to check on him as soon as I can." I handed her the vial.

"Bless you."

"Go straight home, Mrs. Greinhold. The Rebels are still about town," Jonathan said. He ushered her to the door and outside. She hurried from our yard.

Jonathan had only just closed the door when there was another soft knock. And again, and again, for the next few hours. Fear had driven many poor souls from their homes, seeking medicines for ailments that could not be ignored. Chamomile leaves for tea to calm the nerves was the main request. My stores of herbs, teas and poultices were almost depleted before the last few patients left, but my services were repaid in the form of eggs and produce from almost all who visited. I made a mental promise to see my pregnant patients who hadn't come. Rebs or no Rebs.

With the influx of visitors, we heard a generous amount about the actions and intentions of the Confederate army.

Upon arrival in town, Generals Gordon and Early went directly to the Burgess and Town Council to negotiate terms. They demanded that our town bring them a large supply of flour, meat, groceries, hats, and shoes, as well as ten barrels of whiskey. Or five thousand dollars, if these items were unavailable. But all of Gettysburg's wealth had been shipped to places of safety in Philadelphia and York weeks before. We could not meet their demands for food either — as private stores had just been ransacked. After, an order was issued by General Gordon: ransacking was prohibited, and any soldier found doing so would be severely punished. Any items already taken would be paid for with Virginia money — which was worthless this far north.

The same few stories were retold again and again by my visiting patients. We have seen nothing to prove them false. We were lucky enough to have had the early warning from Mr. Buehler, but many in town weren't.

We have nothing to give, so why would the soldiers of the South stay? Will they wait until we can come up with their monetary demands? Will they kill us all to arouse the anger of the North?

The hour is late. Rosie, Mary and I have retreated to her bedroom to try and sleep. Jonathan returned to his study — I believe he will remain there for the foreseeable future. Rosie hasn't the heart to argue with him to come and take refuge upstairs with us, and I haven't the patience. From our shuttered windows, I can see the Rebs campfires. The faint sound of a fiddle and harmonica drifts on the air from the encampment. I pray they will see reason and leave, but if they leave our town, they will only go on to molest another to our border. And if that is the case, what does this all mean for the future of the war?

Tomorrow will be another day to worry.

– A

June 27ᵗʰ, 1863

I woke this morning feeling very out of sorts.

I examined Rosie's bedroom in disbelief; in the darkest part of my soul, I believed the house would be burned around us during the night and we would all perish in its flames. I rose from the bed—careful not to wake my sister— and went to the window. I shifted the drapes and looked out onto the street. The buildings stood just as they had the day before.

I sighed and some of my apprehension left me.

I wrapped a shawl around my shoulders and went downstairs. The door to Jonathan's study was still closed, with him—I assumed—still inside. He'd need to go out and see his parishioners today. Our neighbors would need reassurance that God is still among them. I opened the front door and stepped outside—the morning was beautifully bright; the air was cool and smelled of sweet summer rain. It was early—barely seven—but the street was quiet. Eerily quiet.

I sat down on our front stoop and reveled in the morning peace. I closed my eyes and tried not to think of the Confederate encampment—though the faint sounds of clinking tin and the smell of cooking meats reached my ears and nose. I focused on what the day held for me: visits to the patients who hadn't sought me out the day before. And I had to keep my promise to Mr. Buehler and visit Fannie; try and restock my medicines and herbs, as yesterday nearly cleaned me out and I did not know what emergencies would arise; and Rosie wanted to bake, use the flour and the eggs—that I received as payment—before the Rebs came back and took it all. I'd visit my patients first and then head into the woods to scavenge for plants and herbs.

I opened my eyes and had the fright of my life.

Standing before me was a Confederate soldier, staring at me with a boyish grin. Though I wanted to scream, I held my composure—and his gaze—as I shifted on the stoop and wrapped my shawl closer to my body. I became horribly aware of my lack of proper clothing.

"Sorry if I'm interruptin' your mornin', missus," he said as he tipped his gray, dirty cap. "I was a walkin' by and I saw you so peaceful-like and thought I'd stop and say good mornin'."

"Good morning." My voice was little more than a whisper; inside I was battling my worst fear—that of being raped by a Confederate soldier.

"May I sit and talk for a spell?"

Before I could reply, he sat down on the stoop beside me. All I wanted to do was dart back inside, but I feared he'd follow. I shifted away and prayed Jonathan would come to my rescue.

"I've never been this far north. It sure is beautiful. Makes me want to pull up roots and plant them right here." I looked at him. He was young—younger than I, at least. His hair was the color of sand, his eyes were a piercing blue, and if I stood up next to him he would tower over me. But he was horribly thin, his clothes were rags, and his feet were bare—like the soldiers I had seen from the window the day before. And there was a strong stench wafting from him—a mixture of rancid body odor and spoiled eggs.

"Isn't your home as appealing?" Perhaps if I keep him talking, he'll take pity on me, I thought. But I was also curious. It was strange to hear a southern man commend a northern town for its beauty. The divide between North and South was a very real thing, one that very few crossed. Even with compliments.

"Why, you've got these little brick houses all neat and tidy. Lots of food to eat and more to spare. Farmland to raise your cattle and grow crops. Nice clothes. It's heaven. I'm glad we saw it all durin' summa," he explained, grinning from ear to ear.

My guard came down. For some reason I liked him. "Where are you from, sir?"

"Georgia. An ant of a town, twenty miles from Atlanta. Nothing like this." He went on for quite some time—his face lighting up as he described his parents' home in vivid detail. He called Gettysburg heaven, but the joy in his eyes told me a different story. Slowly, I relaxed into the stoop, listening attentively. Eventually, he sighed and looked around again. "But I'm glad to have seen a town like this. I'll be sad to leave."

"You...you aren't staying?"

"Naw. We'll be pulling out of here in just a few hours. Matter of fact," he said, lifting his body slightly and looking further down the street, "I should be gettin' back." He stood and brushed his pants off. His vacated seat was now ringed in dirt. "It was sure nice speakin' to you, missus. I hope we didn't scare you much yesterday. Us being here must've given ya'll a fright."

"I wish you well, sir." It seemed the polite thing to say, and I partly meant it. I held my hand up to him. He shook it heartily before turning and walking back to the court house.

He was the first southern man—and soldier—I'd talked to since the war began. No, the toothless raider from the day before does not count. This man surprised me with his kindness and generosity.

Realizing I was still only in my shift, I stood and stepped back into the house, feeling enlightened.

Rosie was awake and working in the kitchen like hot coals were lit beneath her feet. She was rolling out dough and was covered in flour, but her foot was poised on the edge of Mary's cradle—which she must've hauled into the kitchen—so she could rock it as she worked. I stepped into the kitchen and stopped her foot. "Oh, there you are," she said, adding more flour to the dough. "Were you outside, sister?"

"Yes. I needed some air." I picked up Mary.

"Oh, I don't know how you can breathe with all the Rebs. Them being in town is suffocating."

"Yes…yes. I think they are leaving, actually." I cradled Mary close to my chest.

"I do hope so. They're such…monsters!"

I walked from the kitchen, still cradling Mary.

Before noon, the Confederate army packed up their camp, supplies, and newly acquired contraband, and moved out. I was visiting patients as they mustered and started their march towards Chambersburg Street. As they filed past, I searched for the young man I'd conversed with that morning, but there were too many similar-looking soldiers. I hope he remains safe and is able to return home when this is all over—no matter the end result. The Southern army was headed towards York, twenty-five miles to the northeast. A much bigger town with, undoubtedly, more to offer.

I am glad to see them gone, but I fear for what will happen next. They have invaded the North, and that cannot be undone. I pray the war ends soon. Now more than ever.

June 30th, 1863

I am being tossed between realities. From confusion and madness, to calm and order, then back.

It was close to noon when I crossed Washington and High Streets. I was heading home from visiting Fannie—she was well, but anxious for news of her husband, whom she hadn't heard from since his flight four days past—when I came across Union cavalry hurrying through town. The horses clambered past with such fury that I looked ahead, half expecting to find that they were pursuing criminals down the street.

The horses rode with purpose, driven by their masters, who were outfitted in navy blue, military uniforms. Their numbers were many—too many to count—and they spread out and separated, going down different streets. The largest group circled to a stop in front of me, with one man sitting at the center, giving orders. I could tell from the way he sat tall in his saddle and the assertiveness in his voice that he was their leader. Though he looked young, the hair on his head and moustache was gray. His look was stern as he spoke quickly; his men listened intently. I wanted to move closer to hear. But before I could move, the group headed in haste towards the Seminary.

Congregated on the further side of the road were some young girls—two of whom I recognized. They heard the conversation, as they were closer to it. I crossed the street and approached them.

"Who were they?" I asked, pointing to the dust they left.

"That was General John Buford and his 1ˢᵗ Division Cavalry brigade. They're here to save the town."

"Save from whom?"

"The Rebels of course!"

"The Rebels have moved on." I almost laughed, looking around to see what these silly girls were speaking of. The Confederates had left four days before. I saw it with my own eyes.

"They've circled back. We've heard just now—General Buford gave the order to fan out, saying the Seminary cupola would be his look-out. He has sent word to General Reynolds and the rest of the Army of the Potomac. They're all headed here. How glorious will that be?"

I stared at her in astonishment. The girls gaily chattered on, but I was deep in thought. If they were putting claim on ground and informing the Union Army of their location, this could not be a false alarm.

Another group of cavalry streamed onto Washington Street, and the girls turned to them, singing "Our Union Forever" and then "Yankee Doodle Dandy." Hearing the words of the patriotic songs, the soldier's faces lit with appreciation, and they smiled down at the girls from their tall steeds. I stood among the lovestruck girls, frozen and silent. More soldiers flooded the streets and more citizens came from their houses to see. The bystanders asked for news and food and declared their allegiance to the Union. I returned home—to break the news to Rosie and her family once again.

But the news had already been broken. Jonathan had heard and seen all that I had, but he took no stock in it.

He was sitting in the parlor with Rosie. She held Mary; he held her hand. Rosie was as white as a ghost, terrified at the news of Union troops stationed in town. He was calm — or at least was trying to be for Rosie.

"It will be as before. They will come and leave again," he said in a hushed tone.

"I heard talk that Gettysburg is ideal for battle," I said, stepping into the parlor.

"I'll believe it when I see it," he said, acknowledging my presence. "When I hear the gunshots and see the wounded." He gave a reassuring pat to Rosie's hand. "I will be in my study. Supper at four, I presume?" He stood and walked from the room.

Rosie looked from his vacated seat to me. I sighed and shrugged my shoulders — we both knew her husband's mind was set.

"We will store provisions, candles and blankets in the cellar. Just in case," I said.

Rosie prepared supper as I gathered our meager food-stores and carried them down into the cellar. I am thankful that I was able to obtain some pork and more eggs, and that the raiding Confederates hadn't found the produce we stored in the cellar.

Now the hour is late, but sleep will not be mine this night. Beyond my own, immediate safety, and that of my family, my thoughts drift to my home in the woods, my animals, poor Barley, and our neighbors. If this war is fought on our fields, we're all in perilous danger. And there is no way to flee. We would not get far on foot—especially with Rosie and Mary.

I pray this battle does not come to pass. I pray this danger passes over us once again and we can return to peace. I know I'm not the only soul in Gettysburg begging for God's mercy this night. My only hope is that He is listening.

—A

July 1ˢᵗ, 1863

The singing of the cannons began close to ten this morning.

We were sitting in the kitchen at a late breakfast. Jonathan was ravenous and ate his fill of Johnnycakes and fried apples. Rosie and I were dead on our feet and ate very little; neither of us had slept. At all hours, I could hear voices outside my window. My terror grew with every hour, and I prayed for daybreak. I must've dozed off at some point because when I opened my eyes, the sun was bright. I dashed downstairs and threw open the front door. Outside, the street was bursting with Union soldiers hurrying to and fro. More troops had arrived; cavalry, followed by wagon after wagon, carrying supplies and bloodied soldiers, wounded from their last encounter with the Southern army. The wind brought the sounds of patriotic songs from the street beyond; from more young girls aiming to provide confidence to downtrodden soldiers.

Prayers circulated over and over in my mind but never crossed my lips. I sat down on our stoop and watched for a few minutes, until I heard the stairs creak and knew Rosie was coming downstairs. I jumped to my feet, stepped inside, and shut the door behind me. I said nothing of what I'd seen. But she knew; the bags beneath her eyes told me she, too, was afraid. Wordlessly, I followed her to the kitchen and helped prepare breakfast.

As we sat eating, one cannon blast confirmed all our fears.

The ground beneath our feet shook, and the blast...I have nothing to compare it to. I could feel the impact in my chest. Jonathan's eyes shot up from his food, and he was Doubting Thomas no more. He stood and walked with a quick stride to the front of the house. Rosie and I followed. He opened the door. The scene outside was like one described in Revelation: apocalyptic.

The perfect blue sky from hours before was now a hazy gray. All of our neighbors were out and clustered on the cobblestone street, looking west—towards the Seminary. The air was tense and thick with silent, shared emotion; we were waiting for the hot lava of hell to wash over us and obliterate everything in its path. Everyone stared—the whites of their eyes bulging— waiting for the next blast. Rosie remained in the doorway with Mary, but Jonathan and I stepped into the crowd.

"A misfire? Perhaps a fuse lit by mistake?" Jonathan whispered to me.

Another cannon fired in response, the explosion louder than before. And the firing continued—blast after blast, followed by the pop-pop-pop of gunfire. Smoke was rising from the west. The smell of gunpowder was pungent and strong. Then a roar of sounds erupted—screams and the thumps of stampeding feet.

Suddenly, from behind, a pair of hurried hooves bounded towards us.

"Get in your houses!" screamed the soldier atop the massive steed. "Get to your cellars. Rebel snipers are everywhere. Stay off the street until dark!" We made way for him to ride through and past us, continuing to scream his warning for all to hear. Immediately, everyone on the street dashed back to their houses. Jonathan grabbed my hand and pulled me towards the house and to Rosie. There were tears in her eyes as they met mine.

I took her face in my hands and wiped away her tears, "Let's get to the cellar."

She was shaking but managed to nod. Jonathan said nothing as he deadbolted the front door behind us, then ran through the house to do the same to the back door. I ushered Rosie into the dank cellar as Jonathan frantically shuttered and then boarded up the windows on the first floor with planks. Except for the pounding of hammer to nail from above, the cellar was silent.

We lit candles, Jonathan brought down Mary's cradle, and we tried to make ourselves comfortable. Trepidation enveloped us. Now, even below the surface, we can hear the battle. With every crash of a cannon, the walls around us shake, and dust rises in the air. We can hear glass shattering. I hope it is from the impact of the cannons and not from ammunition being fired into the house.

We were told to stay put, that we would be safer in our homes. But crouching in this hovel has raised my fear. I feel helpless, like I am sitting on the edge of a sharp blade. I fear this house will be shelled, and we buried beneath its rubble. I fear again for our neighbors and hope they all found safety in their cellars.

Please, let this be over soon.

July 1st cont'd

The sun was low in the sky when we emerged from the cellar. Artillery and fighting had ceased for the day, to be picked up — I assume — tomorrow.

Though the house was mostly intact, the front windows on both floors were shattered, and everything hanging on the walls of the first floor was on the ground and destroyed. Besides the abundance of broken glass, all else seemed to be in order. As Jonathan searched the upstairs for further damage, I opened the front door and stepped out. The street was quiet but filled with the remnants of battle. Riffles lay abandoned, a water canteen hung from a tree on our corner, a Confederate flag was ripped to shreds, and a thick, brown liquid stained the dirt right below our stoop and stretched to the right. I stopped my mind from thinking of it, even though I knew the stain could only be one thing. My eyes were dragged back to that stain again and again, and horror rose in my chest.

Then the stream of wagons began, bringing the wounded down our street, towards the church. The wounded hobbled past, helped along by their comrades or using makeshift crutches. They were dirtied, exhausted and bleeding from every extremity. They had rags and makeshift tourniquets tied to their wounds. Their eyes were bloodshot, and they looked ahead with glazed eyes, seeing nothing and no one.

Before me, a soldier tripped and stumbled to his knees. I leaped from the stoop and helped him to his feet. "I have you now, sir," I said. "There you go." He settled his feet and took a labored breath. Our eyes met. His were large, black orifices filled with sadness. He readjusted his satchel and kept moving ahead, like a walking corpse.

I looked down to the hand that had helped him, and it was dripping with blood. Terror struck me. The pressure of my grasp reopened his wound. I looked up and found him, a few paces away. His dirtied shirt was turning crimson with every step he took. He would surely die.

I write this in haste at Rosie's kitchen table, as I will leave shortly for Christ Church. A field hospital has been established there. Jonathan is accompanying me; medical and spiritual help go hand and hand in times like these. Rosie assured us that she will be fine on her own. "My needs are nothing compared to theirs," she said, kissing my cheek.

"We'll only be gone for a few hours," I assured her.

I don't know what to expect. I know the principles of wound care and surgery, but I've never practiced them in this capacity. I fear I won't be able to stomach what I see.

I will write again when I return.

−*A*

July 2nd, 1863

The sun was rising at my back when I returned to Rosie and Jonathan's home. The house was quiet. I hurried to the water pump in the backyard to fill a basin with water. After doing so I rushed back inside and then up to my bedroom, hoping not to find Rosie in the hallway. Once inside my room, I looked at myself in the washstand's looking glass and gasped.

My brown cotton dress was in tatters: one of the sleeves hung by a single thread on my shoulder, the white of my apron was a distant memory, and every inch of the skirt beneath it was stained with blotches of blood. My hair was matted to my skull, and stray strands hung loose from the bun at the base of my neck. My face glistened with sweat, and the soles of my shoes were completely detached.

I was a breathing embodiment of Gettysburg's mayhem.

I stripped down to nothing, piling my ruined clothes by the door to take outside to burn; no cleaning or mending would remove the stains—or memories—from them. I returned to the washstand and began scrubbing my arms and neck with clean water and lye soap. I refilled my basin again, to wash my face, hands, feet and underarms. When I was through, the water was murky brown. I changed into a fresh shift and then went to the window to toss the water outside.

From my window, I saw soldiers beginning to muster and march towards the Court House. They looked like a fresh regiment—their uniforms were still crisp and clean. They chanted as they marched, but I didn't stay to listen. I closed the shutters and hurried back downstairs.

I sat down at the kitchen table, letting my face rest in my hands.

The emotions I had kept at bay rose to the surface. I gripped the table to hold myself still, and that was where I found you, my diary, beneath my fingers—left there from when I'd last written. I must write again now, before the days meld together.

Jonathan and I arrived yesterday as the wagons carrying the wounded converged on Christ Church.

No one could move on or off the street; the soldiers who weren't grievously injured jumped down from the wagons and started unloading the stretchers, as the wounded screamed in agony; the surgeons hurried down the steps of the church, looking overwhelmed; townsfolk stood to the side, gaping at the horrors the day's battle left behind. Then the soldiers driving the wagons started screaming at each other to move. The wounded were still on the cobblestones, blocking access to the street. Others not as badly wounded, sat or leaned against buildings, waiting to be told what to do. Blood stained the street, and the cries got louder. Confusion bred inaction and chaos.

Like a strong wind during a winter storm, one voice sounded loudly above the others. The power in his voice made up for his short stature and his advanced age. He sent the wagons at the back down to the court house, where another hospital was being established. He put the bystanders on the street to work helping the walking-but-wounded soldiers into the church. He went from wagon to wagon, briefly assessed their baggage, and told the soldiers how to bring the wounded in. Then he turned to the stretchers laying on the cobblestones and gave orders on where to take them. He organized the lost boys into a productive system. Then he swept back into the church.

"Shall we?" Jonathan took my hand, and we walked through the throngs of people.

Once inside, Jonathan dropped my hand and approached another pastor, who was standing in the vestibule. I could tell I was not welcome in their conversation, so I searched the pews for the man who I now assumed was the lead surgeon. The church—which consisted of two aisles of twenty pews on each side, high vaulted ceilings from which hung a modest chandelier, four stained-glass windows, and an ornate altar at the front—was filled almost to capacity, but I picked out the surgeon immediately. He was standing at the podium on the altar, addressing a group of men; he was assigning sections of the church to each man and sending them on their way. As I confidently walked up the center aisle, he was screaming for more lit candles — one at the end of each pew — and sending soldiers into the church's cellar in search of supplies.

When I stepped onto the altar, his back was turned. I tapped his shoulder. "Sir, I've come to assist — " I started, but he brushed past me to address a soldier sitting in the first pew. I followed, determined. The man was holding a rag to a large gash on his forehead. The doctor bent down and removed the bandage; the gash was a minor graze to his temple and a few stitches would send him on his way. The surgeon's diagnosis was the same as mine, and his annoyance showed.

"Sergeant," he bellowed. A young man scurried up the aisle like a servant answering his employer. "I told you all minor wounds at the back of the church. I need this area clear."

"I...I..." stammered the young soldier.

"Never mind. Please escort Mister — " He looked back to the wounded soldier.

"Leeds," the man replied in a daze.

"Right. Please escort Mr. Leeds to the back of the church. I will need this space for amputations."

Mr. Leeds looked instantly relieved to be moving away from the surgery area. The sergeant helped him to his feet, walking him slowly towards the back of the church.

"I could've stitched that for you," I blurted. "Probably in the time it takes Mr. Leeds to reach the back of the church."

He turned towards me with an incredulous look. He stifled a laugh, looking me up and down. "This is quite different than embroidery, my dear." He moved past me and back to the altar to assess his equipment.

I followed. "I am quite aware, sir. I work as a midwife in town and was training for medical school before the war. I wish to be of service."

"Midwifery is not surgery. And this is not the time for an overzealous maiden to test her aptitude. If you want to be of help, there's a pile of bandages over there. I need them cut and distributed to the other surgeons. We need fresh water; the wounded are parched and in need of sustenance. Stay out of my way." He dismissed me and started barking orders to others.

Undeterred, I went to work. If he needed a scullery maid, I'd be one.

The day was hot and humid, and many were suffering from dehydration and delirious from the heat inside. The poor soldiers eagerly gulped down the water I brought them. They grasped my hands as I dipped the ladle back into the metal bucket and thanked me for my kindness. I wanted to embrace them all and take away their pain. I returned again and again to the well outside, knowing it wasn't bottomless and hoping it wouldn't run dry. I stayed towards the back of the church—with the minor-wound patients—and was able to assess them without interference. The surgeons were concerned with the serious cases at the front of the church, but these men still needed care. I began to dress and clean wounds with my own store of red oak bark; if infection was present I employed butterfly root and kept a close eye on the soldier. I set broken fingers and toes in splints made from twigs I stored in my kit, soothed burns with aloe balm, and stitched gaping bayonet wounds. And I did the menial tasks—I cut and distributed bandages to the surgeons, mopped the floors surrounding the surgery tables, and kept the wounded cheerful. No matter how gruesome the wound, I kept a smile on my face and the conversation light.

Cheerful amidst the blood-curdling screams coming from the front of the church.

Surgeon Major Miller—the head surgeon who had taken charge and dismissed me as an overzealous girl—was performing the amputations. The aisles were lined with stretchers holding the wounded who awaited evaluations. One by one, the stretchers were placed on Major Miller's table, and there he decided the care he could provide. His decisions were brutal and instantaneous: the wounded either stayed for surgery or were taken off to die of their wounds. Absolutely no emotion came from him; he assessed the situation, started the surgery if it was deemed necessary, and screamed "Next!" when he finished. The sound of the amputation saw echoed in the church, and the screams—oh, I'll never forget the sound. The pain was beyond measure; the patient would buck on the table, trying to break free from those holding him still. The surgeries were merciless and barbaric. They had to be, given the situation. But it was still harrowing to listen and see from afar. He was the butcher my patients were glad to have escaped.

Eventually, my mop was needed nearer to the altar, so I made my way closer to the surgery station. I was in the second pew when the body of a limp soldier was placed on the operating table.

"The cannon ball came down, inches from his legs," began the soldier who brought him in. "It blew him sky high and he landed on his feet, ten feet away. His bones come right through his skin, sir."

I looked up from my mop to the poor boy. He was breathing. Barely so, but I saw his chest rising slowly.

"Right. His tibia and fibula bones have protruded through the skin right below the knee. The blood has coagulated so he will not bleed out more than he already has. But the infection has started to fester. We must remove both legs below the knee. Hand me the scalpel." Major Miller held out his right hand, waiting for the requested instrument. Clearly, the soldier to his right did not know the difference between a scalpel and a kitchen knife. He looked down at the knives in front of him and picked up each individually, perhaps hoping the name was written on the blade. Seconds ticked away.

I dropped my mop and stepped onto the altar to hand Surgeon Major Miller the thin, short-bladed knife. His fingers clasped the metal and briefly brushed mine. When he saw me, he rolled his eyes but didn't tell me to leave; he took the knife and motioned to the tourniquet lying next to the soldier's knee. I stepped fully into the surgery circle, lifted the man's knee, and slipped the tourniquet beneath it.

"I need that tight," he explained.

"Has the patient been given anything for pain, Doctor?" I turned the side screw of the tourniquet, and the strap tightened.

"Do we look like we have anything for pain?" With the scalpel, he made the initial incision below the knee to mark his place. "No morphine, no ether, no laudanum. Give him a swig of that whiskey and a piece of leather to bite down on. If he doesn't die of shock, pain will be the least of his worries."

At my feet was a small drum of whiskey. I poured some down the soldier's throat and he managed to swallow before I gave him the leather to bite. Then Major Miller deepened the incision and began dividing the muscle and skin. He made quick work of the amputation prep—raising the skin to dissect the muscle, blocking off the blood vessels with small forceps—and then took up the bone saw. As he started sawing into the right tibia, the closest stretcher-bearer turned green and stepped back, allowing me to step closer. The wounded soldier woke and squirmed. When he started screaming, the stretcher-bearer and the doubtful soldier held his shoulders down to the table and I held tight to his other leg. A few minutes passed before the bone was cut through, and thankfully the soldier had slipped into unconsciousness by then.

"Take this." Major Miller handed me the severed leg.

It was heavy in my hands. And to hold it felt so...wrong.

"There's a pile over there," he said. He pointed behind the altar, by the door that lead back to the vestry. I walked over to the unlit area, and the smell—putrid flesh—hit my nostrils, causing me to vomit in my mouth. I averted my eyes and dropped the severed leg atop the mounting pile of amputated, rotting limbs. It landed with an audible thud. I breathed through my mouth and managed to swallow the vomit before I walked back to the operating table.

This went on and on for hours. Eventually, Major Miller allowed me to cut the silk suture thread for the skin flaps and wrap the stumps of men's limbs in cotton bandages. I was not allowed to handle the instruments, but he dutifully explained what he was doing.

Each stretcher-bearer brought a new patient and news. I learned that the McPherson farm — near Chambersburg Street — had been overrun and that the fiercest fighting took place in the wheat field nearby. Edward McPherson was a longtime resident of Gettysburg and a politician, but he'd moved to Washington when he was appointed the Deputy of Internal Revenue by President Lincoln. I hoped the Slentz family — his tenants — were able to flee before the battle began. Repeatedly I heard the name Buford — the graying General I'd seen atop his steed the day before. General Buford defended his "high ground" and set his men to meet the Confederates as they entered town on Herr Ridge; there he ordered his men to dismount and attack, which the Confederates were not prepared for. The death of Major General John Reynolds' was particularly devastating. His unit arrived to reinforce Buford's cavalry and he urged his men forward into the fight, when he was shot in the head and fell from his horse. From the way the wounded spoke of him, General Reynolds was dearly loved by his men.

In the end, the Rebels took the day; the Union pulled back into town near Cemetery Ridge, and the Confederates were now well nestled in Cashtown, ready to attack with all their force. The Union army simply didn't have enough men.

From several soldiers, I heard the name Meade. "General Meade will make it right," was the common phrase. I do not know who General Meade is, but I pray he arrives.

The wounded kept coming. Stretchers took out the men already seen, and if the treated soldiers could walk and hold a rifle, they'd rejoin their regiments and fight another day. New arrivals — fresh from the field — quickly took their place. It was a merciless circle. The church was at capacity and the journey from the battlefield killed many of the wounded. It felt like years since I'd parted from Jonathan in the vestibule. I could see him praying over the bodies of the dead and organizing a group of men to handle burials.

Fatigue and pain crept upon me, as the hours stretched on and a new day began. I couldn't hide my yawns and the muscles in my legs had liquefied — multiple times, I had to grip the operating table to stop from falling. Major Miller sent me home — demanded, in fact that I go home — to sleep. "This day's battle will rage harder than yesterday and these walls will be filled to the brim, again," he said. "I will need your steady hand and head. Come back tonight, after you've rested."

His compliment touched me, and I wanted to argue but I hadn't the energy.

So, I walked home, trying not to think of what I was leaving: the dying men, the conditions that bred infection, the

ever-growing pile of severed limbs, and the constant pro-
cession of wagons with more wounded. Jonathan stayed
behind; he offered to accompany me to the house, but I told
him to stay. He would rest in the vestry and will return
home this evening.

Now I hear voices outside. The nightly ceasefire will end
shortly. I must prepare a hot meal, as Rosie, Mary, and I will
spend the rest of the day in the cellar. I hope I sleep, although
I doubt I will. How can I sleep, knowing tonight I'll return to
similar horrors? I can't tell this to Rosie; I can't let her worry
about my welfare. I am worrying enough for the both of us.

I hear someone stirring on the stairs. I must stop writing.

July 2nd cont'd

I write this now from atop a wooden crate outside Christ
Church. My rest was short, to say the least.

Jonathan came to fetch me around 1 o'clock with a request from Surgeon Major Miller—the Union army was
moving further northeast, and he wanted me to accompany
the medical wagons and ambulances to the front.

"We've had word that the casualties are many. Every
extra hand is needed," Jonathan told me as we climbed
the ladder from the cellar. I grabbed my medical kit and a
shawl from the door peg. Rosie followed us upstairs and to
the front door with Mary in her arms.

"You won't be too close to the fighting, will you? Jonathan,
will she?" Rosie's voice was trembling.

"I'll be with her, dear. And we will be far enough to avoid harm. I promise." He hugged Rosie close and kissed Mary lightly on the cheek. He took my medical kit and walked outside to wait. I opened my arms, and Rosie rushed forward.

"I'll be surrounded by many strong and able soldiers; they wouldn't let anything happen to me. Go to Mrs. Gardener's, she'll be happy to have you both until Jonathan and I return. I'll fetch you once all is clear."

She nodded into my shoulder, then pulled back. I wiped tears from her cheeks. I didn't know if anything I said was true; Jonathan was lying for Rosie's sake, I knew he wasn't accompanying me to the front, but I hoped our little lies comforted her. I joined Jonathan outside, and we scurried to the church in silent meditation—the streets still weren't safe, but our own peril was a secondary thought.

Now I wait for the last of the meager supplies to be loaded into wagons, so we can move beyond the town limit, towards my homestead. I am anxious to get going—I am crippled with fear of what I am about to see. From the little I've heard, today's battle has been bloody and raging for many hours on Little Hill and the surrounding countryside. My heart dropped when Taneytown Road was mentioned as the route we would take.

I'm being called to load into a wagon. I ask God again: please protect me in this endeavor. And protect the lives of our soldiers.

—A

July 4th, 1863

The excessive heat has been broken by rain, heavy and unyielding. Plum Creek has overflowed its banks, and the wheat fields have flooded into a murky mess. But the weather could not dampen the celebration of our country's independence, especially today in Gettysburg.

The battle is over, and the Union Army has won.

After three days of brutality and bloodshed, Lee has retreated from Pennsylvania, taking his badly beaten Army of Virginia across our borders. General Meade—the new commander of the Army of the Potomac, the man I heard much longing for after the first day of battle—arrived with full force on the second day of battle. He rallied the troops from the North again and again and crushed the Southern infantry. It was a strategic and—as the young girls in town had hoped—a glorious victory.

Glorious for those who lived to tell of it.

I write now from a small canvas tent, given to me by Surgeon Major Miller, with orders to, "sit the hell down." So, I am sitting, watching as rain pools on and drips through the canvas above me, unable to rest. The time I've spent in the field hospital at the foot of the Little Hill have all blended together. I haven't had a waking moment of inaction since I left the safety of Rosie's home on the 2nd of July, two days ago. And now, as my small part comes to an end, I fear leaving.

The Union Army is due to move out, but the sick and mortally wounded will stay on or be moved to hospitals in the area.

There are too many to count—we hadn't enough stretchers or beds. More than half of the soldiers slept on burlap sacks upon the dirt. The latrines are overflowing with fecal matter—now made worse by the rain—and are leaking into the nearby creek beds, tainting local water sources. The dead lie unburied, infested with flies and maggots. The smell is abhorrent—indescribable, really—and the bodies are bloating from the heat, their faces unrecognizable, almost inhuman. All able-bodied men—me included—have been assigned burial shifts, but still we have not enough for the job. There are no ceremonies or individual graves; a simple prayer over one of the many large ditches was the most to be done. These boys deserve—and have earned—so much more.

I am getting ahead of myself.

I left Christ Church and headed straight towards the front. Within the limits of town, we were relatively safe. The minute we were beyond the cover of houses, all hell descended. Taneytown Road was littered with broken wagons, dislodged fence rails, ruined food, discarded firearms and personal belongings, and the bodies of fallen men. Thomas Reginald—the young soldier from Connecticut who was my escort—maneuvered the horse and wagon through the debris masterfully. He and his horse were one. But as we got closer and closer to the fighting, sitting atop a carriage became dangerous.

"Ma'am, I think it'd be best to lie in the back-bed," he said. "It's going to be rough until we're among those yonder trees."

Bullets whizzed over my head as he spoke, and I could hear the resounding Rebel yell. I climbed over the wagon bench to the bed of the wagon and lay on my back among the ambulance supplies. The sun above was unrelenting and burned my uncovered skin. With every canter of the horse, my ears ached with intensified sound—I covered my ears and prayed I wouldn't lose my mind or be killed by a stray bullet. True fear—the kind that stalls your breath and makes time eternally drag—didn't exist for me before that moment.

"Whoa," Corporal Reginald called, reining in his horse and stopping the wagon.

We arrived at field camp, and the sounds of battle were replaced with sounds of the sick and wounded. I sat up; Corporal Reginald was already at the back of the wagon, releasing the tailgate and offering a gentleman's hand. I thanked him. He handed me my medical kit, then immediately returned to the front of the wagon to urge his horse away and towards his next assignment. Only after the wagon passed in front of me, did I turn and face the camp.

The scene was like the street outside Christ Church: crowds of wounded, stretcher-bearers scurrying back and forth, aggrieved voices of the wounded, and surgeons attempting to organize it all. But the wounded were tenfold compared to the church. There wasn't a foot of scorched earth unoccupied by a man. I walked among them, careful of my path. I felt disconnected, like I was watching myself from above. I looked into the eyes of the men to my left and right. They were staring straight to the heavens and mumbling softly with tears streaming down their cheeks, begging God to take their pain. Their pain should have affected me — I should've broken down and cried with them — but I couldn't. I kept walking, numbing myself to it all.

Suddenly, my ankle was forcefully yanked.

I looked down and saw a boy tightly gripping my ankle. He was as white as a ghost, ragged, and bloodied. Young. Far too young. He clutched his stomach tight with his other hand, and his eyes were wide with fevered fear. I knelt beside him and gently lifted the blood-soaked blanket that covered his lower half. Beneath the blanket was horror; the boy was holding his intestines. His abdomen had been blown open and torn apart. The wound was mortal. I gently lowered the blanket and took the hand from my ankle, clasping it between my own.

"Mama? Mama?" he asked, looking into my eyes but seeing someone else.

"Yes, I'm here dearest," I said, brushing the hair from his forehead.

"I knew you'd come. Please, I want to go…to go home. Take me home." He pulled me closer, trying to anchor himself to me and this world.

"I will, I promise. Sleep now."

"I love you, Mama…Tell Pa…tell him I'm sorry." His breath came in struggled gasps.

"You will tell him yourself. Sleep now, son."

"I…I…I will." His eyes fluttered and then closed. I stroked his hand and hummed softly, pretending we were the only two people in the world. As he took his last breath, I realized I didn't know his name. I searched his jacket pockets for a letter he might have written to his family, or for anything to identify him, but I found nothing. I closed his eyelids and said a prayer over his broken body. Holding on to that boy as he died should've brought tears. The emotion was there, I was wracked with grief and still am, but tears haven't fallen on my cheeks since Mam. I didn't want to leave his side, but I needed to. I stood and walked away, with the boy's face firmly imprinted on my heart.

I stepped inside the vast medical tent and found Major Miller sitting at a makeshift desk—a wooden board laid across an empty barrel. He was writing down the names of those who'd died on his operating table. He looked up from his growing list, and his face flushed with relief. He crossed in front of his desk and took my arm, leading me out onto the field.

"Today will be the worst of it. We've received dispatches telling us to be ready at all hours. The fighting is only a stone's throw from here—in the fields that way, and in some damned place called Devil's Den. Have you heard of it?"

"Yes." Devil's Den was at the foot of Little Hill; it was a formation of rocks and boulders with little alcoves and caves. It was a favorite hideaway for children. I am unsure of the origination of the name, but I have heard rumors of a fifteen-foot snake presiding within. It was a perfect barricade, but also a deathtrap for anyone caught within it.

"Union snipers are positioned on the Little Hill, firing down at Johnny Reb; they're using those boulders as a shield. It's a massacre, on both sides. And both sides are being brought here."

"Both?"

"We will be caring for Confederate prisoners on top of our own. We cannot deny care to those in need."

I nodded, but I couldn't hide my shock. Caring for both sides of the fight was the right thing to do, but how would that go over with the Union men? And would our men receive the same care from the enemy? "Where do you need me, Doctor?"

"Everywhere," he said with a sigh. "But for the time being, I need you to be waiting for the ambulances as they arrive. Organize the wounded: minor cases, send to the left; surgical care, on through to the tents; the lost cases, to the right."

"You want me to distinguish lost cases? To send them to their deaths?"

"We haven't the staff, supplies, or space to see them all. We need to save those who can be saved, not waste time on those who can't."

"I can't do that, sir."

"You want to be a doctor? This will be required of you on a daily basis." His voice was clipped, dismissive. I nodded again and looked out to the field; ambulance wagons were turning into view of field camp. He trusted me to use my judgment—for that I was flattered—but how would my soul reconcile playing God?

He shook his head and looked out to the littered field in front of him. "This war will not end here. Every day we'll send more boys to their deaths. I don't know how much longer these hands will listen to me." He rubbed his knuckles and stretched his fingers, then put a hand on my shoulder. "If only I had ten of you, then maybe we'd save more." I blushed in spite of myself; his words bolstered my confidence. We stood there for a few minutes longer, both of us deep in thought. Then he guided me back to the canvas medical tent, that stretched for a quarter of a mile.

And my work began.

The wagons were unloaded, and I evaluated the wounded quickly. Gunshot grazes, broken bones, concussions, bayonet lacerations, fevers or treatable infections went to the left. Amputations or simple, but lifesaving surgeries went straight ahead to the tents. Grisly wounds to the head or abdomen or any wound that was already infected went to the right. The medics gave the truly hopeless cases small doses of whiskey to ease their pain, knowing they wouldn't make it through the night. Each time I sent a soldier to the right, my heart lurched. I kept my face stoic, pointing to the left or right, but before long, the stretcher-bearers caught on. With each I sent to the right, their heads dropped in resignation. I couldn't look at them. With time and individual attention, most of the men who I sent to die could've returned to their families.

In the lull between ambulance arrivals, I administered medicines for men suffering from diarrhea or dehydration. Those men were in pain but still had light in their eyes. They chatted on and were polite; they knew they would likely walk away from this battle. It was from one of them that I learned that the 90th Pennsylvania — Joseph's regiment — was fighting in Gettysburg. I was wrapping a finger splint for a man named Robert Robbins when he mentioned General Hooker.

"Yes, ma'am. We're the 90th," he replied when I asked after his regiment. They were engaged at the McPherson farm on the first day of battle, then moved to Cemetery Ridge thereafter. He chatted on about the battle, but I heard none of it. *He's here? He's in town and fighting the Rebels. Why hasn't he sent word to me? No, don't think like that,* I told myself. I quickly asked the man if he knew my husband.

"I don't think so, sorry ma'am. We're a big regiment, and I'm not too good with names. But," he turned and looked over his shoulder, "there's more boys from the 90th back that way. They may know him."

I finished with his splint and saw to the others around him. I didn't want to know but I needed to; my heart was beating fast as I stepped towards the group he mentioned. But before I could speak my husband's name, my own was called from the tents. Major Miller was hailing me down to follow him, to replace his worn-out assistant in the medical tent.

I was relieved, but swore I'd eventually find the courage to approach the men from the 90th.

I never got the chance.

Fortunately, my work at Christ Church had prepared me for the sights of war. Here on the battlefield, the surgeries were much the same—amputation after amputation, bullet extractions, sealing of gaping wounds. Major Miller and I found our pace: I was ready with his instruments, discarded his refuse, and helped placate his patients. There was nothing for pain—the cask of whiskey was depleted—and there was no spare water with which to clean the knives between surgeries. The moment we had a handle on the men in our care, another wagon arrived with more critical cases and I had run out of the tent to assesses the wounded.

And the new arrivals to the medical tent knew what awaited them.

They were scared; their eyes harrowed and when they saw me, they begged for reassurance that they'd survive. They clutched my hands—so hard I thought they'd break—and begged, "Don't take my leg, missus. I can still walk, I swears. Don't take my leg." They'd seen the pile of amputated limbs—discarded like scraps of uneaten food a few feet from the medical tent—and they were panicking. I knew what they were thinking—take my leg, cripple my life. If they returned home, how would they support a family? But a crippled life is still a life.

It was hell. Every waking second. And it only got worse when the sun went down. The dark heightened the fears of the wounded. They were confused and fevered, they screamed for hours: they cried for their mothers, begged them to come and take their pain; to God, for forgiveness of their sins; to their fallen comrades, asking why they were taken too soon. They screamed all night, until either death or exhaustion took them. It was maddening. I'm ashamed to admit, but the doctors and I resorted to sticking cotton in our ears to block out the overwhelming noise during surgery.

I checked our amputees and the wounds under their bandages almost hourly. I wanted to be ahead of infection as much as possible. Which gave me an idea; I snuck out of the tent with a lit candle in hand and approached the discarded limb pile. Though small, the candle cast quite the light. The putrid smell emanating from the pile was just as horrific in the dead of night. I placed the candle down on the ground and knelt close. What I was looking for were small, white specks, wriggling in the light like stars in the sky. A pile of flesh is an ideal feeding ground for maggots because they fed on rotting vegetation and dead muscle. This was a trick of Mam's, noted in one of her medical journals. Major Miller wouldn't agree with Mam's methods, but he needn't know. I scurried back to the surgery tent and placed the maggots beneath the bandages of my patients. After a few hours, I removed the maggots and the wounds were pink and weren't reeking. Even in the darkness, Mam was with me.

The next day, the battle shifted closer to town, but we remained as the wounded and dead were still brought in from the hills and Devil's Den. All those who were able, stood and marched from the field with their regiments; the men were exhausted and dehydrated, but their will was strong. I do not know how they did it; they could barely hold their guns and had no ammunition, but they followed their leaders to fight. We heard the echoes of the cannons, the Rebel yells, and the bugle calls. My heart ached knowing that more boys would never return home.

And now it's over.

Around noon, a rider barreled into our camp and screamed the news for all to hear. "We've won! The Union has defeated the enemy!" Yells of triumph erupted, bringing the doctors and myself from the medical tent to hear the repeated news. We cheered along with them, but our glee was halfhearted. The battle was over, with our side the victor, but the camp before me was still full of the wounded and dying.

The wagons have slowed, and now our able hands are needed to bury the dead. I've spent the last two hours digging trenches. Kindly soldiers argued, insisting I not take up a spade and join them. But this work needed to be done. The rain turned the dirt to thick mud however, and after an hour, we couldn't dig down as far as we wanted—only three feet, when it should've been six. As the bodies were piled in the grave, I looked for Joseph in every face. I prayed I wouldn't find him. I didn't, but that doesn't mean he wasn't here. I don't know how I can discover if he was in Gettysburg. Perhaps I could locate General Hooker. But I would not be the first widow begging for news of her husband—and others are more deserving. I will need to wait, like all the other wives.

Now that I have seen carnage, I will never feel the same about this war. I will never believe in war and violence again. How can our leaders not see this? How? And I saw only one battle; Chancellorsville, Antietam, Fredericksburg all had bloody days of their own and still the fight goes on. So many men will never return to their mothers, wives, families. Surely there is another way to end this conflict. Words hold more powerful than loaded rifles.

Now I think of Rosie and sweet Mary. I hope they've fared well. I haven't seen Jonathan since we parted at Christ Church. I pray God has kept him safe as well.

In the darkness of the last few days, I've been thankful for Major Miller. I've learned invaluable lessons from him: the instant decisions he made after assessing a wound, how he pushed me to think like a physician, the way he treated me as a colleague. He reminds me so much of my dear Dr. Watkins — my instructor and mentor from another life — and I will be saddened when we part.

I wish I could lie down on the cot and sleep. But I fear I will never sleep again. In the quiet, I still hear their screams — the cries for their mothers.

Chapter Twenty

Breanne Walker

F LICKERING LIGHTS ABOVE MY HEAD PULLED MY ATTENTION FROM the diary. After a few seconds, the lights flickered again, this time with a hint of annoyance. Within the library world, the flickering of lights is the universal sign for, "Get the Hell Out." I looked at the time; it was almost midnight. I had fifteen minutes before the doors would be locked, with me inside.

I gathered my things — placing the diary safely inside my messenger bag — and headed towards the stairs. My steps echoed through the stacks. It was dead quiet. *Too quiet, even for Labor Day.* When I reached the stairs, I could see the librarians, waiting for me in the lobby. I frantically looked behind and saw that no one was joining in my exodus. They were waiting on me to lock up. *Or they kicked everyone out to get me alone. Were there cameras upstairs, with someone watching my every move? Does Peggy have access to their footage? Does she know?* I took the carpeted stairs two at a time, clutching my bag tight and hoping I didn't trip. As my feet hit the last stair, I waited for my bag to be snatched away;

I'd be showed to a back office of the library and accused of theft. Peggy was probably on her way.

I'm done for.

As I crossed cautiously in front of the two librarians, one of them cleared her throat. I froze, and we made eye contact. She looked down at her watch and then back at me with an air of aggravation—waiting for me to move. I didn't. I was too scared. She rolled her eyes and walked to the door, holding it open and motioning for me to walk through the metal detector. *Oh God, here it comes.* My feet felt like bricks, but I smiled and crossed in front of her as she turned to her co-worker and asked, "Are you heading right home, Karen?"

"Yes. I'm opening again tomorrow. Barry is a real jerk for making me close and open."

Paranoia and delusion definitely go hand in hand.

I walked through the door and sprinted like an Olympic athlete—urgency and fear pushing me beyond my limits. Thank God for a well-lit campus; otherwise I would've tripped over my feet and never found my car. When I did, I sat down on the asphalt and leaned against my front tire to catch my breath. I put my head between my legs and closed my eyes. *Calm down, no one is coming for you.*

And really, what was the worst Peggy would do if she found out about the diary? Fire me from the museum, arrest me, take the diary—the latter probably being the worst, given my current attachment to A.M.P. They'd have to snatch the diary from my cold, dead fingers. That's how crazy I felt. I'd kill for this diary—*well, maybe not kill, but maybe make someone extremely uncomfortable.* I'm not a violent person—I've never actually laid hands on anyone—but A.M.P's emotion had seeped into my soul: *there is a rage inside my heart that is dying to be released.*

Reading the facts of a historic event is moving, but a first-hand account brings the horror home. The big events were all there: the southern invasion and their exit towards York; Generals Buford, Reynolds and Meade and the Army of Potomac; the battlegrounds of the McPherson farm, Seminary Ridge, Cemetery Ridge, Little Round Top, Devil's Den, and "the fields," which were the peach orchard and wheat field; the field hospitals and A.M.P. stretching her medical legs; and the end of the battle, with the Union victory and subsequent retreat of the Army of Virginia. The information she provided was valid and valuable. And her courage in the face of it all was astounding. She was in the middle of the bloodiest days of the Battle of Gettysburg, and she held her own.

"I need to sleep," I said aloud as I leaned back against the tire. And before I knew it, I was pulling into my apartment's parking lot and, thankfully, into one parking spot. I lumbered up the stairs and unlocked my front door, practically falling inside. My bed had never looked so inviting. I didn't bother undressing. I fell into my bed's comfy goodness. On my nightstand I put my messenger bag, with the diary still safe inside. The last thing I did before I let exhaustion take me was turn my phone off.

Anyone who needed me would need to wait at least six hours.

At least.

Chapter Twenty-One

Breanne Walker

B EHIND HER, THE SUN WAS SETTING. HER JOURNEY ON FOOT HAD been long and she walked through the exhaustion. She walked with her head down; her chin almost touching her chest, like she feared to look ahead. Nevertheless, she knew the way by heart and didn't need to look up for landmarks or streets. Every step was one of determination.

The town around her was a shell of what it had been, and the houses were still boarded up. Debris covered the dirt streets — broken wagon wheels, discarded shoes and clothing, empty canteens, ammunition-less rifles, ripped regiment flags, even a dead horse rotting in the heat of the day. These obstacles didn't stun her or throw her off stride; she maneuvered around the debris and kept her pace.

Her appearance made people stop and stare as they walked by. She looked like she'd stepped out of a tornado: the braid down her back was coming apart and greasy from sweat and god-knows what else; her blouse was torn and stained; the blue of her skirt was now a faded gray; she was dirty from head to toe, with brownish tints *of handprints and smears all over her clothes, and she emitted a horrific scent, a mixture of blood, fecal matter, body odor, and dirt. In the days following the battle, it wasn't uncommon to see many in Gettysburg in similar states — but a woman walking in such a disheveled state was alarming. Yet she didn't appear to be a victim of any sort; in fact, her walk was driven and filled with strength.*

She stopped before a house and laboriously climbed the front stoop to the door. She took a long breath and turned the brass knob. The door was locked, which confused her. She pauses for a second and then lightly knocks. A few seconds pass, then the door opens an inch. A scream sounds from within, the door fully opens and a young woman dashes through and into her arms. They fall into each other in the doorway, clinging like small children. The second woman — the one who flung herself into the disheveled woman's arms — had to be Rosie.

"I was so frightened when you didn't return." Rosie pulled away and held the other woman's face in her hands. "I returned this morning from Mrs. Gardener's. She opened her house to wounded soldiers and…so many died. Rebels came pounding on the doors at all hours, accusing us of harboring Union troops. We had to hide them in the attic. The poor boys…I did the best I could but…I couldn't stop thinking about what you were facing." She pulled her into an embrace, again.

They didn't move from their embrace for a long time and probably would've remained there if a baby hadn't started crying from inside the house. Rosie pulled away. "Poor Mary, moving houses like this has her so confused. Jonathan returned just a few hours ago. When I saw you weren't with him, I sent him right out to the hospitals to look for you. Sometimes he just doesn't think." She offered her hand and helped her sister to her feet. "I heard such awful stories from the men at Mrs. Gardner's. I'm so thankful you were nowhere near the worst of it. What would I have done if I lost you?"

"Complain about Jonathan to someone else, I suppose," her sister whispered. They both laughed.

"Let's get you inside and into a tub. I love you sister, but as Mam used to say 'Dahlin, that smell would choke a rose.'" Rosie stepped into the house to fetch her crying newborn and to boil water for the bath.

The unkempt woman followed her into the house. She stood in the foyer and took a deep breath, holding the air in her chest for a few seconds. When she released the breath, her shoulders dropped, and the tension went with it. She turned back to the door and grasped the knob. Before the door was completely closed, she stopped and looked up.

Straight at me. "Wake up, Breanne," she said.

I gasped and shot out of bed — and immediately crashed to my apartment's carpeted floor in a tangle of sheets and blankets. I lay there for a few minutes, stuck in my cotton sheets, head buzzing. Air wouldn't go to my lungs. *The way she said my name.* I shivered and pulled my blanket over my head; I needed to hide until I calmed down.

It had been a deep sleep; I knew that for sure. How long it had lasted, I couldn't say. I read somewhere that dream lengths are deceiving. A dream that seems to last forever in your mind could only be a few seconds in real time.

But whatever its length, my dream was very intense. I was walking beside her as she trudged down the streets of Gettysburg; felt her exhaustion and pain, as the events she lived came crashing down on her as she returned to normalcy; saw the townsfolk staring at her; felt her anxiety lift the moment she was in Rosie's arms.

Slowly, my heart's pace evened out. The tingling in my fingers stopped, and my thoughts became rational. I pulled the blanket from my head and sat up. The sheets were double wrapped around my legs, like I had gone through the mummification process. I shifted my legs as far apart as I could and started to unravel.

POUND! POUND! POUND! sounded from the front of my apartment.

I leaned forward to peer around my bed. My bedroom door was open, so I could see straight through my living room and to the front door. I froze and listened with every ounce of my being. *Maybe it's the landlord? Is my rent late?* I sat there and waited. Nothing happened. *I guess they left.* I looked to my alarm clock above my head to see the time — nearly 10 a.m. but still an odd time for a visitor during the work week.

POUND! POUND! POUND! POUND!

My door would crash off its hinges if I didn't answer it. I stepped out of the last tangle of sheets and hurried to my front door.

I unlocked the deadbolt and opened the door wide to the blasting sun. As my eyes adjusted to the light, I didn't find my landlord, steaming about a late rent check. Instead, standing in front of my door was a casually dressed Greg, steaming with a similar anger. I stood there in disbelief, staring and waiting for him to say something. He continued to stare right back at me.

"Yes?" I asked, prompting him to start the conversation.

"Where the hell is your phone?" he huffed as he barged into my living room.

"It's off. I've been sleeping. And sure, Greg. Feel free to walk into my apartment and —"

"Vince showed up at the museum with your samples."

My heart dropped.

Greg shoved his hands into the pockets of his jeans. "Peggy knows."

Chapter Twenty-Two

Breanne Walker

I RUSHED PAST GREG AND INTO MY BEDROOM. MY PHONE WAS SITting on my nightstand, charging and still turned off. I snatched it up and pushed the home-screen button. The screen lit up and slowly started to load my settings. The anticipation was causing me to shake.

"Finally!" I said. Twenty-five missed calls! And ten text messages. *Jesus Christ.*

Six were from Vince.

> **Hi Mrs. Walker! The samples took a little longer to analyze, but everything is done and ready. You should see the data! The lab tech was really excited!**

> **I'll be getting on the road lickity split!**

> **Should I meet you at the museum?**

> **Or somewhere else?**

> **Maybe you're in the archives and you don't have signal.**

> **I'll come to the museum.**

"Why did I turn off my phone?" I whispered. Greg was in my bedroom doorway, leaning against the frame.

The remaining four texts were from him.

> **911!**

> **This isn't a joke! Where are you!! Answer your phone!**

> **Vince is here. He went to Peggy with your samples. She knows you sent him to the lab. She's looking for you.**

> **She's pissed. I'm coming to your apartment.**

"Shit."

I looked up. Greg was staring blankly at me. He shrugged his shoulders. I didn't know what to say. But I wanted to cry. Or scream. Probably both. I resorted to crumbling to my bedroom floor and holding my knees to my chest so that I wouldn't do either. *Oh God. Oh God. Oh God.* This was all inevitable, I knew that from the moment I accepted the diary from Greg, but I had hoped to be further along and to present all my evidence to Peggy under better circumstances. Show her my completed work and explain Greg and I's position. Now, all our actions reeked of deceit—like we had no intention of ever clueing Peggy in to the second discovery. *Why had we involved Vince? Why?*

Greg had crossed the room and sat down next to me on the floor. The awkwardness of my boss being in my bedroom seemed miniscule compared to the mental war going on in my head. He leaned back against my mattress and sighed. "I wasn't there. If he'd come to me first, I could've diverted him from Peggy and contained the situation. But he went straight to Peggy. And told her everything."

My stomach turned. "Which is?"

"An easy guess based on the results from the samples you gave him—which he obviously looked at. That you possess an artifact of significant age."

"How much trouble are we in?" I asked through my knees, my voice muffled.

"I doubt there's precedence for conducting archival research in secret while withholding the existence of said artifact from your superiors." He sighed again and let his head fall back onto my bed. He ran his fingers through his hair and shook his head. "Does she have grounds to fire us? Yes. Will she? She'd love to hand me my walking papers—a personal vendetta for my family owning half the collection. Being fired would be the ultimate scandal for my family, and she would lap that up like milk."

"Damn. Damn. Damn!" I really needed to hit something. "How could I be so stupid to turn off my phone? I've just ruined both of our futures!" I resorted to pounding my fists on the carpet.

"Listen, there's nothing we can do. Our secret's out, and there's no pulling it back in." He gripped my shoulders and held me still. "But I'll tell you this—I don't think either of us gave Vince enough credit. I for one didn't think he had two brain cells to rub together, much less the guts to go straight to Peggy, who eats interns like him for breakfast."

I snorted—which only made us both laugh harder. We slunk back against my bed, and my head naturally fell onto his shoulder. A feeling of intimacy replaced my building anxiety. "You took a huge risk giving me the diary—all stemming from something I said at my interview—and this is how I repay you?" I said.

He shrugged his shoulders. "There are plenty of other museums who'd love to have me. But I haven't counted you out yet." He pulled his legs in and stood, then offered his hand down to me. "Prove me right."

I looked at his outstretched hand and then to his eyes. *Man, his eyes are blue.* He smiled, and I clasped his hand and stood.

Chapter Twenty-Three

Breanne Walker

I QUICKLY THREW ON SOME FRESH CLOTHES AND MET GREG OUTSIDE my apartment. He left his car and drove us both back to the museum in mine. Usually, I roll down at my windows and blast music first thing in the morning. Fresh air and the bass bumping works better than coffee. But given the situation, neither of us had issues with tiredness.

Anxiety and adrenaline were racing through my veins, and Greg's hands were clutching the steering wheel like his life depended on it. He played it cool, but I knew he was putting on a brave front for me. He loved his job and having his name on a wing had its own set of pressures. He worked hard to live beyond the Ransome name and being terminated for an infraction like this...well, the stain of it would follow him for the rest of his career.

I buried those thoughts as we pulled into the museum parking lot. Greg turned off the engine and we sat there for a few minutes in silence. I slid my messenger bag on top of my lap and through the fabric of the bag, I could feel the edge of the diary. *Be calm and confident.* I turned to Greg—who was staring straight ahead, into his hypothetical future—and gave him a playful punch on the shoulder. "Let's go." I opened the car door and stepped into the September sun. I walked across the steaming asphalt with a bounce in my step, with Greg hustling to keep up.

The camera vans and crews were still in place, but their presence was miniscule compared to the number of cars in the rest of the parking lot. There were no parking spots to be had—luckily, there were designated employee spaces— and the foot traffic was unusually heavy. A large crowd was converging on the museum—larger than the museum was used to at this time of the year—and we passed many visitors walking the paths from the lower lots on their way to the entrance. A surge in museum attendance wasn't surprising; it's happened with past discoveries.

I weaved among the patrons and took the rear entrance's slated steps at a frenzied pace; I walked with long strides, paying no attention to those I walked past on the stairs. An elderly woman was struggling with the final set of stairs in front of me; in normal circumstances, I would've stopped to help her. But I cut to the right and left her in my dust— karma would find me later for that slight. Once on the patio, I saw that a line had formed—starting at the double-door entrance and back about fifteen feet.

"Wow," I said, mentally counting the heads.

"Great day for ticket sales." Greg guided me to the employee entrance, bypassing the massive line.

We flashed our ID badges to the posted security guard. He allowed us through with a quick wave of his hand.

Inside, the atmosphere was pandemonium. The vestibule was filled with screaming children running to and fro — *why aren't these kids in school?* — even longer lines at the reservation desk, and employees trying frantically to keep control. Trashcans were overflowing, and the air was thick with the smell of burnt pizza — wafting from the jammed-packed saloon. It was a sight — I paused for a second to take it in. If nothing else, the revenue earned from the discovery of the body — *and the diary* — would foster more research and endowments to the museum. The publicity would be invaluable for the continuation of the museum's mission — finding and preserving history at its source. Although chaos in any situation provokes anxiety and creates more work for all those involved, the scene in front of me was job-affirming.

"Hey!" Greg stepped in front of me, waving his hand in front of my face.

"Sorry, spaced out."

"Let's go!"

We stepped, bobbed, and weaved our way through the hordes of people. Once we were past the souvenir shop — mugs, books, Confederate and Union costumes were flying off the shelves — the crowd finally started to thin. My nerves returned when we approached the hallways leading to the back offices. My mind was fixated on dread. *Will I be able to get another job? Will anyone allow me to handle precious documents again?*

Before I could mentally negotiate my doubts and questions, Greg abruptly stopped short in front of his office. "Go on in," he said. "Better to be on my turf than hers." He opened the door, forced me inside, and closed the door behind me. From inside, I could hear his footsteps sprinting down the hall.

For half a second, I wondered if he had locked the door. *He could be afraid I'll bolt.* I tried the knob; it turned and opened with no issue.

"Relax, he's not about to keep you prisoner," I said aloud as I shut the door again. I turned my back and leaned against the door, closing my eyes for a few seconds. *I guess this is how Marie Antoinette felt before the guillotine.*

I pushed away from the door, and my eyes were immediately assaulted with the cluster-mess known as Greg's office. For a man who took such pride in his appearance, Greg's workspace was a complete paradox. Every inch of the room was covered in crap. Beneath the stray notebooks, clothing, trash, and the excessive amount of papers, there should've been a navy-blue carpet — but I couldn't see it. He was a complete and utter slob. I hadn't been inside his office since my interview, so this mess must be three months old. *Or he had shoved everything inside the coat closet that day.* There was a narrow path to his desk, which I utilized by walking on my tiptoes. I sat down in his executive leather chair — expensive and personally obtained, no doubt. Papers, dirty coffee cups, pens, and Post-Its with hastily written reminders about dry cleaning and his mother's birthday were everywhere.

How can he work like this? When my anxiety is on over-load, organizing helps me relax. My hands were twitching, wanting to shift papers to proper order. *This is not my mess,* I reminded myself. Instead, I settled into his leather chair, my messenger bag on my lap, with my twitching hands be-neath me.

I sat there, staring ahead and waiting. My heart raced every time I heard footsteps by the door—they'd either keep walking or were unmistakably high heels, which I knew didn't belong to Peggy Cupples. Vanity was a waste in her eyes. Normally, she stuck to orthopedic clogs that she could easily slip in and out of. Those shoes also helped her roam the hallways of the museum without a squeak, peep or clack. So, I'd have no warning of her arrival.

I leaned back in Greg's chair and closed my eyes. I breathed deeply; I breathed in the positive and out the neg-ative, repeatedly until I could feel myself drifting off to—an unintentional—sleep.

"I hope I'm not disturbing you, Ms. Walker."

My eyes shot open, I jumped from Greg's expensive chair, catapulting my messenger bag to the floor by my feet. Peggy Cupples was standing in the doorway with her hands on her hips, a menacing look on her face. She was back in her normal attire—khakis, a white button-down shirt, and her trademark shovel pin embellishing her popped collar—but her makeup and hair were polished and flawless. She looked beautiful—*in a homicidal way.* She rarely wore makeup, so she must have been coiffed for an on-camera interview about the discovery. Behind her stood Greg, with a look of terror and disappointment painted on his face. "Finding you asleep in my chair isn't helping us" is what his look said.

She strode into the room—like a queen entering her throne room—and, with a flick of her wrist, shooed me away from Greg's desk. I snatched up my bag and scurried from her wake—nearly slipping on a pile of receipts from Amazon. She sat down in his chair; a look of disgust crossed her face. She kept the top of his desk at an arm's length, as if touching the mess would transmit an incurable disease. From behind, Greg grazed my elbow, so I knew he was there—physically and emotionally. He retrieved two wooden chairs and offered one to me before sitting down himself. *A.M.P., please give me strength.* Peggy looked from Greg to me, her maniacal smile continuing. She was holding all the cards and lording her power over us.

"So," she started in a deadly calm voice, looking down at her fingernails, "I hear you have something for me."

I felt myself starting to slide out of the chair, like I was made of water. Luckily, I stopped myself before it happened.

"Well, I guess it depends on how you look at it, Peggy. We—"

"Don't patronize me, Gregory. That wasn't a question," she snapped. "You know the dynamics of this museum and the chain of command. Everything that is on display, everything that is brought into the labs for preservation and authentication, everything that is dug out of the ground passes over my desk. I have earned this position with my sweat and fortitude—do you understand me?"

"Yes, ma'am." Greg looked down to his toes like a scolded schoolboy.

"Now, Ms. Walker." She looked back to me and placed the manila file folder she had carried in with her on Greg's cluttered desk, "According to this datasheet—and might I say, the excellent analysis completed by the forensics lab in Harrisburg—given to me by our wonderfully eager undergraduate intern, Vincent..." She lifted a sheet of paper, looking for his name, "Yes, Vincent McGill—you have a document of considerable age in your possession. And from what I gather from young Mr. McGill, this artifact was found on the same day the body was unearthed near Little Round Top. In fact, Mr. McGill informed me that he caught a glimpse of what you were working on and believes it was a personal record, bound in leather. Am I getting warm, Ms. Walker."

I gulped hard and nodded quickly.

"Imagine my surprise when Mr. McGill knocked on my office door this morning, handing me these documents and jabbering on about the lab in Harrisburg and the call you, Gregory, made to have an analysis rushed." She pulled her reading glasses down from atop her head. "I had no knowledge of an age verification for a small sample of ink, DNA extraction and testing on a single thread of hair and a deer tick, the age on a sinew of thread, a bit of leather, a blade of grass—and the list goes on and on." She pushed her glasses back into her hair and looked up with a smile. "A very expensive list for a pet project, wouldn't you say? I was curious and investigated your network drives and assignments—your last project ended two weeks ago, Ms. Walker, and it is currently waiting on my desk for review. You also haven't been seen in the office since before the holiday weekend. No; you were seen exiting the building hastily after my staff meeting. Security records show that you were in the labs the day the body was found and were also granted access to the archives the same day—you granted that access, Gregory. Your whereabouts have been unknown since. In fact, Gregory here tried to cover for you, saying you had a family emergency." She closed the folder with the lab results and folded her hands-on top of it. "Have I missed anything?"

Big Brother, indeed.

The silence that followed was heavy.

Greg cleared his throat. "Peggy, I know how this looks, but if you'll allow me to explain—"

"Oh yes, Gregory. I know exactly how this looks." Her voice rose into a yell. "This looks like insubordination and theft! Not only could I fire you both, but I hope you realize anything committed on these grounds is a federal offense. I can singlehandedly keep you both from getting a job in any museum ever again. You, Gregory, know better." The pitch of her voice made the glass window behind her whine. I was scared to my core but also in complete awe of her; watching a woman put a grown man in his place was inspiring.

"Yes, yes," Greg stammered. "I know how this looks but I can assure you there was no underhandedness involved. When I got the call from the park rangers about the Witness

Tree, I rushed to the site. The body was discovered, and I saw the...the artifact soon after I arrived. I called Breanne and—"

"And you thought you'd give your girlfriend—who's been here a total of ten weeks—the opportunity to make a name for herself."

My head shot up. "I'm not his girlfriend!" My voice was loud and reverberated off the walls.

She turned to me, a look of curiosity crossing her face. "So, you aren't mute, Ms. Walker?"

"I—no, I'm not. And I don't appreciate the accusation that Dr. Ransome only trusted me with this...this artifact because of a romantic entanglement." My face was aflame. "I am a qualified archivist and preservationist. Dr. Ransome trusts in my abilities and eye. Maybe you'd do the same if you actually took the time to get to know your staff."

The smile on Peggy's face shrank and disappeared. Reemerging a few seconds later, only now with a vengeance.

Too far? I met her gaze; my confidence was back, and I wasn't going to allow her to unnerve me any further. Greg didn't move a muscle. It was a complete stalemate. A battle of wits to see who'd give in first.

She broke. She looked down to her fingernails again. "It seems we stand at an impasse, Ms. Walker. But before we continue this delightful conversation, I think I'd like to see the artifact." She sat back in Greg's chair, folding her arms across her chest, and waited.

I glanced sideways at Greg. *Are we doing this?* His shoulders dropped in resignation, telling me to stop delaying the inevitable. I stood and stepped closer to the desk. I lifted the flap of my messenger bag and pulled out the small bundle—rewrapped in the original cloth and inside a Ziploc bag. I pulled the bundle out of the plastic bag and my fingertips grazed Rosie's embroidered initials.

I tried to keep my face passive, but I was panicking. I couldn't think of a more unpleasant experience than handing the diary over and potentially never getting it back. So deplorable that just showing it to Peggy—and watching her greedy eyes grow bigger and glassy—made me overprotective. In that moment—poised with the diary in my hand—I fully understood Gollum from *Lord of the Rings*. I wanted to run, to hoard the diary and keep A.M.P's thoughts to myself.

Give it to her, save your job.

Keep it and run, protect A.M.P. and her secrets.

Greg cleared his throat. I had no choice. I placed the bundle on the desk and stepped back. I slumped back into the wooden chair to lick my wounds.

To Peggy, the diary was like a massive piece of chocolate cake, placed before a chocolate addict. She stared at the bundle long and hard, salivating, before gently picking it up. Then, with the back of her hand, she swept everything from the desk. Greg flinched as the papers and refuse crashed to the ground, but he said nothing. Delicately, she placed the bundle back on the cleared desk and scanned the cloth. She was drawn to the initials in the corner.

"The initials are—"

"Associated with the diary," I interrupted.

"Diary?" She looked up, her eyes were twinkling.

I nodded.

She held her hand out to me and shook her fingers. Reading her mind, I retrieved my cloth gloves and handed them over. She slipped her hands inside and started to unfold the cloth. Once the leather binding was revealed, she sat forward. "Almost perfect condition," she said under her breath. She inspected every inch of the outside, muttering to herself as she did. Placing it down on the desk, she touched the cover and carefully opened it. She took a few seconds and examined the introduction page—the one with A.M.P's initials. The words registered in her head, and she looked back up at me.

"Talk," she ordered, leaning back in her chair.

I told Peggy about every entry and its contents. I described the key players: Rosie, with her sweet nature but selfish tendencies; Jonathan, with his ego and narcissistic outlook on life; Mam, the god-sent mother figure for the diarist; Mother, the wicked and ominous figurehead; and finally, A.M.P., the diarist. I described the timeline and the major historical events that she witnessed. I relayed the part she played at the Battle of Gettysburg and the medical treatments she administered to the dying and wounded. But I held back on the truly emotional moments from the diary—the relationships with Mam and Mother and her forced marriage. Peggy hadn't earned the right to those memories, not yet. I also kept my mouth shut about the dreams—*she already hates me, I don't need her thinking I'm crazy, too*. Besides, Peggy was more interested in the facts.

When I finally stopped speaking, my throat was raw. I sat back in my chair, exhausted and flustered. Peggy had glared at me the entire time I spoke. She was still glaring when I finished. She nodded her head, deep in thought, and drummed her fingers on the desk. Watching her was nerve-wracking. I started cracking my knuckles, hoping to ease my anxiety.

Finally, she spoke. "So, A.M.P: a female, and notably not the initials of the male soldier found beneath the Witness Tree. But you don't know her full name, yet?"

"No. The diary entries have given no indication of the name behind the initials."

"You haven't finished? And haven't read ahead?"

"No. I make it a habit of reading manuscripts through to completion."

"As do I." She looked down at the diary and carefully closed the cover. "It seems you've accomplished...well, *something* in the short time you've had this."

"Thank you."

"Don't mistake that for a compliment, Ms. Walker. I would've read the diary in full by now and found the connection to the body. I also wouldn't have been caught sleeping on the job while it was in my possession."

Nothing stings more than a backhanded compliment.

She pointed to the folder of data collected from the lab, saying, "But this gives conclusive evidence of its age."

I kept her gaze but said nothing. Nothing would change her mind, regardless of what I said or did; my part to play was over, and I would learn of A.M.P's identity along with the rest of the country. I kept my emotions in check, but the thought of not personally finishing the diary brought tears to my eyes. *I need to know how it ends.*

Peggy sighed and began wrapping the diary back in its cloth. "Today is Tuesday. I expect to see you here, on Monday, with a full analysis."

My jaw dropped. "I—I don't understand."

"Gregory, I truly hope you didn't hire someone who cannot comprehend simple instructions." She pushed away from the desk and stood up. Before walking from the desk, she touched the diary once more—it was a tender caress, like that of a mother to her sleeping babe. Then she walked away from Greg's desk, practically chucked my gloves at me, and threw open the office door.

"Monday, Ms. Walker," she said, pausing in the doorway. "And your job depends on it. Gregory, the first debriefing on the analysis of the body is in one hour."

She didn't wait for Greg to reply; the resounding slam of the door was the only noise that followed her exit.

Chapter Twenty-Four

Breanne Walker

THE SLAM OF THE DOOR ECHOED IN GREG'S OFFICE, TURNING US—the remaining inhabitants—into breathing mannequins. We looked straight ahead, out the window behind the desk. Minutes continued to pass with nothing—nothing but the building glassiness and ache of our eyes.

"Is it okay to move?" I asked through clenched lips.

Greg snickered. "Not sure. She might double back."

Cautiously, he peeked over his shoulder. I could see him weighing out the options before standing and walking to the door. He opened it a crack, then stuck his whole head out into the hallway. He sighed, saying, "Coast is clear." He closed the door and did a little jig. *Has he lost it?*

"I spent my childhood running these halls." His voice was light and jovial. "Learned to tie my shoes in the gift shop, smoked my first cigarette on the back patio. And Peggy...I've known her my entire life; she dated my father before my parents met. But that woman—that woman has always scared the crap out of me. Even when she isn't mad."

I stood and stretched my back. "I've heard the janitorial crew won't approach her office unless they know she's out of the building." I stood and stretched my back.

We laughed.

"Occasionally, she surprises me. I've never seen her pass up the opportunity to toss someone out on their ass. She'll never admit it, but you impressed her. And me."

My head dropped, to hide the redness forming on my cheeks. *Stop blushing, you idiot.*

He crossed the room, back to his desk and started shoveling papers off the floor and onto his chair. "Man, can she make a mess."

I scooted to his side and bent down to gather papers. He grabbed my hand. "What are you doing?"

"Helping you re-clutter your desk?"

"No, you're not."

"I'm not?"

"You're leaving." He stood and marched me to the door. "You have until Monday to finish the diary. And judging by how slowly you read—and your tendency to fall asleep while doing it—we'll both be out of a job come then."

"I wasn't—"

He put his hand over my mouth. "Stop talking, I don't care. None of it matters. Get out of here. Now." He opened the door and unceremoniously pushed me into the hallway before slamming it in my face.

Greg's tempered glass door became my mirror, and I stood staring into it. *What do I do? Where do I go?* Just as I was about to step away, the door flew open again.

Greg was smiling his megawatt, movie-star smile. "I think you'll need these."

He handed me the bundled diary, my cloth gloves and the manila folder containing the sample analysis. "Call if you need anything. Good luck." He slammed the door again.

With the diary back in my possession, I knew where to go. *Back to the archives.*

As I walked past the research and conservation labs, I sent Greg a quick text.

> **I'm heading down to the archives. No cell reception, so don't freak out if I don't answer your 911's.**

> **If the South secedes again, come get me.**

I slid my ID through the card reader. I turned quickly and looked down the hallway, thinking I'd find Vince—Peggy's little spy—cowering in a corner. *If I ever see that kid…* But no. He did what anyone in his position would've done. When he couldn't find me, he went to the next logical person. And he was probably hoping to look competent in Peggy's eyes.

After a few minutes, the elevator button lit green, and the doors opened. I stepped inside, and the doors closed me inside the death-drop machine. *Please don't break today.*

The elevator shuddered to a stop on the ground floor. Once the doors opened, I jumped out and into the alluringly musty scent of archives. The doors clinked shut behind me, and I was alone. Mercifully and thankfully alone.

I took in the archival sights—the crates of paintings, the plastic-wrapped furniture, the glass cases of books, the racks of clothing worn by people long dead. All of these artifacts were from A.M.P's time, maybe even pieces from her own house. From an air-tight garment bag rack in front of me, a light blue cotton skirt caught my eye. Just like the one A.M.P. was wearing in my dream. *Minus the blood and bodily fluids.* I couldn't help it; I walked towards the rack and unzipped the garment bag. I pulled the skirt out and hung it on the rack, then stepped back. In length, the skirt was over three feet—which would skim the ground of a woman over five feet tall. Although it had been repaired and preserved by the museum's staff, I could see that the stitching was clumsy and probably handmade. I touched the cloth—it was stiff with starch and the fabric was rough to the touch. I leaned into the skirt and inhaled. Again, I smelled starch and a hint of mothballs—akin to the dryness of the air around me. But...also a hint of copper—the coopery smell of blood.

Okay, stop. Your mind is playing tricks on you.

I zipped the skirt back inside the plastic and shouldered my messenger bag. Then my legs started to move of their own accord, guiding me in and out of the rows of artifacts and to the work desk. I found the table and chair exactly as I'd left them—my pencil sitting right where I left it. *Just the same but so different.* I put my bag and the manila folder on the table and sat down in the vacant chair in front of it.

I opened the flap of my bag and retrieved the rewrapped diary. A feeling of déjà vu spread over me as I pulled my cloth gloves on and spread the cloth to reveal the leather diary inside. My body was anticipating the strain of hunching for the next few hours, but the pain was necessary.

I now had a deadline. And it was inching closer with every passing minute.

But before I went any further, I needed to read over the analysis from the lab. I opened the manila folder and read over the results. Peggy was right—the research was very thorough. The lab detected a chemical date tag on the ink from the mid 1800's. It was comparable to other inks logged in a national database—so A.M.P. bought her ink instead of making it herself. *Interesting given her knowledge of plants.* The age of the leather and sinew of the binding were conclusive as well—with radiocarbon dating, the cow and deer hides used for the binding and cover also dated the back to the mid 1800's. And the hair sample—the gleam of which caught my eye when I first started reading—was human. The hair had a root and the lab was able to extract nuclear DNA, linking it to a human.

I was giddy. That single strand of hair could possibly link the soldier's body to the diary. *And maybe even to a living descendant.*

Peggy certainly had the capability of knocking anyone down a few pegs, but now I felt vindicated.

And she gave me until Monday to finish.

I checked my phone for the time—it was nearly noon. *Exactly twelve hours since I closed the binding.* I found my acid-free bookmarker in the binding and opened to where I had left off.

Chapter Twenty-Five

A.M.P.

July 10th, 1863

It was time for me to go back to my farm.

Rosie pleaded with me to stay on until the remnants of battle had been cleared away, but I was anxious to be home.

"My sheep and cow have been in my neighbor's care for far too long," I explained, as I gathered my belongings in the foyer of her home. "I'll return, I promise. I need to visit the field hospitals in town and my patients. And really, I'm not that far, sister."

"At least wait for Jonathan to procure a horse. That way he can drive you home," she said, grabbing my satchel and the small bundle of clothes I arrived with—depleted even further because of the battle—and attempting to re-fold them. "You can't possibly carry all of this and a sack of fresh groceries."

"I'm looking forward to the walk." I snatched back the clothes and stuffed them inside my satchel. It was true; I was looking forward to the journey to my homestead. Aside from detailing the last few days in your pages, I haven't had a moments peace to think about all that had happened. A long walk was what I needed.

"But I have grown accustomed to your presence. It's like when we were children. Sleeping under the same roof, spending every waking moment together."

"You know we rarely spent more than a few days together at a time."

"I know." A playful smile lit her face.

I laughed and pulled her into a hug. "The years will never change you, dear one. Always the same little girl begging for treats."

"Always."

I kissed her lightly on the forehead. I shouldered my satchel, medical kit, and burlap sack filled with food. My arms were quite loaded; the four miles would truly test my endurance, and part of me regretted turning down Rosie's suggestion of waiting for Jonathan. But I wouldn't admit that.

Rosie opened the door. "Be careful, sister. I love you."

I turned back and took her hand, "I love you more. I'll see you soon."

She nodded. I stepped out and onto the cobblestones.

When I had left my home to help Rosie in June, I never could've anticipated the events that would follow. I will not recall the events of the battle again; I will not add salt to the wound and feel that pain once more. I fear I am forever changed from those days and I pray every night to forget all that I have seen.

Life needs to begin again. As it has in town. Gettysburg is rebuilding. News of the battle spread, and wagons filled with food, clothing, and able-bodied men and women came to help with the devastation faced by many townsfolk. Houses were patched, fields were cleaned, and pantries were restocked by the generosity of kind souls. Many homes still housed wounded soldiers—and field hospitals are still entrenched on others' farmlands—and those who couldn't be moved will stay until their strength returns. Or not at all. There are so many. So many who will never leave. I've tried to return to my normal visit schedule; my patients are all in good spirits despite the horrors they've experienced. Stress and fear can induce labor, but I am lucky that my two pregnant patients are still stable and doing beautifully.

Within a mile of Rosie's home, my arms were aching under the weight of my baggage. As I dropped my bags at my feet for a brief rest, a man passed me in a wagon and stopped. He was heading in the same direction and generously offered to drive me the rest of the way. I accepted whole heartedly, knowing I wouldn't make the trek otherwise. God dropped that man in my path in my exact moment of need, and I will say extra prayers for him this night.

My heart was brimming with warmth and longing as the wagon turned off Taneytown Road and onto the small path leading to my home. It's no secret that I've never been overly fond of my home, as I considered it my shackle, my term of bondage and the reason for my marriage. The second day of the battle raged on Little Hill and my house sits not far from that very spot, so I wasn't sure what I'd be walking into. I imagined the remains of my home littered in bullet holes and splintered wood. But the grass around my little cottage never looked greener. The trickling of the small creek that ran through our property never sounded more musical. The summer leaves waved in earnest with the wind. And the wooden planks, crooked windowpanes, and sloping front porch never looked so inviting.

I politely thanked the man. I owe much to his kindness—particularly, the strength left in my writing hand. Our goodbye was quick—he tipped his hat and I went running to my front porch.

Tomorrow, I will visit Mr. Larsen—my kindly neighbor who took in my livestock. I hate to admit, but I am looking forward to seeing their itty, fleecy faces. All twenty-five of them. I also need to restock my flora and fauna; June and July completely cleaned out my medicinal supplies. And I will take a closer look at the grounds; something isn't right, I can feel it.

Tomorrow, tomorrow. My life will begin again tomorrow; life away from the gossip of town and with an attempt to forget the events of the first few days of July. I am looking forward to a normal, quiet life. These entries may become fewer.

I hope my days will not be worth recording for a very long time.

—A

July 11ᵗʰ, 1863

I'm surprised to be writing so soon, but my day was filled with many unexpected events.

I was up with the sun—filled with energy and a need to be productive. I threw open the shutters and let fresh air bathe me. Sunshine painted the trees and grass in a warm yellow hue and I could've stood there all morning, watching the beauty of nature. But my long list of chores was beckoning, as was my need to retrieve my livestock from Mr. Larsen's.

I set to work and scrubbed down the entirety of my home's interior—the smell of mold nearly knocked me back last night. I would've stripped, cleaned, and scrubbed every inch of the house then, but I was far too exhausted. Opening the windows helped immensely. With the amount of rain in the area over the last month, there was surely a leak in the roof and water had collected inside the house. As I scrubbed the floor, I found that my hypothesis was correct; mold spores were growing close to the fireplace and I found the cause of the leak—sunlight was peeping in through the roof over that exact spot. Hopefully, I have a few shingles in the barn to repair the damage.

I stepped outside and headed straight to the barn. But my pace slowed when I saw that the barn doors were open. I'd shut the doors before I left—I never, under any circumstances, would've left them ajar. The wind probably blew the doors open, I thought as I cautiously approached. As my hand reached for the knotted rope handle, I heard a rustle from inside. I took a second to contain myself and then flung open the doors.

And my eyes thought my brain was stunted. For surely, I was seeing a ghost.

Inside the barn—pulling hay from the loft above her head—was Barley. My beloved horse stripped of me weeks before. I couldn't believe it—Barley was either dead or on her way south, ridden by a toothless soldier who also possessed Rosie's wedding band. But my eyes found the light patch of black fur beneath her right ear. I knew it was her.

I yelped, startling Barley with my voice. She started uneasily pacing, so I approached slowly and tried to calm her with soft whispers. Her ears twitched in recognition and took a few cautious steps towards me, allowing me to touch her. With her silky fur beneath my fingers and my face nuzzled in her neck, she settled, and I smiled.

She was real. My friend and companion, once again. You may think I am silly for the affection I hold towards Barley, but no one can truly understand the loneliness I have felt in these woods. Barley became a constant for me. I didn't care how she got here. Having her home was all I needed. She was still saddled, though the leather was badly torn and stained with blood—perhaps the toothless man met his demise? I looked through the saddle bags and found nothing inside—stripped of valuables, most likely. I reached beneath her belly, undid the buckles, and pulled the saddle from her back. She snorted in approval. Though thin, she looked to be in good spirits and healthy. I looked over her legs and hooves — they desperately needed to be cleaned — and her hind had a few superficial scrapes.

"We've been down separate paths the last few weeks, old girl. But I'm glad we arrived back on the same one," I told her. She bucked her head lightly into my shoulder. I patted her and grabbed a rake to pull down more hay. She indulged immediately, and I watched her with a happy heart. I left the barndoors open wide, knowing she'd want to graze outside. It'd be easier for me to herd the sheep and Gertie with her help, but I didn't want to push Barley too soon.

I arrived at Mr. Larsen's before noon — like planned. But I found much of his land out of place. The house was still standing, but only just: every window was broken, with the shutters hanging from their hinges; the wooden wall planks were chipped, inundated with bullet holes; the grass was torn up, with wagon tracks leading onto and away from the property; limbs from trees were strewn everywhere and the bowers overhead were thinned and appeared to be badly damaged. I stood back in awe, unsure if it was safe to move any closer. It looked like a war —

Then I realized it had.

The Larsen farm was within a mile of Little Hill. And both armies trampled over these grounds — either to get in position or retreat. I hadn't looked close enough, but my own property would probably show similar signs of the battle. I was further away but the battle left nothing unscathed.

As I stood frozen in the front yard, a horse-drawn wagon pulled onto the dirt path behind me—a wagon manned by Mr. Larsen, with his son, Henry, my hired shepherd sitting beside him. I waved them down, and after a few seconds of strained eye-sight Mr. Larsen did the same. He climbed down from his perch, looking forlorn and utterly exhausted.

"I was a wonderin' when you'd turn up. You doin' alright?" he asked, pulling me into a warm hug. Hugs or affection were foreign to me—besides with Rosie and Mam—but he was a kind man.

"Yes, of course. And you? The house seems—"

"Gone to hell? Yeah, yeah. Spent the better part of two days in my root cellar with my wife and children screamin'. Then we come up to all this. Not that I'm complainin', I know some are worst off. You stayed in town then? Safer in town."

"Yes, yes. Safer." My proximity to the battle would bring questions, questions that I didn't want to answer. I stayed silent and hoped the subject would change.

"Well, we'll make do. Can't say I agree with the army up and leavin' us with the clean-up. Particularly the dead." He pointed back to his wagon, "Don't know where we'll be putting this lot."

I leaned to the left, towards the wagon's flat bed. And I caught a glimpse of what I assumed was a leg hanging off the side.

"I went into town to ask the council about the removal and funeral arrangements for the fallen. I wanted to make sure all our boys found their way home. But I was told I had to deal with it on my own. That anything on my land or within forty yards was my responsibility."

"I've heard this," I told him. The people of Gettysburg didn't ask the Northern and Southern armies to converge in their town, so why should they clean-up after them? But I knew firsthand that the dead were simply too many and fields were still littered with unclaimed bodies. The battle was over, but the war was far from it.

"Henry found another five this mornin'. Don't know where we'll put them but I spect I'll find a spot back behind the house," he said, pointing to the empty parcel of land behind his home.

"I'll help you."

"No, no I couldn't let you do that now. I've got Henry to help, and it's not something you should see."

I smiled and patted him gently on the shoulder. "I've seen far worse, Mr. Larsen. You taking-in my livestock was a great kindness. Let me assist you."

He shrugged his shoulders and relented. We walked back to the wagon, where I greeted Henry, and thanked him for caring for my animals. Then the smell hit me before I saw the bodies. It was noxious, and I covered my nose to suppress the urge to gag. It was a smell I hoped I'd never come across again. "Found these by the creek 'round back. Looks like they were shot but stumbled towards the creek for water," Henry explained, throwing back the burlap cover to reveal the bodies beneath.

They were certainly waterlogged and all five had clear gunshot wounds to the neck, head, and chest. Their skin was gray, and I imagined slippery to the touch. Their lips were blue and eyes still open, staring at their own mortality. And their clothes were—

"They're Confederates." I pointed at the gray hue of their uniforms.

"Yeah, the damn bastards," Mr. Larsen said, climbing back into the wagon. "Buryin' them is more than they deserve. I'd rather a noose around their neck than six feet of dirt on their blasted corpses. I'd a done it too, if I found 'em alive on my land."

I didn't agree—all men deserve the dignity of burial, no matter the side—but I nodded. My opinion wasn't a popular one and Mr. Larsen obviously didn't agree. Henry covered the bodies and Mr. Larsen flicked his whip, urging his horse off the path and towards the back of the house. I followed the wagon on foot, and in silence. We spent the next two hours digging a ditch big enough for five bodies. It was slow going as the ground was rocky and hard to break through. But eventually we made headway and fit all five soldiers into a mass grave.

Mr. Larsen scattered a thin layer of dirt onto the bodies and then—to my horror—he hocked up and spat onto the shallow grave. "Good riddance," he said before turning for home, whistling a song with his son trailing a few feet behind him.

I was shocked. It was wrong, so wrong to treat death with such little regard. I turned to the grave and whispered a short prayer. I asked God to see them safe to the beyond and forgiveness for their souls.

Mr. Larsen helped herd my sheep and Gertie back to my property. All twenty-five sheep were accounted for and Gertie looked well fed. I thanked him and offered two lambs—born that spring—as repayment for his generosity. After I insisted, he agreed. He asked me to be more neighborly in the future, and I laughed a nervous response; the image of him spitting upon the grave still fresh in my mind.

With the sheep—five rams, nine ewes and nine lambs— safely in their paddock, Gertie munching hay in her stall in the barn, and Barley grazing in the field, I finally returned to the house and to you—to record it all and put away the day.

I truly hope this day will be the last that I am reminded of the battle.

—A

July 13th, 1863

It is midday and I just sat down for a short break.

Once again, I was up with the sun. The house was in order—except the shingles I still need to replace—but today I needed to make sure my property had withstood the battle.

I stepped off my porch and it felt like my skin was glowing.

When I entered the barn, Gertie seemed restless. Normally, she didn't care for being milked first thing in the morning.

She'd linger in the back of the barn or step away from the milk stool every time I'd set it up beneath her. She was stubborn. But this morning when I opened the door to her stall, she stepped right up to the milk stool. I laughed and patted down her back, then sat beneath her with a pail and started to milk. A forty-five-minute process was knocked down to twenty. When I was through, I shooed her out of the barn and into the paddock; she needed some sun and I wanted to bring fresh hay down from the loft and muck out the stalls.

After, I got down on my knees and tended my garden. Many of my herbs survived the intense weather of the last few weeks — the lavender, mint, chamomile, rosemary were thriving. Miraculously, my land seemed undisturbed by the battle, as had the vegetables I'd planted a month before I left — the onion, garlic, carrots and turnips were rooted firm and flowering. But the water drainage seemed to be blocked; from the creek at the edge of my property, I had dug a trough to feed water into my garden. The small gully — that collected the creek's water — was dusty and dry; water probably hadn't flowed there in over a week. Once I put down my pen, I will walk up the trail and find the blockage. And while I'm at it, forage for roots, flowers and leaves — my stores of poppy heads, black haw, red oak bark, elder berries, and calamus root were completely depleted. The woods around my home were normally abundant with them, I only hope the woods hadn't been picked clean by wandering soldiers.

After gardening, I walked behind the barn and whistled shrilly. Our land is fenced, which allows Barley to roam freely. I waited for a few minutes and then Barley appeared. She trotted towards me and bent her head, asking for a rub behind her ears.

"Happy to be home, girl?" I asked and obliged her request. She snorted in agreement and I went on scratching. I will take her with me when I forage — I'd like the company.

The sun is shining through my front windows, bringing with it a warmth and coziness that makes me want to retreat to my rocking chair with one of my books. If I wait much longer, I will do just that and waste the day.

July 13th cont'd

I found what blocked my garden trough. And brought him home with me.

Almost four hours ago, I headed into the woods. The sun was still high — the time was close to two — and the July heat was persistent as ever. I unclasped the top few buttons of my blouse for some ventilation beneath my clothes, and the shade from the trees thankfully brought some relief. I guided Barley down a familiar trail behind the house with wicker basket in hand. We walked for some time; Barley nodding her head up and down with each step, as I searched for foliage. Barley seemed pleased to be led by me once again, and that my affection hadn't waned in our time apart.

Within a few yards, I tied Barley's lead off on a switch and stepped from the path. I stripped pieces of bark from a red oak — useful for the treatment of coughs. Then my ears perked to the sound of buzzing. Guided by my sense, I walked some distance before I looked up to find a large beehive hanging from a low-lying tree branch. Besides sweetening tea and atop slices of freshly baked bread, honey has many medicinal uses—particularly in the treatment of sore throats and tonsillitis if gargled with sage. This was quite a find, but one I had not anticipated.

Smoking out the bees would leave the hive intact and the bees would remain unharmed. But I hadn't the tools—a ladder, moss, and tinder—to complete the task this way. Knocking the hive out of the tree was against my morals, but I wanted that honey and was willing to suffer a few stings to get it. On the ground, I found a thick branch that was taller than me and would easily reach the hive. I picked it up and did a few practice swings before feeling confident enough to take aim. If I hit the hive and it didn't fall, I'd have a hoard of angry honeybees to deal with. I stood a few paces back from the tree and steadied my breathing, while firmly gripping the branch between my hands. Then I swung with all my strength. One swing and the hive broke off. I didn't wait to see it drop; I ran as fast I could back to the trail and Barley — who was calm, munching on grass and blissfully unaware of the angry bees. I was out of harm's way, but I heard the roar of angry buzzing behind me. One sting would send Barley into hysteria and she'd bolt immediately. So, I quickly guided Barley further up the trail, just in case the hive started massing. I'd return for the honey on my way home, by which time the bees would be gone and I could safely cut the combs.

The tree bower overhead became thicker. The air was soft and sweet. I loosely held onto Barley's reins and allowed her to stop and go as she pleased. Sparrows and starlings flitted among the tree branches and soon my basket was overflowing with plants and roots. I felt content—no longer burdened by the stress of foraging—and longed to lie on a cool patch of grass and allow the sounds of the forest lull me to sleep. A short nap would be wonderful, I thought. After clearing the debris from the creek, I'd allow myself a short break before returning home.

If only it had been that easy.

My ears perked to the slight trickle of water on stone and I knew the creek's birth was just up ahead. As did Barley. She was thirsty and started to impatiently nudge me forward. "Oh, you're thirsty? Okay, okay girl." I took her lead and quickened my step. We veered to the left of the path. The ground beneath my feet was covered in green and purple clover. I removed my shoes and stretched my toes, wanting to feel the velvety forest floor on my skin. The trees and bushes started to thin, then we stepped into the glen that the creek ran through.

And at the creek's head water, I saw it.

A body. Sprawled between the two banks, head partially submerged, legs flayed and shoeless. He was in a military uniform. A navy-blue uniform.

Barley's lead dropped from my hand and I lunged forward. I didn't think, I splashed through the water and rocky terrain—the water was usually a foot deep but now deeper because of the obstruction—and reached him in two bounds. I knelt in the water; my hands were shaking as I pulled his collar away from his neck. I pressed down into his skin and was surprised to find warmth. And a slow pulse.

"Good gracious," I whispered.

I touched his shoulder and a small moan escaped his lips. Possibly a dislocation, I thought as I adjusted the weight off his injured arm—that was tangled in the strap of a leather bag slung across his body. I'd need a full, unobstructed view of his shoulder joint to assess the damage, but freeing his arm was impossible without lifting his upper torso from the water.

But his shoulder was the least of my worries. I needed to know—was it Joseph?

His regiment was here during the battle and we are within a mile of our home; Joseph may have been trying to reach me. It's been almost three years, but a sense of safety will always be found within the walls of one's home. The voices screaming at night during the battle taught me that much. Gently, I rolled him onto his back. Loose pieces of long hair hung over his face. I hesitated, curling my fingers back within inches of his face. Did I want it to be him? I wasn't sure, so I held my breath and brushed the strands from his face.

I barely knew my husband—I'd been in his presence for less than a day—but the man in the creek was not him. His hair was a dark brown and his hairline was pointed in a widow's peak. Freckles specked his sharp and distinct nose, and his lips were full. I sat looking at him—imagining what color his eyes were and what his voice sounded like.

I leaned in closer and brushed another wisp of hair from his brow. Very suddenly, my hand was grabbed, and the man's eyes shot open. I screamed, pushed away from him and fell back into the creek with a loud splash. Engrossing fear took me, and his dangerous eyes held me as tight as the grip of his hand.

They were deep and brown—darker than I'd ever seen. And wide with a look of crazed confusion. Panic swept his face and he tried desperately to see beyond me and speak.

I had to say something. "Sir, I—"

His grip on my hand slackened and his eyes lolled to the back of his head; he was unconscious once again. I touched his hand and forehead; both were on fire. Whoever he was, I had a matter of hours before fever took him from this world. I needed to get him back to the house where I could care for him properly.

But getting him home wouldn't be an easy task.

He was at least six feet tall and though he was lean, I estimated his weight at close to two hundred pounds—which was much more than I could handle. I squatted by his head and attempted to lift his torso. With all my strength, I was able to sit him upright. But he was dead weight and quickly slipped from my grasp, sending me onto my bottom with his head in my lap. I sat, out of breath and thinking of my next move. Since he was incapable of walking, the only way to get him home was atop my horse. But how would I lift him onto Barley?

Should I fetch Mr. Larsen? No, it would take too long to get there and back. And I couldn't leave him.

I was stuck; as was the wounded man.

Then as I looked out on the forest undergrowth, resourceful inspiration hit me for a second time.

Using two long tree branches, Barley's saddle blanket, twine made of tree bark, and a bit of rope I managed to make a stretcher. I looped the ends of the rope around Barley's pummel and tied them off to the ends of the tree branches; if the stretcher held, Barley would drag the wounded soldier back to my cabin with very little effort. I guided her into the creek and beside the unconscious man, so that the side of the stretcher was touching his arm. I whispered a few words of encouragement to Barley and prayed she'd remain still. With all my strength, I pushed, and the man's body rolled onto the stretcher.

I had to stop myself from clapping; I was that shocked that it worked. With the bark twine, I tied him down to the stretcher to assure he wouldn't roll and checked the blanket beneath him; the cloth was strong enough to hold his weight and the bark twine was looped tight enough around the poles and through the blanket to support him. Mercifully, Barley hadn't moved. I stepped up into the stirrups, and then whispered to Barley, "Slow going, girl." My foot nudged her side and she stepped out of the creek. I took the reins firmly in hand and watched the stretcher drag behind. I held my breath with those first few steps, praying that the stretcher held.

And thankfully, my prayers were answered.

We arrived home within the hour, without the honey — I couldn't risk stopping — but with the unconscious soldier.

I guided Barley right up to the front porch, untied the stretcher from the saddle pommel, and unbridled her. She immediately took off like a speeding train, relieved to be rid of me and my cargo.

"Thank you," I coughed, choking on her dust.

I turned back to the stretcher. The prospect of a strange man in my house alarmed me, as it should. He was unconscious and immobile, but not dead. He could easily kill me in my sleep, but I couldn't leave him outside; the night chill would only worsen his condition. So, I rolled up my sleeves and braced myself to drag the stretcher into the house. I was able to haul him up the two porch steps—without him falling off—and then pulled him inside the house.

With the door closed behind us, I immediately examined him: I stripped him of his wool shirt, breeches, leaving him only in his long-johns. I removed the leather bag slung across his body and saw his shoulder was twisted at a weird angle, and dislocated. Across his abdomen was a large gash, likely the result of a Confederate saber. His face was bruised a deep purple, and there was a rather nasty cut on the side of his head. He was not bleeding, and all the cuts had scabbed, but the gash on his abdomen was deep and looked infected. There was a pungent smell of feces coming from below his torso region and from my time spent on the battlefield, I assumed he was suffering from diarrhea. The combination of the heat and the looseness of his bowels should've caused severe dehydration and killed him; he was lucky to have fallen into the creek. I pulled the long-johns from his legs, leaving him completely naked—which didn't shock or embarrass me. I'd seen many naked, injured men.

I propped his head with a pillow from my own bed and bundled him in quilts and blankets. I put the kettle to boil and then pulled out every vial from my personal store of medicines. Quinine would've abated the diarrhea and fever, but I hadn't any, so whortleberry leaves and boneset would have to do. In my mortar, I crushed the leaves into a paste, putting this and hot water into a mug before returning to his side. With his head in my lap, I propped his mouth open wide. Slowly, I dripped the tea down his throat. He had no problem swallowing, which was a relief but the next hour would be difficult; the concoction caused vomiting, which I needed to be attentive to. I needed to get everything out of his gut that could be causing the fever, while keeping him hydrated. I knew I had a little over an hour before he would start to retch, so I quickly set to cleaning his wounds.

From my basket of forest foraging, I grabbed a piece of red oak bark, a garlic clove and added these to warm water to soften. I retrieved my reserve bottle of whiskey—for medicinal purposes, naturally—from a shelf above my wash basin. Honey was also a useful antiseptic, and in that moment, I regretted leaving it behind. I contemplated going back for it but knew I hadn't the time. With cotton cloth, I wiped dirt and debris from the wounds on his head and abdomen then I poured a small amount of whiskey directly into his wounds. His body immediately lurched off the stretcher and he screamed—as expected. Though unconscious, he could still feel pain. I repeated this four times before I felt secure enough to wrap the bark poultice around his head and abdomen wounds.

Now, the stretcher sits before my fireplace, the soldier is lying on his uninjured side—as I wait for the vomiting to begin. I have built a small fire in the hearth—his body is shivering from the fever. His shoulder still needs to be set, but it will have to wait for tomorrow; the infection, fever, and the diarrhea are my top concern. Once they are appeased, I will readjust his shoulder into its socket.

Now, my head pounds with the implications of bringing this man back to my home. My empathy got the best of me when I found him in the creek, but what now? What will I do once he wakes? His recovery could take some time and the army has left Gettysburg. And as my pen pauses on the page, it has dawned on me; what if he deserted his post? What if he was fleeing in an act of cowardice when he succumbed to his wounds? I've heard the stories of what happens to men who run from battle—prison, if he is handed over to the proper officials, or an immediate lynching. I haven't heard of lynchings in these parts—I'd read reports in the Philadelphia's papers about incidents in the rural counties further south—but a lot has changed since July 1st. I've also heard of the repercussions for those hiding runaways; they, themselves, were treated just as harshly.

I shudder now at the thought.

I hope this man simply wandered from the battle and my nursing him back to health will not cost me my life or freedom. Once he recovers, he will walk from my house on his own accord, I will return to my quiet life, and this will become a distant part of my past. But…what if he dies in my care? What if I cannot contain his sickness and I become ill?

I must stop writing. I have an arduous night ahead of me and I must be vigilant for any changes in his condition. I pray I made the right choice in bringing him here.

– A

July 14th, 1863

It is midday and my eyelids are puffy and burning. Closing them for a few minutes of relief is all I want. But I dare not; I fear if I sleep, I will wake to a dead man on my floor.

As I abandoned my pen last night, he started to convulse and retch, and I had to rush to his side to hold a bucket to his face. He spewed up bile—there was nothing of substance left in his belly. The retching came every twenty minutes and lasted for about twenty-five minutes. Then he'd slump back onto the stretcher, exhausted and sweating. I allowed him to rest for a few minutes before lifting his head, forcing him to drink water. His fever went up and down—he'd sweat through his cold shakes, then it would spike right back up within the hour. I persisted with the whortleberry and boneset but added some butterfly root hoping it would keep his fever down for longer periods.

I have tried to keep him on his side, still fearing he will vomit in his sleep and choke. But the fever has caused him to thrash. His nightmares are horrific — he screams to the high heavens and reaches out, almost attempting to stand with his eyes closed tight. I've seen it among other soldiers; he was reliving the battle. His words were incoherent — they were the babblings of someone who cannot escape the madness of his own mind.

His bowel movements have intensified. I fear he has dysentery, as his stools have been bloody and mucus-filled. Diarrhea only worsens dehydration and in his current condition, he will not last from much more water deprivation. I have tried to be persistent, keep him full of fluids, and — as I removed and burned his undergarments — wrapped his bottom in thick, linen cloth. Typhoid fever was rampant in the army camps because of the poor drinking water and many cases were too far gone for anything to be done. If his fever stays down today, I can rule out typhoid. I am being overly cautious and thoroughly scrubbing my hands with lye soap and disposing of all dirty water that meets his body — to avoid the spread of the contagion.

During all of this, he's had moments of consciousness. In the early hours of this morning, I was carefully reapplying his head bandage when his eyes popped open. I was inches from his face and fright stole the breath from my lungs. He looked as if he wanted to speak; I could see his chest draw in and his throat quivered with the words forming. But his eyes fluttered shut once again and his head slumped to the side.

In writing to you, I have taken a few minutes to sit down and escape the monotony of his care. I hope today has been the worst of his sickness—I believe it is, but I still question my diagnosis, and if I am providing adequate care. I've only left the house to milk Gertie, but I cannot neglect my other animals and eventually I will need more whortleberry and boneset.

I hope tomorrow will be easier on his poor, broken body. God, please let him live.

—A

July 16ᵗʰ, 1863

Three days have passed since I found the soldier and he has finally turned a corner.

Within the last twelve hours, his fever dropped, and his bowels have settled. The wounds to his head have scabbed. The laceration to his abdomen was deeper by far and was grossly infected, but the red oak bark has worked wonders and the skin around the wound has turned red and puffy—the signs of health returning.

The sickness coursing through his body has taken every ounce of his energy, so still he sleeps. I have managed to feed him some vegetable broth, hoping to build his strength. Thankfully he hasn't vomited this day, so I no longer fear him choking in his sleep. I was able to leave the house for an hour this morning to see to all the animals. After milking Gertie, I grabbed a few empty oat burlap sacks and filled them with fresh hay. I carried them back to the house and slipped them beneath his stretcher, hoping to bring some comfort to his back.

Soon, I will set his shoulder; the joints have started to fuse incorrectly and once this is finished they cannot be manipulated without cutting into the joint and muscle. I've already waited too long, and it will be less painful if he remains unconscious. The sound of the joint popping back into place is rather alarming. The sight is worse.

I've also made a decision that may seem barbaric.

I've decided to strap the man down to the stretcher. Take some rope, tie his legs to the poles of the stretcher. Possibly another across his chest to tie him down. In his weakened state, he hasn't the stamina to cross the room and violate me. Honestly, I doubt he could stand without assistance. But I cannot be too careful, and this is the only way I will feel safe in my home.

Reading this passage back, I know I sound crazed. But I need sleep.

July 16th cont'd

I set the shoulder back into its joint. I am rather proud of the result, which is why I write now.

Standing with my feet on his torso, I took his hand in mine and I firmly pulled on his arm. With the right amount of traction and his arm at a ninety-degree angle, the head of the humerus should slide under the bone of the shoulder blade and back into its socket. I've done it many times — especially in the last month — but never on the floor of my home. After three maneuvers, I finally heard the pop of the shoulder joint and his arm hung in its proper place.

And the figure beneath me barely made a peep.

I rewrapped his arm in a sling, as the muscle will be sore for a few more days. Hopefully there isn't an internal tear or bleeding — that will require quite a bit more than a few arm maneuvers. I will know better in the morning based on the bruising around the joint.

I also managed to wash his clothes. They are outside now, drying on the clothesline. I accomplished much today, and I feel fulfilled.

— A

July 18th, 1863

Greasy pots from broth, hot water bottles, cutlery and glasses were piled on the kitchen table. The pile was staring — jeering at me from across the room — reminding me that there weren't any clean dishes left in the house. With my patient's health stabilizing, I couldn't neglect my household maintenance any longer. So, I stepped into the kitchen, grabbed the tin washtub and headed outside to the water pump. I filled the tub to the brim and brought it back inside and added soapy suds.

After a quarter of an hour of scrubbing, I tossed the dirtied water outside. I stood in the doorway for a few minutes to breathe in the fresh summer air. The day was hot. My house was nestled beneath the shade of many poplar trees, but I could feel the heat on my face. It'd be a nice day to go down to the stream and soak my feet. The daydream of wading through cool water lingered in my mind as I closed the door. I turned back to the interior of my one room home, shrieked, and dropped the water tub with a loud crash.

For the unconscious soldier was no longer unconscious. Head turned to the side, he was staring at me from the flat of his back. In the heights of his fever, his eyes were wide with mania, screaming from the fire that burned within him. But this wasn't a frenzied stare. His pupils weren't dilated; he was looking at me and not through me to the demons of his dreams.

Everything I had done over the last few days sped his recovery, so seeing him awake was a relief. But I was caught unawares. Even though he was tied to the stretcher, he was still a soldier trained to kill. I didn't know what to do, so I continued to stare into his deep brown eyes.

Then he blinked, turned his head away and let out a sigh.

I took a hesitant step further into the room. I picked the tin washtub off the floor and placed it on the kitchen table, keeping his form in eyesight. His chest rose up and down with deep breaths, and he started shifting his torso on the stretcher. His muscles had been dormant for so long, undoubtedly, he was checking to see if he could still move at all.

He realized he was tied down when he couldn't lift his legs.

I stepped closer. "Don't...don't move. You'll only re-open your stomach wound," I said, my voice sounding like a forced squeak.

He turned to me again. He was a mouse caught in a trap, vulnerable, and probably more scared of me than I was of him. I realized I had nothing to fear, but he did. I stood and waited for a sign—a sign that I could approach. His gaze stung, and I could tell he was reading me, as I had been reading him.

Then he blinked and with a slight nod, turned his head away, again.

My heart was beating fast, but I strode across the room and knelt by his side. From the corner of my eye, I could see beneath my bed—to my shotgun. If things went horribly wrong, it was within reach. Avoiding eye contact, I loosened the knot across his chest and the rope released. The soldier pulled his uninjured arm up to his chest.

"You'll understand my precautions." I released the rope binding his legs and he flexed his legs at the knee, grimacing as he did. "Don't try anything drastic, sir. Your muscles may feel wobbly until we rebuild your strength."

He lowered his legs and looked to the arm sling. When he shifted the joint in his shoulder, his eyes went wide, and he wailed. I rested my hand gently on his shoulder. "Your arm will be sore for a while yet, I've had to reset your shoulder blade. It'd be best to not move it from the sling. Or at all."

Then his nakedness became apparent—and I felt very different about seeing and being so close to his body. I averted my eyes and shifted the blanket balled by his feet over his form and stood. I retreated to the fireplace and took the tea kettle from the small burning fire in the hearth and placed it on the kitchen table. From my medical kit, I took a few poppy heads and crushed them into the bottom of a mug. I poured hot water from the kettle into the mug, let it seep and cool for a few minutes, and then returned to my patient.

I knelt and lifted his head ever so much. "This will help with the pain," I said. The mug touched his lips and I tipped the liquid into his mouth, and we made eye contact once more. But this time it was different. His eyes were soft, full of gratitude. The warm liquid hit the back of his throat and he closed his eyes. The poppy would take a quarter of an hour to take full effect, but the first few sips brought a tingling sensation. I laid his head back down, grabbing additional pillows from my bed to prop up his back and head.

"Is that better?" I asked, as I fluffed the pillow.

He nodded.

I moved to his side and placed two fingers by his throat, making him flinch. I counted the beats of his heart; his pulse was normal. He winced when I straightened his sling and then checked the poultice on his abdomen.

Suddenly I felt a bit out of place, like I was the naked one. I sat back on my knees and looked down at my hands. "I...I found you in my creek bed. Not far from here. Five days ago. Do you...do you remember anything?"

I expected a prompt reply. He stared back, silently. His throat shook, and his mouth cracked open, only then to tightly shut. His brow furrowed, and his eyes looked over my head. Almost like he thought better of responding or knew he couldn't.

"No?" I asked.

He nodded in agreement.

"But you were at the battle?"

He nodded aggressively and then turned his head, as if the acknowledgement dug up a memory he wished he'd forgotten. Traumatic events along with injury can affect normal bodily functions, memory, and the healing process. Which made me wonder. "Can you...can you not speak, sir?"

He gave me a long, hard look. The whites of his eyes widened and then he slowly nodded.

Compassion replaced my lingering fear. His pain went beyond the physical. His eyes started to flutter with heaviness; the poppy was taking effect.

I patted his shoulder and stood. "Rest now. You're safe." His eyelids immediately dropped; my words gave him permission to relax.

It has been several hours, and the soldier still sleeps. I am relieved he woke and was able to communicate—in the way that he could. I see no bruising around his neck, so I don't believe his throat or vocal cords have been injured. But I cannot be sure and have been reading up on the anatomy of the throat.

I am keeping dark thoughts at bay—thoughts of safety, tomorrow, and implications of the soldier's wakefulness. Tonight, I am glad that I nursed a poor young soul back to health. I will sleep easy this night.

Easy, with my shotgun close beside me and the soldier tied again to the stretcher.

– A

July 20ᵗʰ, 1863

The last two days have seen vast improvements. He has been awake for longer; he's been able to eat more broth and even a bit of buttermilk with every meal; his temperature peaks at night, which is normal and easily combated with butterfly root; the wound on his abdomen still needs time to heal but there is no trace of infection.

The issue of his speech is still a mystery to me.

Though I haven't the instruments or proper lighting to do an adequate internal evaluation, he allowed me to look down his throat and I couldn't see anything obstructing his airway or infection on his tonsils. I am starting to believe an emotional trauma is the reason for his silence. Many men were brought from the field, staring straight ahead with glazed eyes. They were in shock and unable to speak; the trauma of battle stole their voice. So, I will not force it— when he is ready, his speech will return.

Today, he sat up for the first time. And as the heat wasn't harsh, I helped him stand and move to the porch and into a deep-seated rocker. His legs were shaky, and he had to lean on me for support, but I got him outside without issue. The change of scenery did wonders for him and he leaned back into the chair with ease. Sunlight hit his face and a slight breeze rustled his hair, and all the cares he carried seemed to melt away.

"The heat has finally passed," I said as I sat down on the wooden porch steps.

He nodded, his eyes closed.

I looked forward and did the same. "The people of Gettysburg will never forget the heat of July in 1863."

Realizing the absurdity of my insensitive statement—of course he'd never forget July of '63 in Gettysburg!—my hands flew to my lips. Shyly, I looked over my shoulder; his shoulders were raised, and his face muscles tensed. Then, he cracked one eye open and his mouth turned up into a small smile.

I hoped his smile showed understanding of my slip of the tongue. I was grateful for his lack of voice and ashamed of my inability to think before I speak. Casual conversations are foreign to me, especially in my own home.

We sat outside for quite some time, he for longer than I, as I went to the backyard to work in the garden. When I returned, he was asleep with a stern look on his face. I had seen similar expressions cross his face during the height of his fever. Then, his face would screw up as if he was concentrating very hard, and his mouth would twitch. Then he'd start to thrash. This dream was different; the look on his face wasn't as troubling. I hadn't the heart to wake him. I stood there, staring at him, wondering what was replaying in his mind. With every day, I grow more and more intrigued.

I am glad of his company, and my voice has filled the four walls of my home in a way it never has; now, I am speaking for two.

As I write, he sleeps a few feet from my desk—still on the stretcher upon the floor. I watch his chest rise and fall, no longer scared about the prospect of his death during the night. Or my own vulnerability; I no longer fear for my safety and will not tie him down to the stretcher tonight.

Now, I am looking forward to the morning and the day to follow.

—A

July 21ˢᵗ, 1863

"I must go into town. To see some of my patients," I told the soldier.

I was gathering my medical kit and he was sitting at the kitchen table, carefully spooning grits—his first solid food—into his quivering mouth. His injured arm was still in a sling, but he was quickly becoming dexterous. He put down his spoon and listened as I spoke. His eyes glistened with worry, as this would be the first time I'd left his side.

"I won't be long. A few of my patients were in rough sorts after...after those first few days of July. And I need to look in on my sister."

He nodded his head in agreement. I shouldered my kit and he attempted to stand to walk me to the door.

"No, no," I said, motioning for him to return to his seat and meal. "I can make it safely to the door without your assistance. There are enough grits for another meal, and there is bread in the box. If you'd like to go outside for some air, please do. But be careful of your injuries and don't—" his eyes rolled in a playful annoyance. "Okay…I'm talking too much. I'll go and be back."

He nodded and settled back down at the table. I crossed the room and opened the front door. Pausing in the door-way, I watched him. His posture was straight in the chair, not hunched or pained with sickness. He slowly lifted the spoon and tipped its contents into his mouth. I imagined the buttery grits traveling down his throat and coating his stomach, and the contentment a full belly must bring to one who was starved for so long.

He sensed my lingering presence—and hadn't heard me shut the door—and he turned slowly to find me staring.

A small smile crossed his lips, and—with spoon still in hand—he waved at me. My heart fluttered.

"Yes, I'm going." I laughed. I stepped out onto the porch and closed the door.

Several hours later with the sun setting, I returned to an empty house. And I panicked.

In a one-room house, there are only so many places an injured man could be. I checked beneath my bed and inside the wardrobe—he wasn't in or under either. Visions of him scampering through the woods, injuring himself further, or crossing the path of someone who may question who he was made my mind race.

But how could he leave? How could he run off without a word—not that he could speak, but without making a gesture of thanks? No, no, he'd never do that.

My eyes drifted to the fireplace, to the makeshift stretcher that was still his bed, then to the leather bag still beneath his pillow. He wouldn't leave without it, would he? His only belongings were in that sack.

Then I heard Gertie call out. I looked out the window above my bed, to find the barn door open wide. Which was curious. I had shut it tight when I bridled Barley and walked her into the yard earlier that morning. I stood and walked from the house, towards the barn. Gertie called out again and again, mooing more fervently then I'd ever heard her before. My steps hastened and by the time I reached the barn, my anxiety was bursting. I stepped into the barn and found an unexpected sight.

Inside was the soldier; he was sitting with his back to me on a low stool, holding a bucket between his feet and milking Gertie with his one good hand. He hushed her calls, touching her fur gently and cooing.

I sighed. He turned suddenly, a look of fear mingled with surprise—the reaction of a man who doesn't like to be walked up on. Once recognition crossed his face, he awkwardly waved and then returned to his chore.

I felt like a complete fool to have panicked. Sheepishly, I left the barn and returned to the house, so he could finish without an audience.

I sit now at my desk, still feeling bashful. I can see him from the window; he is walking back and forth in the yard, trying to strengthen his legs and stamina. His pace is slow, and every step tests his limits but every day he is a little more independent.

Before I forget—I learned something unpleasant in town today.

I visited each of my patients and my two expectant mothers. No further complaints, no surprises or new fatigues. I am also happy to report that Mr. Buehler—the postmaster who fled town when the Rebels arrived—has returned. He practically tackled me in the street as I guided Barley on foot past the Post.

"I can't thank you enough for checking on Fannie!" he exclaimed. "I had half a mind to turn back and surrender myself to the enemy. But I knew she would fare well under your watch."

"Surely, Mr. Buehler, I really did nothing but look in on her after the battle." He was grossly exaggerating my involvement with his family, to the point that I felt guilty for not having done more.

"You did much more for my peace of mind. Thank you." He shook my hand vigorously. "I must repay you. I will hand deliver your mail. It will save you a trip to town."

"Mr. Buehler, really that isn't necessary. I—"

"I insist." He shook my hand again, inviting me for supper in a few weeks.

We'd never had a great affinity towards each other—in fact, I'm sure there was a mutual distaste. But the battle brought neighbors closer and gratitude was abundant.

Then I quickly visited Rosie. And she sensed my urgency.

"You are making the floorboards shake, sister. Is something the matter?" Rosie reentered the parlor and placed the tea tray on the small table before me. She sat in the plush armchair on the other side of the table and served the tea.

"Oh, it has been a long day and I am anxious to get home," I replied, consciously trying to steady my shaking leg, but also staring over Rosie's head at the grandfather clock in the foyer.

"I won't keep you long," she said with a smile. She chatted on for close to twenty minutes about the latest achievements of sweet Mary—who was down for a nap in the nursery—then continued with news of the continued recovery in town. I was happier to hear news of the baby; gossip has never interested me, and I didn't need to hear anything further about the battle. I listened, waiting patiently for the conversation to dry so I could take my leave.

" —and you know Mother will be here within a fortnight."

Rosie's words made the tea in my mouth bitter. I put my cup down—no longer thirsty. "I didn't know."

"I had a letter from her this morning—Mr. Buehler has returned. It was postmarked from a week ago, but she wrote to let me know she was able to secure train tickets for the first week in August."

"Oh." To hide my grimace, I retrieved my teacup and pretended to sip.

"You know she probably hasn't the faintest that Mary was born so early. I sent a short reply, telling her of Mary and how very elated I am to see her. Maybe you could make sure you're in town that week. Maybe a supper? With the whole family."

"Maybe." I lowered my cup, and we made eye contact. She cocked her head, and her eyes pleaded with me to at least give the notion of a meal with Mother a chance. I rolled my eyes and nodded. She smiled sweetly, bouncing her shoulders as she did, knowing she won.

Then I excused myself, with no further objections from Rosie. We embraced, I left my regards for Jonathan — who, thankfully, wasn't home for my short visit — and stepped from their doorway.

My temper was boiling before Barley turned from Rosie's street. Mother hasn't crossed my mind since the battle and Mary's birth — with the letter that remains in my possession, still un-mailed. Rosie has taken that burden from me — none the wiser — and announced the birth herself. And now she was coming for a visit, under the guise of concern for her grandchild. In truth, curiosity booked her rail ticket; she wants a dramatic, Gettysburg story to tell her social circle. I felt such anger that I rode right by the Lists — which I had intended on stopping at. I was anxious to read the death notices, which were building daily, as more men were being found and identified. Joseph's whereabouts and fate were still a mystery to me, and my heart was troubled. The soldier's care has clouded my concern for my husband, which should not be. I will write to him once I finish this entry; I will write to the last place I heard from him, in hopes that the army will forward it on to wherever his regiment is stationed.

Then my guilt and anger were replaced by panic when I arrived home to an empty house.

But now I am happy to be sitting at my desk, finishing this entry and watching the soldier lead Barley slowly into the barn, to remove her saddle and bridle.

Until next time.

– A

July 24th, 1863

The day has been rainy.

Gushing raindrops have poured from the sky, off the roof, and pooled on the lawn; now unblocked, the garden trough has overflowed and flooded the garden. The sheep are huddled beneath a large oak at the corner of their paddock, hoping for protection from the soaking rain. Gertie is safely stabled, but my clothes are soaked from running out to the barn and milking her. Only Barley seems to be enjoying the downpour—I can hear her whinnies and the wet plop of her hooves on the ground as she gallops around the property.

I now have proof of the leak in my roof. A pot sits below the rotted shingles, filling every few hours. The drip-drip-drip of the water hitting the metal pot has almost a melodic quality — and for hours, it has been the only sound that fills the walls.

Summer rains are sweet and refreshing, but not on days when you'd rather be outside. Except for my short excursion to the barn, we've been stuck peering out the window like poor children; disappointed at the waste of a day knowing of the fun to be had outdoors. Boredom seeped in soon after breakfast and it seemed like the day would be long and uneventful.

I was cleaning dishes in the washtub, when I found the soldier lingering at the side of my bed. The sight of which made me initially uneasy — my heart was beating fast as his hand touched my pillow — until he turned back to me and gestured inquisitively to my book shelf.

My heart slowed, and I smiled. "Not as many as I'd like, but my collection is growing."

I dropped the plate I was washing in the tub, dried my hands, and stepped to his side. "They are mostly medical texts, of course. But I have a novel or two in amongst them. Would you...would you like to read one?"

He nodded eagerly.

I kneeled on the edge of my bed and from the shelf I pulled my copy of *David Copperfield* — a very expensive birthday gift from Rosie. "My sister told me it is quite good. Reading is not considered a noble art. Especially for women. My mother, she...she didn't...well, she doesn't approve of much I do, really."

He raised his hand and nodded; he understood, and I needn't speak further. He took the book from my hand and his fingers lightly brushed my own. Skin to skin for just an instant but I could feel blood rushing to my face. He turned from me and took to the rocking chair in front of the fire, where he has been for the last few hours. We have passed much of the day in a comfortable silence, both reading.

My interest in this man has piqued. I've had to stop myself from staring at him longer than I should. He has caught me twice. The first, I quickly looked away. But the second time, I held his gaze. He stared back, challenging me. It became a game of wits and our mutual stubbornness prevailed. When it felt like we would remain locked in a stare for the entirety of the day, he crossed his eyes and stuck out his tongue. I snorted, and my hand flew to my mouth in embarrassment. "Okay, you win," I said through my fingers. His chest vibrated with a laugh and my face flushed once again.

I look at him now, *David Copperfield* abandoned in his lap as he naps soundly. His face is peaceful. I've grown accustomed to his presence. Admitting it now, on your pages, makes it so. And that scares me.

I try not to think of the day he will leave. I know that day is fast approaching.

August 5ᵗʰ, 1863

Mother has arrived.

Around noon, I heard a horse and wagon driving up my path. Rosie had sent Jonathan—with their new horse—to bring me to supper. Rosie rarely takes no for an answer and I couldn't say no if Jonathan stood on my doorstep, ready to drive me back to town. When I peeked from my windows and saw his wagon, I forcibly pushed the soldier out the backdoor.

"It's my brother-in-law. He can't see you. He—" the soldier raised his hands and nodded. He pointed to the barn and walked towards it. I exhaled my held breath and turned back inside the house.

Jonathan's fist was poised to knock when I flung open the front door.

"Oh, there you are," he said, lowering his hand. "Rosie sent me to fetch you. But...you're not dressed." He looked at my dirtied skirt and blouse.

"I wasn't expecting you, Jonathan."

"Yes, well you'll need to change but do so with haste. I have an appointment at two and can't be late." He turned on his heel and walked back to his wagon to wait. I rolled my eyes and closed the door.

Ten minutes later, I emerged from the house. But I wasn't joining Jonathan in his wagon.

"I'll ride Barley to town. Then you won't need to bring me back tonight." I quick stepped to the barn, not waiting for his response — or questions about how Barley was back in my possession.

The soldier was in Barley's stall brushing her down with a brown brush when I walked in. His arm sling was draped over the stall door and he was testing his injured arm: stroking her up and down, cautiously flexing his bicep; his face grimaced, feeling the pain of the strain in his unused muscle. Sweat was pouring from his brow and his shirt was soaked but I knew he was glad to be of use. As I approached, he stopped and leaned against one of the beams in the stall.

"I need to visit my sister. And my mother. I will be back after dark."

He nodded and wiped his brow on the sleeve of his shirt.

"Will you be okay without me?"

He shook his head no, but his smile said otherwise. He retrieved Barley's bridle and slipped the bit into her mouth, then buckled the noseband.

"Alright, I know you'll survive for a few hours. Just don't leave the property?"

He dramatically nodded in agreement. He turned and opened Barley's stall, guiding her past me and to the front of the barn. He grabbed her saddle and slung it over her back, buckling the bottom straps and adjusting the stirrups. Then he turned and offered his hand — his freckled, long-fingered hand. I took it and climbed up into the saddle.

"Don't come out of the barn until I'm gone."

He slapped Barley's behind and she jolted forward, into the yard. I didn't look back, but I knew the soldier was watching me from the shadows of the barn doors.

After a hurried journey, Jonathan guided his horse to the back of their house. He helped me down from Barley and took both horses to his stable. I crossed the gravel yard, straightening my skirts as I stepped up into Rosie's kitchen.

And before my feet were comfortably on the hardwood floor, my ears were assaulted with Mother's voice.

"No, no... I don't need to hold her, dear. I can see her perfectly well from here," I heard her say. I stood in Rosie's kitchen and imagined Mother physically recoiling as Rosie tried to hand her the child. Mother hasn't suddenly become affectionate just because of a baby.

Behind me, the kitchen door slammed. "We're back dearest," Jonathan called as he removed his riding gloves and hat. He marched past me and into the foyer. "I'm just grabbing my notes, sweetling. I'll be back for supper at four? Yes, she's in the kitchen," he said pointing over his shoulder to me. I walked into the parlor; my head was high, but my soul was cowering in the corner.

"Oh, sister. I'm so glad you could join us." Rosie stood and kissed my cheek.

"I hadn't much of a choice." I took Mary from her arms. I wanted to kiss every inch of her and probably would've if my attention wasn't pulled away.

"Don't spoil her now, you silly girl," Mother said. "Children must earn affection, or they'll come to expect it."

My body stiffened, but I turned to face her. Mother was dressed in extravagant silk and her jewelry glittered with the summer sun. The Confederate occupation aside, Rosie's household was impeccably decorated, and Mother looked out of place. But she always did; she held herself beyond those she kept company with. Even her own daughter. The years — over three to be exact — have not changed her; she was as cruel as she was beautiful.

I handed Mary back to Rosie and crossed the room with weighted steps. "Mother," I said. She turned her head slightly and allowed my lips to graze her cheek. She was frigid to the touch and I wanted to be away from her. When I took a step back, she grabbed my arm to prevent me. Her hand gripped me like a vice; her fingernails were digging in my skin, threatening to draw blood.

"You look positively gaunt. Have you been eating?" She looked me up and down — like she did when I was a child.

"Yes, ma'am."

"You know she nursed our sick soldiers during the battle, Mother. She was on the front for the worst of it," Rosie explained.

She released my arm. "Oh, I'm sure she did." She wiped her hands on the napkin in her lap before picking up her teacup and sipping. "Can never pass up the opportunity to make a spectacle of yourself, now can you?"

On the ride to Rosie's, I had mentally prepared myself for the condemnation I knew I would receive from Mother. She never had a kind word for me. Critiques on my dress or appearance were mainstays in her repertoire. But I wasn't expecting judgment for doing what was right—like saving the lives of injured men. I was dumbfounded and appalled that my actions during the battle would be deemed self-serving. There was so much I wanted to say but arguing with her was fruitless.

Rosie changed the subject without a beat and handed me a teacup.

The day continued with very little mind paid to me. Rosie and Mother chatted on about the latest gossip in town and in Philadelphia. Mother talked of Benjamin's latest business ventures, her wish for him to retire to their house in France, of the fashions she had seen whilst traveling, and the weather. Rosie told her about the battle—all which Mother had already read in the paper, which she was prompt to explain—and then spoke about her labor.

"I have never felt such pain in my life, Mother."

"I've experienced childbirth, Roseanna. Once was quite enough."

"Twice, Mother." She glared at her.

"Yes, twice. But once would've been enough."

Mother smiled into her tea, enjoying the effect of her latest dig. Rosie mumbled, desperately trying to think of what to say. In my head, I started listing the bones in the hand just to keep myself from going mad. Twenty-seven in all and I repeated them backwards and forwards, counting them on my fingers and toes. I remained silent for the rest of the afternoon, until Jonathan returned, and supper was served.

Supper was dominated by Jonathan's musings on the parish and the need for industry in Gettysburg—neither of which were very interesting. But Mother was captivated. She listened, agreed, showed empathy when appropriate, and laughed infectiously at things that truly weren't funny. Jonathan thrived on it; Rosie and I exchanged side-ward glances, in silent agreement that Mother was over the top. She turned on the charm, as if she were a debutante looking for her first suitor. Every man was a personal conquest and she strove to be adored by them all.

The meal was delicious, and Rosie spared no expense or effort: whole roasted chicken, rubbed in butter and rosemary; cabbage salad, dressed in vinegar and oil; fresh summer vegetables; steaming-hot bread, served right from the oven with melted butter; and a fruit tart for dessert. My stomach was bulging when I finished—it was the best meal I had eaten in quite a while, especially considering the scarcity of certain produce since the battle. I looked down at my clean plate and felt guilty, knowing there was someone waiting for me at home who would've enjoyed a meal of this quality.

"That was simply divine, dearest." After three helpings, Jonathan finally put down his fork and inched his chair away from the table.

"I don't know how you manage without a servant. Or at least a cook," Mother added, though a plate of food still sat before her. As was usually the case, Mother talked much and ate little. She was always conscious of her figure and rarely ate her fill. "I can't imagine who taught you to cook." She took a long swig of the red wine Jonathan had procured for the evening.

Rosie looked at me and smiled. "A woman should always have one dish perfected. Or so my sister has always told me."

A girlish giggle passed Mother's lips, attracting my gaze. "I didn't realize you had a kitchen in that hovel you live in."

I'd had enough. It took everything in me not to jump across the table and claw her eyes out. "The hovel that you banished me to, Mother. Or do you not recall the circumstances of my marriage?"

She knew this, and it seemed to please her. She continued to smile. Unflinchingly.

The chair legs scraped against the wood floor as I pushed away from the table and stood. "Rosie, Jonathan: thank you for your warm hospitality and wonderful meal but really I must be heading back to my hovel in the woods."

"Sister, please I—"

"Don't let us detain you. You have very important things to do, I'm sure." Mother raised her glass and took another long drink. She placed the emptied glass in front of her and stroked the table lightly with her fingertips. "Roseanna, where did you find such a fine tablecloth? Such material, it must be from New York."

Rosie opened her mouth, looking from me to Mother and then back. Conflict tore her in two—she was always the bordering country between two enemy nations. She looked down to her hands and mumbled softly to herself.

"Roseanna? I asked you a question," Mother insisted.

With that, I was forgotten. I didn't stay to listen to Rosie's explanation on where the fabric was special ordered from; I whisked out of the room—with Jonathan a few steps behind—and didn't stop until I was outside.

My anger was white hot, and I could feel myself shaking. Jonathan led my horse into the yard and helped me into the saddle. He handed me the reins and then turned from me to return to the house without even a polite farewell. Part of me hoped Rosie would dash out to hug me goodbye, to say something to comfort me. I sat there atop Barley, waiting. When the door remained closed and Mother's giggle carried through an open window, an overwhelming feeling of loneliness filled me. No matter what I did, I would always be an outsider—an intruder even—to their world. They were my family, but I'd never belong.

"I shouldn't have come," I whispered to myself.

I nudged Barley's flank with the back of my heels and leaned forward in the saddle, signaling to her that I wanted to move. Barley trotted from the yard and into the street. Her pace was calm until we reached the town's limit, then she showed me the strength of her legs. She became a steed from hell—fiery and full of wrath. I clung to her neck, trying not to fall off as dirt and her mane whipped my face. It seemed my pain and loneliness had leaked into her being. She felt my emotions and took it out on the road.

And as her legs pumped harder and harder, my anger fell away. I pulled out the pins and comb from my hair,

letting it come undone and stream through the air like ribbon. Cautiously, I sat back in the saddle and closed my eyes,
letting the rush of air take me. I felt free. Free of everything
building inside of me.

Barley's speed cut our journey in half, but she slowed once
we were under the cover of trees; nature became whole again,
instead of a blurry mess of colors. The forest was quiet—quiet except for a faint hammering in the distance. Maybe it's Mr.
Larsen fixing his fence, I thought as I straightened my blouse
and pulled my hair away from my face. But as we turned
off Taneytown—and away from the direction of Mr. Larsen's
farm—the hammering grew louder.

The tree bowers opened, and my house was before me,
cast in the light of a beautiful sunset. With the soldier on my
roof, hammering new shingles into place.

My jaw dropped, as did the reins from my hand. Barley
threw back her head and let out a loud whinny, startling the
soldier upon his perch.

"Why...why did you...you didn't need to do that," I
stammered, my voice caught in my throat.

He lifted his hand, wiggling his fingers in a downward
pattern.

"Yes, the shingles needed to be replaced but you're not
well. I would've—"

He put his hand up and turned his head to the left to stop
me. When he looked back, he was smiling. I melted beneath his
gaze and I didn't want to look away. But Barley made me—she
turned her head and started towards the barn and her supper.

"Please be careful up there," I called over my shoulder. The sound of hammering answered my request.

And the hammering continues, even now as I record the day's events. I'm not sure if he intends on putting an entire new roof on the house, but he has been working for quite some time. He seems determined to finish the job—even after sunset and nothing but a lantern to light his work.

After today—seeing Mother and being subjected to her continued verbal assaults—I am happy that I've returned to my hovel. Especially to a kindly face, welcoming me back into its fold. My smile seems permanent these days—as is the blush on my cheeks.

—A

August 8th, 1863

I am a fool. A stupid, stupid fool, blinded by compassion.

The smell of buttery grits and toasted bread woke me this morning. I rolled over—my cheeks dimpling—to find I was alone. The backdoor was open wide, but the table was laden with waiting breakfast. And at the center of the table was a single sunflower in a clear glass. My heart leaped, as did I from bed and to the table. I leaned forward and smelled the fresh flower, feeling light and giggly. The soldier was nowhere in sight, but I knew he wasn't far. Since finding his stamina again, every waking moment has been spent outside and at work. Free of the sling, he has been chopping wood and fixing fence rails for the best of two days. Undoubtedly that's what he was doing at that exact moment, as I could hear the distinct sound of the chopping of wood in the distance.

I sat down at the kitchen table to my still warm breakfast. No one had cooked for just me since Mam. A hazy steam rose from the bowl as I dipped my spoon into its contents. The grits were creamy, and the bread was golden and crunchy. I was famished and licked the bowl clean. I lazed in my chair and closed my eyes, letting the calm bathe me.

Eventually, guilt took hold. If the soldier was hard at work, then I needed to be productive.

I stood and pulled the chairs away from the table. It had been at least a week since I swept the house, and the floors were filthy. The bristles of the broom swept back and forth, capturing all the dust and food crumbs that had fallen from the table. A small pile accumulated in the center of the room, and I had only gotten through the kitchen. Next, I turned to the area in front of the fireplace — where the soldier found his rest.

The soldier still slept on the handmade stretcher — cushioned with straw and blankets. I offered my bed or suggested taking turns, but he wouldn't accept my proposal; he shook his head, and obstinately crossed his arms over his chest. I knew nothing of his past or background, but he obviously adhered to chivalry.

With my foot, I pushed the stretcher a few feet to the left of the fireplace, so I could sweep beneath it. As I repositioned the broom in the now clear area, my nose was smacked with a pungent smell. "Ugh," I cried. My hands instinctually covered my nose and the broom toppled to the ground. I stepped away from the fireplace, looking left and then right in search of the smell. I knew there were no spoiled foods in the kitchen and the wash tub was empty. So where...

I leaned towards the stretcher and the smell wafted to my nose, again.

The stench was coming from the crumpled blankets and cushions in front of the fire. I removed the top quilts, flicked them out and then, cautiously, sniffed them. They smelled of fire and sweat—the soldier's personal musk. When I picked up his small pillow, the smell became intense. Beneath the pillow was the soldier's leather bag—the same he was wearing when I found him in the creek bed—and the flap was open.

The closer I got, the more evident it became that the smell was coming from the bag; I tapped it lightly with the tip of my big toe and the smell intensified.

My first instinct was to take the bag and toss it outside—remove the smell by force. But whatever was inside was his property and going through it, or removing the item entirely, would be a complete intrusion of his privacy. I peered out the back door, hoping he'd walk by and I could take the bag out to him. I waited for a few minutes to no avail; wherever he was on the property, he wasn't returning anytime soon.

Then the smell hit me again.

"I'll find whatever it is, clean it and put it right back. He won't even notice," I professed, as I bent down and picked up the leather bag.

I took the bag to the kitchen table and laid it flat. I averted my nose, taking a deep breath of clean air, and then looked inside the leather satchel. On top was a book; the cover was well worn, a deep brown and nameless, but I opened it and read from the first page, "*The Commentaries on the Laws of England.*"

My eyebrows rose in question. I knew the soldier was bright, but I assumed his education stopped at the ability to read. I shook the flawed assumption from my head and placed the book on the table. Next was a toilet kit, inside was: a razor, a broken comb, a cracked mirror, and a small vial. I took the vial and removed the stopper. Hesitantly, I put the vial up to my nose and inhaled.

I laughed. "Cologne." That was curious, indeed. I don't know of many country boys who were conscious of the way they smelled. I corked the vial and placed it next to the book.

Then there was a cotton-cloth wrapped parcel about six inches wide. Inside was a gold pocket watch — still ticking — a silver cigarette case — with nine cigarettes packed inside — a small pocket-knife, an ink pen with a half empty jar of ink, a bundle of what appeared to be letters wrapped in a black ribbon and last, a tintype photo. The tintype was of a bearded, older man seated with a gun across his lap and standing at his side — with her hand resting on his shoulder — was a well-dressed woman. Pearl beads adorned her neck, and the wrap around her shoulders looked to be of fine lace.

"His parents?" I fixed my gaze at the two figures, looking for similar features. She had the same widow's peak and flare in the nostrils. And the soldier's eyes were undoubtedly as dark as the man's pictured. Suddenly, the feeling of intrusion crept upon my heart and I hastily wrapped everything back in the cotton.

I removed the remains of a rotting apple and a piece of moldy bread—neither of which produced the obtrusive smell. Only one thing remained.

At the bottom of the bag was a thread-bare, red blanket. The wool was wrapped in a tight ball—perhaps done suddenly, when his regiment moved. It was surprisingly heavy; heavier than a simple, wool blanket should be. It was knotted on one end, concealing whatever was inside. Carefully, I unknotted the bundle and the sides fell open like flower petals.

I gasped and stepped back. Not just from the smell—which filled the room with all its gusto—but from what was inside the red blanket.

A short-waisted jacket and trousers—both of a grayish-tan hue. The colors of a Rebel uniform.

My hands grasped for the top of the chair and I stumbled into it, as my mind whirled with flashes of how I found the soldier: how he grabbed my hand when I initially touched the leather bag slung over his shoulder, the murderous look in his eyes, that the hem of his pants were a few inches too short and didn't cover his ankles, how the bag was hidden from sight, his lack of speech with no visible signs of trauma. All things that I should've questioned and am now seeing so clearly.

The enemy is in my house. He is a Confederate soldier.

My hands acted of their own accord and touched the rough fabric of the uniform and my fingers felt something firm and concealed within the jacket's arm. Into the uniform sleeve, I inserted my hand and grasped the smooth, cold metal of a pistol.

The floorboards creaked. Instinct made me grab the cool, smooth metal and stand, pointing the pistol directly at the backdoor.

It was him.

My stance made his eyes pop and he reactively raised his arms above his head, palms out. My breath came in short bursts, my heart was thumping from my chest, and my finger was poised heavily on the pistol's trigger. His brown eyes held confusion and hurt until he stole a glance at the contents of his leather bag poured out on the table. He knew what I'd found. The charade was over, and his stare burned my skin.

We stood there in stalemate — a complete juxtaposition to the playful staring game of a few days before. This stare was dangerous.

"Madam, please let me explain."

His voice — that I heard for the first time — was tinged with the accent of a Southerner.

"Get out," I said through gritted teeth. I pointed the pistol and aimed directly for his heart.

He shuffled back and forth on his feet, silently debating what to do; should he rush me and take the gun, or retreat?

Resignation made him lower his hands. He turned and walked out of the house, closing the door behind him.

My hand went slack, and the pistol dropped and smacked on the floor by my feet.

I stood staring at the door, long after it was closed. Every piece of my anatomy was tingling, and I couldn't recognize my own body. The only thing that brought me out of that trance-like state was the smell. I inhaled and felt the vomit rise in my throat. Because I didn't know what else to do, I picked up the soiled uniform and took it to the wash tub; I filled the tub and scrubbed the uniform clean of muck.

It is now several hours later. The uniform is drying before the fire — taunting me from across the room. The house is quiet, and he has not returned. Where he is, I don't know. Truthfully, I don't want to know.

I brought this man into my house without a second thought, when I should've left him where I found him. I should've searched that bag at the first chance. I should've handed him over to the authorities. Everything he's done since I brought him here was contrived and planned — he kept his voice from me, knowing his accent would reveal his secret. He took advantage of my compassion and now... and now what?

He is a Confederate soldier, sent here to invade the North. And his mere presence has put my life in danger. Oh my God...I'm harboring a deserter.

I'm no longer protected by the rules of engagement; I cared for this man in my home, not on a field of battle. If I am found out, my life will be forfeit. The war is still raging away from Gettysburg and this man is not one of us.

He is the enemy.

Chapter Twenty-Six

Breanne Walker

"HE IS THE ENEMY." I LET THE GRAVITY HIT ME. The chair scraped across the cement floor as I pushed away from the diary. I raked my fingers through my hair, pulling at the knots and scratching my scalp. I'd been reading non-stop since I returned to the archives hours before. No water breaks, no bathroom runs, or pauses to stretch my legs.

And now that a big piece of the puzzle had fallen into place, I felt like a marathon runner on the last mile stretch. With the appearance of an unnamed, voiceless, injured soldier, the story has been propelled to a different stratosphere.

I never saw this coming. And neither did A.M.P.

What could she do? Would she throw her burgeoning affection for this man aside, kick him out, and act like the last few weeks never happened? Or does she trust her heart? See the man who has not harmed her, but has become her companion and confidant?

I let my neck elongate and fall back so I was staring up at the water pipes. My nerves couldn't stand much more. The story was good; too good, that at times I've had to remind myself that it wasn't just a story. This was a real woman's life and turmoil.

Now what?

I pulled my chair closer to the table and leaned back over the pages. The next entry was dated the very next day. "No cliffhangers here."

"My eyes – "

Two words in and the ringer on my phone went off. It wasn't a missed call or a text—cell service couldn't penetrate the depths of the archives. I grabbed my phone, as the ring reverberated off the walls. It was an alarm—the alarm to remind me it was almost the closing time of the museum. It was 8:45.

I had fifteen minutes before the doors would be locked and the alarms turned on. I sat staring at the diary, quickly trying to decide whether to stay overnight or go.

I'll be reading anyway; the locked doors won't matter.

Seconds ticked away, inching closer and closer to nine. I could feel my anxiety growing.

"Screw it." I packed up my belongings—the diary included—and hustled towards the elevator. I pushed the button and the sound of bells beckoned me inside the elevator. I stepped inside and willed the doors to close and rise fast. *Really, I can read at home.*

"Last one out," said the burly security guard—who I didn't recognize—as he ushered me through the rear exit.

"Yeah sorry about that. I—"

"Great. Great. Goodnight." He barely waited for me to cross the threshold before he locked the glass doors and turned back into the museum to do his final checks.

I idiotically waved after him, readjusted my bag strap and walked towards the parking lot. The lot was empty; even the news vans had retreated for the night. Mine was the only car left in the lot and it seemed that the guard was correct.

Except he wasn't.

The employee parking spots were in an unlit area of the lot and as I got closer to my car, I could see someone was perched atop my hood. Fear rose in my chest; I could see a pair of legs hanging off the front bumper. *Why didn't I buy pepper spray?* I clutched my bag to my chest in a defensive position and kept walking. As I got closer, the form sat up and his features became clearer.

There's something familiar about that floppy, red hair—

"Mrs. Walker? Is that you?" squeaked a voice.

"It's Ms." *Oh great, just who I want to see.*

My eyes finally adjusted and there was Vince—the intern—sitting on my car, surrounded by empty Coke cans and candy bar wrappers. I rolled my eyes and started rummaging inside my bag for my keys.

325

"I figured you'd be here late. I recognized your car though — no one else drives a red — "

"Vince, get off my car." My voice was brusque, and I meant it to be.

"Oh, right." He looked embarrassed, glancing to his sides quickly. He grabbed his trash, stashed it in his backpack, and then jumped down, almost falling flat on his face in the process. He settled his feet and stood up straight. "Sorry, I didn't...yeah. Let me just — " he reached forward for the remaining Coke can and tossed it over his shoulder. *He's a snitch and a litterer.*

"How long have you been here, Vince?" I touched the dent left in my hood, hoping it wasn't permanent.

"Um...a few hours I guess?" He pulled up his sleeve and held his watch up to the light, trying to read the time. He shifted his body left and right before giving up, dropping his arm back to his side and looking down to his shoes. "It was after five. But I went back in for some snacks around seven."

"Right. Well I need to get going so...was there something you needed?"

"Well yeah. I...I wanted to apologize for ...you know for Peggy..." He paused, took a large breath, and then looked me right in the eye. "You weren't answering your phone and when I got back from the lab, I didn't know what to do and I assumed you didn't want me to just leave the envelope and samples on your desk. Here they are by the way." He picked up the cardboard box — filled with my samples — and placed it on his vacated seat on the hood. "I looked all over for you and asked the people who sat around your cubicle—some didn't know who you were, let alone where you were. Then I panicked and went to Peggy. But I—"

I cut him off by raising my hand—like the solider had with A.M.P. His words were dizzying. "It's done. Don't worry about it. You just sped up the inevitable and there's no point in rehashing it. Really...I should thank you."

"Why? I screwed everything up."

"Because...well yeah, you almost got me fired. And Greg—Dr. Ransome I mean—too. But facing Peggy wasn't so bad. Well, yeah it was bad—I'm pretty sure her voice reached a glass-shattering octave. But I survived, and it ended better than I expected."

He gulped and kicked an invisible rock.

"Don't beat yourself up. It's done." I patted him on the shoulder. He looked like he needed a hug, but the awkwardness of a hug would be too much for me. I jangled my keys and turned to the driver's side door, hoping he'd take the hint.

"Is there...is there anything else I can help with?" he asked meekly.

"No... I—" he was giving me puppy dog eyes; all big, watery and pathetic. My heart went soft. *I hope I don't regret this.* "Yes, there may be something. I have a name. Well, a last name and a general location of where he lived in 1863. I need a land deed or mortgage documents with the exact location. That way—"

"You can trace the name and location to the Witness Tree?" *Greg was right; Vince was smarter than we thought.*

"Exactly." From my bag, I retrieved a piece of paper and a pen. I quickly scrawled, "*Larsen*" and "*Little Round Top*" and handed the paper to him. "Anything you find will be helpful."

His face was beaming as he read the paper and then folded it carefully in half. "I won't let you down, Mrs—I mean Ms. Walker."

"It's Breanne."

"Thanks, Breanne."

I turned my keys in the car door and opened it. "But first, go home and sleep. You look like the walking dead." He laughed and handed me the box of samples which I sat on my passenger side seat.

"Can I ask you something?"

"As long as it's no more than six words. I really need to get home."

He paused before he spoke—I could see he was counting the words before he uttered them. "It's a diary, right?"

I smiled back and said, "It is."

With a broadening Cheshire cat smile, he put his hand to his forehead and saluted me. I returned the favor then shut my door. He stepped back and waved, then immediately turned and jogged off.

I laughed to myself and started my car, heading to my apartment and A.M.P.

Chapter Twenty-Seven

Breanne Walker

I TRUDGED UP THE STAIRS TO MY APARTMENT, INDIFFERENT TO THE amount of noise my elephant feet were making. I inserted my key and turned the knob, opening the door to my pitch-dark home. Inside, the air was frigid and stale; in my rush to leave that morning—which now seems like a lifetime ago—I hadn't turned off the air conditioning and the smell of Freon wafted through the door. I stood there motionless, staring into the darkness, waiting for my eyes to adjust and the air temperature to regulate.

As I stood there, a realization crept upon me.

My life had become a scratched CD; the disc was scuffed beyond repair and stuck on a single song verse. There's no fixing it—no amount of elbow grease or buffing to remove those scuffs and move your favorite song forward. Instead, frustration leads you to eject the disc and throw it across the room.

Since A.M.P. was thrust into my arms, my life had pivoted between two points: the museum and my apartment.

I'd been running from one place to the next at a maniacal pace without a minute to think. On and on and on, trying to finish the diary—safeguard my job—and reclaim my sanity. Both places had melded together and at times, I looked up from the diary and been at a total loss for where I was sitting. Fatigue and total absorption in the words have rattled my brains. Everything has been forfeited to her.

I didn't know if I could keep up this pace without throwing something across the room. And hopefully, it wouldn't be the diary.

As I stepped into my apartment, my foot slipped on the carpet. Adrenaline rushed to my heart and stole my breath; I had to grab the doorknob to stop from face planting. I dropped to my knees and reached for what I slipped on. The ground beneath my fingers slid; something white was scattered in the doorway. *My mail.* My mail had been slid beneath my door, no doubt it was given to my landlord because my mailbox was full. This has happened once before; when I first moved, I had a few things shipped that didn't fit in my mailbox. My landlord promptly marched up to my apartment, dumped the boxes in front of my door with a nasty note telling me to get a PO Box or a personal assistant.

Which I hadn't.

And there was a lot of it—an influx after the holiday weekend. I gathered up all the envelopes and stood with arms overflowing. With my elbow positioned beneath the light switch, I pushed up and the lights illuminated my living room. Everything was as I left it—the television in the living room remained off and I could see the bedding still on the floor in my bedroom. I took a few wide steps and dumped what was in my hands onto the coffee table in my living room. But before I walked away, one small envelope caught my eye. Particularly, the handwritten address scrawled across its front.

It was Mom's writing.

Beautiful, tight, and perfect; her letters were a calligrapher's dream and I always envied her penmanship. Growing up, my teachers compared my own handwriting to that of a serial killer's. I worked tirelessly in grammar school to correct my sloppy hand, to no avail. And every time I handed back a signed assignment or a note from my mother, they'd comment on the perfection of her hand and wondered aloud why I hadn't inherited the trait. That comment always sent me reeling and depleted my — already dangerously low — self-esteem.

If my life depended on it, I'd be able to distinguish her writing among a group of hundreds. I sat down, placed my bag gently on a clear space on the coffee table and picked up the envelope.

We've barely spoken since I left. The extent of our communication was a few texts about boxes I left in my old room, then a curt e-mail two weeks ago. But I've never received a card from her my entire life — birthday cards were a "scheme dreamed up by corporate America." My birthday wasn't for six months. And Christmas was still way off. *Why else do people send cards?* So, this was unprecedented, and I hadn't a clue what could be inside the thin, sealed-white paper. I turned the envelope over and broke the seal.

Inside was indeed a card—the background was beige with a single, purple orchid in the center. There was no greeting or words on the outside, just the single orchid. I had no reason to think the worst, but it felt inauspicious. I opened the card. The inside was also blank except for a short, handwritten note.

Breanne,

I hope everything is working out in Gettysburg.

I just got word and thought you'd want to know. Daniel had a heart attack a week ago. He's dead. I'm sorry.

—Mom

I had to read the paragraph three times before it fully set in. *Daniel is dead.*

The words processed at a snail's pace but finally it hit me like a wrecking ball against a brick wall.

Daniel is dead.

My father is dead.

My hands grasped for the corner of my couch and I caught myself from crashing to the carpeted floor. I sat back into the couch cushions and put my head between my knees to stop my hyperventilation. The man I never knew — the man who my mother dismissed, kept from me, affectionately referred to as her "sperm donor," and the man who destroyed her life — was dead. I didn't know him from a stranger on the street, and now that would always be the case.

Her short note was drenched in hatred. The words were cold, unemotional, flat, and her one statement of condolence was out of obligation, not from any true regret or sadness. She sent a card — a greeting card — to tell me that my father was dead. She should've called, sat on the phone with me for hours and talked me through my pain. Even a text or an e-mail would've been appreciated, but instead she chose the most impersonal way to let me know the news — via snail mail, so there would be no immediate reaction from me. This was vengeful and utterly cruel. She didn't care how this would affect me. She didn't care about anyone but herself.

My ears were ringing with rage. My chest felt tight and I was heaving under its weight. I lunged into the kitchen with the card still in hand — unsure if I was going to puke or do something more dangerous. I stood in front of the sink and reached for the garbage disposal switch. I flipped it on and raised the card before my face.

I've never liked purple.

I ripped the card in half. Then in quarters, and even smaller. The cast iron sink vibrated with the force of the blades, and I held the ripped pieces of paper over the drain and let them drop — like snowflakes from a winter sky. I wanted the card to disappear, and it did with the ferocity of sharp blades.

I wouldn't call her. I wouldn't give her the satisfaction of knowing how upset I was. The last time we spoke of Daniel was enough.

I was twelve.

My middle school was having their annual Father/Daughter Dance. I'd been dreading the date announcement and for the fliers to start littering the halls. The chatter among the girls in my class would start and then I'd be the odd girl out. Again, as I was for just about everything. I didn't have a father figure who I could beg to take me, so it'd be another Friday night where I'd sit home while my classmates were out dancing.

Unless...I could find a way. Unless I could find my father and convince him to come.

Mom kept a binder of all our important documents at the top of her closet; I saw her organizing it once, specifically our birth certificates right at the back of the clear-paged binder. If my father's name was anywhere, it would be on my birth certificate.

So, two weeks before the dance—when she worked an extra shift on a Saturday and I was left to my own devices at home—I snuck into her closet.

Standing in the doorway, I felt like I was somewhere forbidden and reaching for the fruit that I wasn't meant to taste. But I was desperate for a bite; I reached for the binder and sat Indian-style inside her closet with it in my lap. And on that second to last page, there it was, with the Arizona State insignia emblazoned on the page. I reached inside the clear, plastic pocket and pulled out the certificate.

And there was his name.

Daniel Cook.

I always knew his first name; "Daniel" was referenced in drunken rages on numerous occasions throughout my childhood. But I never knew his surname. My last name, Walker, was my mother's maiden name. My existence was enough of a reminder that he existed but bearing his name and hearing it daily would drive the knife deeper. Truthfully, I couldn't blame her for that.

"Breanne Cook," I whispered to myself, testing the sound of it.

Inside the page before was Mom's birth certificate and the address of the hospital in Littleton, Colorado where she was born. If my parents were high school sweethearts, most likely they lived in the same town. I imprinted the spelling of his name and the town on my brain—said it repeatedly until I could see the formation of letters in my mind—and then quickly put the binder back in its place.

And right in time, as I heard Mom's keys jingling in the front door.

The next day at school, I started my search for Daniel Cook in Littleton, Colorado. Using the library's computers, I was able to access the *Yellow Pages* and find the listings for Littleton. In the search bar, I typed COOK and waited for the results to load. My dedication to research traces back to this moment.

After a few seconds, thirteen phone listings popped up on the screen.

Thirteen.

Thirteen wasn't bad. I expected over a hundred. With two weeks, I could contact each and still have time to convince my dad to come to the dance. There weren't any direct listings for a DANIEL COOK but I knew it wouldn't be that cut and dry. If his family were still in the area, they could fill in the blanks. I was happy; happier than I'd been in a long time.

I printed the page and planned to start calling each listed number that afternoon. I had a pocket full of quarters—the remnants of my broken piggy bank were scattered on the floor of my bedroom—and would use the payphone across the street from school. I had exactly three hours before Mom would expect me home—*plenty of time*. I walked back to class believing I'd speak to my father. That my father would know my name and become my real, living and breathing father, rather than the figment my imagination created.

Naturally, I was idealistic.

I called all thirteen numbers: four were no longer in service, the dial tone sounded quickly after I finished punching in the area code and the seven-digit number; two answered, but weren't familiar with a Daniel Cook; and I left messages on the answering machines of the six remaining, giving my home phone number and an explanation on who I was looking for. On my bike ride home, I assured myself that it was early, and many wouldn't be home from work to answer the phone. I'd wait a few days and call again.

The second day of calls crossed off another three from my list; all three answered and still no one knew Daniel Cook. I left messages again on the remaining three and crossed my fingers and toes that one would be the right Cook. *I only need one*, I reminded myself when disappointment crept in. I knew he was out there.

Things sure looked grim when the dance was only a week away. Our answering machine remained blank day after day — I even replaced the batteries — and still I couldn't reach the final three Cooks. With my last quarter, I punched in the number of the last Cook from the three remaining and prayed someone picked up. But they didn't, and I hadn't the heart to leave yet another message. I hung up the phone with a loud clang of plastic on metal and jumped atop my bike to pedal home in defeat.

I nearly fell off my bike when I pulled onto my street and saw Mom's car parked on the driveway. Seeing her home this early never boded well for me. I pulled onto the front lawn and dumped my bike, quickly wracking my brain for an excuse for my lateness. *I stayed after to…to study for a geography test,* was what I decided on as I opened the door and stepped inside.

She was waiting for me. Sitting in an armchair, with the cordless phone in her lap and a drink on the side table beside her. She didn't look at me, just stared out the window next to the front door and lifted her drink to her painted lips. My feet shuffled back and forth and the book bag on my back grew heavier by the minute. She finished her drink with a loud smack of her lips and put the glass back on the table. Her fingers reached and pushed the green play button on the answering machine to her right. The button clicked under the weight of her finger.

"You have ONE new message," said the machine. Her eyes found mine as the message played back.

"Hi…um I'm returning a call from Breanne Walker," said a female voice. I flinched, knowing I was caught. *Please don't say your name, please don't say your name.*

"I've gotten a few messages here. I've been out of town and only just got them. Here is my number: 555-9869. I'll be home after four tomorrow if you want to call back. I…I think we need to speak. Oh yes, this is Dorinda Cook."

Mom watched me as she pressed the red button on the machine. "Message DELETED."

My breath came in quick spurts and I suddenly felt very hot. Still she stared at me, without revealing any emotion. A sob gurgled in my throat and my head dropped to my chest. I heard her stand and cross into the kitchen.

"You are never to contact that woman again. Or her son. Do you understand me?"

"Yes ma'am."

"Go to bed."

I cried myself to sleep that night and would every night until after the Father/Daughter dance.

Dorinda called twice after that—leaving messages that were like the first. The third time she called, we were home. Mom swiped up the phone. "Never call here again," she screamed into the receiver.

And that was the last time Daniel Cook or his mother were ever talked about. Until I received the purple orchid card, now torn to shreds in the garbage disposal of my sink. But I never stopped thinking about them. Daniel and his mother became this fairytale enigma in my life—like Santa Clause or the Tooth Fairy. I couldn't see them, but knowing they were out there gave me hope. I knew they could love me the way I so desperately needed, and someday I'd be able to reach out and take it.

As the memory filled me, I stood with my hand on the faucet and water swirled into the tub. I turned off the water and watched as the sink drained.

I still know Dorinda's phone number. It became almost a prayer to me; in dark and lonely moments, I'd recite it to myself forwards and backwards. But I never contacted her. I was too afraid Mom would find out. Her wrath was venomous, and I never had the nerve to go against her. With one fowl swoop, my mother stripped me of any chance of having a relationship with my father, let alone my grandmother.

That was why I felt so passionate about preserving history—because everyone deserves the chance to know their roots. And why I cut myself off from the world—if my own mother couldn't love me, how could anyone else? Better to not even try.

The loss of Daniel, the memories from my childhood were hitting me hard and I was that little girl, crying into her pillow all over again. Crying for what could've been. *No, I won't cry; how can I cry for a man I've never known?* Emotion and I have never mixed, and it was easier for me to push it aside, flee from it and fill my head with something else. Now that's exactly what I'd do. A.M.P. was worth so much more than anything going on in my life. I couldn't let my own family drama curtail my progress with the diary. *Six days until Peggy's deadline.*

It was stupid. I was being stupid.

"Get back into it, Walker."

I retreated to the living room and sat down on the carpeted floor. With the coffee table before me, I retrieved the diary from my bag and found where I left off.

Chapter Twenty-Eight

A.M.P.

August 9ᵗʰ, 1863

As my eyes fluttered open, the room was blurred and engulfed in a bright haze; almost like I was opening my eyes under water. I rolled to my side, pulled my quilt tight around my body and waited for my surroundings to become clear. I blinked the sleep from my eyes, and then the memory of the day before flooded back in.

I pulled the quilt over my head, hoping to hide from everything. I wanted to forget the betrayal and agony; pure exhaustion was the only reason sleep had taken me in the wee hours of the morning. I closed my eyes again and hoped sleep would return.

CREAKKKKKKKK echoed through the house.

The sound made me shoot out of bed and crouch defensively on the floor. My hand reached for the shotgun beneath the bedframe and I stood hesitantly, with the gun outstretched before me. Nothing before me was out of place; the one-room house was silent, and I was utterly and miserably alone.

CREAKKKKKKKK sounded again.

My eyes darted to the two windows on either side of the front door. Sunlight beamed, casting a golden light on the wooden floor and furniture. But the left was darkened by a shadow. Someone was on the porch. I walked towards the door, shotgun firmly in hand.

I opened the front door and poked my head around the doorframe.

It was the soldier.

He was sitting in one of the low-back rocking chairs, staring ahead with a stern look. Quickly, I ducked back inside. Unsure of what to do, I lingered in the doorway. He was back to full health, and he could easily overpower me, take Barley, and run. The possibility of other things he could want didn't escape me; his carnal desires frightened me the most.

I was trying to recall the last time I used the shotgun, when he broke the silence.

"I know you're there."

The sound of his voice made my heart freeze and then thaw in quick secession. It was clear, a low baritone tinted with a southern drawl. The sound of it was soothing and for a short moment, my fear was forgotten. Of its own accord, my grip eased on the shotgun, momentarily making it slip in my hand. My head caught up to my heart and I gripped the gun, positioning the butt into my armpit and aimed onto the left-hand side of the porch.

"I am armed, sir. And I do not fear killing a man who has trespassed on my property," I stated, faking strength and tenacity.

From my position in the doorway, I could see his feet—shod in a pair of my husbands that I'd given him the week before. I shuffled uncomfortably from one foot to the next, questioning if the gumption to kill an unarmed man was truly within me.

"I assure you, Madam, I have every faith that you'd kill with a single shot. But—" he took a breath, waited a beat then finished, his voice almost a whisper, "we both know I haven't trespassed on your property."

I stepped onto the porch and pointed my shotgun directly at the man sitting tensely on my porch, anger oozing from me. He was disheveled and unrecognizable: his hair was greased and matted to his scalp; his clothes were wrinkled, and grass stained, from sleeping outside; and he looked beaten down. He reeked of defeat and melancholy, and normally compassion would've quieted my rage. But compassion can't cool a burning barn once the flames are out of control.

Slowly he turned his head to look at me and once again, his dark-brown eyes seemed to sear my soul.

"I see you've found your tongue," I snarled. "And you are trespassing, sir. You were brought here under false pretenses; if I had known who—no, what you are, I never would've pulled you from that creek. Undoubtedly, you are a spy and caring for someone like you puts my life in danger. I never would've devoted so much time and energy in—"

"And who do you think I am?"

"I don't think; I know. I trust what my eyes have seen."

He blinked twice, his face emotionless. "What have your eyes seen?"

"No more questions! I want you off my porch and away from my property!"

He continued to stare and asked his question once again, "What have your eyes seen?"

Without moving the gun from his direction, I shifted my hips slightly and pointed inside the house to the uniform drying by the fire. "I saw that; the second uniform balled up among your possessions. I have seen and know the color and badge sewn onto its sleeves; 'Liberty, Equality, and Fraternity' is the motto of secession and Southern soldiers wear it with pride."

He leaned back in his chair, his eyes returning to the trees in front of him.

"Will you deny it?"

"You don't understand," he whispered.

"Understand what? That you are a Confederate soldier: that you and your comrades invaded my town, tore and pillaged as you went, and killed many good and honest Northern men? I can take a guess at the rest: once the battle was lost you deserted, stole a Union uniform—from a dead or dying Northern soldier—in the hopes of escaping capture; you ran and tried to go undetected, so you could slink back to whatever town in Virginia that bore you."

"Alabama."

"What?"

Slowly, he turned his head towards me. "Haleburg. Henry County, Alabama is the town that bore me. And that," he leaned forward and pointed to the same spot inside the house, "that uniform stole my dreams and destroyed everything for which I stood. I didn't want any of this; to be in this god-forsaken town, to take up arms and kill men I never had a quarrel with." He slammed his fists on the arms of the chair—beating his frustrations into the weather-worn wood.

His eyes were glaring with heat and intensity. But he seemed to be seeing something beyond. Like the past had seeped into the present and was playing in an awful pantomime on my porch. My finger was no longer lax on the trigger and I was ready for him to lunge at me.

The rage within him passed and he sat back with a sigh. "I have scared you and that was not my intent. You've shown me a kindness I have not deserved and I'm alive because of your care. But it's not fair to lump me with my southern counterparts. You've judged me the enemy when you know nothing of my character. You have no idea what brought me here."

A personal revelation came with his words: I was a hypocrite. Only a few weeks before, I'd been hard in my condemnation of Mr. Larsen; his refusal to give the fallen southern soldiers an ounce of respect in their final resting place was deplorable. He didn't see their humanity and buried them as traitors, lower than cattle. Was I not treating him similarly? Was I not throwing the half inch of dirt and spitting on his grave? Just the day before I believed this man a Northern soldier and didn't I believe he was a genuine, trustworthy man? Shame filled me.

I closed my eyes and asked, "What do you want from me?"

No immediate answer came, so I peeked through my eyelashes to find him staring at me. Slowly, his eyes drifted to the double barrel still pointed in his direction. Sheepishly, I released the trigger, bent my elbow and dropped the gun to my side. The tension instantly lifted and he visibly relaxed.

"What do you want from me?" I asked, again.

He looked straight ahead. "You must think me a scoundrel."

Frankly, I did; after his trickery, how could I think otherwise? I offered no rebuttal and remained mute, shifting uncomfortably.

"This war has destroyed much that was good in this country," he continued. "It has turned us against each other from the inside and forced many to take up arms. Young boys pledged their allegiance to one side or the other, in the hopes of bringing honor to themselves and their families. I was no different. But none of us knew the toll of war; no one can know what war takes from you until you're in it."

He paused and shook the thoughts from his head. "I assure you, my allegiance is with my country—a whole country, not divided by points on a compass. Circumstance forced my hand and yes, I enlisted with Colonel Oates' 15th Alabama. I've struggled with that decision every day—with every footstep that's taken me from Henry County. I believe, wholeheartedly, that change is needed—that the South needs to change—but not at the cost of young boys."

A thousand questions formed in my mind. I opened my mouth to ask but he continued.

"I can't, in good conscience, ask anything of you after what I've done. But...I humbly ask that you give me the opportunity to gain your trust; to prove that I am not the uniform I wore in battle. And with your trust, I hope you will allow me to stay."

His words were drenched in vulnerability, and his eyes were big, glassy and pleading; he was scared I'd refuse. I realized the power—with or without a gun pointed at his head—was all mine. Gettysburg was not a safe place for anyone in either uniform of his age; the local militia was actively looking for deserters and he wouldn't get far. He'd be sent to a military prison or shot on sight. He knew this; I knew this. Without me, he was as good as dead.

Power is a funny thing; eagerly sought, but you stumble beneath its weight. In forcing a man from my property, my hands would be forever soaked in his blood. How could I trust him? How could I see past the Confederate uniform?

"I will need time to think on this. I don't—"

Like a light-footed rabbit, he stood from the chair and pounced off the porch. With the grass beneath his feet, he turned back to me and said, "I'll work your farm while you think."

"How can chores prove your character?"

He grinned. "I'll do whatever it takes."

There was no arguing with his proposal; his help over the last few weeks was irrefutable. But were his intentions pure and not just another ploy to take advantage of my guilty conscience?

I released the doubts building in my chest and looked deep into his eyes and asked, "What is your name?"

His eyebrows raised in question.

"What is your name, sir?" I asked, again.

"Emmet. Emmet Conroy."

"Well, Mr. Conroy I expect you're hungry."

He nodded slowly.

"Gertie will need milking. I'll have something ready when you're through." I turned and closed the door behind me.

And flicked the dead bolt for good measure.

Soon, there was a soft knock on the backdoor. With a plate filled with golden johnnycakes, I answered the door. The soldier—Emmet, his name is Emmet—was smiling, standing on the top step with a pail filled with creamy milk. His foot lifted to walk inside the house, but I didn't budge and only allowed the door to open a crack. The smile fell from his lips. I handed him the johnnycakes and he passed the pail through the doorway.

"Thank you." His words were short—like the look he gave me when he walked from the door.

My curtness struck him. But what did he expect from me? Nothing had changed. I wanted to return to the congenial repartee we established in the weeks since he had been living under my roof, but to do so would take time and further explanations. I still knew nothing about him—nothing of his character or what brought him to

Gettysburg. And until I had those answers, trust couldn't be reestablished.

But staying cooped up in the house all morning and avoiding him was doing nothing to soothe my growing anxiety. If I had questions, I needed to ask them.

I stepped from the house with a glass of cold water and intent in my heart. The barn was filled with hay and Gertie noisily chomping away, but there was no Emmet. Panic crept into my heart; had turning him away changed his mind? Had he run off? The not-too-distant sound of chopping quelled my fears. I gathered my skirts and followed the sound of the axe.

Within a mile of my property, I found him. Two felled oaks lay on either side of him and he was busy stripping bark from their trunks with a drawshave. He was intent in his work as he sliced away with precision and force. Finding him so—chopping down the trees that were my towering guardians—sent my emotions into frenzy. Those trees were my companions; the first thing I loved about this homestead, my protection in the unknown around me. And seeing them—cut at the root, dead—struck me. He had no right to destroy my property!

"Hey!" My voice echoed among the still standing oaks.

He looked up, momentarily startled but then went right back to his work. He ignored me, even started whistling a tune I didn't recognize.

"What are you doing? Those trees are—"

"Your paddock needs new rails. The ones standing won't make it through winter and the gate is termite-ridden," he said, stripping a large piece of bark and tossing it over his shoulder.

"Oh."

He laughed to himself then continued. "I said I'd make myself useful."

"I see that." I stepped closer and handed him the glass of water. He dropped the drawshave and accepted the drink, quickly gulping down its contents. Then he handed back the empty glass. "The bark will come in handy, I expect."

"Yes," I said, looking at the pieces strewn across the ground.

"Stay awhile and collect what you need," he said, taking back up the drawshave.

I organized the pieces into piles: the bigger pieces for kindling and roof shingles, the smaller pieces for poultices and teas. As I gathered, I watched him from the corner of my eye. Though the canopy of tree limbs shaded us, the sun found him, and he glistened beneath its rays.

We worked separately and in silence. He stripped the last piece of bark from the second log, dropped the drawshave and sat down with a big huff. From his pocket, he retrieved a handkerchief and wiped his brow. "These trees," he said, patting the cleaned log beside him, "they're bigger this side of the hill. Heartier, too."

"This side of the hill?"

"Yes. I thought the trees on the other side were the biggest I'd ever seen, but these," he patted the log, "are taller, thicker and have fewer branches. Do you know their name?"

"Honey locust," I answered. Slowly, I stood and stepped closer to him. "Are you familiar with another part of this hill?"

"As familiar as an invading solider could be. Were you here—in your house—during the battle?"

"No," I took a seat on the soft grass beside him. "I was with my sister when the fighting began—she'd just given birth. After, I was called to help the wounded in town and then at the front."

"Your men were well tended I expect." He absently passed a hand over his stomach—where he'd forever have a scar. "I imagine those days are etched in your brain."

"I'll never forget them," I answered truthfully. I smoothed the folds of my skirt and stared at my hands folded in my lap. "Was this your first engagement?"

Silence followed. I peeked at him; his eyes were big wells of grief. There was an inner struggle as well; he needed to talk about it, even if reliving it would be painful. He turned his head from me and looked straight ahead. He extended his long fingers, one by one; he was counting. "Gettysburg was my sixth campaign."

"You mentioned your brigade—"

"The 15th Alabama."

The air around us was tense and the conversation would quickly die if I didn't urge it forward. I needed to keep him talking.

"The men in your regiment—were they friends from home?"

"No. My childhood friends enlisted when the war began but I held out, hoping the war would end. But come August I gave in. The men of the 15th were complete strangers to me. Most were Irishmen from Henry County and hearing their

Gaelic — my parents native tongue — made me feel welcome, but truthfully I kept my distance from them."

"Why? I imagine that would be hard to do given the camaraderie within brigades?"

"My opinions wouldn't have been appreciated. And I knew if spoke, I'd be ostracized. It was hard, but a solitary existence was far better. They tried to engage me, but after a while they gave up all together. They called me 'Witless'; they thought me dumb." He chuckled. "It's never been hard for me to keep my tongue."

I plucked a blade of grass from the ground, held it firmly between my index finger and thumb. Much of the grass had yellowed with the heat of the summer months but the rain had found its way to this patch of grass. I focused on the thin piece of green between my fingers, careful not to look at him. "Your wounds; how did you come by them?"

My question made him wince. He leaned further in to the log and stretched his legs. His hands were on his thighs, tightly gripping the fabric of his trousers. Memories raced through his head and he was deciding how best to approach this subject.

"I'm sorry I just—"

"No." He waved away my concern. "My story is part of our agreement." He closed his eyes.

"We'd been stalled in New Guilford, Virginia for close to a month, waiting for our next orders; I wasn't sure they'd ever come. Then on the 2nd of July, we were roused shortly after midnight, told to decamp with haste. Nothing was known for sure, but naturally whispers and gossip spread—mostly tall tales told by half-asleep men. Two hours later, we marched out and into the early morning hours of the day and further. With the sun came oppressive heat and canteens were emptied with no chance to refill. There were no clouds or hope of protection from the sun. Many dropped from heat sickness, only to be scooped up by their fellow soldiers and forced to keep pace. Our commanders urged us on and though they hadn't whips, they treated us like cattle going to slaughter."

"Hours later, I thought my eyes deceived; we were standing on the bank of the Potomac River—I knew it from the town on its shore. Men hurled themselves into the icy-cold water; their bodies were cooled, and they drank their fill. I cautiously stepped into the swirling waters, wondering why no one else was seeing the significance of where we stood. The Potomac was the gateway to the North and there I was standing in its waters. Though the sun blazed on my back, my body felt chilled."

"The water of the Potomac momentarily cooled my tongue, but its relief was fleeting. We marched on to our destination: Gettysburg, a quaint town in Pennsylvania with brick houses and cobblestone streets. We arrived late in the afternoon on the same day; the 15th were bone-tired, thirsty, covered in sweat and a thick layer of dirt that filled the air like smoke. All I wanted was to remove my shoes and stretch my sore feet. Maybe find a tree and nap beneath its limbs for just an hour. But Colonel Oates received our orders almost immediately.

"Lee means to end this war today," Oates told us, as we mustered before him. Deep exhales reverberated through the crowd of men. To thrust men into battle after a twenty-mile death-march was cruel. Just standing caused the muscles in my legs to seize and spasm, and the thought of another march turned my stomach. But the look on Colonel Oates' face was pure exhilaration. He was just as beaten down as we but taking part in this battle — the battle to end all battles — gave him the energy to push forward."

"His impassioned speech inspired me to raise my fist and scream, 'Hoozah!' The men — the men who knew me as the regiment's mute — looked on in disbelief. I yelled again, this time louder. And the 15th answered my call. Our chant filled the air like a raucous chorus. I didn't believe in the cause — that hadn't changed after all I had seen — but now I'd fight for the men of the 15th. To protect their lives was my only objective. I shouldered my rifle, shook the pain from my legs and marched out with my comrades."

I could feel my heart beating fast as he described the arduous trek through town — my town, where his army helped inflict the wounds I had tended to. He could hear the cannon blasts and the screams of men and the shots of ammunition all around him, but his focus was solely on the back of the man before him. As they crossed onto the Emmitsburg Road, two large hills loomed ahead. He wondered if they were headed to the base of those hills — the ground seemed ideal for an offensive assault. As they got closer, he could hear the shots of sharpshooters nearby.

"The sound is...unforgettable. It's a single shot, a pop-pop-pop of the gun then a shrill whizzing as the bullet searches for its target. The bullets hit the dirt around us and the men scrambled away or hit the ground for cover. Atop horses, the officers were easy prey—many jumped down from their steeds and walked alongside us. Colonel Oates screamed orders and we diverted away from an open field, surrounded by a rocky hill, with a rock formation at the center. The sharpshooters—positioned on a rocky hill that looked down on the open field—were aiming for that formation. From our distance, I could see many Confederate men were trapped among the rocks; hiding among the boulders, firing their own rifles when they could and hoping the Union sharpshooters would miss. We trudged on, but I said a prayer for the trapped men."

The rock formation he described was Devil's Den. I knew where his regiment was headed. And it was close to where we were sitting.

"We were on the eastern side of the Emmitsburg Road when we started our ascent of the smaller hill. The terrain was rocky, and the trees were thick." He looked over his shoulder, at the log at his back. His eyes traveled its length, and then he turned back to continue. "To be out of direct sunlight was a relief but every step was uncertain and many around me slipped upon rocks or a tree roots. It was rough going and only got worse the higher we climbed. Many other regiments had already arrived: from the badges on their shoulders, I saw the men from the 4th and 5th Texas, and some Alabama brothers from the 4th and 47th. They were as dirty and rundown as we in the 15th, but all had a nervous energy. We joined ranks with Maj. Gen. John Hood's division. We continued to follow our officers onward and upward, unsure of what we were marching into."

"But before any of us properly adjusted our footing, shots rained down from every direction. Bullets found their quarry and men fell, their bodies were ripped open in ferocious rage. Screams filled the air; we looked ahead for Union troops and saw only trees. Then the onslaught started again. Blood sprayed my face as a man at my side fell with bullets in the head and chest. Behind a thin tree, I found cover. My stomach rose, and I retched up everything — little that it was — and I closed my eyes for a moment to settle my mind, stomach, and racing heart. In that time, the shots stopped. The Yanks were reloading."

"Cautiously, I peeked from behind my cover and gauged my surroundings. Sunlight glinted and sparkled in the forest ahead of me; sunrays were catching the metal of Union belt buckles. From my guess, the Yanks sat fifty yards in front of us. They were positioned higher on the hill, looking down at us from an angle. To my sides were the remnants of my regiment: either crouching in fear, dead with blood gushing from their mortal wounds, or wounded and desperately trying to stop their blood loss. Officers tried to regain control. I couldn't see Colonel Oates, but I heard his voice above all others. Telling us to stand and fight; not to cower in fear."

"The 15th stood from their barricades and fired back at the Yanks. Shots rang out again, battle cries sounded, and bullets whistled by my head. I loaded and reloaded my rifle, aimed down its barrel and pulled the trigger. The brush and trees were too thick to see if my bullets found a home; I didn't want to kill anyone, but I didn't want to die either."

He paused for a few minutes again. To save his pride, he turned his head and wiped the tears from his cheeks on the shoulder of his shirt. My empathy was with him and building steadily.

He cleared his throat and continued. "After that first volley, we were thrown back by more Union troops. We hammered at them again and again, but nothing could dislodge them from their position above us on the hill. The 15th needed to reposition and spread out from the other regiments. Oates called us back and gave quick orders. 'That hill is the high ground and we need it. Lee is counting on us,' he said, looking into the eyes of the men directly in front of him. If the Yanks were heavily engaged with other brigades at the center of the hill, we could slip in unbeknownst and flank their lines; we could take the field with this one decisive tactic."

We maneuvered to the right of the fray. Bullets still whined at our heads, but our focus was ahead and not back. Our officers halted, and we formed two lines; I stood in the first, close to the center. The sounds of battle rushed, and my ears bled from the noise: indistinguishable words were coming from everywhere. We knelt behind boulders, hugged trees and loaded our guns with shaking hands." His hand drifted to his chest and for a medallion that wasn't there. "I...I prayed only to walk away from battle with my life."

Daylight was fading fast, and darkness was approaching. He loaded, shot, reloaded, and shot in a deadly cycle. He advanced with his line closer to the Union's position, only to be pushed back. Nothing succeeded in pushing the Union. Four times, he had to replenish his ammunition — and the 15th was running low. The bodies of the dead were sprawled on every open surface and the dry ground became muddy with puddling blood. The air was thick with gunpowder and smoke, so breathing and seeing became harder and harder.

"It was hell. Hell, in every sense of the word."

There were longer pauses between rounds and the line was able to squeak a few feet closer; the Union forces were running low on ammunition, too. It was just a matter of who ran out of gun power first.

"We were far fewer than we'd been, but we had enough men to hammer the Yanks and take the high ground. We were sweat drenched, bloodied, and walking on dead legs but we formed ranks one last time. A thunderous yell erupted and then we — the 15th Alabama — dashed forward. We threw ourselves forward in the hopes of glory."

"We ran through the woods like Satan's fire was burning behind us. We aimed straight and fired shot after shot, with no return volley from the enemy. Their silence was puzzling after hours of returned defensive actions. Then I heard a voice, a voice louder than all the others, "Bayonets!"

A chorus of voices repeated the words again and again. Ghostlike, the Union men appeared at full height, and pulled their bayonets off the front of their rifles. Others around me slowed their pace and gaped at them in confusion. For one, stretching second it was marvelous to behold; I have never seen such bravery. The order went up again, and the Yanks plunged forward and into the confused Confederate line. They crushed into us; men fumbled with their rifles and couldn't fire a single shot. The Union troops ran the men from the 15th through with their bayonets or shot them with pistols at close range."

"I shot blindly until my rifle held no bullets. Desperately, my hand fumbled for the leather bag slung at my side; for inside was my revolver—the very same you pulled on me yesterday. I dropped to my knees to retrieve it. Before my shaking hands could grasp the single barrel, I saw a man rushing for me. My hands snatched up the empty M1841 and I thrust the butt into the face of the man standing over me. Blood sprayed from his broken nose and he fell onto his back beside me."

"I feared I had struck one of my own; but the blood that was gushing from his nose stained a blue uniform. I felt for his pulse and there was a steady beat under my fingertips. He held his musket firmly in his hand and would've killed me without blinking an eye, but I wouldn't do the same to him. Five steps I took before another man in a blue uniform crossed my path. With his sword, he swiped through the air and the cool steel shredded the front of my uniform and sliced the bare skin of my stomach. I screamed in pain, my knees gave out and I fell, gripping my stomach. My hands were soaked in blood. My assailant strode off immediately and I desperately searched the woods for medical aid. I screamed for help, to no avail; my voice was swallowed up by the chaos of battle."

"The last thing I remember — before the world around me blurred and then went to black — was seeing what was left of the 15th kneeling on the forest floor, their arms raised in surrender."

He sighed, and his hands lifted from his legs to his stomach. "I'd be food for the grubs if you hadn't found me."

I nodded and looked back to the blade of grass in my hand — now yellowing in the heat of the day. Stories of what occurred on Little Hill made their way back to town but hearing it from the Confederate perspective was quite different.

A chill erupted on my skin and I pulled my legs close to my chest, hoping to find some warmth.

"The day is late. We should — you should get back to the house," he said, as he stood and offered me a hand. I took it and looked up into his dark, brown eyes and the chill left me immediately. I stood, brushed the grass from my skirts and turned to pick up one of my piles of bark.

"Don't worry yourself with that; I'll carry the piles to the barn. And I'll be careful not to combine them."

"Thank you," I said. He bowed his head.

I turned and walked back to the house alone. With every step, my mind swirled with images of the story of Emmet's encounter with the Yanks on Little Hill.

Now, night hugs the woods around my house and I am alone once again. Emmet returned for supper some hours past but did not try and enter. He knocked and waited on the grass by the backdoor. I handed him a bowl of roasted summer vegetables — squash, tomatoes, snap peas and bell peppers — served in a thick broth with a chunk of brown bread. I apologized for the lack of meat, but promised I'd make my way to town to buy some pork; he only nodded, accepting the plate before he turned back to the barn. I closed the door and ate my own meal in silence.

As I sit here, the intensity of his memories strikes me once more. To recall those horrific memories must have pained him, as it did me in simply hearing them. If I had taken part and witnessed it all firsthand — as Emmet had — I don't believe I'd ever sleep again. His heart must be filled with such turmoil. From my window, I can see a small fire burning on the side of the barn; where Emmet must be finding his rest for this night.

My heart is torn in two: strung between feeling loyalty towards the Union army and the empathy for the man whose life I saved.

He spoke of circumstances that "forced his hand" to enlist, but what could possibly force a man to fight against his conscience?

I must blow out my candle and retire for the night.

— A

August 10ᵗʰ, 1863

Yesterday, I'd have stayed the whole morning in bed if the creaking sound from the porch hadn't scared me from my quilts. But today, curiosity — not a mysterious sound — impelled me from the comfort of my bed.

I dressed quickly and was ashamed to realize that the morning was almost through — the hour was close to eleven. In all my years, I'd never slept that late. Even in illness, Mam forced me from bed soon after dawn and set me to menial chores in the kitchen. "Nothing will quicker force the blight from your blood, dahlin'," she'd say. Her voice is always with me; I filled the kettle and put it to boil, thinking of Mam and missing her dearly.

I stepped outside with a cup of bark tea and a bowl of buttery porridge for Emmet; I was hungry myself, but I'd wait until he was fed. As I approached the back of the barn I could hear the trot of Barley on the path from the woods. Emmet sat atop her, looking over his shoulder and holding a thick metal chain in his hand; Barley was dragging the two felled logs from the day before — now stripped of their bark.

Barley stopped a few paces from where I stood, and Emmet jumped down with ease.

"I'm sorry about the hour," I said, handing him my bounty.

"Don't worry yourself." He took the bowl and mug and sat down on a stump. "This was kind of you."

"Really it's not." I handed him a spoon from my apron.

He shrugged his shoulders and practically inhaled both the oats and the tea. "Thank you all the same, I was hungrier than I thought." He stood and passed back the utensil and bowl before returning to Barley.

"Were you up with the sun?" I asked, placing the cup and bowl on the vacated stump.

"Yes. I milked Gertie, brought down hay from the loft, and mucked the stalls." He unhooked the chains from Barley's pummel and tossed them to the ground. "But this girl," he said, as he patted Barley's backside, "she wanted me all to herself. She's been following me all morning."

"She's taken a liking to you," I said as I approached Barley and stroked her velvety neck.

He moved along her flank and ran his fingers through Barley's mane. "She and I are old friends." She bucked her head into his arm, almost in agreement.

"Since you've been here, you mean?"

"No," he said as he knelt next to the logs.

"I'm not sure I understand?"

His hand paused momentarily on the thick, steel chain. "After the battle," he said.

"How's that possible?" An explanation of Barley's reappearance—after being stolen by the toothless soldier on the first day of battle—started to take form in my mind.

He took Barley's reins and led her to the paddock. I followed like a duckling after its mother and watched as he unbuckled the saddle and dropped it to the ground.

He opened the paddock gate and ushered her inside. We watched as she galloped away.

"After the battle," he continued, wiping the sweat from his brow, "I'd been left for dead. I knew we'd lost—I heard the Union bugle calls and the shouts of joy from far off. So, I wandered through the woods, collecting half full canteens and food, and then I crawled beneath a dense holly bush. I hoped sleep would set all right and that I'd wake renewed. But you know that was a fool's hope: my body was failing, and death was creeping ever closer. Slowly, I crawled from the bush and found a welcomed surprise munching on the grass in front of me: your Barley."

"She didn't startle in seeing me; she looked me over and approached like an old friend. I took her as a gift from God. I gripped the saddle, pulled myself up into the stirrup and steered her onto a path away from the hill. But my legs hadn't the strength to hold and I had to wrap the reins tightly around my wrists. With every minute that passed, I could feel life slipping from me. Then the world started to spin with bright colors. I recall the sound of splashing water and that I fell onto Barley's neck, gripping her for dear life. My body suddenly became weightless and I remember the blunt impact of rocks. But nothing else until I woke here."

He looked back to Barley, who was still happily trotting around the paddock. "She has some power in those legs," he said with a smile before turning back to the logs. He crouched down and started unraveling the chain links. I squatted beside him and began on the matching chain.

"And the uniform?" I couldn't see his face, but his shoulders flinched. Perhaps he'd been hoping I wouldn't broach the topic. As if on cue, the chain loosened around his log and it fell onto the grass with a soft thump. His response needed my complete attention, so I laid down my still tangled chain and sat on the log.

"Before Barley, before the bush, before the end of southern assault on your town — I opened my eyes and I was still on the hill. I don't know how much time had passed but the world was pitch dark and the air was ripe with death. My body felt foreign and my entire torso was covered in congealed, sticky blood."

"I had the urge to move and started shifting my legs to stand; but then terror gripped me like a vice and I froze. The sound of shuffling leaves and loosened stones echoed through the trees around me; something — or someone — was slinking its way up the hill, inching closer and closer to where I lay. Before I could decide what to do, the shuffling paused by my feet and something started tugging at my shoes. Pure survival instinct made me kick into the solid form kneeling between my legs. My feet connected with something soft, a voice yelped, swore and then crashed back onto the ground."

"It was a man — a dirtied, shadow-shrouded man. He was pilfering through the belongings of fallen soldiers — as I've seen many do after battle. I stared him down and waited, hoping he'd realize his mistake and slink off to defile another body. But he had no intention of retreating; he lunged at me with such force that the air was knocked from my lungs. I howled in pain as the weight of his body came down hard on mine. I fought for my life as his fingers clawed at my face, looking for my neck. I thrashed my arms and kicked him swiftly in the groin. He grunted, and I managed to dislodge his grip from my neck. Momentarily free, I forced our bodies to roll until I was on top of him. I tried to restrain him and speak some sense—I'd give him anything to secure my life. But he wouldn't be restrained or spoken to. With balled fists, he aimed hard for my stomach and his punch made my wound bleed anew. I fell back between his legs and he jumped atop me, clenching my neck between his hands. I beat on his back again and again, but his grip did not slack. I could feel my heart slow and my arms no longer had the strength to pummel him. After one last punch, my balled fists dropped to the ground beside me. Soft earth didn't cushion their fall; no, there was a large rock nestled in the dirt beneath. My mind reacted fast, and I yanked the rock from the earth, and slammed it into his skull. The force of the impact with his head—I heard the loud crack of rock on bone—made his grip loosen from my neck. I hit him over and over until his body went slack and he rolled off me. He was dead."

I inhaled deeply and held the air in my throat.

"It is one thing to kill from yards away using a pistol. But to kill with your bare hands—like a savage—and watch as the light extinguishes from your victim's eyes...is brutal. There's no turning back once you've started."

Silence dragged on for what felt like an eternity. Then he continued.

"After, I sat and stared at the deep cavity my brute force left in his skull. The rock was heavy in my hand; it was steeped in blood and pieces of his skull dripped from its sides. War made a monster of me—something I swore I'd never succumb to. He wasn't the first man I'd killed during this war, but he's the only man who still haunts my dreams."

"The realization of my plight brought a new fear. The 15th were gone; the hill was silent, and the dead were the only ones left. Soon the hills would be teeming with men loading bodies onto wagons. I had it in mind that all I needed was somewhere to hide for a few days then I'd cross back over the Potomac and rejoin what was left of my regiment. Or I'd head further north and wait out the war. But I knew I'd be spotted and taken for a deserter."

I nodded in agreement and looked at my hands. "The man you killed; you stripped him of his uniform?"

"Yes," he said with a heavy, ashamed breath. "There was simply no other way. If my wounds didn't kill me, that blue uniform was my only chance. I took his uniform and stuffed my soiled set into my bag. I searched the pockets and his possessions for letters; once I reached safety, I would send word to his people. But I found nothing; I don't even know his name."

"I placed his body beneath a tree and prayed over him, asking for his forgiveness. Before leaving, I placed my threadbare shoes on his feet. Though it would hinder my escape and tear my feet to shreds, that would be my penance to God."

I understood why he had killed the man and took his uniform; it was the 'killed or be killed' notion of war. But the brutality of his actions — words he used himself — was a stark contrast to the man I'd come to know. Emmet was gentle and considerate, not capable of killing a man with his bare hands to save his own life. And who knew what else could trigger such brutality? I was frightened. I stood and stepped a few inches to the right; he noticed immediately.

He stood slowly. "I…I'll finish with that chain."

I returned to the house and have stayed ever since. He has kept his distance for the rest of the day; I left food on the top step, and an hour later I found the plate clean. He knew not to push me any further.

I still know very little about Emmet, the man; I know the mind of the soldier, not the man. I'm no closer to understanding him and what caused him to enlist under duress. Tomorrow, I will ask more questions.

—A

August 11th, 1863

Sleep avoided me last night as it never has.

Every time I'd slip off, a vision would jerk me back into wakefulness. One crept upon me again and again — that of a man lying against a tree, naked but for a pair of shoes.

In the vision, his face was shadowed so I crouched down, positioning my face only a few inches from his. But then I'd fall back in fright. For it was Joseph staring back at me with dead eyes and gaping wounds that turned my stomach. I'd wake, screaming uncontrollably. It was horrific. Again, and again, I returned to the same tree, hoping the dream would be different; that another man's face would appear on the shod soldier. Each time it was worse; the pain on Joseph's face was amplified, the gore of his wounds more defined.

Were these visions a manifestation of my guilt or the heavens telling me that Joseph was in peril? My wakefulness only increased my fears. Eventually, I gave up on sleep and from the shelf above my bed, I grabbed down one of my medical texts and read until dawn.

When the sun rose, I was out of bed, dressed and standing in the open doorway looking out on the backyard. In my hand, I held what I assumed was an important possession of Emmet's. Today, I had questions.

Soon after, he appeared from the barn with my husband's tools dangling from a belt at his hips. For some reason—perhaps the lingering dream—seeing those tools at his waist stung me. It felt like a second violation to my property. But I'd never seen Joseph use those tools—or any tools. I stood, stewing in my emotions on the top step, as he crossed the yard and walked behind the barn.

I pocketed my small treasure and stepped from the house to follow him. With each step, I breathed deep and let the anger slip from me; I needed to control my emotions for what was coming next.

When I turned the corner, the tools were laid on the ground and he was maneuvering the felled logs. He lifted each log, flexing his muscles and carefully swinging the log's weight. I took a seat on a tree stump a few feet from him and waited. I won't be the first to speak, I said to myself. But impatience bubbled within me; I felt I would scream if he didn't acknowledge me.

"Beautiful day," he said finally, without turning to face me. The casualness of his speech irked me; had the day before not happened?

"It is." Emotionless was my voice.

In one hand, he took up an edge chisel and in the other a mallet. With the edge set firmly against the top of the log, he smacked the mallet down on the metal and into the wood. Again, and again, he did this and moved further down the log. Slowly, the log started to split. After some time, he sat back on his legs, the wind tousled his hair and he let his head fall back and revel in the breeze. "Did you sleep well?"

"Not very," I replied flatly.

"I do apologize if I had anything to do with it. I'm sure the last few days have been...taxing." He turned and finally looked at me; his brown eyes, the color of darkest soil, were full of contrition. In his throat, I could see his quick beating pulse; he was nervous my heart had changed, and I was going to banish him from my property. As I looked deep into his eyes, the nerve I'd built disappeared. His eyes—though sad—still held heat and I was butter, melting. My face blushed, so I averted my eyes.

"You seem to be skilled in carpentry." I needed to change the subject.

"Skilled, I am not. A knowledge of the basic principles: yes, I have that. Reggie—my father's chief Negro—taught me how to handle timber." The sound of the chisel and mallet started again. Two last strokes and the first log split in half.

"Did you work in that trade before the war?"

"No." He stood and laid the two halves side by side. "I was in Boston before the war."

"Boston?"

He wiped the sweat from his brow and turned back to me. "Law school. Harvard Law."

My eyebrows lifted, and my chin jutted forward; a dumb-founded reaction that I couldn't help. Though his speech and manners revealed a man of education, I had assumed he was a lowly soldier and nothing more.

He stifled a short laugh. "The south holds her sons close, so your surprise is warranted. I believe I was the only southerner in my class, and the only native-born from my county to leave in many a decade." He turned his attention back to the log.

"Did your father practice law?"

He stopped and turned to me again. "No. My parents didn't have the same educational advantages as I. They weren't born in America."

I crossed my arms over my chest. "Where were they from?"

"Ireland."

"I thought the hills of Ireland were green and bountiful?" I asked.

"Not as bountiful as you'd assume. My father—Malcolm Conroy—wanted more than empty pockets and bellies. When the opportunity arose, Daddy sold his land and brought his new bride, Margaret, to America."

I stood and stepped closer to the log halves. I laid them flat on the grass and dusted wood shavings from their surface. He split the second log and sat down beside it, wiping his sweat on the sleeve of his shirt.

"He'd heard tales of Alabama; the bountiful soil, the rolling hills of unclaimed land, and the prosperous opportunities were everything that Ireland wasn't. Cotton farming was like pulling gold from the ground. So, he bought a small piece of land in Haleburg and enough seed to get through one season."

I took a seat beside him on the grass.

"It was a stiff gamble, but the land was good—one of the best in the county. Three years passed, and he bought the neighboring property, rented out parcels to other farmers who grew for him, and filled the fields with enough Negroes to pick the crop. Then I came into the world."

Emmet would be their only child and they doted on him. He never knew the hardships they faced in Ireland and had the finest of everything from a young age. But at the end of every season, he helped bring in the crop and worked the land. He worked side by side with the slaves and picked until his knuckles bled. His father wanted him to see how their wealth was made and know that it was the result of hard work.

"Did you not want to follow his path; own a farm and raise a family?"

"Daddy knew I was a waste behind the plow. My private tutors suggested an education up North. And Daddy's money could pay for the best."

It was a family decision for Emmet to apply to law school; a life in politics was the goal. "Daddy was thrilled, thinking his son — the son of an immigrant farmer — would write the laws of his surrogate homeland. I received my acceptance letter from Harvard on June 2nd, 1857. My 18th birthday. The taste of freedom had me salivating."

I could feel myself smiling, recalling Philadelphia and my own taste of freedom.

Life up North was an adjustment. He'd never been to a big city, nor away from his parents. For two years, Emmet attended lectures in great halls with the brightest men in the country: he devoured the lessons, listening intently to his professor's experience; he worked hard to gain the respect of his peers; he excelled in political philosophy and Constitutional history, whereas Greek and Latin were troublesome; and the classics, like Virgil and Cicero's Orations, became his favorites and he was anxious to learn more. While the South held to its traditions, the North challenged and questioned. He finally felt part of something bigger. The Southern boy was fast becoming a Northerner.

Then a telegram arrived from his mother.

The smile drifted from his face. "It was the spring of 1860. I still remember her words. 'Daddy's sick. Come home, Emmet.' The situation had to be dire if Mama went to town to send a telegram. So, I got the first rail home and leaped from the still moving railcar when she pulled into Haleburg station. I ran straight to the family farm."

He sighed and looked at me, his eyes were glassy. "Daddy was stricken with an attack of apoplexy. Have you ever seen someone after such an attack?"

I nodded — I had cared for someone in town just that past winter.

He continued. "The cheer had been drained from the house and there he was, laying on a daybed in the first-floor parlor. He was alive, but only just; his body was as stiff as a board. His face drooped, like the muscles couldn't support the weight of his skin and drool poured from his lips. His eyes were frozen, as was his entire body. Mama told me to talk to him, that he could hear me. But to see him like that... it was pitiful. I sat at his side, day in and day out, hoping he'd return to us. The doctor could do nothing and explained that if he survived, he'd never be the same. As the months went on, he made slight improvements; he could sit up and strength returned to the left side of his body and he could walk with the assistance of a cane. But his speech never returned. It still hasn't, to my knowledge." His voice was choked with emotion. Solemnly, he crossed himself.

"I couldn't leave Mama. She didn't ask, but I made the decision and didn't return to Boston. The South engulfed me once more." He looked away from me, to the wood at his side and stroked the length of it.

From my apron's pocket I pulled what I'd been carrying. "I found this among your things." I showed him the tintype.

His hands were shaking as he reverently accepted the photograph. "They are my parents."

He stared at the tintype for quite some time before speaking again. "Mama insisted on having this taken." I scooted closer to him, to better see the picture. "Daddy thought it vain and absurd, refused to dress for it until she hauled him in from the fields. 'I know what I look like, Peggy darlin'. Who else will be wantin' my likeness,' I heard him complain from the copper tub in the kitchen. Their voices carried all the way to my bedroom."

"'I'll be wantin' to show me grandchildren one day. Now clean yerself and stop fussing about it.'" As he impersonated their Irish-tinged accents, his face lit with a glorious smile. "They sat for six different poses and gave me this one before I left for Boston."

Silence followed. Digging into the pain was callous of me but I had to know. "Is that what forced your hand in enlisting against your conscience: your father's health?"

"Not directly, no." His hand dropped and gently he placed the tintype on the grass in front of him. "Perhaps… things would've been different if he had fully recovered. I certainly wouldn't have come home without my degree. But…no, I don't believe he would've agreed with my enlistment if other options were to be had."

"Why then?" My voice was higher and louder than I intended. "You've spoken at length," I continued, tempering my voice below a roar, "of your conflict in fighting for a cause you don't condone; that the weight of the gun you carried for the South was an overwhelming burden. You killed men who stood for your ideals; you killed a man with your bare hands for mercy sakes! What made you choose this path?"

"Because I had no choice, damnit!" His face held a ferocious rage that was unsettling. "Haven't you ever had a decision stripped from you? Haven't you ever had to choose between two evils?"

My life has never been my own. But in that moment, I wasn't ready to divulge my painful past—it was the one part of me I wouldn't readily give to anyone. I stared back at him blankly.

"Daddy couldn't manage the farm without his speech. My father's legacy and my mother's welfare were my chief concerns: I wouldn't let either fall to the wayside while I had breath in my lungs. So, I took up his mantle and became his voice. I stayed on and made sure the farm made it through the transition. One, maybe two years and then I'd hire someone to take my place, and then I'd head back to Boston and take the bar."

I looked up at him. "Then Fort Sumter."

He nodded. "The outbreak of war changed everything. Quiet farmers who cared nothing for the world beyond their borders, suddenly became very impassioned about their rights and the injustices forced upon them by the North. There was no stepping into town, without being accosted with fiery opinions. And when I didn't enlist with the rest of my friends, those opinions only worsened and were directed at me."

"'The North has rattled young Conroy's mind,' I overheard one day as I passed the butcher's shop. I quickly realized that Haleburg was too small a town for anything to go unnoticed. I believed my convictions on the war were my business, but I was sorely mistaken. To serve in the Confederate army was an honor, and for anyone to dodge that honor was questionable. After a series of confrontations—one, outside the tavern, where a man came within inches of my face and deemed me a coward—I distanced myself from my neighbors. But southern pride has no bounds and will not be ignored. Two months after Fort Sumter, one of our cotton fields was set on fire. Initially, I believed it a coincidence, that the fire had nothing to do with the aggression I'd experienced in town. Then a week later, a word was painted onto the side of our barn; in large, white letters it read, YANKEE."

I held my breath.

"Setting our field on fire and scribbling a word on the side of a building weren't idle threats. Both were messages of retaliation, and the next time it would be worse. My parents' safety was now at risk, all because of my convictions. I considered selling my father's properties and moving the family up North. But since Daddy's sickness, Mama had become fearful of the world and refused to leave the house. There was only one solution; one I'd have to grin and bear."

Gray was the uniform he was issued, emblazoned with a secession badge and a cap with a county insignia: "HP" for "Henry's Pioneers." On the morning of his departure, the cloth of the uniform was heavy in his hands and on his body. He dressed, belted his short-waisted jacket and stood up straight, looking at his reflection in the standing mirror on his bedroom wall. He barely recognized himself. This man looked defeated and hollow; like a breathing ghost. He felt like he was already dead. He wondered if every man felt their mortality before leaving for war — that the uniform staring back at them would be their death garment.

He shouldered his M1841 Mississippi rifle and stepped from his childhood bedroom. His mother was waiting for him at the bottom of the staircase, hands clasped, and eyes closed tight. Her lips were moving at a furious pace, and as he walked down the stairs he could discern a few distinct words of prayer to the Holy Mother.

When she looked up at him — in his uniform — her face was beaming. "My handsome boy," she said, taking his face in her hands. From around her neck, she pulled a chain and draped it around his. "Saint Michael the Archangel will protect ya in yer endeavors." She put the medal to her lips, kissed it lightly and then laid it down upon his chest. Her hand lingered upon the medal, as she closed her eyes and whispered another short prayer. When her eyes opened again, she looked straight into his. "Trust in Saint Michael and come home to me."

Emmet's hand instinctually went to his chest. With a tinge of guilt, he said, "When I woke on the hill—after I fell—the medal was gone."

He brought the tintype closer to his face and I watched as his eyes drained of sadness, replaced by happy memories of days long past. I felt my conflicted heart ease. Our pasts weren't so different: both of us were forced to make decisions because of the love of another. For him, it was enlisting to ensure his parents' safety. For me, it was entrapment in a loveless marriage or be stripped of my last semblance of family.

Our souls were kindred.

A newfound shyness made me want to rush back to the house. I wrapped my arms around my chest and stood, saying, "I'll make us some breakfast."

As I turned to leave, he caught my hand. His grip was tender but firm, and my breath was lumped in my throat. Slowly, I turned back to face his brown eyes. He stared through me and a guilty smile formed on his lips. He released my hand and said, "Thank you."

I returned to the house and he worked steadfastly on the paddock posts. As I handed him plates of food, we spoke very little and nothing more about his past. But there was a definite shift in the air; we didn't avoid each other's eyes, nor did I feel uncomfortable in his presence.

Which is why—when the sun was low in the sky and supper was laid out—I left the backdoor open and allowed him to eat at my table once more. The talk between us was congenial and continuous. Almost like we were meeting for the first time. I liked it—our starting fresh and moving forward.

I will not forget his past nor his initial betrayal. But now I will see past the Confederate uniform and to the man beneath it. I am no fool; I know he is still a rebel soldier and I am at risk for harboring a deserter.

My heart has softened, and I feel I must help.

—A

August 14ᵗʰ, 1863

Like a fistful of sand, the last few days have slipped from me, grain by grain. The daylight hours have been packed full of work and activity. Every inch of my body aches but the tangible reward is worth every discomfort.

Emmet continues to sleep under the stars but has taken every meal with me. We have worked together in preparing the farm for fall and winter: four more trees he felled, replacing more paddock posts; we've planted the fall vegetables, and pickled what was left of the summer; and in two days, I will take a few of the sheep to town to be butchered. I will also check the Lists for news of Joseph.

For the past three mornings, Emmet has come to breakfast with chores for the day. He has been making mental lists of what needs to be repaired or improved. And though he's spent years behind a desk in the pursuit of a law degree, his knowledge of running a farm is vast. Working side by side has brought an intimacy that I didn't know I was missing.

Yet fear grows within me day by day; I fear for his discovery. My ears are constantly perked for the sound of hooves and I am always jumpy. I know his secret — and have come to terms with it — but others will not be so kind. The war has moved back beyond the Potomac, but the danger is still very real.

We don't speak of it.

Oh, when will this war end?

— *A*

August 17th, 1863

This morning I was sitting on the front porch — rolling bandages from freshly cut linen — when I heard wagon wheels on gravel. I knew it wasn't Henry; I'd gone back to the Larsen's and told him I wouldn't need his help for a while. So, I froze, and my mind rushed with fear for Emmet. Please stay wherever you are, I prayed.

When Mother's covered carriage pulled into view, my heart rose in my throat and I practically choked on it.

William — her long-employed butler, who traveled wherever she went — nodded his head in welcome as he pulled up in front of my house. He climbed from and stood to the side of the carriage, preparing to open the door.

"That won't be necessary," she said, dismissing him with a wave of her hand. "We shan't be long." Her face was hidden beneath a large, flower-embellished, purple hat that perfectly matched her silk gown.

"Yes, Madam." He bowed and returned to the horses at the front of the carriage.

I stepped from the porch like a frail, elderly woman. I wanted so desperately to rush inside and bolt the door. Refuse to see her and dismiss her like she so easily did her hired help. But I hadn't the gumption to deny her when she stood on my property for the first time ever. I stepped closer to the carriage.

"I wasn't expecting you, Mother," I said, believing it more appropriate than what I was truly thinking. I'd been to town only the day before, but I purposefully avoided Rosie's, knowing Mother was likely still there. "I didn't know you knew where I lived."

She turned her head and looked down on me like I was the lowest of low. Purple was her color, everyone told her so; her wardrobe was filled with pieces from all over the world and she sought out the hue in most shops. She was a beauty — even now in her forties — and purple played to her dark eyes and hair. She looked me over critically, pausing on my unshod, dirty feet and stained apron. A grin of condemnation pursed her lips as her eyes made their way back to my face. "I didn't. Roseanna let me know...which path to turn down."

"I'd offer you some refreshment, but you don't seem to have the time," I added, ignoring her tone.

"We are booked on the noon rail for Harrisburg. Benjamin waits for me there. We are on to New York and then Europe. But Roseanna insisted I pay you a visit."

"Well," I said, gesturing to the house behind me, "it seems you've fulfilled your obligation."

She leaned out from the carriage and took in her surroundings; dissecting each corner, pinning it to her memory to recall on days she needed a hearty laugh. How pathetic the existence of her unwanted, eldest daughter, she'd think slyly.

"How quaint." Her gaze fell back to me and her eyes were light and airy—misleadingly so, as I knew the mockery circulating in her head.

"I'd hate for you to miss your train. Goodbye, Mother." I turned but before I could saunter away, she reached out of the carriage window and grabbed my hand to force me back.

"I thought you might want to know that Roseanna and I have been discussing her living situation." She released my hand—mentioning Rosie would keep me at her side for a few moments more.

"I'm not sure there is much to discuss, Mother. She lives with her husband after all."

"Yes. But the birth of my granddaughter—"

"Mary. Her name is Mary."

"—has changed her circumstances and she must look to the future of the child." She brushed her fingers along the metal frame of the carriage.

"I'm sure Rosie and Jonathan will raise their daughter adequately without interference from others."

"Which is my point."

My head cocked to the side in question.

"Your interference," she continued, "is not wanted. I've been lenient with your continued and unnecessary relationship with my daughter, but I will not allow Mary's blossom to be tarnished. She will not become a scamp in the forest, as your grandmother guided you to be. I've made some inquiries in Philadelphia and I believe I can secure Jonathan a new posting."

"You would have them move to Philadelphia all to avoid my interference?"

She folded her hands in her lap and chose her words carefully. "Further north would be safer, given the current state of the country."

"You would lie and manipulate your own daughter just to separate us? Why?" I waited for a reply, but she stared at me blankly. "Why do you hate me so? All of this cannot be from jealousy." My voice rattled through the woods; my anger was a steaming kettle, ready to whistle and burst.

"Jealous? Of all this? Silly child, who'd ever be jealous of you?" Her eyes were hurtfully joyful.

"Rosie is my family. You are my family." My voice croaked with the pain her poisonous barbs inflicted.

She turned her face frontwards, into the carriage and away from me. "Your family is buried in Cashtown."

I wanted — so badly — to reach inside the carriage and slap the joy from Mother's face; to inflict a pain similar to what she was hurling at me. But I believe that was what she wanted; it would be another reason to further disown me.

I stepped back from the carriage. "Goodbye, Rachel."

Her eyebrows arched in amusement—as I'd never addressed her so—and her chest burst in a short giggle. She called for William who clambered up into his carriage seat and retrieved the reins. With a slight flick of his whip, he guided the horses from my yard and out of view.

A tide of emotion swept me, and my legs crumbled beneath me. But as quick as a lightning strike, Emmet was beside me and sweeping me like a ragdoll in his arms. He carried and gently placed me down on the porch steps. He rushed inside and returned with a glass of water. My hands were shaking as I accepted it gratefully and took a long swig, savoring the coldness against my parched throat. He hushed my profuse apologizes and took a seat beside me.

"I'm only thankful I was close enough to aid. I'd be useless if you truly hurt yourself."

I emptied the glass and handed it back to him. We sat in silence for a few minutes; enough time for my hands to stop shaking.

"Those folks you were speaking with—not your neighbors, I expect?"

"No, not neighbors," I answered meekly. "Did you listen to—"

"No, no." He shook his head defensively. "I'd only just stepped in the house when I heard the horses. Scared the lights from me and I dropped to the floor like a sack of potatoes. I managed to crawl to the front window and watched you talking with the lady. Figured it was safer to stay put."

I nodded and looked away.

"From the little I saw, I made out a bit of a resemblance."

I rolled my eyes in aggravation. Looking like my mother was not a compliment I ever wanted to hear—not matter how beautiful she was. Innocently, he shrugged his shoulders.

"She is my mother," I explained.

"Ah. Your meeting didn't seem cordial." He inched closer to my side. "I don't mean to pry but...seeing how I found you; I assume you heard something unsettling?"

I sighed. "She means to keep my sister from me."

He sat further back on the wooden planks of the porch and his eyes searched my face. He was inviting me to continue; he wanted my story. He needed to understand me, just as I needed him. Only once—in your pages—have I recalled my full, pitiful past and not another soul—save Rosie—knows the extent of my sorrow. I feared telling him everything, but I owed it to him.

What's more, I trusted him.

I closed my eyes, inhaled deeply and the dam of my emotions—plugged and protected with all my willpower—broke. My eyes remained closed as images danced through my mind with vicious clarity. I described my triumphs and my pain: the story of my childhood and Mother's abandonment and her seething hatred for my existence; how Mam took me into her home, loved me unconditionally and bestowed on me the knowledge of medicine; the birth of Rosie, the sister I always wanted, and the close bond we share to this day; how I met Dr. Watkins, my formal education and my trip to Philadelphia; and finally, how all of my dreams were stripped from me after Mam's death and the circumstances of my marriage.

When I finished—hours later, it seemed—my throat was dry, aching, and my voice's whispery tone irked me. I was spent and all I wanted to do was flee—hide in a dark corner of the barn and pretend I had never existed. I dared not look at him. Perhaps I couldn't trust him not to judge me too harshly?

Cautiously he reached into my lap, took my right hand and held it between his. His touch caught me off guard; I turned to look at him and his face was adorned with compassion and acceptance. And the warmth of his touch renewed me.

We stayed there in a silent intimacy. Our thoughts were aligned, as were the sorrows of our separate pasts that brought us to my porch.

I've never known such happiness, and as I recall it here—in your pages—I feel it once more. He's taken my pain—pain from my past and my new fear of losing Rosie—and wrapped it with affection. For those few moments, all I felt was peace.

For the first time since Mam's death, my heart is open, and I don't feel so alone.

Chapter Twenty-Nine

Breanne Walker

N OTHING FEELS STRANGER THAN THE FIRST ATTEMPT AT MOVEMENT
when parts of your body have fallen asleep. You
urge and urge your dead limbs to shift, but they remain
locked, stubborn and immobile. So, you physically force
movement—you lift one of your dead arms just to get the
blood flowing. But that first exertion brings the pins and
needles—that's what Mom called it. Pins and needles for
the prickling sensation that surges through your limbs.
"Shake them out, Breanne. Like a pebble in your sneaker,"
she'd say when I yelped in pain. I'd jump around the room
like a wobbly monkey, screeching until the feeling slowly
crept back in.

The diary was opened atop the coffee table in front of
me and my legs were folded and curled beneath it. From
the age of five, this was my preferred reading position. I
leaned back against the cushioned legs of my plush, gray
couch and contemplated standing. But I was numb from
the waist down. I scraped my fingernails up and down my

legs, hoping to rub the life back into them. I shifted my torso to the side, stretching my legs out and wiggling my toes.
The prickling sensation began, and I knew I had to stand.

So, with gnashing teeth and cringing from the pain, I
braced myself between the coffee table and couch, and lifted
my lifeless body to a standing position. "Jesus," I grunted
as I took my first unsteady step and almost toppled to the
carpet. I sat down on the couch's arm and flexed my toes.

I glanced at the coffee table and could see the progress I
had made; the unread pages on the right were significant-
ly less than when I started. In fact, there was only a short
stack of pages remaining. Peggy's Monday deadline was
achievable. And I was inching my way closer to solving the
mystery of A.M.P. and the Witness Tree. I was fairly certain
I knew who the man was — the Confederate soldier thrust
into the diarist's life, Emmet Conroy. But how did he end
up buried in an unmarked grave? How did the diary end
up there? Their relationship — building every day — left me
desperate for more; I secretly wished A.M.P. would appear
to me again and include Emmet. Minimally she described
his appearance but...in my mind he closely resembled Greg.
Okay...stop it, I told myself.

Again, I looked down at the small bound stack of pages
remaining and a feeling of disappointment crept in. Though
I wanted to solve the mystery, I didn't want to lose the connection to A.M.P. I didn't want her story to end.

Slowly, circulation returned to my legs, and I was
able to stand unassisted. No longer immobile, a surge

of energy hit me, and the room felt very small. I started pacing the apartment like a football player waiting to
take the field before the Super Bowl. It was a jittery, "*I
could probably punch through a wall*" kind of energy that I
couldn't quite place. Around and around I went, and the
diary stared up at me.

My intensity needed to be put back to the task at hand:
finishing the diary.

Once more, I shook out my body and then returned to
the coffee table. I sat with my legs out straight in front of
me—hoping to avoid the dead-leg syndrome—and carefully, I flipped the page to the next entry.

But I found something else.

Nestled inside the crease was a folded, yellowed piece
of paper that was not sewn into the spine. It wasn't the
first addition to the diary—the first had been a letter from
Joseph. I shifted the diary forward and tugged at the piece
of paper until it was free in my hand.

It was another letter.

June 20ᵗʰ, 1863

Dear Madam,

I am unsure of your connection to Corporal Joseph
Pritchard but yours is the only letter I found among his belongings and I was unsure who else to contact. I know him
only as a nurse who sat by his bed but thought it my duty
to write you a few lines regarding his state.

For the last month, he was under my care at Harewood Hospital in Washington — he was brought in on a wounded convoy with many others after the battle in Chancellorsville. His wounds were minor and easily mended by Dr. Burgess, one of the best surgeons in the army. A bullet was lodged in his knee, but the foreign matter was found and safely removed without fear of post-op amputation. Soon after, unfortunately, he was afflicted with typhoid. He was assigned to my ward — C Ward on the west wing of the hospital. Joseph was one of the few patients who never had a visitor, so my Christian charity kept bringing me to his side. The fever kept him unconscious for much of his stay, but I took to reading him passages from the bible and I found comfort in those moments. At night, he was restless and — in his delirium — believed he was still serving with his regiment. His screams were something awful and I tended to him the best I could.

With a heavy heart, I now write to inform you of his passing two days past — on the 18th of this month. I held his hand as his soul lifted from his body and went on to meet God in the thereafter. I can attest to the level of care he received at Harewood and want to assure you that everything was done to save his life. But his duty was served on this earth and God chose to call him home. He died nobly and with the belief that he aided in the cause of the Union Army. He joins the ranks of many stalwart men.

I hope this letter brings you solace and closure. Again, I do not know your connection to Joseph Pritchard but I hope you will extend my condolences to his family. You are all in my nightly prayers.

Yours,

Sarah Paulson

My neck could not hold the weight of my head; it fell back onto the couch cushions behind me as I whispered obscenities. I opened my eyes and stared straight up at the cracks in my apartment's ceiling. *Every time I try and catch my breath, something else slams into me.*

Joseph was dead almost two weeks before the Army of Potomac arrived in Gettysburg. He never set foot in his hometown, again. How would the diarist react to the news? She had little affection for him, but her life was tied to his fate.

And what would this mean for her relationship with Emmet?

That question spoke the loudest. So loud in fact that I almost missed a major revelation: Joseph's last name was PRITCHARD. When I reread the letter, my eyes bugged out of my head and if I wasn't sitting on the floor with my legs spread under the coffee table, I would've triumphantly leaped into the air. Assuming the diarist took her husband's last name, I finally had the *P* of *A.M.P.*

I took my pad of paper and pencil and started jotting notes of where I could find a listing for the Pritchard family—birth, death, baptismal, and marriage certificates then land deeds, public notices, and census reports—then a secondary list of where to pull the documents. But I stopped myself before I got carried away; I had to put the pencil down before I forgot my main objective.

"Finish the diary, Breanne."

A.M.P's story was more important than finding out her full name. I needed to know what happened between A.M.P. and Emmet after receiving this letter.

I pushed my notepad aside and leaned in closer to the diary to read.

Chapter Thirty

A.M.P.

August 23rd, 1863

I KNEW.

I knew the moment I opened my door to Mr. Buehler.

I was kneading dough and humming a tune Emmet had taught me the day before. I was on the second verse of "Abroad as I was Walking" when a loud rap on my front door interrupted me.

Shivers erupted down my spine. Emmet and I were past the pretense of door knocking, so I knew it couldn't be him. I stared at the door, hoping a wisp of wind had knocked the window shutter against the pane. A minute passed, silence returned, and I'd almost convinced myself that I'd imagined the whole thing. I pressed my palms into the fresh dough, again.

Then a heavier, more pronounced knock sounded.

I wiped my hands on my apron and walked to the front door. As my hand reached for the door handle, a sense of foreboding struck, and my hand froze. I couldn't place the feeling; I knew Emmet was at a safe distance from the farm, deep in the forest felling more trees for fence posts. No, the feeling of dread was connected to something — someone — else. I opened the door to find Mr. Buehler. That's when I knew it had to be about Joseph.

I didn't speak; I stood like an ancient Grecian statue, staring wide-eyed and ahead for eternity. One nudge and I would've fallen over and shattered into a thousand pieces.

His arms were behind him and his gaze was firmly planted on the floor beneath his feet.

"I told you I'd bring your mail. We're behind, terribly behind after the battle." From his vest pocket he produced a letter and from the flapping seal, it had clearly been opened. "This should've been here weeks ago. I'm sorry...I know I shouldn't have but I saw the return address and...I opened it." He looked up and his eyes held shame. I felt nothing.

He placed the letter into my waiting hands. I stared down at it, at my name printed in ink, and it felt heavy — if dropped, it would have thudded on the hardwood floor like a piece of metal. Only when Mr. Buehler cleared his throat did I remember he was still standing on my porch.

I looked up and took a step back into my house. "Thank you." I reached for the handle and inched the door to a close.

"I'm sorry. I truly am," Mr. Buehler said before I closed the door entirely on him. He stood on the other side, perhaps debating if he should linger and say more. I waited there—leaning against the door—until I heard the trot of horse hooves on the path.

Once more, I looked down to the letter in my hand, a letter with a Washington return address. All letters concerning the fate of Union soldiers came from Washington, this I knew firsthand; I've been called to help calm widows after the letters were received. The words in those letters broke the hearts of the recipients and the aftermath was brutal.

Slowly, I tore my eyes from the letter and found Emmet standing in the back doorway, staring intently at me. I walked towards the table and sat. Emmet mimicked my actions, taking a seat across from me.

Carefully, I laid the letter flat on the wooden surface and opened it. I read it. Twice. Let the news soak in. But I felt nothing; like a blank slate covered my body. Emmet was patiently waiting for me and when I finished, I met his gaze head on.

"He's dead." Hearing the words as they fell from my mouth—not just reading the facts on the page—felt final and real.

Emmet released his held breath. He looked down at his hands and asked, "How? When?" He feared it had been here; that he'd played a part in my husband's demise.

"Typhoid. After Chancellorsville. He never returned to battle." I handed him the letter.

He took the letter from me and I watched as his eyes scanned the page, lingering on the closing remark. The tension released from his shoulders and his eyes lifted to mine.

"He served and died with honor. I am so very sorry for your loss," he said, meaning every syllable of it.

But loss hadn't filled the emptiness Mr. Buehler left when he handed me the letter. For in that moment, all I felt was… relief. Like the invisible chain binding me to my present life had dropped and my body was now weightless. I felt like myself again; like the woman I was before my forced marriage.

Emmet wanted to speak — I could see his throat wobbling with emotion and his fists were tightly clenched. His pain looked realer than my own — which I couldn't allow. In that moment I knew exactly what I wanted.

Resolution made me stand from the table and step towards him. Our bodies were so close — the fabric of my skirt was brushing against his legs. We stared at each other, not speaking, and time seemed to slow. My breath was leaden and caught in my throat, and his eyes pierced me. The chair legs scratched against the wooden floor as he leaned back and raised himself to my height.

Only a breath of air separated us.

I uncurled my left hand and reached out, laying my palm directly on his chest. Beneath the cotton of his shirt, I could feel his beating heart. I watched in fascination as my hand vibrated atop it. Was I doing this to him? Cautiously, I looked up. His head was tilted to the side, like he was questioning my intentions. I stared back, unable to breathe and afraid to move. He placed his own hand over my heart and I could feel every hair on my body stand on end.

And the space between us became even less.

He reached for my neck and pulled me towards him, covering my mouth with his own. My body felt weak in his embrace, and if he hadn't been holding me I would've fainted. All of it was foreign: the way he held me, his hot lips on mine, his wet tongue in my mouth. I allowed the kiss to deepen, but my eyes were firmly closed. My mind raced with questions: was I meant to kiss him back; did he want me to grip him close; was this wrong? I'd never experienced an embrace of this type—Joseph and I were never intimate. But before I could calm myself, my lips were deserted. I dared open my eyes and found him staring at me, ashamedly.

He released his gentle grip and backed away from me. "I'm sorry." His eyes dropped. "I've wanted to do that from the moment I laid eyes on you. It's wrong...you've had such awful news about your husband, and I shouldn't take advantage of—"

The thought of losing his touch answered my lingering doubts; I grabbed his shoulders, pulled him to me, and feverishly kissed him. I wrapped my arms around him, pulling my body up against his. My forwardness shocked him, and initially, his body stiffened. Then he melted into me and we became one. Everything was how it was meant to be. Our kiss became more of a primitive need, and to separate our lips would have been a torture most cruel. Our fingers explored, grasped and touched with no bounds.

Now he sleeps, wrapped in the quilts of my bed.

The curve of Emmet's naked back is towards me and by faint candlelight, I can just make out the rise and fall of his breathing. My body is still abuzz with emotion. I turn every few minutes to be assured that it really happened; that I haven't imagined giving myself to him in every way possible. My body answers me with rushing blood and heat.

Oh, how I yearn to be beside his warmth once more, so I will end this passage quickly.

The letter from Washington sits beside these pages, and though my thoughts are occupied, I have not forgotten about Joseph. I have reread the letter; like an itch needing to be scratched, the contents of the page remind of their existence. I will pray for Joseph's soul and hope that his pain wasn't too great. My life is once again my own, and I will not live another day under someone else's expectations.

It may seem queer for me to have written down what is considered perverse and explicit, but I care not. This day was altering—in more ways than one—and I will want to recall these events in the years to come. For this day has been the best of my life.

—A

August 26ᵗʰ, 1863

"I've been thinking," Emmet said, propping himself up against my bed's headboard.

"I thought thinking was meant for waking hours." I pulled the quilt over my shoulders and snuggled into the crook of his arm.

It'd been three days since I received the letter concerning Joseph's death. Three days since Emmet and I stopped denying our feelings for each other and gave in to our longing hearts. And three days since we'd left the confines of my bed for more than a few hours. Passion has wrapped its arms around us and kept a firm hold. Every boundary, every internal defense created over my years of solitude, fell and I gave in to every desire. He knew every inch of me: body and soul.

"Thinking about leaving this bed—now that is a dangerous thought. No, my thoughts have wandered to the future."

He was so deliciously warm. I kissed his chest and wrapped my arms around him. "I haven't thought further than a month for years."

"You've never had to, my love. You've been a prisoner on this farm—in this town—for far too long. And now, you can have anything you want. So, what do you want?"

"Just this." I kissed his chest again. "Just you."

He rubbed my back and kissed the top of head. "I'll never leave your side. But we cannot remain in this cabin forever."

I sat up. "Why not? What else could we need?"

He smiled and brushed my hair behind my ears. "A life where I can step from your door without fear. A life far away from the torments of your past."

"But the war—"

"Peace will return to this country and the states will unite. Gettysburg proved that the South cannot win. And I want us to start over."

"Where?"

"Further North. We could get lost in a big city. No one would ever look for us."

"Boston?"

He smiled again and pulled me back into his arms. "You've read my mind, you little witch." He pulled me back into his arms. "Yes, Boston; I can take the bar and provide a fine life for us."

"Shall I just be keeping your house? At least in Gettysburg, I can practice medicine and still have some independence."

"Isn't that obvious?" He rolled over on his side and our faces practically touched. "With your experience in battle surgery and midwifery, any medical school would be a fool not to accept you. And I'll sue whoever objects."

"But how—"

"No." He put his pointer-finger to my lips. "No questions. No thinking, remember? At least not tonight."

"You are mad," I laughed.

"Could be." He smiled and pulled me closer. "Just say yes and I'll figure out the rest."

The practical part of me—the part I've been shushing for the last few days—wanted to list out the multiple ways his plan couldn't happen. It was a dream! A fool's dream that could never come to be. But as I saw the sincerity in his eyes, my reservations evaporated. All that mattered was he and I. "Yes. Yes, a million times yes."

And he pulled me in for a kiss that lasted hours.

His dream was more comforting and warm than the real world, and in it I wanted to remain always. We stayed there, painting a picture of a perfect life away from Gettysburg. Together, we will make it happen.

I love him.

−A

August 30th, 1863

Last night, my dreams were blanketed with a harrowing dread—a dread that shook me to the core and woke me from a deep sleep. Words escape me now, as I sit here and try to recall what my subconscious was dwelling on. It wasn't a common nightmare; I wasn't running for my life or witnessing a horrific scene of pain. But the feeling…the feeling of hopelessness strangled my heart. Oh, it was awful and consuming.

I woke with a start in the wee hours of the morning and hoped for sanctuary in the real world. Wakefulness only brought further darkness. Perhaps I'm still asleep, I thought as I blinked my eyes furiously. My mind jumped to the worst possible assumption; your life will be an abyss of darkness and you will never escape it. My recent happiness was only a façade and misery would cling to me like a persistent cough. The walls started closing in and my throat tightened. I needed air.

I kicked away the strangling quilts and peeled myself from the mattress. I stepped towards the backdoor and flung it open, let the fresh air and moonlight wash over me. But that wasn't enough; I crouched in the doorway and hugged my knees to my chest, rocking back and forth in silent prayer.

Just as I was about to fall apart entirely, Emmet was there, wrapping me in a protective embrace. I'd forgotten about him; my dream had pushed every good thing out of my head.

He rubbed my back and asked, "Do you feel ill?"

"No, I...I just...can't breathe," I whispered into my knees between gasps of air. Every part of me was convulsing.

He stepped in front of me and grasped my knees. "Your dreams: were they horrid?"

"I feel like I'm not really here. That...that I'm not in my body. I think...I think I'm going mad."

"No, no. You aren't awake yet. Look at me, darling. Look at me." I obeyed like a meek child, begging her mother to kiss away her pain. "Pick something on my face, dissect it. Stare until you feel your mind settle."

With the moon shining behind him, I could make out the line of his jaw, the point of his nose, and finally the corners of his eyes. I looked straight into those dark brown orifices. I imagined where the specs of gold were—circling his pupils—and the long, velvety touch of his eyelashes on my cheek. Then the way his eyelids fluttered when he was excited or happy. Slowly, the haze on my brain lifted, my vision cleared, and I could feel my mind reconnect to my body. I sighed, and the tension released from my body.

"Welcome back," he whispered as he leaned forward and nipped my lips.

"How did you...how did you know what to do?"

He wrapped his arm around me. "I know the look: like a rabid animal with eyes wide and halted breath. My sleep has been plagued with such nightly terrors, as was my father's. When I was a child, he'd hear my screams and rush to my side. He'd bring me back from the dream world, asking me to concentrate on something in my bedroom."

Relieved, I laid my head on his shoulder. "Was it every night?"

"No. When I went to bed worried about something, it always hit me within an hour or two of falling asleep."

I nodded into his shoulder and my heart's beat synchronized with his.

"Anything vexing you?" he asked.

"Everything," I laughed. "But...I suppose my mind has been preoccupied with thoughts of the future. And this house."

"The things I told you not to worry yourself with."

I leaned away from him. "I've been on my own for quite some time, Emmet," I said, not bothering to hide my annoyance. "And it's been even longer since someone has taken care of me."

"Tell me then." He scooted in front of me, so our faces were practically touching.

"Too much of your plan is dependent on chance. Journeying up North is certainly dangerous but the issue of your soldiering for the Confederates puts you in even more danger. How can we flee with this hanging over your head?"

"I cannot deny either. But I have friends in Boston—friends who will gladly take us in and publicly vouch for us."

"But if we're going to start over we need money: for lodging, schooling, and sustenance."

"I agree."

"I have a bit, but nothing close to what we'll need."

He rubbed his thumbs into my shoulder blades. "This land, your flock will bring a hefty profit."

"You forget that the land, the house on it—none of it belongs to me. All of it will go to Joseph's nearest male kin once his death is known." Joseph's death freed me from my marriage, but soon I would be destitute. I held no stake in the farm and surely Joseph hadn't the foresight to include me in his will.

"You forget, my love, that I'm familiar with the laws of the land."

"You never finished," I reminded him.

"That is hearsay and—aside from the ramblings of a desperate solider—you have no proof," he mocked, tweaking the tip of my nose as he did. "After my second year, I worked as a clerk at a small firm. I transcribed legal documents until my fingers were blackened with ink. And many of those documents dealt with property law."

"But that's Boston—"

"Yes, there are variances from Massachusetts and Pennsylvania law, but I'll take the bar in Pennsylvania if I must. The flock of sheep: your dowry procured them, did it not? That is partial ownership—and considering recent events, that has changed to full ownership."

I opened my mouth to offer a rebuke—more out of habit than anything else—but I was speechless. In fear of looking ridiculous, I closed my mouth tight and scrambled for a clear thought to add.

He cocked his head, begging me to debate more.

"Please don't patronize me, Emmet. I'm allowed to be worried about things as vital as my future. There is no security when it comes to you and I."

He huffed and pulled me into his arms again. "What security do you require? Marriage?"

I pulled away and looked at him with a hard expression. "That's not...that's not what I—"

"That's my intent."

I looked at him like he had just spoken a foreign language. I couldn't have heard him right.

"Don't look at me like that," he said. "Marry me! Be mine always!"

Blissful happiness overwhelmed me. "Of course! Of course, I will," I cried, pulling him hard against my chest.

We kissed with renewed fervor.

"Back to bed," he said, breaking our kiss. "Conversations like these are better suited to daylight."

He stood and offered his hand. From the floor, I looked up at him — to savor the moment, commit it to memory and remind myself that I wasn't dreaming. The glisten in his eyes made it even more real. He winked and helped me to my feet and then to bed.

Darkness still clung to the room around me, but now it wasn't so lonely.

— A

September 4th, 1863

Twice this week, I've pried myself from Emmet and visited my patients in town. One is nearing the end of her term and she was glad to see me both times, as was her husband. I've assured them both that I will be at her beck and call once her labor has begun.

Visiting my patients also gave me an excuse to visit Rosie and darling Mary.

"She is growing like a beansprout, Rosie! What are you feeding her?" As I balanced her on my thighs, Mary wiggled and kicked her strong, long legs. She will be crawling before Rosie has time to store away her valuables, I thought as I struggled to hold on to her squirming form.

Rosie stood to clear the tea tray. "She loves the breast almost as much as her Papa—" she gasped and put her hand to her mouth. She scurried to the kitchen with the tea tray, mumbling words of embarrassment as she went.

Before, I would've shrunk from talk of the carnal nature; Rosie and I never spoke of intercourse and her gasp was an expected reaction. Things were now different. I thought of Emmet and blood pumped to parts of my body that I hadn't known existed. Part of me wished I could confide in her, speak openly about Emmet and all that had transpired between us. I sighed, knowing I couldn't. At least not yet; his existence was still a delicate issue and it needed to remain a secret until...well until we figured out our next step.

I refocused on Mary, littering her cheeks with kisses. I bounced her up and down on my knee and her innocent giggles filled the silence of the house. Her laugh was contagious, and my own voice joined hers.

"Why sister," Rosie said as she reentered the room, "I can't recall the last time I heard you laugh. Has something happened?"

"Nothing comes to mind." I sat Mary down on my lap and stared at the crown of her head, avoiding eye contact with my sister.

"Have you heard from your husband?"

Her question stung. I looked at her; Joseph was another subject we never discussed. How odd for her to bring him up? "No, not a word," I lied.

"Curious." The look in her eye was queer. "I only assumed something would've arrived; even if he wasn't engaged here, surely he'd be concerned for your welfare after learning of the battle?"

"There has been nothing, sister."

"Curious," she repeated, slowly annunciating the syllables.

The lies were compounding. The words were forming on my lips, but I closed them and kept the thoughts circling in my mind. She'd have understood—I know this, without a doubt—but I couldn't tell her. It would only lead to more questions or possibly an unannounced visit to check on her now widowed sister. I couldn't risk it. I'd deal with Joseph's death once the news was made public.

I took my leave soon after. The day was waning, and I wanted to stop at the Lists—to see if his death was indeed public knowledge.

I made my way to the center of town and stood in front of the announcement board. The constant crowds in the weeks following the battle had diminished to a trickle and today no one was in sight. Today, I had the time and privacy to leisurely scan the death notices. My future clung to the public news of his death. I lifted my hand and traced down the names—read them each, one by one—until I found his.

Pritchard, Joseph of Gettysburg, PA

It was real; no longer in a private letter, only read by myself, Emmet, and Mr. Buehler. The whole of town would know — perhaps Rosie knew and that's what prompted her question. The rolled yarn of my life would start to unravel and now, my life could begin again. Begin with Emmet as my husband. Atop Barley, I rode back to my little cabin in the woods with a happy heart.

Straight into Emmet's loving embrace.

— A

September 9th, 1863

My patient's — Catherine Russel — labor had begun a few weeks early. Two days ago, her husband rushed to fetch me in the wee hours of the morning, urging me to follow him back to town. Luckily, the curtains were drawn, and Mr. Russel was too frazzled to look inside my home — to Emmet curled up in my bed.

"I'll return as quick as I can," I whispered to Emmet after gathering my things.

"I'll be waiting," he said, pulling me into a farewell kiss that left my lips tingling and head reeling.

Four hours after my arrival to the Russel home, I was handing a beautiful baby girl to her mother. As she had three sons already, a girl was a welcome sight to Catherine.

"Isn't she lovely?" she asked me.

I replied the way I always did: "The loveliest I've ever seen."

She studied every inch of the infant's face, kissing each of her fingers and the crown of her head. I watched as I usually did during these precious first moments, but this time it was different.

I will know for sure in a few days' time. My heart flutters merely thinking of the possibility growing in my womb.

I tidied the room and made sure she was comfortable. With three children already, Catherine needed very little instruction. So, I gathered my things and took my leave.

Outside the Russel home, I was met with a torrential downpour. The heavens had opened, and Gettysburg was being pounded with all its blustery might. But I was determined as ever to return home—and a little rain would not stop me. I stepped to the hitching post and untied Barley's reins. I climbed up into her saddle and trusted she knew the way, as I could barely see my hand in front of my face.

Sometime later, I forcefully kicked open the front door of my home to find Emmet piling fresh logs onto the hearth. He took one look at me and his jaw dropped, and he keeled over in a fit of laughter. For I was a sight to behold: my clothing was drenched and muddied, my hair was unkempt, windblown, and standing on end. Undoubtedly, I resembled a drowned cat.

"I'm glad you find this funny," I said with chattering teeth. I stepped into the house and my shoes squeaked, leaving little puddles on the hardwood floor.

"Come inside," he laughed, ushering me into the fold. "Let's get you out of those clothes."

He built up the fire, sat me down in the rocking chair before it, wrapped me in the quilt from our bed, and boiled some water to warm my feet. With a dry towel, he stood behind me, combing out my hair. His fingers were gentle, and my entire body warmed to his touch.

"Mam brushed my hair out every Sunday. I don't think anyone's touched it since."

"Not even Rosie?"

"No. After Mam died…it just didn't feel the same."

His hands froze. "Do you mind that I'm—"

"Of course not." I grabbed his hand and brought his fingers to my lips. "It's heavenly." His fingertips grazed my scalp and I melted beneath his touch.

"Well then." He leaned in, sweeping the hair away from my ears and whispered, "perhaps you'll find other places heavenly." With his tongue, he pulled my earlobe into his ear and suckled. I grasped the arms of the chair and let the quilt fall to the floor. His hand wandered down to my neck and exposed chest, where he continued to litter my skin with kisses. He spun the chair around to face him and said, "It's been far too long since I touched you."

"It's only been—"

He covered my mouth with his and I succumbed to his unadulterated need.

Hours later—and Emmet's appetite for my flesh abated—we were lying on the quilt before the dying fire. The embers cast a comforting orange glow across the room, and shadows danced among the beams overhead. My head lay on his chest and the sound of his breath was lulling me to sleep.

"There's a lot in this house. A lot you could sell."

"Hmmmm," I mumbled, only half listening.

"No really." He leaned up on his elbows, waking me fully with his movements—annoyingly so. "Your bed, the tables and chairs—anything that isn't nailed down could bring a good price. Even your produce and stock of hay." He looked around the room, seeming to make inventory.

"I suppose," I yawned.

"We'd never be able to take any of this with us, but we could sell it in town."

"To who?"

"To anyone willing to pay. It matters not."

"I like when you say We."

He settled onto the quilt and pulled me back down onto his chest. "I'll say it all day if it makes you smile." He traced the curve of my spine with his fingertips.

"But you're right—we don't need any of this." I swept my hand around the room.

"We just need we," he said.

I nuzzled back into his chest and we continued to talk— dream about the future of we.

September 16th, 1863

When I woke this morning, I was alone.

I rolled over, reached for Emmet and my hand found air. My hand dropped and the mattress beneath was cold; he had been gone for quite some time. I wasn't alarmed — I assumed he had only gone to milk Gertie.

But the sun wasn't up; my eyes drifted to the front windows before me and it was still dark outside. My brow furrowed, and I turned my head towards the kitchen in deep thought. Where could he be?

Sitting against a flower vase on the table was a letter with my name on it.

I slipped out of bed, wrapped a shawl over my shoulders and sat down at the kitchen table. The letter was from Emmet.

My love,

I hadn't the heart to wake you — you looked so lovely, which made it harder for me to leave your side. I decided to get a start on our future and thought it better that I leave now and send for you once I'm established. You never would've agreed to this — I know you, darling — and this seemed the most logical course of action. You must trust me, I will send for you as soon as may be. These days will fly, I promise, and then we will never part again. Sell the sheep and anything else of value.

Beneath this page is another letter — please mail it to my mother.

> *I love you,*
> *Emmet*

Three simple words and my shock cooled.

His notion was true; I never would've let him leave without me. Even if he did, I would've shadowed his steps, followed him like a carrion scavenger, ducking behind trees and into bushes, and only revealing myself when it was too late to turn back. My imagination created the romantic scenario; he'd turn to find me within arm's length and his initial annoyance would melt into a reluctant acceptance of our reunion, then there'd be a passionate embrace. The notion — even just in my mind — brought a smile to my face. I seriously considered going after him; he couldn't be too far, and his tracks wouldn't be hard to find.

But leaving now would keep us penniless — the sheep needed to be sold.

I sighed and pushed away my daydreams; Emmet was being logical, as I needed to be. I needed to stay, sell the sheep, and wait for him to send for me. I missed him already. Without him, the house seemed so much gloomier.

I picked up the second letter. It was addressed to his mother, at their home in Haleburg, Alabama. But it wasn't sealed.

My palm itched, and my curiosity ached.

Surely, he would've sealed the page if he didn't want me reading it? In fact, he would've asked me not to read it. No, I thought, he left it there wanting me to read it.

Thoroughly convinced, I opened the letter and read.

Mama,

I am alive and well. I cannot tell you where but know that I am safe. I've left my regiment and have no intentions of rejoining them. I tried, Mama, I really did. But I cannot lie to myself or to the men I served with. Let people think I'm dead— you'll be safer that way. I intend on restarting my life, exactly where I left it. And once this damned war is through, I hope you and Daddy will join us—me and the woman I intend to marry. She is kind, intelligent, and my equal in every way. For the first time since Daddy took ill, I feel like every- thing is as it should be. I will write soon.

Your son

I brought the letter close to my face and kissed the ink. His words silenced my doubting heart. A tiny piece of me believed he had used me for his own gain and had fled when he had enough of the pretense. But this letter proved his conscience. He wrote to tell his parents about me! He hadn't been feeding me a story of the future with no intention of fulfilling it! True, he could've written the letter as a decoy but...no, I will not allow my heart to linger on the negative.

He loves me. And our life will start the moment he sends for me.

— A

September 30ᵗʰ, 1863

After reading Emmet's letter, I was lightheaded with glee.

The sun rose, I was dressed, Barley was saddled, and we were on Taneytown heading to town with Emmet's letter stored in my pocket. The early hours of the morning — when the mist and dew clings to the muted earth — has always been my favorite time of day and I drank in its beauty from atop my mare. Even Barley could sense my happiness; she trotted with a bouncy vigor. If I wasn't so anxious to get to town, I would've let her gallop as fast as her legs would take her. I'll let her do just that on our way home, I thought. She deserves to enjoy herself as much as I.

But my errands in town were paramount and my first visit was to Mr. Ricgard's butcher shop.

Though I've cared for them since my wedding day, I've no attachment to my sheep. So, I confidently walked into his shop and haggled, using the last year's reaping from the wool — almost four dollars a pound, with each sheep producing three pounds of wool — to reckon their value. If he didn't butcher them for their meat, Mr. Ricgard could easily resell half the flock for their wool value. My knowledge of past wool prices stunned him; when I didn't accept his low offer, I watched as his face turned purple with frustration. He wasn't accustomed to bartering with a woman but eventually he agreed to my sum. A hand shake sealed our pact.

Though I felt no remorse selling the sheep to a butcher, I couldn't do the same to Gertie. She'd been a companion, rather than a hindrance and I wanted her to go to a home where she could live out her natural life, grazing in a bountiful field of green grass. There was a small dairy farm off Chambersburg Street—owned by the Daley family—and that was my next stop. They were good people and in the market for a milk cow. Though I'd miss Gertie, seeing their property eased my conscience. I'd deliver her myself in a few weeks' time.

My morning had been productive, but the most important task still sat in my pocket: mailing Emmet's letter.

After tying Barley's reins off to a hitching-rail in the center of town, I walked towards the Post, repeating under my breath, "He loves me; he's telling his parents about me." Saying it made my heart swell to twice its size. I wondered what he was doing, how far he was from Gettysburg, how long it would take until he sent for me. My daydream was so engrossing that everything else was background scenery—so much so that I slammed right into Mr. Larsen outside the Post.

My feet slid on the street's stray gravel and he grabbed my elbow to steady me. "Hold on there, girl," he said.

"Oh Mr. Larsen!" I called out after he righted my feet beneath me. "I didn't see you there."

"That's pretty plain," he said with a laugh. He brushed the stray dirt from his pants—he was wearing what looked to be his best suit, which was a stark change to the work clothes I'd only ever seen him don. "Well, you be careful now," he said, tipping his hat and stepping aside. But before I could extend my foot onto the Post's steps, he grasped my elbow and forced my attention back to him.

"Stay clear of that oak tree on the edge of our properties. I know you like goin' up there to read."

"Has something happened to the tree?"

"Nothing you need to be botherin' yourself with. I'm headin' on down to the militia encampment now." He straightened his coat jacket, then took his hat off and ran his fingers through his greasy, grayed hair. "I thought we were through with all this battlin, Rebel-snoopin nonsense. But here I found one on my property this very morning. Sneaking around, up to no good. Knew he had to be a spy."

"A rebel?" My voice squeaked like a prepubescent boy's. I cleared my throat and started again; "You found a Rebel spy on your land?" My hand instinctually drifted to the letter hiding in my apron pocket.

"You betcha. I snuck up on him and fired a warning shot into the air. He froze right quick," he laughed. "He didn't look familiar—I don't forget faces—so I asked who he was and what he was doin'. But he wouldn't open his mouth. I screamed, hollered, and said all sorts of nonsense this close to his face," he said moving within an inch of mine. "Should've angered any red-blooded fella. Still he didn't say a word."

My heart was in my throat and dark thoughts were streaming into my mind, but I had to stay calm. "A mute doesn't make a man a spy. Nor does it mean he's a Confederate soldier."

"But I didn't tell you what I found on him."

My fingers pinched the letter inside my apron and I started repeating my affirmation—he loves me, he's telling his parents about me. "Go on," I urged.

Slung over his right shoulder was a satchel bag made of leather; he pulled it forward and said, "This." The bag looked very similar to—no! Emmet was on his way to Boston! He was nowhere near Mr. Larsen's farm. Why would he cross—no!

"These were issued to all the boys—after the battle, I found 'em all over my property. My barn is filled with 'em; gonna clean 'em up and sell 'em back to the army. Brought this with me to prove my case." He motioned for me to take his bounty. I accepted the bag and felt the weight of its contents.

"When he wouldn't talk, I pointed my shotgun between his eyes and ordered him to turn out his bag. I wanted to be sure he didn't have any guns on him, you see. I thought he was gonna bolt—young boy like that, he could've taken off and I never would've caught him. But he was scared and shakin' in his boots. Eventually, he dumped out the bag and you know what I found?"

"No." My fingers went numb and my grip on the leather bag was weakening. Again, I repeated my affirmation and steadied my breath.

A smile crossed Mr. Larsen's face. "I'd know it anywhere—saw them by the thousands for three days straight and then every time I found a body for weeks after. I'll never forget those Confederate gray uniforms and there one was, lying in a ball at my feet."

His eyes glittered triumphantly. Mine were blank; outwardly, I kept my composure, but my mind was battling horror, confusion, and denial. His uniform was draped over the rocking chair in my home; I saw it before I left...yes, I remember seeing it. Maybe? But if...no, he wouldn't have taken it with him. He never would've taken it with him—he was smarter than that. It was a coincidence.

"Now I ask ya: what man would carry a uniform that wasn't his own?"

"I...I don't know, sir." The words stumbled from my lips and into the air.

"Well I asks myself the same question and there was no way around it: he was a spy. I made him strip down and put the damn thing on. It fit him like a glove. And there's only one thing to be done with spies. So's you stay clear of that oak for a few days til the militia cuts down the body."

"The body?"

"Oh, sure. Had to lynch him. He fought me a bit—had to put a bullet in his arm just to overpower him. The bastard—'scuse my language ma'am—finally opened his mouth once I tied the noose around his neck. Begged for mercy and told me some sob story about a woman."

The words registered in my brain, my shoes slid on the gravel and I fell forward, dropping the bag and Emmet's letter to the ground.

"Oh, watch it there." He caught me by the elbow again and hoisted me back to my feet. "Let me grab that for ya."

He picked up the letter and turned it over, slowly reading the address. "You have kin in Alabama?" The look on his face was queer, almost questioning.

"Yes...yes an aunt." I snatched back the letter and returned it to my pocket. "I must be going, Mr. Larsen. Have... have a pleasant morning." I turned and gathered my skirts to walk away, with the composure of a person just struck by a runaway train.

He yelled after me, "Aren't you wanting to mail that letter?"

I waved my hand but didn't acknowledge him further. I ran through the now crowded square—pushing my way through the throngs of people going about their daily business—and found the hitching post where I'd left Barley. My fingers were shaking as I took her reins and undid the knot. "It's not him, it's not him," I said as the leather strap came loose, and I pulled myself up into the saddle.

But I had to know. I had to see with my own eyes.

I kicked my heels forcibly into Barley's flank and she lurched forward. Fearful desperation bled from my pores and Barley ran like a pack of wolves was hot on her trail—a stark contrast to the gentle trot of a few hours past. I clung to her neck like a child at her mother's breast.

All the while I prayed repeatedly that my destination—the white oak on the border of my and Mr. Larsen's property—would resolve the fear in my heart. My affirmation had to be correct; Emmet was on his way to Boston, he loved me, and had written to his parents about me. It wasn't him. It couldn't be him. Emmet was alive and safe, far from the dangerous wiles of Mr. Larsen's assumptions.

The ride—fast as it was—helped settle my nerves and when the trees of Little Hill rose above my head, my confidence crept back in. I slowed Barley's manic pace and found myself humming, "Abroad as I was Walking." The song helped me think of happier times—times that I'd have again, I reminded myself.

The path to my house branches off from the left of Taneytown, but I guided Barley to the right. She needed no more urging and knew exactly where to go—the grass on the small hill was one of Barley's favorite grazing grounds. I loved that tree; its thick trunk was perfect support for my back, and the heavily-leaved branches provided shade for a reading retreat on a spring day.

After a short while, we were at the base of the hill and Barley started to climb up the small incline to the flat surface where the oak was rooted. For the rest of the journey, my eyes remained on Barley's mane. My convictions were strong, and I wasn't afraid to see a dead body—I'd seen hundreds over just a few days in July—but I focused on her velvety neck and continued to hum the song Emmet taught me.

"One quick look and you're going straight home. You can't dwell on the death of an unknown man," I whispered to myself. But my soft words became loud and reverberated in the silence that surrounded me.

When Barley's steps leveled out and then stopped all together, I took a deep breath, swung my right leg over the back of the saddle, and stepped down onto the cushy grass below. I faced Barley and patted her down.

"Good girl. Go on now," I said to her. She trotted away greedily, looking for a patch of sweet grass to munch on. I paused, took two long breaths and then slowly turned to face the oak.

And then my whole world fell apart.

One look—a half a glance—was all I needed. My guttural, ear-splitting, anguished scream filled the silence of the forest and I crumbled beneath my pain. My heart, my happiness, my world, my dreams were ripped from me with one, short look. For hanging from the branches of the oak tree was Emmet—my Emmet, my love, my life.

"No, no, no please no!" I screamed, again, clutching my chest and falling to the ground. He was dead. There was nothing I could do to save him. My life was over—our future was over. I gripped the ground beneath me and I succumbed to darkness.

The ruthless midday sun found a crack in the tree bower above me and bore its rays down on my uncovered face.

Lazily, my eyes drifted open. Sweat was beading down my face, my tongue was as dry as sand, and every part of my body was sore. I lay there on my side in a daze, staring horizontally at the forest before me. I couldn't recall where I was and how I'd gotten there. The beauty of nature—the last green of the summer season, the rolling hills, and bright blue sky—started to lull me back to sleep. I rolled over and hoped to drift out of consciousness, again.

But from behind me, the whine of stretched rope brought it all back.

Emmet was dead.

And no matter how painful, I needed to face it.

I sat up and hovering just a few inches from my face were Joseph's brown, leather shoes—the pair I'd given Emmet weeks before. He was so thankful for those shoes, I thought numbly, trying to contain my emotion. The wind was twirling his lifeless form—like a hunter's twisted prize—and the rope whined again and again, strained by the weight of Emmet's body. I flexed my fingertips over the smooth leather of his shoes; they were warm to the touch. A glimpse of a bare ankle caught my eye and my fingers drifted to the spot of exposed skin. Beneath my fingers, his skin was clammy and cold. Tears welled in my eyes. I leaned forward and kissed his shoes and bare ankle. Then I stood and wrapped my arms around him. Deeply, I breathed in his scent—a musky sweat with a tinge of wood—and his death became real.

"My love, my love, my love," I sobbed anew. My dammed emotions burst, and my tears were glass; slicing and cutting my cheeks. I clung to him and my tears soaked the tails of his cotton shirt. I hoped, I prayed, I wished this was all an awful, painful dream; that I would wake at any moment, safe in my bed and roll over to find Emmet. I would tell him about the dream; we'd laugh, and then make love for hours. I picked a spot on the tree—the way Emmet taught me to settle my mind after a nightmare. But no matter how hard I stared at the one small knot on the oak's trunk, the nightmare didn't go away. The twang of the rope sang a death song and I gaped up at the awful, jutting angle of Emmet's broken neck.

I crumbled into his torso in a fit of hysterics, again. "This... this is...all my...fault."

And it was.

I was the reason Emmet was dead: if I'd made him leave the moment he was well, if I'd burned the uniform after hearing his explanation, if he hadn't fallen in love with me, if I'd sold the sheep sooner and left with him—he never would've met this fate. Mr. Larsen tied the noose but meeting me cursed him—as it has with everything and everyone I've touched.

"I'm so sorry." I apologized again and again until my throat was raw.

After some time, peril dawned on me. When I had left town, Mr. Larsen was on his way to inform the local militia of what he'd done and task them with dealing with the body. If they believed him, they'd come to that exact spot. Every passing minute put me in danger and I couldn't be found there—nor did I want anyone touching Emmet's body. I'd seen firsthand how Mr. Larsen treated Rebel soldiers—a shallow grave, a few inches of dirt, and a dollop of spit—and I didn't trust the militia to be any more discerning. The mere thought filled me with rage and then a new purpose.

I pushed my emotions into the furthest part of my soul and got on with it—like Mam would've wanted.

I kissed Emmet's torso then stepped back from him. "I'll be back, my love." I whistled for Barley, who appeared obediently. I swung up into her saddle and urged her towards home.

I returned to the tree with a burlap sack filled with supplies: a knife, a tablecloth, a canteen filled with water, a small bundle of clean linen, a packet of sewing needles and thick thread, and a shovel. I jumped down from Barley and set to hiding Emmet's body.

My first task would be the easiest: I untied the rope from around the tree and looped it around Barley's pummel; I urged Barley to take a few steps forward; and using her as an anchor, brought Emmet's body carefully to the ground. After, I untied the rope from Barley's pummel and let her walk off.

I started my next task: the grave.

Moving him would not be easy—I couldn't lift or carry him very far—and he was my heart and the reason it beat. I needed him close, always. Though this tree was the bane of his fate, beneath its branches was as good a place as any for a final resting place. But it was still Mr. Larsen's land and I knew he begrudged the existing burial sites scattered around his property. This grave would need to be a secret.

I took up my shovel and struck shallowly into the ground. Carefully, I lifted the top, grass-filled layer of earth and placed it to the side. I repeated this again and again until I had firmly outlined the grave. Then I dug down and deep. I was covered in dirt and barely able to pull myself out of the hole, but I managed and allowed myself to sprawl out on my back for a few minutes respite.

The third task was still ahead: preparing Emmet's body for burial.

I stumbled to my feet, retrieved the burlap sack and from inside, I took my best tablecloth and a needle with thread. The tablecloth was the finest thing I owned; it was my wedding present from Rosie. It'd been years since I used it, and there was no better purpose for it than as a funeral shroud for my love.

I laid the fabric flat next to the grave—like a picnic blanket—and rolled Emmet upon it. I positioned his body at the center of the fabric, making sure there was an even amount of slack on either side of him.

Then I could avoid it no longer; I had to look at him.

My eyes paused on every inch of his body, traveling from his shod feet, up his long legs, his torso and strong arms, and then finally to his beautiful face. I could've stared at him all day: his strong jawline, his plump lips, the brush of freckles on his nose. Everything about him was still perfect; perfect, except for the distorted angle of his neck and the congealed gunshot wound in his shoulder. He looked handsome—even more so dressed in his Confederate uniform. The one and only time I'll see him wear it, I thought as I hesitantly touched his chest. My emotions bubbled to the surface, but I shook them away and retrieved my canteen from the burlap sack. I set to cleaning his body; I knelt beside him, cut away the noose, and threw the rope over my shoulder. Using a piece of linen, I cleaned his shoulder wound and then his face. The skin of his neck was purpling and burned from the rope. There was no way to disguise this—or the turned-out angle of his neck— but I managed to maneuver his neck to a straighter position and buttoned his top collar. His face was angelic—the look he so often had when he was in the deepest sleep. He was still himself; still my Emmet and my greatest love.

I sighed and crossed his right arm over his chest. As I went to repeat the same with his left, I noticed his hand was fisted—frozen in the last action of his life. This was curious; with extreme distress—like a lynching—a defensive reaction would be to flail and reach for the noose. Emmet's fist shouldn't have been clenched. I pried open his fingers. Concealed in his hand was a balled handkerchief.

Carefully, I pulled the edges of the fabric loose. Wrapped within was a lock of hair.

Instantly, I reached for the ribbon that tied back my tendrils, letting my hair fall loose by my shoulders. My fingers searched my scalp, and right at the base of my skull I found it: a small patch of shorn strands.

My heart lurched. He must've cut it while I slept.

"Oh Emmet," I whispered. I brought the hair to my lips and kissed it. Tears fell from my eyes again, wetting the auburn lock. I wrapped the hair back inside the handker-chief and placed it back into Emmet's fist.

"A piece of me will always be with you," I murmured as I crossed his arm over his chest. And in turn, I took my knife and cut a lock of his hair. I stowed his hair in my apron pocket; it will remain my most precious ornament.

Taking up my needle, I sewed the ends of the table cloth around his feet then worked my way up to his chest. Emmet would have no coffin, but I hoped the cloth would offer some protection from the elements. Before closing the cloth over Emmet's face, I paused.

This would be the last I'd look upon his face.

I rested my cheek against his—imprinting the feel of his skin to memory. I kissed his cheeks and brushed the hair from his brow. To see his eyes, darkly shining back at me, was all I wanted. I smiled despite myself, recalling the way his face lit up every time I returned home after a prolonged visit to town; the way he'd sweep me into his arms with ease. I closed my eyes, let my tears fall onto his still form, and kissed his lips once last time.

Then I sewed up the cloth.

I whistled for Barley, who appeared again. Around her pummel, I tied off the rope and draped both ends down her back. Standing in front of her and holding tight to her bridle, I guided Barley towards the grave. She strategically stepped around the hole and then halted. Cautiously, I al-lowed Barley two small steps and the bundle fell smoothly into the grave. I untied the rope from the pummel, jumped down into the grave beside Emmet, and laid his body flat. Then with the last of my strength, I pulled myself out of the grave.

Using every bit of removed dirt, I filled the grave and then layered the grass-filled soil atop it. I took off my shoes and stomped on the grass—so the roots of the blades would again find a home in the soil. I did this for quite some time; until I was sure my excavation would go unnoticed. After, I picked up a branch and brushed out the grass surrounding the grave; so, there would be no suspicion of a dragged body or anyone's presence there.

Then there was nothing more to do. But I lingered at the foot of the grave.

There would be no funeral rite for Emmet. No words of prayer, sung to God to secure his place in the hereafter. No one would stand and speak of his many good deeds or of the man he was. All he would get was me, staring down at him with tremendous guilt and emotion. There was so much I wanted to say—so much that I needed to say to quench the pit in my stomach—but no words would come. I had no tears left; the bounty I had stored up since Mam's death were already spent. So, I stared down and uttered three sentences: "I love you. I love you. I'll never love another."

I knelt and kissed the earth—knowing his lips lay beneath that exact spot.

I whistled for Barley for the last time, slung the empty burlap sack over the saddle, and pulled myself atop her. I nudged Barley forward and she turned for home.

It's been two weeks since I left Emmet beneath the white oak. I've only now had the strength to commit this to page. Since that day, I've heard nothing from Mr. Larsen nor the local militia. If they investigated Mr. Larsen's claim, I know not. But no questions have been asked or inquiries made at my home.

I haven't left my house and have no intention of doing so. Some of my patients sought me out, but I sent them from my door, telling them to fetch Cashtown's midwife. I've remained in bed, preferring sleep and my dreams where Emmet is alive and well. My waking life has become a nightmare; I have nothing, I am nothing, I want nothing but Emmet.

I don't know how I will go on.

How can I live without my heart?

−A

October 4th, 1863

Mr. Ricgard called today—to fetch the sheep I'd promised him. Truthfully, I had forgotten about this transaction; after everything that had happened, the sheep and Mr. Ricgard were the least of my concerns. So, I wasn't expecting anyone. I answered the door in my nightgown—the garb I'd been living in, day and night, for the last few weeks—and I didn't need a looking glass to know I was haggard and dirty. His jaw dropped at the sight of me and he turned his face out of decency. I didn't grab a shawl or attempt to cover myself further; I hadn't the energy to care about his comfort, so I stood there watching the veins in the back of his bald head twitch as he explained that he'd come to collect the sheep.

"Yes, of course. They're penned out back." He bowed his head and said he'd take half of the flock now and return in a few days for the rest. He handed me a small pouch with the money we'd agreed on.

I stood in the doorway as he and his son herded eleven of my sheep into the front yard. As each ewe steadily climbed a small plank into Mr. Ricgard's large flat-bed wagon, their cries hurt my ears and I looked on in a stupor. I never felt anything about the sheep, but I cared even less about the weighted pouch of money in my hand. I was tempted to chuck it into the wagon.

What do I need money for?

Mr. Ricgard climbed into his wagon and — without looking directly at me — waved. I didn't return his salutation; instead, my freehand drifted and came to rest on my stomach.

I'm pregnant.

– A

October 5th, 1863

Though I've known for weeks, I haven't outwardly admitted it until the last entry in your pages. I sit here, reading and rereading my closing statement and its meaning is defined more clearly.

I'm pregnant.

I'm no fool. I'm a midwife; I know how the reproductive organs work and I know the implications of lying with a man for weeks on end. The possibility of a pregnancy has always been in the back of my mind. If Emmet was alive I'd be overjoyed—he would've sent for me by the time I started to show, and I'd have nothing to fear. Now...I pray daily that my courses come.

God has forsaken me. Emmet's death has taken my faith.

I feel crazed. Everything reminds me of Emmet; I see him sitting in the chair by the fire, outside chopping wood, and his voice drifts among the rafters of the ceiling. His ghost has become my constant companion and my only respite has been in my dreams—where I can touch him and he me. I wake every morning, disappointed that I'm alone, only to crawl back beneath my covers to return to his embrace.

Oh, how I wish I could dream him back into being!

I can't do this without Emmet—this pregnancy and life. I can't have his child without him. I won't! In my bleakest moments, I think of the tea I can brew to put an end to what is growing in my body. I know where the plants grow, and the exact combination needed—the recipe is in Mam's journal and I've opened to that very page nearly every day.

Emmet would understand; I could never love the child, nor look at it without my heart breaking. It would be a constant reminder of what I've lost. No, I don't want this child. I can't have this child.

I've become my mother; resentful of an innocent after the death of its father.

–A

October 18ᵗʰ, 1863

Another unexpected visitor drew me from my bed.

This time, it was Rosie persistently knocking on my front door.

"Sister, you look dreadful. Are you unwell?" she asked, barely waiting for me to open my door as she breezed by me and into my house.

"Yes, I've been in bed all week with an...awful ache in my head," I lied.

"I can see that." She scanned the room, seeing my unmade bed, the refuse and dirty dishes piled in the wash tub, and the dirt and dust accumulating on the floor. It was eerie how much she reminded me of Mother; inspecting the room with dignified horror as she attempted to not touch anything. Suddenly, I became very ashamed at the mess my life had become; my house looked like bedlam incarnate, a mirror of my emotional state. Quickly, I started clearing and cleaning the kitchen table, offering her a freshly cleaned seat.

"What brings you, sister? I can't recall the last time you rode all the way out here." I stoked the fire to put the kettle on for tea — I had little else to offer in ways of refreshment.

"I could ask you the same question: where have you been? It's been more than a fortnight since I've seen you last."

"I...well, I haven't been—"

"I know about Joseph."

With my back turned and iron poker still in hand, I froze. My heart's beat rose, and I could see it pulsing beneath my cotton nightgown. From behind, I heard the chair scrape against the wooden floor and Rosie's soft steps crossed the room to where I stood at the fireplace. She put a comforting hand on my shoulder and waited for me to speak — which I didn't. It was obvious that Rosie assumed my appearance and the disarray in my home was due to the death of my husband. She had no clue the true cause of my sadness.

"I know you're grieving, sister," she continued, "and his death must be hard to bear. But please do not shut yourself away from the world for a man you hardly knew. I hope you will realize the sadness you feel is only for the thought of him and the shock of the moment."

I took a deep breath and placed the poker back in its stand. "You're right, sister." I turned to her and forced a small smile. Her eyes were gentle and motherly; I reached for her hand and squeezed it three times before turning back to the fire. I put the kettle on and then returned to the table with two clean teacups.

"Look at this as an opportunity," she added, with cheery disposition. "You can begin again. And find true love."

I nodded quietly. If only she knew the impossibility of my ever starting over. My emotions were on the cusp of spilling over but letting Rosie talk kept the tears at bay and my mind occupied. She went on for almost an hour — about many topics, thankfully — and I remained silent while I cleaned.

"Well, this has been delightful," she said as she took one last sip of tea. "I must be off before Jonathan worries about me. He's had Mary all to himself this afternoon — he looked perfectly panicked when I announced that I was coming to visit you. It's the first time he's been alone with her for more than a few minutes."

"He is her father after all," I replied, taking a seat across from her.

"Naturally. And I can't possibly juggle two without a little help from him now and again."

"Two? You don't mean..."

Her smile was broad, and she pulled her dress close to her stomach. "I'm only a few weeks along, can you tell? I've promised Jonathan a boy."

I stood, crossed in front of the table, and hugged her close. "I'm happy for you, Rosie."

"As am I. I'm excited to give Mary a little brother."

She pulled back from our embrace to look at me — a long and lingering look. I felt my muscles tense and I feared she could sense my secret — pregnant women have a way knowing these things. Her eyes squinted slightly in question but then her mind cleared, and she was on to another topic. "Come visit me. Some sunshine will do you good. And please—take a bath. I love you, but you smell like death."

A smile cracked my lips. "I will. I promise."

She affably squeezed my arms and then let go, turning towards the door. "I expect Jonathan will never allow me to leave the house, again." I opened the door for her and she stepped outside. "Leave that open," she said, pointing to the door. "Trust me."

She crossed the yard, unhitched her horse, and climbed up into her small carriage. She flicked her horse's reins and blew kisses to me. I remained on the porch, watching as her wagon pulled out of sight. With one last glimpse of the back of Rosie's head, I felt the smile she had given me fall back into a miserable scowl; I could not escape the oppressiveness of my dark thoughts.

I envied Rosie—returning to a home filled with a blossoming family and blissfully happy about the baby growing in her stomach.

—A

October 25th, 1863

Since Joseph's death, I've known two things: that his death granted me my freedom, and that eventually my home would be taken from me. The last has been a hefty, prod-ding splinter in my thumb.

And this morning, that shard of wood came loose.

I was outside, digging up the last of my fall vegetables and preparing my winter bulbs when I heard my name called from the front porch. I stood, brushed the dirt from my apron, and walked back inside.

Someone was standing on my porch. From where I stood in the back doorway, he didn't look familiar; in fact, his suit looked far too expensive to be anyone from Gettysburg. My heart fluttered with an old fear — deeply rooted since Emmet's death—as I crossed the room and answered the door: had someone found the body and made the connection?

"Can I help you, sir?" I asked.

"Yes...I'm looking for a Mrs. Joseph Pritchard?"

He certainly wasn't from town; I was known only by my first name and the sound of my husband's surname nause-ated me. I concealed a shiver but told him I was she.

He reached within his suit jacket and produced a thin, rectangular envelope. "I was hired as a solicitor by the late Mr. Joseph Pritchard before he enlisted with the 90th Pennsylvania. In the event of his death, while serving in our country's military, he wanted to be sure his assets would be adequately distributed among his living relatives." He passed the envelope over the threshold and to me. "Inside, you will find a copy of his will."

I looked at the envelope, then back at him. He expected me to open the document and read it in front of him, but

I already knew what was committed to page. "Thank you, sir." I started to close the door, but he stuck his foot in the doorway gap to prevent me.

He flinched as the door smacked his foot. "I...um...yes, Mr. Pritchard has bequeathed this land to his brother," he continued, unabated. "I've spoken to Mr. Edward Pritchard and he wishes to sell. I've convinced him to give you until after the New Year to settle your affairs." His head dropped, and his eyebrows arched; he wanted me to thank him for that small concession. And though I wanted to be smug and shut the door forcibly in his face, I just hadn't the energy.

"Thank you," I said dryly.

He nodded quickly and removed his foot from the doorway. "I've written my Harrisburg address on a small piece of paper inside the envelope. Please don't hesitate to write or visit if you have any questions about the division of assets. Additionally, I have Mr. Edward Pritchard's address in Emmitsburg if you'd like to reach him for any reason." He tipped his hat and retreated from the porch.

I closed the door and turned back inside the house. I had no desire to read Joseph's will—nothing inside pertained to me. I stepped to the fireplace and tossed the letter atop the dull flames. I watched as the paper curled, turning orange then purple, and melted into ash.

I envied the paper.

In two months' time, I'll be homeless.

−A

December 13th, 1864

There was no delaying the inevitable, so I was packed and out of Joseph's house by November.

I sold Gertie to the Daley's—the family I promised her to—and tried not to be emotional as her new owner tied her off to his wagon and left. She was the last thing tying me to Joseph's farm and once she was gone, I had little left to do. All my possessions fit into two cases and one wooden crate; aside from Mam's rollout desk, all the furniture was in the house before I arrived, so I felt no responsibility for anything too large to carry. I'd send someone later to fetch the desk, but my books were my only treasured possession—that and the lock of Emmet's hair that I've been using as a placeholder in your pages.

It was a strange feeling, standing in the doorway and looking in at my home, knowing I'd never return. My mind danced with the happy memories created within those four walls—the happiest being those stolen, passionate moments with Emmet. But then bitterness seeped back into my heart and I needed to get away from everything that reminded me of what I'd lost. I took one last look and closed the door on my past.

Rosie and Jonathan—mostly Rosie—had graciously offered me a place to stay.

"Only until the spring," Jonathan emphasized as he carried my cases into their home. "We will not become your crutch."

"Never mind him," Rosie whispered as she welcomed me with a big hug. "You stay as long as you need."

I don't know what I would've done if Rosie hadn't offered. Accepting charity has never been easy for me, but this is far better than going to Mother.

I've tried to find the positive side of my new living arrangement: I'll be here to help Rosie and I'll be readily available to my patients.

Until I start to show — which is the new splinter in my thumb.

I've done everything in my power to conceal my condition — even asking Rosie for privacy in the kitchen while I bathe. I've come to terms with my pregnancy, but I know the repercussions and the questions that will be pointedly asked, especially now that it is common knowledge that my husband is dead. Carrying a bastard child will only bring judgement and condemnation that I'm not ready to face.

I fear Rosie's reaction most of all.

— A

January 6th, 1864

I was changing from my nightgown this morning when my naked reflection in the washstand mirror stopped me. I'd been avoiding mirrors for weeks, but the change in my body was fascinating. I twisted my hips back and forth, peering at the curve of my belly from both angles. This was how Rosie found me when she entered, unannounced.

"I have fresh—"

Our eyes met in the mirror and the pile of linens she was carrying dropped to the floor. I crouched to the ground, protectively wrapping my arms around my naked body. All I wanted was to hide; crawl into a dark, dank hole and pretend I'd never been born. The bedroom door creaked shut and with a few quick steps, she was beside me.

"Please don't look at me," I whispered.

She retrieved the bed's quilt, draped it over my shoulders, and then knelt beside me. "Are you with child?" she asked in a hushed tone.

I didn't need to admit what she could easily guess, still she waited for my response. I nodded into my knees and I heard the breath she exhaled. With my downward gaze, I saw her bare feet flex and then tighten. She sat down beside me and draped an arm around me.

"And the father?"

I shook my head defensively; I couldn't tell her about Emmet. I'd take that secret to my grave; I still feared repercussions for helping a deserter, feared a connection being made between myself and the man Mr. Larsen had reported. The less she knew, the less she would have to lie.

She asked nothing more.

"I will protect you. Don't fret," she said as she pulled me close. I laid my head down on her chest and we sat there for quite some time. Inside my bedroom — and in her embrace — I felt safe. But I knew the outside world would not be so kind.

— A

January 28th, 1864

There's no denying it any longer. My clothes no longer fit, and I am visibly heavier. Rosie, without asking, added additional panels to my skirts and dresses to accommodate my growing size.

Bless her heart.

I'm acutely aware that my condition puts her in a precarious situation. She has kept my secret and yet, Jonathan hasn't noticed my growing belly—mostly due to my deliberate avoidance of him and to his busy schedule outside the home. It is only a matter of time before he realizes it on his own or someone from town informs him. I've tried to maintain weekly appointments with my patients and I've been the recipient of many sideward glances in the street. And once Jonathan discovers the truth, I'm sure he will look to his own house for an explanation—and anger will ensue if he believes Rosie lied to him.

Rosie cannot shoulder this blame. I won't allow it.

I'll tell him myself.

This very week.

—A

February 1st, 1864

February has brought a staunch chill to the air—outside as well as in.

We'd just finished our evening meal—a silent one, tinged in an awkward, hovering tension between the three of us. As soon as his plate was cleared of food, Jonathan stood from the table and coldly stated, "Please meet me in my study, sister. We've a matter to discuss."

He turned on his heel and walked from the dining room without further explanation.

My eyes drifted to Rosie's place at the table, but she'd already taken her own exit to the kitchen, laden with dirty dishes. I surmised that the proposed conversation wasn't one she wanted to be involved in.

Just breathe, I reminded myself as I stood from the dining room table and walked the few feet to Jonathan's study. The door was closed, so I rapped on the wooden door with my knuckles.

"Enter," he answered from the other side of the door.

I took one last breath, pushed open the door, and stepped inside.

The bible was open in front of him and he was copying out verses on a blank page—tracing the line in the holy text as he did. I shut the door and stood waiting for him to acknowledge my presence—which took almost a full five minutes.

Finally, and without tearing his eyes from his work he said, "After today, you aren't to leave this house."

"Pardon?"

Slowly, he put down his pen, closed the bible, and looked up. His eyes were stoic, but his face was tight with a reserved—but pulsing—anger. He repeated himself, pausing distinctly on each word; "After today, I forbid you to leave this house."

My mouth suddenly became very dry. I stood there, panicking and shuffling my weight from one leg to the other. He continued. "As a Christian, I cannot—in good conscience—dismiss you from my home, but I will not allow your wantonness to blight my family's reputation. Gossip will be fueled by your presence and appearance; therefore, you are not to leave this house." He picked up his pen and started writing once more.

I felt myself shrink to the size of an ant. Jonathan's position—a pillar of faith and an upstanding citizen in Gettysburg—made him more susceptible to harsh condemnation. Shame bathed me, and I wanted nothing more than to flee. To run from Jonathan's home—from Gettysburg and its condemning eyes—and start over somewhere far away. I'd adopt a story for the child's father—he died in battle in a no-name southern town—and create a new life for myself. All I had to do was walk from Jonathan's study and out the front door.

But doing that would take strength and mine was buried beneath the white oak. I was little more than a breathing corpse without Emmet. There was nothing to say in rebuttal. My head dropped in defeat and I turned from him to go lick my wounds in private. But as I gripped the brass doorknob, he spoke again.

"I've sent some inquiries to Harrisburg; the child will be placed in an orphanage."

My blood turned to ice and my stomach seized; his words were a fisted punch to my gut and I was left bereft. I didn't want the child, but I thought the decision would be mine to make. I could hear the scratching of his pen against parchment, as he went on writing. I was forgotten — the pain he had just inflicted was forgotten — and our conversation was over.

Silently, I opened the door and crept from the study like a wounded animal.

Once again, my freedom, my control have been stripped from me.

−A

March 11ᵗʰ, 1864

Doldrums have stripped my life of color and light. Days trapped inside with nothing to distract myself with, my thoughts have been consumed by the troubles of my past. There's no escaping it.

But today was different.

Today, I felt you kick.

I was lying down — as I typically do in the afternoon — and beginning to doze when I felt a swift jab in my left side. My eyes shot open in godawful pain and I looked around my bedroom, fearful that someone had snuck in unawares. But nothing was out of place; I was completely alone. I sat still and waited for something else to happen. When nothing did, I convinced myself that it was just a trick of the mind and I pressed my fingers into my side, rubbing the pain away. As my hand lifted from my stomach, it happened again—a firm, more pronounced kick—and only then did it dawn on me. You were making your presence known.

A light fluttering in my stomach had quite often accompanied meals. But this kick was so much more.

I sat there and willed you to move.

And you did; three more times, and before the last, I lifted my shift over my stomach and watched as my skin bubbled in and out in quick rhythm. I saw the faint outline of your foot and I felt...electrified. Like the part of myself that was suffocated within these four walls—the part that I'd almost forgotten—was awakened. I palpated my abdomen, feeling the curve of your bottom, the slight ripple of your spine, and the head-down position you'd taken in my womb.

In that moment, you—my unborn love-child—became real. You were no longer a burden or a dirty secret, but a blessing; you were our baby—mine and your father's. We never spoke of children but now—hours later—I close my eyes and I see the life we would've made; there's a rustic cottage, nestled and protected by thick, oak trees—very similar to my home on Little Hill; inside, your father and I are sitting in rocking chairs before a blazing fire; you are in my arms, dozing after a hearty meal; and Emmet is reading aloud from a book—one of the many that lined shelves around the room. We look blissfully happy. Happy in a way neither of us had ever experienced. And I wanted it, more than anything.

Before, I couldn't think of such things. My heart was consumed by loss and anger. But now, thinking of what could've been doesn't make me so sad; now, I feel determined to give you the life you deserve. I will not become my mother and take my loss out on you. I promise to protect and love you with my whole heart. No matter what society thinks of us, you can always be confident of my love. I'm keeping you, my precious baby, no matter Jonathan's plans or objections. Emmet may be gone, but our plan can still take fruit; I don't know why I didn't think of this before. I've the money from the sheep and Gertie—an ample amount to make a start somewhere. In fact…I'll write to Doctor Watkins—my old mentor and friend—I'm sure he'll help establish me in Philadelphia. Perhaps he'll even hire me as an assistant. And I'll tell people I'm a widow and your father died in the war—no one has to know the truth about Emmet.

My heart is brimming with deep-rooted love for you, my child.

I've started thinking about names. Something with an E for your Papa.

May 2nd, 1864

My Dearest Sister,

I have intruded on a very private part of your life. Every entry—every page—is saturated with aspects of yourself that you never revealed to anyone. When I found this diary—the very one I gave you so long ago—I debated long and hard on whether to read it and in the end, my inner conflict conceded to my overwhelming sense of loss. I had to read it. And given the circumstances, I know you would have understood and forgiven me.

Seven days have passed since your labor pains began; seven days since you left this world for good. Six since I found this diary. And one day since I decided to write this letter and finish what you started.

Your baby came a few weeks early.

The hour was going on ten and still you hadn't emerged from your bedroom; I've never known you to sleep in, so I had reasons to be concerned. I climbed the stairs—clutching my own very pregnant belly—and knocked softly on your bedroom door. After some time, I called your name and pressed my ear to the wooden door. Still no answer came. When I could no longer stand the anxiety building within me, I barged into your bedroom. As my eyes adjusted to the darkness—the shutters and curtains were still drawn tight—I realized you weren't in bed.

"I'm here." Your voice was labored.

I found you on the floor on the far side of the bed, tangled in your bedding, writhing in pain, and sweating profusely. "I tried to get up—" I shushed your words and knelt to unravel the bedsheets from your legs. A powerful smell hit me.

"Your water has—"

"I know." You smiled and brushed the hair from my face.

"What do I...should I—"

"Get me to the bed, Rosie. All will be well."

Your labor was intense and quick; within the hour, your beautiful baby girl plopped into my waiting arms and squealed like a newborn piglet. We both cried—you from exhaustion and euphoria, and me from the accomplishment of bringing your child into the world. As I cut her umbilical cord and cleaned the blood from her tiny body, I looked up and caught your eye. You were smiling, looking eagerly from your daughter to me. You mouthed the words "Thank you," and I returned the sentiment with "I love you."

"My heart," you whispered as I handed over your child, cleaned and wrapped in cloth. You kissed her lightly on the crown of her head. "Little one," you cooed. "She's beautiful, isn't she sister?"

"Like her Mama," I added.

"No." You looked long at her face and ran a finger over her cheek. "She looks just like her Papa."

Your words were an invitation to pose the question plaguing my heart since I discovered you were with child— but I closed my mouth tight. It wasn't the right moment.

"Have you any thoughts on a name?"

"Yes." A minute passed—a minute of you kissing her head and each of her tiny fingers—then you named her; "Emily." On cue, the darling little girl in your arms jutted her balled fists towards the heavens. You laughed. "I think she likes it."

"I think so, too."

The afterbirth still needed to be delivered, so I turned from your gleaming face to retrieve the wash basin from the washstand at the corner of the bedroom. I've replayed the next events in my mind repeatedly; at the most, my back was turned for only a few minutes but when I returned to the bed, everything was lost.

Your head was slumped to the side, drained of all color, and Emily was screaming with the might of a grown man. I took Emily from your limp arms; I rocked her and called your name over and over. Your eyes were large, dark pools—they didn't blink or acknowledge my voice. I took Emily to the nursery and placed her in Mary's cradle—Mary, thankfully, was fast asleep—and then returned to your bedroom. It was then that I pulled the blanket back.

Your legs, shift, and the bed beneath were soaked in blood.

"Sweet Jesus," I gasped and covered my mouth.

I lifted your shift and blood was still trickling down your thighs, but the afterbirth was nowhere to be found; you were hemorrhaging. I reached for your hand—you were still warm, and I could feel the faintest heartbeat. I can fix this, I thought frantically, urging my mind for a memory of Mam. I was never allowed in the room for difficult births, but I knew she had remedies for bleeding. There was always a brew or a tea—

I hauled your medical kit from the wardrobe and ransacked the small vials inside, looking for black haw root and partridge berry—you brewed this same foul-tasting concoction for me after Mary's birth. Finding both, I waddled downstairs to the kitchen. I grabbed the kettle off the stove, snatched up a mug and placed the root and berry inside, and then poured lukewarm water atop it. With mug in hand, I breathlessly reclimbed the stairs and to your side.

"Sister? Can you hear me?" I implored, looking deep into your blank expression. I tilted your head and parted your lips. I drained the mug down your throat and waited. Half of the tea dribbled down your chin, but I thought you swallowed enough. Mam's brews were always magic; I half expected that you'd instantly sit up and laugh at me for jumping to assumptions. So, I waited. I returned to the kitchen, brewed more tea, and repeated the process. And then waited some more.

But nothing changed.

Desperately, I returned to the nursery and fetched Emily; breastfeeding, I remembered, helped abate excessive bleeding after labor. I placed her on your bare chest and held her there securely. Instinct made her suckle and she was persistent—tried for quite some time to feed—but eventually she cried out in discomfort and hunger. In defeat, I returned her to the nursery.

That's when I heard the front door slam and Jonathan's voice call my name.

I ran downstairs and into his waiting arms. Through hysterical sobs, I told him what had happened, and all my worries disappeared. Jonathan would know what to do, he always did. He guided me to the parlor and gently placed me in a chair. "Stay here, my love. I'll be back." I heard his heavy steps on the wooden staircase and then on the floor above my head. I sat there, rubbing my swollen belly and praying harder than I ever have.

After a long while, I heard Jonathan's footsteps on the stairs and then I turned to find him standing in the parlor's doorway, wiping blood from his hands on a rag. "She's gone, my dearest," he said flatly.

"Are you…are you sure?"

"Quite." He threw the rag to the ground with a look of disgust.

What had I done wrong? Could I have prevented your death? What would you have done if faced with the same dilemma? Each question led back to one, dark answer: your death was on my hands. And I crumbled into myself, cried and howled like a pained dog. Each breath inflicted more grief; grief that covered me like a maelstrom of snow.

Jonathan appeared beside me, placing his hand on my shoulder. I expected — and needed — kind words that only a husband could give to ease the shattered heart of his beloved wife. What I got was the exact opposite.

"Buck up now." His voice sounded like he was speaking to a child. "Really, this is for the best."

My hysterics stopped short and I stared up at him in bewilderment. "What could you possibly mean?"

He stroked my cheek. "This was God's will, my sweet. Her indiscretion tarnished her soul and God punished her for it."

I swatted his hand away and stood. "How can you be so cruel?" I walked out of the room and towards the stairs.

"A man of faith cannot see this any other way. We are better off," he called after me.

I paused, my hand firmly grasping the baluster. I couldn't believe what he'd said—he talked as if you were refuse on the street, that you and your life meant nothing. He sauntered into the hallway and his presence revolted me.

I turned from him. "I must see to the child and prepare my sister for burial."

"Where are you expecting to bury her? Not in our family plot, I hope?"

My anger was seething, and I replied through gritted teeth; "Where else would we bury her?"

"Not in our plot. Or in the town's cemetery." He calmly walked through the hallway and placed his hand atop mine on the baluster. "Hallowed ground will not accept someone like her."

I recoiled from him in disbelief. "She is our sister—what would you have me do?"

He sighed. "We should not involve ourselves in such matters. Call on the coroner and have him decide what is best. I know of a pauper's field beyond town that will—"

"She isn't—wasn't some common criminal! She deserves a proper burial. If you won't see beyond your damned beliefs and do right by our sister—"

" — your sister, not mine."

" — then I will handle the arrangements myself." I stomped up the steps, leaving him silent and stunned in my wake.

I'd never spoken so harshly to my husband — never even raised my voice to him. But I couldn't let his total disregard go unchallenged. We didn't speak about it again; Jonathan avoided me for the remainder of the day as I fed both children — I am blessed with enough milk to feed both our daughters — and then left the house for an hour. First, I went to the coroner and purchased a wooden casket — which would be delivered to the house under the cover of darkness. Next, I found a day laborer looking for a few days' work. He asked very few questions — only how many days he was needed and how much he'd be paid. Two days, I told him and in exchange for his discretion, he could name his price. He could've named a small fortune — he didn't — and I would've dared Jonathan to oppose me. My anger empowered me to stand my ground.

Once home, I prepared your body.

I cleaned you, brushed out your auburn hair, and dressed you in your favorite blue gown. My tears fell freely — as they are falling while I write this now. Once finished, I crawled into bed beside you — like I so often did when we were children and you were spending the night at Mother's — and pulled your motionless body close to mine. Your skin was losing its warmth, so I wrapped my arms and legs around you, hoping you'd steal my heat. I laid my head on your chest and pretended we were those same children once again—whispering and laughing late into the night—and that all of this was a bad dream. I prayed it would be so until a knock at the front door echoed through the silent house—the laborer had arrived to help carry your body to the cool cellar. I sighed and sat up, knowing I had to finish. That's when I found the lock of hair closed tight in your fist—the hair that I now know belonged to your love. It remains there still and will be with you for all eternity. I took up a thread and needle and sewed up your funeral shroud—made from my finest tablecloth. But before finishing, I paused over your face and kissed both your cheeks. That one last embrace, one-sided, was what I needed. And will need for the rest of my life.

Now it is done.

After reading your diary, I had you placed where I know your heart belongs.

I cried bitterly at your gravesite: I apologized for not being a better sister to you, for not coming to your aid sooner, and promised wholeheartedly that I would love and protect Emily. I promise this anew in your pages; I will raise your daughter as my own. She will not want for love and affection. Jonathan will not send her to an orphanage—he will not broach that topic again. I will protect and cherish Emily with your memory in mind. And one day, I will tell her about you.

And Emmet.

Reading your diary has opened my eyes but crushed my heart. Why, oh why did you keep so much to yourself? I knew so little of your daily pains—the anguish you carried silently for so long. I could've helped you, sister! You felt—and were—so alone, but I was always here. Why didn't you ask? Why didn't you confide in me? Why did you shut out everyone who truly loved you? I would've listened. I'm so angry with myself for being so blind and selfish. And I'll never forgive myself for it.

I'm so sorry, Abigail.

You wrote that those who crossed your path were cursed and that this was to blame for Emmet's untimely end. I hope you didn't truly believe that. You were a blessing in my life; you were my family, the stable ground that my life was built on, the purest form of love and without you, I would've been lost. I know not how I will go on without you; raising our babies and growing old seems the harshest of punishments. I feel your absence hourly, but I take comfort in knowing that a piece of you remains in Emily.

Tomorrow, I will return this to you. This diary is not for me to keep. But I will keep your story, and when the time is right, I will tell Emily.

Your Loving Sister,

Rosie

Chapter Thirty-One

Breanne Walker

"ABIGAIL PRITCHARD," I SAID AS I TYPED INTO THE SEARCH ENGINE. It was nearly 11pm on Saturday and me and my growling stomach were back in the library at Gettysburg College—surrounded by darkened windows—using their computer databases and hoping their resources would be better than my phone. I pressed enter and the site started to buffer; adrenaline rushed to my heart, sending my senses into overdrive. I stood and paced the area in front of the computer station, frantically trying to calm my nerves that had been on perpetual alert after reading the diary's final page.

The diary was the air I breathed and now I found myself stripped of oxygen; Rosie's letter was the final, gut-wrenching entry. A.M.P. deserved a happy ending; given her past, the karmic energies should've been in her favor and I wanted it so badly for her. I was left numb and reeling from the loss. I flipped the diary's last written page over and over, hoping through tear-clouded eyes that a magic entry was going to appear to redeem the diarists' exorbitant pain.

The tiny hour glass symbol froze and then three results loaded on the screen. I queued up the documents to the printer and three sheets of hot paper spewed out: a birth certificate, a wedding license, and a death certificate.

"Birth, life, and death," I mumbled as I sat back at the high-topped table.

I pulled out my ever-growing folder of evidence and added the license and birth certificate, leaving the death certificate on the desk before me. Her death and the events that occurred immediately after were still obscured in a bit of mystery; specifically, where she was buried.

Modern standards for death certificates in the United States weren't applied until the early 1900's. It was the job of the local church to log deaths in their parish. Which was why Reverend Jonathan Anderson, himself, completed the official document—*that and he could bury the truth.* The hastily recorded—based on the sloppy slant of the Jonathan's penmanship—and official reason for the death of Abigail Pritchard on April 24th, 1864 was childbirth. I hoped for a personal annotation from Jonathan; something about his personal connection to Abigail. But there wasn't—A.M.P's death was lumped into a basic category, with no particulars or personal reflections.

But what about her child? What happened to Emily?

For close to an hour, I searched databases for Emily Conroy—or Pritchard—using the birthdate and region. I found nothing. Then I started combing through adoption records in Gettysburg, in case Jonathan had forced the issue.

But that returned nothing. Exasperated, I sat back in my chair and stared up at the ceiling—knowing I had very little time before the library closed.

What am I not seeing?

My eyes drifted to the manila folder and the printouts that were peeking out from the inside.

"Wait." I snapped forward in the high-top chair and pulled out all the pages, finding the census report from 1870 Adams County. In it was the listing of the Anderson household. My finger traced down the household listing, to the two females—age six—listed as dependents of Rosie and Jonathan.

"Emily and Elizabeth."

I'd assumed these two little girls were twins. But Emily and Elizabeth were cousins! Elizabeth was Rosie's child, born a short time after Emily's birth. Rosie kept her promise and Emily was still under her roof six years later.

I sighed heavily, feeling like I'd just narrowly missed a massive cosmic blow to my psyche.

But something is still missing...

I leaned over the desk, head in hands, trying to mentally grasp the one nagging question hovering in the bleakness of my fried brain. Then the ringing of my phone jolted me back into reality.

I answered it. "Yes?"

"Mrs.—I mean Breanne, its Vince. The intern," said a breathless, squeaky voice on the other end.

"Oh yes... hi! What did you find?" I asked, recalling the task I'd given him: finding the deed for Mr. Larsen's land.

"It took some digging, but I found something. Actually, there's not much of anything here—"

"Okay, okay." I cut him off knowing he would go on a declarative tirade if I didn't. "Where are you?"

For the second time, a short phone call in the dead of night made me venture out past Little Round Top.

But now, I had a GPS pin-drop—provided by Vince—to guide my way. I gripped my phone in my left hand, steering the car clumsily with my right, checking the directions every few seconds to be sure I wasn't veering from the GPS path, and hoping my low battery wouldn't deplete. I knew roughly where I was going—past the tourist drive on Sykes and towards Taneytown—but then the blue direction line on my GPS veered off the asphalt road and into the woods.

I had voiced my concern about getting lost and walking in the woods aimlessly for hours. But Vince assured me I'd be fine.

"Just look for a flashing light," he explained.

Driving towards lights. Again.

I pulled over, got out of my car, rummaged through my trunk for a flashlight—stored along with my spare tire, jumper cables, and washer fluid—and immediately tested the batteries. The bulb flashed and gave off a steady stream of light. "Alright, Casper," I called to Abigail, my friendly ghost. "Lead the way."

For close to twenty minutes, I walked aimlessly through the forest. Tree branches blocked the stars and there weren't even fireflies floating around to offer additional light. I was literally fumbling and stumbling in the dark. I looked for Vince's beacon and tried not to freak out about the eerie circumstances surrounding me. But every creak, every rustle of leaves, every slight animal shriek set me more and more on edge.

Then up ahead, I saw a quick, crisscrossing dart of light—reminiscent of air traffic control. I strained my eyes and recognized Vince's lanky arms—flapping in the air—and wisps of his fire-red hair.

I shouted his name and signaled back with my own flashlight.

"My arms were starting to hurt," Vince's bodiless voice yelled back.

"How long were you doing that?" Carefully, I maneuvered my way through the bramble towards him.

"Since I got off the phone with you?"

Once I was close enough, I saw that he was bouncing from one foot to the other—like a child playing hopscotch on the playground—but the massive, pink bags under his eyes indicated he probably hadn't slept since I saw him last.

"What am I looking at?" I asked.

"I looked for ownership deeds under the surname Larsen." Hearing his name—the name of the man who took Emmet from Abigail—made my stomach lurch. "I narrowed down the search to 1840 to 1865; I assumed twenty-five years was a long enough spread. I called in a few favors—I have a cousin who works for the government. I can't tell you where but he's—" he put his hand over his head and mouthed the words, "high up." I nodded emphatically, pretending I was impressed. But I didn't care how he got it, I just wanted the information.

"Anyway," he continued, "he got me a copy of the land deed for a Mr. Daniel Larsen." From his pocket, he pulled a piece of paper and pointed his flashlight at it. "You see." He pointed to the names and dates.

"Yes, right." It was an Indenture Deed, like ones issued to homesteaders on the Oregon Trail—I'd seen countless in grad school.

"His piece of land was a half mile west of Taneytown Road and twenty-one-and-three-quarter degrees south. Taneytown obviously stretches for a good way through town, but luckily you added Little Round Top to the equation." From his other pocket he pulled a map and laid it flat on the ground. I took his flashlight and we both crouched over the map.

"So that narrowed down the area to about here." He pointed to a small square between Taneytown and Emmitsburg Roads. "And according to the coordinates, Daniel Larsen's property line ends about here." He pointed to a nondescript green mass on the map.

I passed back his flashlight and looked at him with genuine admiration. "Are you a geography enthusiast, Vince?"

He laughed. "Boy Scouts got me hooked."

"So, are we standing on the Larsen property?"

"My cousin provided a bit more context and there were only two landowners listed by the 1860 census for this parcel of land. Daniel Larsen and Joseph—"

"Joseph Pritchard!"

"You know him?"

"Yes...well sort of....by association."

He stood and blazed his flashlight into the open space behind us. "I can't know for sure, but if we walk over here..." he offered his arm. As I'm an exceptionally clumsy person, I gratefully accepted, and we walked out into what I assumed was an empty field. Then he stopped abruptly and pointed his flashlight down to the ground before us. "Can you see the stones?"

I bent over and ran my hand over the ground. As my hand hit a hard surface, a scene flashed before my eyes; I saw a man and woman, standing on the wooden porch of a small cabin and wrapped in a warm embrace.

I've seen her before.

"Oh God," I whispered as the porch from the past was swallowed up by the empty field of the present.

"Pardon?"

"Nothing...sorry." I stood and shined my light across the dark, open space in front of me.

"The stones form a square. Like the foundation for a house. And over there," he pointed to the left, "is another, large formation of stones. I assume it was a—"

"Barn." I walked into the middle of the first stone foundation. The energy was electric; a warm, buzzing feeling coursed through my body. It felt...like home.

"I can't know for sure, but—"

"No, this is it. This is where she lived." I looked around and everything I had read—every emotional record—came to life. Even in pitch darkness, I could see the events that took place there: the happy along with the sad. Though she'd left in duress and the house itself became a painful reminder of all she'd lost, her soul was ingrained on that piece of earth. Very suddenly, that nagging question from the library came to light.

It was something Rosie wrote in her letter: *I had you placed where I know your heart belongs.*

Standing there, near the foundation of the house where their love was born, everything became very clear.

Abruptly, I turned back to Vince. "How close is the Witness Tree?"

Chapter Thirty-Two

Breanne Walker

I'D NEVER BEEN SO THANKFUL FOR VINCENT MCGILL, SUPER-INTERN extraordinaire. Not only had he found the approximate location of Joseph Pritchard's farm, but he'd also mapped out the entire surrounding area and knew—even after dusk—where the white oak was.

"A happy coincidence, right?" he chuckled. I clung to the crook of his arm as he guided me to the second location.

"Sure," I lied, trying to contain my excitement.

Abigail Marie Pritchard wasn't buried in hallowed ground. There wouldn't be a registered grave for her in the National Cemetery—which, before the battle and dedication on November 19th, 1863 was a cemetery for the townsfolk of Gettysburg. Jonathan was correct in his declaration that no religious cemetery would accept the remains of a woman who had a child out of wedlock. So, Rosie found somewhere unsanctioned and buried Abigail in secret.

Abigail's heart belonged with Emmet—she said so herself after his burial—and Emmet was buried beneath the

Witness Tree. So, I was returning to where this adventure all began: to the site of the toppled, one hundred and fifty-year-old white oak.

"And here we are," Vince announced after thirty minutes of my carefully placed feet and his nervous chatter. We stood on the outskirts of the yellow, caution-taped perimeter—the opposite side of the area that I'd slipped under days before.

Vince lifted the tape and I ducked beneath it. Without waiting, I sprinted up the small hill and found the glade exactly as I had left it. Tools from the excavation littered the ground, the tree was still on its side, and the grave was gaping beneath. Using my flashlight, I was able to find the power switch for the portable generator; I flipped the switch on, and the hill was flooded with light.

"Good thinking," Vince chimed in, appearing beside me and looking around like a child at Disneyland.

With a sort of reverence, we both stepped towards the tree. "Oh wow," he said, running his hand over the trunk's smooth surface, "I've never seen tree rings this defined."

"An increment borer wasn't needed; the tree was already on its side. The arborist cut a whole chunk; see how smooth it is," I explained. He knelt, rubbed his hand over the polished, cleaned wood. I peered into the grave, finding it empty and deep without Emmet's body. I shrugged off my messenger bag and jumped down inside the hole to get a closer look.

"Hey! Are you okay?" Vince hurried to the side of the hole and leaned over with concern.

"Yes. I'm looking for something." I kneeled in the moist dirt and ran my hand over the walls of the hole.

"Anything in particular?"

"I'll know when I see it."

After ten minutes of picking up mounds of dirt and chipping away at the walls with my fingers, I conceded defeat; there was nothing proving another body was buried nearby. Vince offered his hand and helped me climb out of the grave.

Where now?

Abigail's grave wouldn't be above or below Emmet's—so finding nothing in his grave meant the same. I jogged over to the abandoned excavation equipment, snatched up a shovel, and returned to the ground above Emmet's vacated grave. Even though I knew it illegal on an official dig site, I raised the shovel above my head and struck down into the soft turf a few inches to the left of the grave.

"Do you want help?" Vince questioned.

"Yes, please."

He grabbed another shovel and started digging a few paces to my left.

Two hours, five completed holes—in a circular pattern around the felled Witness Tree—and both of us were depleted of energy. For the briefest of seconds, I stopped to catch my breath. My grip on the shovel slipped, it fell out of my hand, and the handle landed with a loud CLANK! on the ground. I stepped back into the center of the hole and retrieved the shovel. Hesitantly, I tapped the iron tip into the ground again, feeling a blunt hardness beneath.

I froze, staring down the length of my arm at the spot in the dirt.

"I found something," I yelled to Vince.

He grunted in response and hoisted himself out of his hole. His feet scurried on the grass above and then he plopped down beside me. We started digging, again. Three inches of dirt separated our feet from whatever lay beneath and we cleared it within minutes. When finished, I tossed my shovel out of the hole and knelt, brushing away the last thin layer of dirt with my hand. We both stood back, breathing heavily and looking down at the same spot. And then, like a serendipitous scene from a movie, the sun rose and beamed a stream of light into our hole.

We were standing on a six-foot-long by six-inches-wide piece of trapezoidal wood that sloped gently from the top to the bottom; a cross was etched into the middle.

We found her.

"Crap," Vince whispered beside me.

"Exactly." I turned and hoisted myself out of the hole—Vince followed suit—and I snatched up my messenger bag. I dug through the contents and found my cellphone with five percent battery remaining. I closed my eyes, exhaled my held breath, and tapped on the icon for Greg Ransome.

"Hello?" he answered groggily after an extended ring.

"It's Breanne."

He paused for a beat and let the thought register in his brain. "Yes...right...what's wrong? What time is it?"

"Early. You need to see something at the Witness Tree. Bring a crowbar."

Chapter Thirty-Three

Breanne Walker

G REG ARRIVED WEARING SWEATPANTS, AN OLD, CRUMPLED TEE-
shirt, and one brown and one black shoe. His hair and
eyes were wild—from the thrill of our short, non-explana-
tory conversation—and he was carrying a rusted crowbar.
"Had to dig through my dad's old shed," he said, handing me the heavy iron tool. "You'll probably need a tetanus
shot after handling that."

Seeing Greg so unkempt did something to me; my concise,
methodical thoughts were clouded with visions of Emmet
and Abigail—one very particular scene. My face flushed,
and I started stupidly, grinning and twirling my ponytail
like a girl beside her schoolyard crush. *Stop being ridiculous,*
I scolded myself. I motioned for him to follow me. He shook
hands with Vince and they exchanged pleasantries as we
trekked up the hill and towards the clearing. When he saw
the state of hill—especially the mounds of turned up dirt
and the multiple holes circling the Witness Tree—his eyes
bulged, and he froze, mid-step. His head darted around the

field and I watched as his stare bounced from hole to hole, mentally counting them. He started to say, "What the—" but Vince and I didn't wait for him to finish the phrase; we crossed behind Emmet's grave, towards the obstructed side of the Witness Tree. Greg scampered behind us but stopped short again once he saw the casket.

"That's not—" he craned his neck back to the first grave and then back in confusion. "What is this?"

I jumped down into the grave. "We're about to find out."

The lid was nailed shut at the four corners, so I wedged the sharp edge of the crowbar under the bottom left corner and used my weight to press down. Three hefty shoves later, the top rose slightly, pulling the nails from the wood. Oxygen was sucked out of my lungs.

Vince jumped into the hole beside me. We stood on either end of the wooden box and then—after exchanging a look and a slow nod—we pried the lid off. Hovering above me, I heard Greg's inhaled breath and my eyes dropped.

There was no mistaking it. Right there, by my feet and inside the wooden box, was a cotton-wrapped body. Tears welled in my eyes.

"I got it, Breanne," Vince calmly whispered, motioning to the lid. "Let go."

I allowed Vince to take the full weight of the casket top. He turned, hoisted the lid up into Greg's waiting arms, and then climbed out of the grave. I knelt in the dirt and with trembling hands, touched the yellowing cotton shroud. An image flashed through me and I gasped like I'd just been electrocuted; I saw a woman standing in front of the white oak, clutching a cloth bundle close to her chest and sobbing uncontrollably. She looked familiar. Especially around the eyes.

Rosie.

The vision cleared, and I was back in the grave, but my hands had wandered to a small square of embroidery at the center of the linen. I leaned forward and found a pattern of initials. I traced the letters and my finger's read; "R.M.A."

Just like the linen the diary was wrapped in.

"It's her."

Things happened very quickly after that; like someone pressed the fast-forward button on the remote control of my life.

Greg called in the troops: The National Park Services, local police, all the curators from the museum, and the forensic team from the Harrisburg lab. They all showed up like an obnoxious, history-obsessed cavalcade. The quiet of nature was replaced by the sound of footsteps, car door slams, and excited conversations. And Peggy Cupples — in all her glory — was close behind. She barked orders at anyone within ear shot, and anyone meandering was quickly sent scurrying with a new task. She stayed clear of me — avoided standing within earshot and wouldn't cast her eyes in my general direction. Which was just as well; I wasn't quite ready for the aggressive onslaught of Peggy Cupples.

I tried my hardest to melt into the background of the chaotic scene. At first, Greg included me in the initial debriefings, but I was on complete autopilot; I don't know if my uttered, strung-together words were coherent or just the mumblings of an exhausted mad-woman. My chief concern was the handling of Abigail's gravesite and I kept the excavation in my direct line of vision. When the backhoe's engine was ignited and positioned next to the grave, it took everything in me not to pry the operator out of the equipment and insist on raising the casket myself.

Not that I have a license to operate heavy machinery…

Eventually, Greg dismissed me. "Peggy wants you and Vince to go home." He pointed behind us — to the passed-out form of Vince, curled around and harmoniously snoring with the portable generator.

"There's a car waiting on the street for you both; leave me your keys and I'll have someone bring your car around later today. You're spent and of no more use here."

That last part stung a bit — professionally and emotionally — but I conceded; I was dead on my feet and my eyes were beginning to sting. I would've argued but I knew Peggy's word was law. "You'll call if—"

"Yes, we'll call if we need anything. Peggy wants you at the museum tomorrow morning at nine sharp. Bring the diary and your research. We need to discuss next steps."

"Next steps? The diary needs to—"

"No more questions. Just go," he said, ushering me towards Vince. Using the tip of his mismatched shoes, he poked Vince's side. Immediately, Vince startled awake and smacked his head on the metal generator. Rubbing his head, he turned to us with puppy-dog eyes. "Where...what...I don't know where I am."

Greg looked at me and huffed his aggravation. "Give him a couch to sleep on. It's bad PR if he passes out behind the wheel and kills someone." He bent down to help Vince to his feet, but I waved him away, hoisting Vince up under his armpits myself. His legs shook like Jell-O and he was still half asleep, so I had to basically carry him down the hill. It was the least I could do; without him I never would've found her. *But he better get a job out of this, too,* I thought as I supported his deadweight and cautiously made my way down the hill.

Back at my apartment, Vince woke twice during the day: once in confusion as to where he was — which I quickly cleared up — and then again to use the bathroom. The fact that he was sleeping on a co-worker's couch — one he barely fit on — didn't seem to bother him, but then again, he was a college student and had probably fallen asleep in worse places. From my bedroom, I watched his socked feet — dangling off the couch — twitching with his dreams and I knew he was harmless. But I still couldn't sleep — and it had nothing to do with the awkwardness of a coworker passed out on my couch. Unlike Vince, I couldn't just turn-off and pass out wherever I flopped. I lay in bed, propped up with pillows and the lights off, staring at the crisp, white wall in front of me as scenes from the diary came to life. The wall became the movie screen, and my brain the projector. I couldn't escape Abigail's life. Her life melded into my consciousness.

But comparing my life to hers—*the parallel between us made it impossible not to*—left me feeling very defeated about my own future.

Eventually, I must've drifted off because at 8am—when my weekday alarm sounded—I jolted to wakefulness and toppled out of bed, blankets and all. I stared up at the ceiling and waited for my brain to reset and calm. It was Monday—Peggy's deadline to complete the diary and exactly twenty-four hours since Greg forced me to leave the Witness Tree. From my position on the floor, I could hear Vince still snoring away in a comatose state.

Today's the big one.

I pulled myself up, showered, dressed—blue jeans and a cotton, button-down shirt was as professional as I could get—and made myself a quick cup of coffee. Peggy hadn't requested Vince join the meeting, so I left my apartment silently, armed with all my research, the box of samples, and the diary.

At quarter to nine, I was sitting outside Peggy's office, waiting for my audience with the queen. I was early, but not nearly enough; I heard voices—hers and Greg's—in a heated discussion inside her office.

What are they arguing about?

I was tempted to lean against the door and listen, but it'd be my luck that the door would open without warning and

I'd tumble right inside. With every ticking second and the continued raised voices, my imagination wandered to the extremes. *What could they be debating without me? Was I in more trouble than I thought?* Both were very likely—more so my dismissal, considering the number of additional holes left up on that hill. *Unauthorized digging on an excavation site was not exactly allowed.* I leaned back against the wall and rested my hand on the flap of my messenger bag. Beneath my fingers, I could just make out the spine of the diary. I should've been nervous—the "biting my nails and pacing the hallway" kind of nervous—but I wasn't. Sleep had centered me, and I felt more focused than I had in days. And inside my bag was closure—closure for Abigail, Emmet, and Emily.

"You got this," I whispered to myself.

Suddenly, the door flung open and Greg stepped out, looking fresh and poised.

"Ah, great! She's here. Come in, come in," he said ushering me inside.

I'd never been inside Peggy's office, so I took in my surrounding voraciously. Hers was the biggest in the building and everything inside was meticulously organized. Shelves lined both walls, rows upon rows of categorized books ranging from history and geography to anthropology. The shelves had recessed lighting, installed to emphasize the books and their titles. Two leather armchairs provided seating—*perfect chairs to curl up and read in.* And the window sill behind her desk was lined with framed pictures; I spied one of a much younger Peggy standing in front of the pyramids of Giza and another of her at the Taj Mahal. Her antique mahogany desk was clean—unlike Greg's—bearing only two neat piles of paper on one side, a small potted succulent, and her computer. Natural sunlight lit the room, but there was also a single lamp in the corner; it was bronze and had a fancy, vintage shade.

It was warm and inviting—the type of office I'd design for myself.

Greg sat down and gestured for me to fill the vacant armchair beside him. He was wearing a three-piece navy-blue suit, brown leather shoes, and his gold Rolex, glinting under his sleeve—identical to the outfit he wore at my interview. *Handsome, as always,* I thought, trying to conceal my blush. I sat beside him, with the box of samples at my feet and my bag laid across my lap. Peggy was sitting at her desk. Her back was to us; her window had a perfect view of the National Park and of the beautiful, sunny day outside. *Is this some sort of scare tactic?* I looked to Greg for some direction. He mouthed the words, "Just breathe." I smiled and did just that, shifting my gaze back to Peggy.

Eventually, she spoke; "Do you have the diary?"

The dryness of her voice made my anxiety spike. My hand fumbled with the flap of my messenger bag, but I managed to pull the diary from within, rewrapped in the original cotton cloth—the handkerchief with Rosie's initials—and inside a Ziploc bag. Only when I laid the small bundle on her desk did she turn and face us.

She didn't pick up the diary; with a sort of reverence, she placed her right hand on it, closed her eyes, and flexed her fingers over it. Her eyes twitched beneath her eyelids, almost like she was absorbing the contents through her fingertips. Finally, she opened her eyes and looked right at me. "Greg's given me the details on what led you back to the felled Witness Tree. You believe the second grave contains the body of the diary's owner?"

"Yes, it's her. I have no doubts."

"We'll need to prove beyond—"

"No, it's her." Finding my confidence, I dumped everything from my bag onto my lap and handed Peggy the file of printouts. "These are the official documents proving the existence of Abigail Marie Pritchard and that of her close family members: birth certificates, marriage announcements and licenses, census records, death certificates, and the land deed that Vince tracked down. Also, the military record of Emmet Conroy—the Confederate soldier found in the first grave. Yes, that's his name. Here are his enlistment papers, various campaign data, and the newspaper clipping that lists him as missing, post Gettysburg." Peggy thumbed through the papers; she tried to keep her face stoic but was failing miserably. With every page, her eyes grew bigger, her lips moved as she silently read the material. She couldn't contain a tiny smile from taking form on her lips. Only when she looked up and caught me staring did the smile fade. She cleared her throat and nonchalantly handed the folder to Greg. Undeterred, I retrieved one of the vials from the box of tested samples. "This is a single strand of hair; it holds the DNA link between the body and the diary."

Greg raised his hand, "But how do you—"

"This was found in the spine of the diary. Once she is examined, another lock of hair will be found in her hand. It was cut from the Confederate soldier post mortem."

"How do you know that?"

I nodded towards the bundle beneath Peggy's hand. "Something similar was found in his hand, was it not?"

Peggy and Greg exchanged glances and ever so slightly, she nodded.

"The hair samples from both will help in identifying any living descendants," I continued.

Abruptly, Greg faced me, his brow furrowed, his lips pursed. "Why would we want to find living descendants?"

I returned his questioning look.

"That," I said, pointing to the diary, "is someone's family history. Only one person was privy to the truth after the fact; the story may have been passed down, but the diary is the actual living record of what transpired, and we have no right to withhold that information. The descendants of Emmet and Abigail—Emily's children's children—have a right to know their lineage and decide what's to be done with the diary."

"Well." Greg sat back in his armchair with a smug look. "*What's to be done* has already been decided."

I looked from Peggy—whose eyes were glued to the diary—back to Greg. "What do you mean?"

"This is more than a family history; this is American history. The Gettysburg Military Park is national property, so anything found on its land is the property of our government. You've seen the signs around the park: NO ARTIFACT HUNTING—this is why! We can't have people walking off with artifacts pulled from the ground."

"The Board is very excited at the prospects of adding this discovery to the collection," he continued. "Our ticket sales will surge to new heights and this story will pull at the hearts of all demographics across the country—even the world—and, most importantly, breathe life into the mystique of Gettysburg. I've started drawing up the plans for a permanent exhibit—I'm tossing around the idea of calling it, *The Star-Crossed Lovers of Gettysburg.*"

The urge to vomit made my body tremble. But still he went on.

"We'll showcase the diary; plaster the walls with blown-up pictures of its entries, maybe construct a real-life panorama of the cabin in the woods—a day in the life exhibit, where you can walk through a replica. And then we'll bring the story full circle and conclude with the excavation site, the bodies—"

"What? No, no no!" I pulled my chair away from him and shook my head in disbelief. "You want to use the depths of a woman's soul for its entertainment value?" *What are you doing,* I silently mouthed.

He looked at me and cocked his head—an action that reeked of condescension. "This is the stuff of movies! Why wouldn't we use it?"

"But this isn't a movie! She wouldn't want this! She'd want the diary to go to her family and for them to decide its fate! She'd want them to know the truth! They deserve to know their roots and have privacy to process the information." My voice cracked with my own personal outrage.

"Have you asked her that specifically?" he questioned with a laugh.

"Come off it, Greg. Obviously, I—"

"Breanne." He shifted in his seat, faced me dead-on, and—in an overly familiar manner—placed his hand on the arm of my chair. "I know you've come to think of Abigail as a friend and that you have her best interest at heart. But this is the reality: the diary will be placed on permanent display in the museum and will be the centerpiece for my proposed revamp. Of course, your name will be associated with the discovery and authentication; this is a huge career accolade, one that you should be thankful for."

That same cocky smile cracked his lips and his blue eyes—which once gave me butterflies—bore into me and twinkled with a hidden message. *Be thankful I handed this to you, Breanne,* they said. As I looked at him, a newer reality took form; Greg Ransome was not the man I'd thought. He was not my friend, not my counterpart in the need for historic preservation and truth over money and prestige, and he certainly didn't give a damn about how I felt. He was a perfect stranger, too consumed with living up to and surpassing his family name to do what was right. Notoriety was within his grasp and he threw his ideals away—if he ever had them.

My eyes dropped to my hands, folded tightly in my lap, and I shook my head in resignation. "This isn't right."

"*This* is business."

His words froze and shattered above me, piercing my heart piece by piece. I cringed and shifted away from him. The air he breathed became deplorable to me. My face was blank of emotion, but inside I was scolding myself for ever having trusted him—and for thinking that our relationship was more than a business transaction. *He isn't my Emmet.*

My opinion was stranded on a desolate island and I desperately needed rescuing. But there was no one to save me from Greg. Peggy still wouldn't look at me and that was more damning than any words she could've said.

"What about the bodies?" I grasped at anything for Abigail's sake. "Will they be returned to their graves?"

He sat back in his chair and unbuttoned his suit jacket. "There's a lot of red tape to jump over when displaying human remains. Our lawyers have started the paperwork, but approval can take up to six months. In the meantime, the bodies will be kept in temperature-controlled storage."

Emotionally, I curled into myself. Emmet and Abigail deserved to be returned to their original graves; to spend eternity side by side in peace, not behind Plexiglas, gawked at by anyone with twenty-five dollars to spare. The fate of the diary was taken from me—eventually I'd come to terms with it—but this...this was too much. *I shouldn't have called Greg; none of this would've exploded if I'd let Abigail stay where Rosie placed her.* I blinked away my tears and tried to keep my composure.

"Naturally," he continued, "you're the only staff member who's read the diary—so you will be front and center for the publicity campaign."

"You want me to do what?"

"This story will be picked up for feature pieces across the country, so we're putting together a press junket. You will be the focus of these interviews; the responsibility of telling her story will be yours."

A brawny voice—one that I couldn't control and hardly recognized—gurgled up in my throat and I spat out one word: "No."

He brushed off my abruptness with a laugh. "I know this isn't your forte. Don't worry; we'll get you an interview coach. We'll script out the narrative and all you have to do is—"

I cut him off. "I don't want any involvement in this. Any of it."

He looked at me, dumbfounded. "Excuse me?"

I stood and shouldered my messenger bag. "I'm out. Strike my name from the research. Forget you ever called me. Get another employee to stand in as your lackey and paint whatever narrative you want for the national scene. I don't care what you do, but I'm out. My integrity is all I have, and I won't use Abigail or the diary to boost my career."

I intended on turning and whisking myself from Peggy's office in a dramatic fashion, but Greg snatched my wrist and stopped me. His grip was tight, and I felt violated—so violated that I froze. "You're making a mistake; walking away is a mistake," he said in a strained whisper.

I looked down at his hand and then straight at him. My eyes were white hot and slowly he realized his mistake; his grip loosened, and his hand dropped. "Thank you for the opportunity, Dr. Ransome," I continued. "But I respectfully decline your offer. Please consider this my resignation."

After my words registered in his brain, his shock turned to irritation. He turned from me without another word. Peggy's eyebrows were arched in surprise and her lips were a thin line. Our eyes met for the briefest of seconds and before she looked away, I swear she nodded.

I stole one last look at the diary, still wrapped and sitting on Peggy's desk. That little, leather-bound book had dominated my life and I knew it'd be the last time I'd see it without a reinforced obstruction. Visions swirled in my head of all that the diary had given me—all Abigail had given me—and I wished I could do more for her. A crazed part of me wanted to dive over the desk, grab the diary, and dart out of the museum; I'd find Abigail and Emmet's family myself.

Illegal, yes but I could do it.

But I came to the same conclusion as Abigail had when Jonathan threatened to take her child; I haven't the courage or strength to fight. So, I turned my back on the diary, walking out of Peggy's office and away from Abigail's story.

Chapter Thirty-Four

Breanne Walker

W*HAT DID I JUST DO?*
The sound of my footsteps bounced off the hallway's walls as I hustled away from Peggy's office and towards the general concourse of the museum. Though my feet were moving, air was entering my lungs, and loud voices swirled around me, my brain was scurrying a few feet behind — desperately trying to reunite with my body and reconcile what just happened with Greg.

Then, as if I'd gotten a forceful slap to the back of my head, my brain jolted back online and started processing all that had occurred.

"You just quit your job. You just quit your job," I said, as I maneuvered through the crowds of people waiting to purchase tickets for the day's exhibit. The words — spoken out loud — took life: I had just given Dr. Greg Ransome, Assistant Director of Exhibits and Collections at the Gettysburg National Military Park, a verbal resignation. Termination was my fear — and push — to finish the diary. But instead of rejoicing in the fact that I was keeping my job AND being given the opportunity to make a name for myself in the archeological field, I decided to double down and spit in the face of ambition. *What is wrong with you?*

My first instinct — after closing Peggy's office door — was to flee, like I had when Greg first handed me the diary; to run as fast as my short legs would carry me. Only this time it wasn't from the shock of an otherworldly vision, this time I was running from a rash decision. Greg wouldn't run after me; he wasn't going to scream my name, overload my cellphone with voicemails and text messages, or attempt another conversation in hopes of swinging my allegiance to his plan. I could run all the way home to Nevada and make the news while doing it, but Greg Ransome would remain glued to the leather of Peggy's armchair and never speak my name again. He was done with me, I saw it in his eyes when he let go of my arm. Our relationship — friendship or romantic — was something I dreamed up. My reality was blurred by Abigail and Emmet — I had wanted Greg to be my Emmet. *I yearned for it.* But now the truth was very evident: Greg was nothing more than a gear in the money-making machine. That hurt, more than I wanted to admit.

I needed to be alone — to put space between myself and the museum — and think.

I pushed through the museum's glass entrance door and walked briskly to my car. Only when the driver's side door was closed did I know where I was going.

The area around Little Round Top was heavily guarded. Park Rangers were stationed on both ends of Sykes Avenue leading up to the battlement, with strict instructions that the "attraction" was closed until further notice. Given the beautiful day and the line queuing at the museum, the hill would've been teeming with history buffs. Protecting the Witness Tree would've been a tactical nightmare, so it was smart to close off the entire area until everything was secure.

Luckily, rules don't apply for museum employees — even if you quit twenty minutes prior. When I drove up to the roadblock at the junction of Warren and Sykes, all I had to do was flash my work ID and give the young Park Ranger a big, toothy grin. He lifted the barricade without question and let me drive past.

Past the checkpoint, there wasn't a soul or a car in sight. I expected to see museum activity, as the area was still an excavation site. I parked my car on the side of the road, trekked into the sunlit forest, and found the Witness Tree's hill completely desolate.

Did I not get the memo?

I walked around the small hill, looking for an indication of what had transpired over the last twenty-four hours — and why the site was completely empty. After doing a walk of the perimeter, I surmised that the crew hadn't yet arrived for the day. Standing there, looking at the site and destruction left behind, I felt very much like an outsider and an intruder.

Daylight has a funny way of making things very clear — especially the negative impact man has on nature.

The grass beneath my feet had lost its buoyancy and greenness; long strands were browned and flattened from being traipsed on repeatedly, and tire marks stripped parts of the ground down to the dirt. Leaves and branches littered the ground, as construction equipment being hauled onto the hill had hit the topmost bowers. Even the Witness Tree was a slayed carcass; once rooted deep and towering high above, it was now rotting away. Everything was forfeited in the pursuit of historical significance. And—as I sat down and dangled my feet into what had been Abigail's grave for the last one hundred and fifty years—I couldn't help but reflect on the amount of damage my own involvement had created.

I sighed and peered into the gaping hole. Her grave was now several feet wider and deeper; from the precision and clean lines of the hole, the backhoe was used to do the job my shovel couldn't. In the earth remained a perfect indent of where the wooden casket had lain; my eyes traveled over the perfectly curved corners and I imagined her lying there, within arm's length of her love.

My hand drifted to my messenger bag—slung over my shoulder—and instinctively felt for the imprint of the diary. Naturally, my fingers found nothing. The small, leather-bound book was no longer in my possession and never would be again. The only thing I had left were the pages imprinted on my memory. Without the diary, I had no way to make a direct connection to Abigail other than sitting at her grave. I just wanted to feel close to her. My mood plummeted into an even lower melancholy. Part of me wanted to fall forward into the hole and...

"I thought I'd find you here."

I shrieked and clutched my chest. I turned to find Peggy Cupples standing a few feet behind me, removing her sunglasses, and looking slightly bemused at my reaction.

"I...am I still allowed to—"

"Your resignation terminated all museum privileges, including access to dig sites," she said, stepping closer and peeking over my shoulder into the grave. Then she looked me right in the eye and a grin formed on her lips. "But frankly my dear, I don't give a damn."

"Rhett Butler?"

She clapped in glee. "*Gone With The Wind* is the reason I fell in love with history. Are you a Margaret Mitchell fan?"

"Does the movie count?"

"Read the book! You're a historian for God's sake! I read it four times the summer I turned thirteen. Glad her work—at least in movie form—hasn't been totally lost on your generation."

She reached out a hand to me, which I stared at for longer than she appreciated. She rolled her eyes, shook her hand and struggled to bend her knees.

"Oh right," I said, realizing she needed my assistance.

"Never get old," she said as she settled into a sitting position in the dirt beside me. "You'll wake up one morning and your body will start creaking in all sorts of weird places." She rolled back her shoulder blades and sighed; not from exertion or annoyance with me. Her face showed joy and vitality, the kind of look a kid has when they're finally tall enough to go on their first roller coaster.

Her casual demeanor was really freaking me out. *Am I on one of those hidden-camera shows?*

"You know, it's very peaceful," she said, admiring the surroundings. "The tragedy aside, I understand what drew her here."

Minutes passed with no words between us. I didn't know what I was supposed to say; I felt like an overgrown gold fish, with my mouth inaudibly gaping open and then shutting. With every second that passed, her presence and relaxed attitude confused me more and more. *Shouldn't she be raging with anger?* I just threw a wrench into the museum's expansion plans; she should want nothing to do with me. And she definitely shouldn't be sitting beside me.

"Look," I said, clearing my dry throat in the process. "If you're here to convince me to come back, you're wasting —"

"I don't beg." Her voice was clipped and abrupt. "Never have, never will. A lesson to take with you; begging is for the weak."

I nodded because it seemed the only suitable reaction when receiving advice from Peggy Cupples. "So then —"

"Why am I here?" She repositioned herself to face me. "I'm not quite sure. Two weeks ago, Breanne Walker was just a name I occasionally saw on department email chains. After the last few days and a handful of conversations, you intrigue me, and not many people can say that."

Am I in another Abigail-influenced dream sequence?

"I...I don't know what to say."

"How about starting with the real reason you quit your job?"

"I...I told you why back in your office. I just...I can't—"

"'*My integrity means everything to me*,'" she mocked. "Yes, I know. But that's a fluffy bunch of bull; there's more going on in that head of yours than concern for your integrity. You're running from something, and it isn't just Greg Ransome. Stop the mumbling, and spit it out."

I drew back. One conversation and she'd nailed me. I looked down at my hands, staring long and hard at the veins pulsating with blood, and searched my psyche for a response to her question. Embarrassment—on top of the sun rays streaking from the cloudless sky above—flushed my face. There was no running from her—*she'd probably hunt me down*—and even if I didn't know what was going on in my head—*which was the case*—I needed to say something.

"I just pictured all of this ending in a different way," I blurted.

"With what? A joyous family reunion, hugs and kisses all around, and you receiving the gratitude for closing the gap on a long-lost family history? It's a lovely dream, but a fool's one—and you're smarter than that. The diary was always going to end up on display in the museum—even if only to collect dust in some dark corner. And now that we know there's some meat in those pages, there's no way around it." A condescending half-grin was painted on her face—the kind I imagined an older child would give a younger sibling just to escalate a disagreement.

And it worked.

"You're right," I said, throwing my hands up in resignation. "I'm not that naïve; the public has a right to hear this story and I can't expect anyone to feel the way I do. But I'm obligated to her in a way I can't explain. I need to try and make things right." I looked back into the grave.

"Abigail's life was a long, sad story. She never got a chance to find long-lasting happiness—almost like she was doomed because of her mother's rejection. I can't believe—I won't believe that good people are doomed because of their past."

"That's what you're running from." I turned back to face her, and she was pointing at my invisible words. "You're running from your own sad past."

Could she read my mind?

I let my eyes drop. Running crossed my mind for the second time since she'd sat down, but I stayed beside her and quietly hoped she wasn't going to pry into my "mommy issues." She already thought I was a bit crazy for quitting my job for no apparent reason, but an emotional mess would be icing on the cake.

"The past is a tricky thing." Her voice was soft, nurturing even. "Everyone has one—it binds us as humans. But what makes us different is our reaction to the past; you can run from it, strike out the memories and deny it ever happened; live in fear of it, never take any chances because you feel your future is predestined; or you can strive to live in spite of it, never letting it define you and map your own course. Running was my expertise."

Discreetly, I looked up. She was twiddling a long piece of grass between her index finger and thumb, looking deep into Abigail's grave. She sighed and looked at me; her green eyes were swimming with memory. "You see my success—the long-standing accreditation in my profession, my tenured position at a premier museum, the respect of my peers, and the god-like look of awe from my subordinates. And I love every second of it. But—" She paused for a beat, staring long at the blade of grass between her fingers before continuing. "Those pictures lining my office windowsill—I saw you looking at them—did you notice anyone standing beside me?" She threw the piece of grass down into the grave. "People like us—people obsessed with history—have a hard time seeing the world in front of us. The past becomes more important than the present. Like you—and Abigail—my life wasn't always so easy, and in my darkest moments, my ambition was the only thing I could count on. I ran to the past of others and away from the living, so my pain wouldn't consume me. But that was a mistake—one I think our friend," she gestured towards the grave, "would agree with."

Again, looking at her became uncomfortable. I barely knew this woman, but she was reading me like a diary—and revealing parts of her own story in the process.

"Your similarities to Abigail," she continued, "which I don't need to know the extent of, have given you a very passionate sense of obligation: you want to fix what she couldn't, bring closure to her pain. But closure won't bring her back; learn something from the mistakes she made.

Embrace your own past and live! Because eventually, your past will outpace you and come bursting into your present. That's the true curse of life."

I choked down the sob forming in my throat and turned my head to brush the tears from my cheeks.

"Alright." Peggy slapped my knee. "I'm done preaching for the day, and some of us have jobs to get back to."

I laughed—and it sounded like a snort.

She shifted her body and stood, groaning as she did. She brushed the dirt and grass from her pants. "Oh, Gregory gave me your grad-school thesis. I gave it a read last night. Oregon Trail, huh? You know, the curator at the National Museum in Idaho is a colleague. If you're serious about your resignation, I could make a call?"

My jaw dropped. "I...yes...yes, thank you! You really don't have—"

She raised her hand, brushing away my thanks like they were an irritating fly. "You've got talent and I'd hate for that to be wasted—even if it's at a subpar establishment."

I reiterated my thanks as she walked away. "Think about what I said," she added from over her shoulder. I watched as she cautiously stepped down the slant of the hill and disappeared into the trees. Even after she was gone, my gaze stayed in that direction. But my mind was above the trees, spiraling like a crashing airplane.

Learn something from the mistakes she made.

Abigail lived a solitary life, cut off emotionally from everyone, and trusted no one. She blamed herself for every bad thing that happened to those around her—including Emmet's death. And all of it could be connected back to her mother's rejection and insatiable need to prevent any semblance of happiness for her daughter. Her cruelty had long-lasting ramifications for Abigail's psyche; she believed she wasn't worthy of love or kindness, so she secluded herself and wallowed in her mother's condemnation. But she had the power all along to make a better life for herself.

That was Abigail's mistake: she listened and obeyed Mother.

She should've challenged her mother's monetary and familial threat and joined Dr. Watkins in Philadelphia. She shut out the world when she should've jumped into it. She should've gone to medical school. Period. True, she wouldn't have met Emmet or had Emily, but her life could've turned out differently—a fact that she realized much too late.

That was why she was reaching out to me. She wanted to fix *my* life.

Sadness crept upon me and made its way to my lungs. I leaned forward and hugged my knees to my chest as memories from childhood flooded me: the loneliness; the sullen looks from my mother; the drunken rages, where she flung hurtful assertions my way; the lack of hugs or affection; the way I always knew my existence had ruined her life. All of it sent me down the same rabbit hole as Abigail—books and learning were my only friends. Professionally, my life was full—*well, it was until this morning.* But would I look back with regret? I realized I was punishing myself for my mother's inability to love me.

Learn from the mistakes she made; take control of your life.

I stared even longer into Abigail's grave and I realized there were two things I needed to do: forgive and build upon the wreckage.

No more running.

I took a deep breath and pulled my cellphone from the pocket of my jeans. She wouldn't answer, I knew, but I typed in my childhood phone number and waited while the line connected. Eventually, the answering machine picked up; claiming in a computerized message that no one was there to answer the call, and to leave a message after the beep. The prolonged beep nearly made me vomit.

"Hi Mom, it's um…it's Breanne," I stammered, anxiety oozing from every uttered syllable. "I'm sure you're at work and not just screening my call." I nervously laughed. "Um…yeah I got your card…about Daniel. Thank you for that. I know how you feel—felt about him so I appreciate the gesture."

Oh god this is awful, I started pacing around the Witness Tree. If a machine was making me this nervous, I probably would've had a full-on panic attack if she had answered. As the dead air ticked on, I tried to grasp what I wanted to say.

"I quit my job today," I blurted out in a high-pitched, semi-crazed voice. "Yeah, a lot happened this week—really weird things—and I thought—but I might have a prospect closer to home. Your home, not mine. Well, if it pans out…I don't really have any guarantees but…but it could bring me closer to Nevada."

You sound like Vince McGill. Get it together, Breanne!

"Sorry, I'm rambling and I'm sure the machine is about to cut me off. Um… I was hoping we could talk and maybe catch up? It's been awhile and there's a lot I want to say. You know my number; give me a call when you have a few minutes."

"I love you, Mom." I moved the phone from my ear and hung up.

Those four little words held power; I'd never uttered them to my mother — nor she to me. This was a start. It was my cliché-filled version of an olive branch.

After ending the call, I wondered if Abigail would appear in a fuzzy, dreamlike form. She'd smile, and Emmet would emerge beside her. He'd been waiting all these years for her; closure was the only way they could finally be together — and my olive branch had given her that. Their love would radiate, and they'd clasp hands. A sense of fulfillment would cleanse my sadness and they'd walk off into the afterlife in total bliss. It'd be a total *Wuthering Heights*, Catherine and Heathcliff moment.

But you know what they say about assuming.

I looked expectantly across the field for my miracle moment, but nothing supernatural happened; the sun went on shining, the birds went on chirping, Abigail's grave remained empty, and the Witness Tree still lay on its side. Worst of all, I was completely alone, and the same anxiety-filled sadness hung at my back.

My head dropped back, and I asked the cloud-filled sky; "What else could you possibly want?"

As questions circled the drain of my mind, I felt my nerves and confusion gradually ease—like both emotions were siphoned out of my body. Everything abruptly became clear. She didn't appear, but Abigail spoon-fed a memory into my consciousness. I spoke the words she gave me.

"555-9869."

This was the phone number I'd repeated like a prayer since I was a young girl: the phone number of my paternal grandmother, Dorinda Cook, the woman who returned my call when I was searching for my father. Fear of my mother's anger had kept me from ever reaching out. But now, standing in the eaves of the tree that had witnessed such pain, I knew that something new—something terrifyingly good—needed to take fruit. I needed to learn about my father—in the way Emily and Abigail never got to.

The screen of my phone lit as I typed the number and pressed send. After a few seconds, the line started ringing, and it continued for quite some time. I resigned myself to leaving another voicemail.

Then the ringer silenced. I stifled a gasp.

"Hello?" asked the voice I recognized from so many years before.

Acknowledgements

A SCHOOL FIELDTRIP DIDN'T BRING ME TO GETTYSBURG FOR THE first time, nearly six years ago. A free weekend and a need to experience something different drew me from Philadelphia, along the Pennsylvania turnpike, and to the town that became infamous in 1863. Crossing the border felt like I had stepped back in time, and as I made my way around the town and battlefields, I couldn't believe I was still in Pennsylvania and that this place—filled with such momentous history—was in my backyard.

To say I was inspired is an understatement; that night, I had a very vivid dream that became the framework for this novel.

Thank you to the town of Gettysburg. I am indebted to your history.

I started writing this novel during one of the most heart-breaking summers of my life. Three months of death and family health issues should've crippled me—and in many ways it did. But writing this story kept me from crumbling into a bottom-less pit of depression. Breanne and Abigail needed me to push through. I owe so much to these two fictitious women, and I hope their lives give something to all who read this novel.

To my parents, Bob and Jane, and my family for your years of undying support. Especially for tagging along on "research trips" — one of which will remain infamous in our family for lifetimes to come. Next trip, I promise I'll do a bit more research into the Air B&B rental.

To Janet Benton, my editor, writing therapist, cheerleader, and friend. Working with you has made me into the writer I am today. Your tutelage and influence produced much of this novel, and I can't thank you enough for encouraging me to hone my craft and believe in myself. I hope my usage of the semicolon passes your test.

To Ken Ford and Lyndsay Mahalis, my perpetual beta-readers. Your opinions and input have been indelible. There's no one I trust more with my work.

This novel would not have been possible without hours upon hours of research, and I'd be remiss if I didn't give due credit to those who completed the grunt work for me: the Gettysburg National Military Park; *A Journal of Hospital Life in the Confederate Army of Tennessee: From the Battle of Shiloh to the end of War* by Kate Cumming; *Flames Beyond Gettysburg: The Confederate Expedition to the Susquehanna River, June 1863* by Scott L. Mingus Sr.; *At Gettysburg: or, What a Girl Saw and Heard from the Battle* by Matilda "Tillie" Pierce Alleman; *Recollections of the Rebel Invasion: And one Woman's Experiences During the Battle of Gettysburg* by Fannie J. Buehler; *The Great Battles of the Civil War* by John MacDonald; *Brought to Bed: Childbearing in America, 1750-1950* by Judith Walzer Leavitt; *The Killer Angels* by Michael Shaara.

Endless thanks to those who read my first book and have been eagerly awaiting its sister. I'm sorry it took so long, but I hope it was worth the wait.

To my husband (and "business manager") Justin. From the beginning, this book was the "third person" in our relationship; for the first year and a half that we dated, we rarely saw each other during the week. You understood that writing took up most of my free time and were nothing short of encouraging and supportive. I could not ask for a better partner in life and love. You are truly my soul mate. Wyatt and I are so lucky to have you.

To Wyatt, my son born well after my manuscript was completed. Motherhood is at the center of this novel, and I truly didn't understand the power of it until I held you in my arms. Everything I do—every breath I take—is for you.

About the Author

J ena M. Steinmetz graduated cum laude from DeSales University in Center Valley, Pennsylvania, with a BA in English/Creative Writing. Her non-fiction articles have appeared in the Lehigh Valley's *Morning Call*, the *Bucks County Herald*, and the *Bucks County Courier*. Her first novel, *Codename: Sob Story*, was called "a notable debut" by Kirkus Reviews and was included in their Best Indie War Stories of 2013. Jena works in the suburbs of Philadelphia, where she lives with her husband and their son.

CPSIA information can be obtained
at www.ICGtesting.com
Printed in the USA
BVHW041823120821
614303BV00014B/520